Shaping Shannon

Jo Ann Swahn

TREATY OAK PUBLISHERS

PUBLISHER'S NOTE

This is a work of fiction. Except for authentic historical persons, none of the characters or events is based on actual people, living or dead, or their lives or circumstances. Any similarities are a coincidence and purely unintentional.

**Printed and published in
the United States of America**

TREATY OAK PUBLISHERS

ISBN: 978-1-943658-93-0

Available on Amazon

DEDICATION

To Lou, my best friend

TABLE OF CONTENTS

I. SEED

The ground must be prepared before the seed is dropped in. Yours to prepare the soil—Mine to drop the seed-blessing into the prepared soil.

From "God Calling,"
edited by A. J. Russell

The sounds are what stuck in her memory. Dull thuds, marked by sounds like air forced from lungs. Shouts and screams had ceased a good bit before. Now it was just the thuds of fist against flesh with occasional moans. "Oscar, please not there. Not in my stomach."

At last, Shannon could stand it no longer. She summoned all the courage her fourteen-year-old petite frame could muster and dared to enter her parents' bedroom sanctuary, breaking a strict rule never to come into their room when the door was closed.

Her first sensation was the heat from the open-flame gas heater hitting her in the face. No windows were open, and the room was stifling.

Shannon was shocked to see her mother, Beth, lying prone on the bed, naked, with her father weighing her down, straddling her. Beth's pregnant body was exposed, and her father was pounding her swollen belly, causing the dull thuds Shannon had heard, sounding something like hitting a drum.

"Shannon, please turn off the heater," her mom pleaded, her voice husky, little more than a whisper. "I can't breathe."

Her father glared at her, rage distorting his once handsome Swedish face, cold blue eyes boring into his daughter. "Get out of here," he hissed.

Shannon turned off the heater and, without saying a word, returned to her room.

But the sounds stopped.

Shannon lay in her bed, wondering why and when this all started. She couldn't remember her mother without black eyes or bruises or a time without the shouting. Her mother Beth was either furious with her father Oscar or hysterical, crying. Was her father ever sober? She'd peek out the window each night, at the sound of his truck on the driveway, and study him as he got out and staggered to the door. His walk and his expression told her if he were in a silly mood, if he would pass out, or become a raging bull. Then she would rush into her room, hide under the covers, and pretend to be asleep.

Their lives teetered from soberness to drunkenness and what lay between.

Unable to return to sleep, Shannon struggled to understand why her parents were this way.

"How can people live like this?" she said aloud. "When Mom was little, did she ever think she'd be lying in her bed, pregnant, with her husband beating her? Did Dad ever see himself as a drunken excuse of a man, his family terrified of him? What kind of man hits his unborn child?"

That night proved to be the death of her innocence. Born in its place was a force of nature. Determined. Defiant. Disciplined. She would invent the person she wanted to become.

"Someone has to be in control," she vowed, "and that person will be me! I will never be like my mother or father. And no man will ever frighten me."

II. ANCESTORS

The Great Swedish Migration

"You don't need to starve in Sweden and work yourself to death with nothing to show for it," he bellowed from the church pulpit in the tiny village of Ljuder. "If you're willing to work hard and take risks, you can have a bountiful life and freedom in America."

The century was new—1908.

Lucas Berg was resplendent in his well-tailored frock coat and enormous wide-brimmed hat, never before seen by the Smaland farm folk. While he spoke fluent Swedish, his 40 years in the Americas had imprinted a strange accent, influenced by the many languages spoken in the New World.

The pews were packed. Everyone in the Ljuder farm community had heard of the imposing, wealthy Swede, one of the many thousands of penniless but hopeful immigrants who had fled poverty and famine in Sweden for the American dream. *American fever* had gripped the entire country. Someone knew someone who knew someone who had immigrated. Now here was one of their own who had answered that call. And he was rich, successful, powerful.

"I was among the early ones to go," he said, "those who left Sweden in the 1850s. I entered the United States through Ellis Island in New York, but I sought my fortune in Texas."

Land lured him, that lasting legacy that tugs at the heartstrings of all Swedes. In his years in Texas, Berg created an empire amassing 600,000 acres in land grants in the Texas wilderness, vast, empty spaces hungry for homesteaders.

"Texas doesn't have the lure of gold in California, or the safety in numbers of the Swedish settlements in the Midwest." His fervor increased as he talked about the land he loved. "What Texas has is unbridled enthusiasm for freedom. Freedom to own land and be lord of it. Freedom to practice any religion or none. And perhaps most of all, freedom from church and government. You'll be free to pursue the American Dream."

One parishioner dared interrupt Berg's presentation. "We've heard it is a long and dangerous journey, Mr. Berg. What can you tell us about that?"

"My first few crossings were on old wooden sailing ships. It took two to three months to cross. Many got the seasickness. Some died on the journey. Now the trip is on steel-hulled steamships, safer and faster, and you can get from Liverpool to New York in six to eight days. For us, another week to the port of Galveston, Texas."

He continued, his blue eyes boring into every man seated. "I need people to tame and work the land I own, and I know no more hard-working or trustworthy people than my fellow countrymen."

Wilhelm Nils Lindberg, sitting in his customary pew with his two sons, Simon and Oscar, listened to Berg's every word. His wife Tilde, four daughters, daughter-in-law, and infant grandson sat across the aisle with the other women.

"Here's my offer," said Berg. "Come to Texas. Work for me for two years as farmers, and I will pay passage for you and your family. After two years, you can buy your land, 177 acres, for $1 per acre."

Wilhelm shot glances at both Simon and Oscar.

"Come to Texas and become the farmers you were born to be, without the oppression and restrictions imposed by Swedish authorities." He waited a few moments. "This is the last group I'm sponsoring. I'll only be in Sweden another month. If you're interested in joining my last pilgrimage, talk to your bishop and start your immigration papers."

On their walk back to the farm, the Lindberg men led the way while the women trailed behind, chatting about that evening's dinner and the week's chores ahead.

Simon broke the silence. "Father, what did you think of Berg's talk?"

"It's given me much to think on, Simon. I had a difficult time swallowing my anger, listening when the pastor announced yet another tax the government expects from us. They must enjoy watching us starve."

Both Simon and Oscar murmured, "Yes, Father," knowing the timeworn tirade was coming.

"Except for the Neutrality Acts and keeping our sons out of foreign wars, our monarchy has done nothing to help its people." His anger heated up. "Even during the potato famine when so many Swedes starved to death, our King did nothing except fill his own coffers!"

The boys listened with the characteristic respect young people showed their elders.

"And now after two bad harvests, one destroyed by drought, and the next finished off by a harsh winter, the government levies yet another tax on us. If it's not the King, it's the bishop." His voice was raised now, and the womenfolk stopped their chatter. "The rich landowners and the magistrates are in league with each another, mark my words, to keep themselves fat and comfortable off the backs of the poor."

"But what of Berg's comments, Father," Oscar said, hoping to stem the list of grievances all farmers shared about the unfairness of the government and the church.

"I'm getting to that, Oscar!" snapped Wilhelm. "What have I told you about holding your tongue when I'm talking!"

Wilhelm stopped walking and looked at both his sons. "Until Lucas Berg talked today, I had no hope. No hope for me to feed my family this winter." He paused. "Berg gave us the answer. Four of you are immigrating to America."

Simon and Oscar stared at each other as their father continued walking toward home.

* * *

The Lindbergs

WILHELM KEPT HIS SILENCE the rest of the afternoon, while his uneasy family worried about what troubled him. That night and in the privacy of their small bedroom, Wilhelm discussed with Tilde his plans for four of their children to immigrate to America.

Tilde gasped. "How can you even think of such a thing? Why, we'd never see them again."

"What other choice do we have, wife? I'll call a meeting with some of our neighbors," Wilhelm said in a firm manner.

No other conversation occurred between them, the two sleeping as far apart as their bed allowed.

The next day Wilhelm made a circuit of four neighboring farms, the Peterssons, Swensons, Anderssons, and Nordins. "Please come to my house next Sunday, after services. I have a proposal to put before you regarding Lucas Berg's offer."

Curious, they all agreed to come.

"Please say nothing to others until we've talked. I don't want to encourage rumors or gossip."

The next Sunday, Wilhelm watched as Tilde cleaned the cottage to spotless condition and prepared a light lunch for their guests. He had not shared his proposal with her.

In customary promptness, the four families arrived and stamped the dust off their feet at the threshold. Tilde and Wilhelm welcomed each couple with formal handshakes, offering them a seat in the small sitting room, furniture rearranged to accommodate eight visitors. Tilde had set out cheese sandwiches, coffee, and some sweet rolls flavored with apples from her tree. After exchanging pleasantries, Wilhelm opened the meeting.

"Welcome, neighbors, to our home. We thank you for spending part of your Sabbath to consider a proposal I wish to put before you." He cleared his throat.

"We all heard Mr. Lucas Berg speak last Sunday. I've thought of little else since then. My farm has not prospered these past years, and this year's harvest will barely keep us alive. No matter how hard we work, our small patch of ground just doesn't provide enough for us. I hope you have been more fortunate, but the talk in our village suggests we all share this fate."

Several of the visitors nodded as they glanced at each other.

"Yet I have two sons, four daughters, a daughter-in-law, and a grandchild to feed. My second son labors for another farmer, my oldest daughter works as a maid in the bishop's home, and we rely on their wages to help us survive. All four of my daughters will soon reach marriageable age."

He shrugged. "When Mrs. Lindberg and I die, our small farm cannot be split into enough pieces to support my children and the families they'll have. Maybe you have the same predicament?" He scanned their faces for any sign of agreement.

"I listened to Mr. Berg with two warring thoughts in my head. One, immigrating to America is my children's only hope for a better life than the one they can have here in Sweden. The other, sending my children away means I will probably never see them again." He shook his head and sighed. "But I have decided that my responsibility as their father is to offer them at least the chance, even if I have to give up…" He paused, and then swallowed hard before he continued.

"My proposal, neighbors, is this. My eldest, Simon, will remain here and inherit the farm. My eldest daughter, Ella, will remain here to care for my wife and me in our old age. The shares belonging to the four who leave will stay with me, my wife, and Simon. We will accept Mr. Berg's stake for four to go to America on the condition our family remains together in the New Land. My four children will farm his land for two years with his promise they can buy that land."

All of the wives shifted in their seats to look at Tilde, who stood in the corner near the hearth.

"The other necessary condition," Wilhelm said, "is that all four will be either married or betrothed before they leave Sweden." He hesitated, then looked at each of his visitors, one at a time. "Each of you has children. I am proposing arranged marriages of my younger son and three of my daughters with the most suitable partners among your children—knowing that you, too, will likely never see your children again."

Wilhelm sat down then to let what he had said sink in.

The group sat in stunned silence. Wilhelm guessed that some might have imagined their children leaving Sweden, but so far none dared let the thoughts pass their lips.

Alva Swenson broke the stillness. "How could I ever part with my children! What would become of us in our old age? Who would work our farm?"

The dam broke then, and the room erupted in noisy discussions. Wilhelm held back and let them talk. "I've said what I needed to say," he thought as he looked at his wife's ashen face, reflecting unmistakable anger at him.

At last, William Swenson stood up and said in in his loud, authoritative voice, "Who in this room would not leave for America if he were a young man again?"

The others stared at him.

"I would have gladly given up my birthright for a chance to go to America. To have all the land I need to feed my family, to be free to do as I want, to worship how I choose, to offer my children a life of their own making. Not one of poverty and starvation laid out for them, no matter how hard they toiled. Now I'm too old. My time has passed. But I'll be damned if I condemn my children to the life of suffering my wife and I have endured."

"But how can you part with our children?" Alva wailed.

"How can you deny them a better life than we have had?" William said as he clasped her shoulders and gazed into her eyes. "We don't have to send all of them. Just those whose share in the farm will be too little to matter. Think about their future, what lies ahead for them."

Another wife spoke up. "How do you think our children will feel about being sent away to America? Do you think they will so easily accept a person in a marriage that we choose?"

Wilhelm turned toward her. "You have to search your hearts and know your children. They are at first obedient to us as parents, and we as their parents must do our best to make a suitable match. I would not want a single one of my daughters married to a slacker, a blasphemer, or a man with uncharitable character. It's my job to make sure your son deserves one of my daughters. And your job is to make sure our daughters will be loyal, obedient, and hard-working wives for your sons—and good mothers to the grandchildren we will never see."

"How do you propose we go about these arranged marriages?" said Peter Andersson, a disagreeable man known for his skepticism and distrust.

"I don't have all the answers. You each must talk, husband and wife. Think about my proposal. Pray about it. Let's meet next Sunday to see who is interested in doing this. Then we will work together on a plan. But I am writing to Mr. Berg that within the year, the Lindberg family of Ljuder will have eight people ready to immigrate to America."

Wilhelm thought about the hearths in these four homes, imagining bouts of shouting and shunning, wives turning cold shoulders to husbands, and husbands scolding wives. The Lindberg sons and daughters learned of their father's proposal and surprised him in their reactions.

Simon, the eldest, spoke first. "As the eldest," he said angrily. "I should have a voice in this decision and be the new head of the household for our family going to America. I should be the one to start a Lindberg community in the New World."

"But you have a wife and a small child and another on the way," Wilhelm said. "The trip could be dangerous for your family."

"Because I am married is the reason it should be me who goes," Simon said. "As husband and father, I must try to make a better life for my children in America."

Oscar, the second son, was eager to take Simon's place. According to Wilhelm's plan, he would be the sole heir to the farm.

The daughters expressed different reactions.

"What if I'm married to someone cruel and unkind?" Stella said.

Both Stella and Olga wanted no part of crossing the ocean and settling in a land rumored to be full of savages and men of ill repute.

Alma, the youngest at fifteen years old, refused to go. "I will not leave my mother." She stamped her feet, tears flowing. "I'll take care of you and father when you're older," Alma pleaded. "I'll even sleep in the kitchen and won't be a burden to anyone."

"This one is my biggest problem," Wilhelm thought to himself.

As the youngest, she was her mother's favorite. Her mother coddled and shielded Alma from the work of the household that fell to her older sisters. Alma escaped tutoring on cooking, cleaning, sewing, and embroidery. While most girls Alma's age imagined their futures as wives and mothers, Alma showed no interest in anything beyond being cared for like a small child. Her saving grace was her natural beauty. She was by far the prettiest of Wilhelm's daughters, with bright blond hair, piercing blue eyes, and milk-white skin.

"Boys are already noticing Alma," Wilhelm said later to Tilde.

"She ignores them," Tilde hissed.

"Well, they must think her aloofness is evidence of her virtue. At least we'll have no trouble finding her a husband," Wilhelm murmured. His daughter's pampered, spoiled nature convinced him that Alma must be separated from her mother if she had any hope of becoming a responsible wife for a future husband.

"How dare you concoct this plan without my knowledge or acceptance!" Tilde growled through clenched teeth.

Wilhelm sighed, then straightened his shoulders. They had not had intimate relations since Alma's birth, but he realized Tilde's accusation sealed that fact for all time.

In the end, the Lindbergs decided which four children would

immigrate: Simon, eldest son and his family; daughters Olga, Stella, and Alma. Oscar, the second son, would remain and inherit the family farm. Ella would stay behind to help her parents in their old age, and in all likelihood, remain a spinster.

As the weeks wore on, news of the Lindberg plan became common knowledge throughout Ljuder and spread to surrounding communities. People spoke of little else. The list of marriageable candidates for the Lindberg daughters shifted back and forth.

The Anderssons rejected Wilhelm's plan outright, declaring they would not give up their children to the risks of the journey and settling in a new land. "We will all stay as a family in our native Sweden until we die."

As time passed, three of the four families offered up children as marriage prospects for the Lindberg daughters. Parents agreed to discuss the merits of each marriage before introducing the couples to each other and to allow a time of chaperoned courting so the couples could get acquainted. Since the girls were not yet of marriageable age, they had to accept their parents' wisdom in selecting their future husbands.

No one, least of all the Lindbergs, expected men and women from beyond the four families to present themselves as candidates for immigration. After word spread of Wilhelm's plan, young men and women throughout Smaland made their intentions known. Several came from the cities beyond Smaland, offering their trades as carpenters, bakers, butchers, and ironworkers, desirable skills to add to a farming community.

When all was said and done, not just eight people, but a total of 36 young men and women and ten small children signed up for passage and an unknown future in Texas. To Simon Lindberg fell the responsibility of group leader and spokesman. Both men and women would vote on major decisions, but as peacemaker and judge, Simon would have the deciding voice. Most picked up Swedish-English dictionaries to learn English.

Parents allowed betrothed couples to court according to Swedish customs, and under the strict supervision of parents or older siblings. All the pairings seemed promising except for Wilhelm's youngest daughter, Alma.

Olga, just becoming of marriageable age, was betrothed to Joseph Nordin, to be married in Sweden before leaving. Stella was betrothed to Noah Gustaffson, and Alma to Liam Swenson, and both would marry in America after they turned 18. Until then, they would be under the protection and supervision of Simon and his wife, Brigitta, who reasoned she would get two household workers in the bargain.

Alma erupted when her parents announced her engagement to Liam Swenson. "Of all the boys in Ljuder, Liam Swenson is the last person I want to marry!" she stormed.

Tilde said to Wilhelm one evening, "Liam is a stark contrast to Alma."

"Give him time, he's only seventeen. Plus he's shy. His parents agree that one strong personality within a couple is enough, and perhaps Liam's gentle manner will temper Alma's petulant nature." Simon shrugged. "Alma turns 18 in three years, time for her to grow accustomed to her new life in Texas and, we hope, acquire some domestic skills under Brigitta's guidance."

A somewhat frail and sickly girl, Alma became an even heavier burden on her mother, demanding care and attention for all manner of real and perceived ailments. Wilhelm was unmoved. Of all his children, Alma was the one child he didn't want living under his roof as a spinster. Though he wouldn't dare express these sentiments to Tilde, shipping Alma to America would be a blessing rather than a sacrifice.

"You will go, Alma, and your tantrums will not change my mind," Wilhelm said to her, summoning all possible authority as head of the household.

Alma never relented in her disapproval of the arranged marriage and immigration to America and did her best to make life miserable for those around her. When the parents planned supervised visits between Alma and her betrothed, she treated Liam with complete disregard.

The families agreed to host one combined wedding for couples of age, a practical Swedish decision as the costs and legalities could be shared and accomplished in one fell swoop. Olga was among those brides and married Joseph Nordin in the group ceremony.

By year's end, Wilhelm sold the forested portion of his land to the parish's largest landowner, who was acquiring tree-covered land for his forestry business. That money provided Simon with a purse for the journey.

Lucas Berg had established an elaborate support system to help the immigrants resettle, from embarkation in Sweden to arrival in the Port of Galveston and all the way to their final destination in Texas. To begin, Berg lent wagons and teams of draft horses. Once the families arrived at the coastal port of Karlshamm, their point of embarkation, the teams were reserved for the next group of immigrants. In Karlshamm, the immigrants purchased provisions for the sea journey at a general store along the wharves, also owned by Berg,

At last, the day arrived for the group to leave their farms and homes. The travelers packed as little as possible, but everyone brought precious keepsakes to remind them of their home, heritage, and culture. Family Bibles. Traditional costumes. Special tools. Handmade quilts. Heirlooms passed down for generations.

Stoic even now, the Swedes kept their emotions in check as families said final farewells, their excitement of starting the journey tempered by sadness at leaving their parents, never again to see the land of their births.

The scattered group converged at the Akerby Crossroads—a dozen wagons transporting the immigrants and their meager possessions—eighteen married and betrothed couples, ten small children—forty-six souls in all.

They set off in the summer of 1909.

Their group was the last of the Great Swedish Migration that had stripped the country of its young men and women, abandoning

Sweden for an uncertain future in America.

* * *

The Crossing

NONE OF THE Smaland group had ever seen the ocean, much less crossed one.

"This port at Karlshamm is nothing but a foul-smelling, unpleasant city," moaned Alma.

"Well, after three days onboard that old wooden sailing ship," snapped Brigitta, "you'll be relieved to be on dry land again."

"Just looking at the *Carlotta* makes me sick," said Alma as she stared at the docked boat that would take them to England. "How long will we be on that awful ship?"

"I'm told the *Carlotta* will take three days to get to Liverpool. Then we switch to the SS *Norna* for the transatlantic voyage." Simon said.

"I can't imagine being on a boat like that for months, much less a few days," whined Alma.

Simon's group spent a night in the Karlshamm harbor town, gathering provisions and ensuring their trunks and possessions were loaded and stored. That night they enjoyed their last Swedish meal in their homeland.

At first light, all forty-six passengers lined up at the embarkation point, both eager and anxious to walk up the gangplank. Even Alma was giddy with excitement. After the crew guided the passengers to their quarters below decks, they made ready to cast off, timing their work to catch the outgoing tide.

The Lindberg group jostled about below with other immigrant groups.

"There!" Simon called to Brigitta, pointing. "Toss your things on that bunk before someone else claims it."

"But it's only one," Brigitta said.

"How will we stay together?" wailed Alma.

"In these crowded conditions, some of us will be separated," he said. "Just try to do your best to stay together."

After a few hours at sea, a few already felt the effects of seasickness, but it wasn't until nighttime when people were trying to sleep that the worst grips of the cursed malady hit them. The humiliation didn't reserve itself for just the women. Even the stoutest men fell victim. Staying topside in the fresh air was the best treatment, though some couldn't even rise from their bunks.

Three rough days later, the *Carlotta* sailed in view of Liverpool, and the anticipation of setting foot on land raised their spirits. Granted two nights ashore before their next scheduled departure, Simon and his fellow travelers rented rooms in an inn and slept in beds that didn't move. They walked along the waterfront and visited shops and restaurants where signs were posted on windows warning the travelers: Do not immigrate to the Americas unless you are accustomed to hard work. You are not guaranteed success.

"Hard work is second nature to us," Simon said to his family members, "so don't let these warnings intimidate you."

"On the contrary," said Joseph as he clasped Olga's hand, "this two-day reprieve will bolster our spirits and prepare us for the journey ahead."

"Yes," said Olga with a smile, "we can't imagine what crossing the ocean will be like until we really do it."

* * *

THE *NORNA* WAS far more comfortable than the old wooden brigs. Though still staying in inexpensive steerage three flights below top deck, the Lindbergs and other families found more spacious quarters with comfortable bunks, electric lights, and hot and cold running water.

Alma flopped onto her cot and moaned. When Liam reached out to pat her shoulder, she pushed him away.

"What a contrast from the *Carlotta* to the SS *Norna*!" said Brigitta.

"I met a member of the crew who is half Swedish and half English," said Simon. "His name is Basil, and he has agreed to tell us more about the ship when he has some free time. He speaks Swedish."

Later that evening, after dinner, Basil met with Simon's group on the top deck.

"The *Norna* measures hundreds of feet from bow to stern," Basil said.

"That's as wide as the fields we left behind," said Joseph.

"The ship can hold as many as 1,000 passengers with a crew of 125-150 seamen," Basil continued in his curious, cockney-influenced Swedish.

"How many times have you made the crossing?" Simon said.

"This is my eighth voyage, all on the *Norna*," Basil said, boasting, "and she's the tightest ship afloat."

"How long will it take us to get to Galveston?" said Liam.

"The ship's route follows the coast of the Eastern seaboard, then through the Caribbean between Florida and Cuba, and into the Gulf of Mexico to the Port of Galveston, adding a week to our journey."

"How does the ship handle rough weather," said Stella, already anticipating the seasickness she suffered just three days on the *Carlotta*.

"Ahh, she handles the weather just fine," said Basil. "In fact, she was the lone survivor of the Great Hurricane that hit Galveston in 1900. You know about that, don't you?" Basil scanned his small audience, looking from one to the next. "We were harbored in Galveston when the hurricane hit, maybe one of a dozen other ships anchored in Galveston Bay. We were expecting a gale, but that storm hit without warning."

"What's a gale?" Noah said.

"A gale is a bad storm with lots of wind. They're pretty common on the seas, and Galveston gets lots of those. A hurricane is ten times worse," Basil continued. "This one struck the island with 120 mile-per-hour winds, catching everyone unprepared. Citizens there even went to the beach to watch the waves come ashore when an unexpected tidal wave over 15 feet tall crashed ashore. Over 6,000 people drowned, and 10,000 were left homeless."

The Lindberg group couldn't believe a storm could be that vicious.

"I was on board the *Norna* when it hit. She was the only ship that didn't break its moorings. All the others were washed ashore, battering everything they hit. Some went as far as ten miles inland before they dry-docked, and they'll remain there always."

The immigrants looked around them at the ship that was taking them across the ocean.

"Nay, don't worry about the *Norna*. She was beat up a bit, but she was the only ship that could be salvaged and made seaworthy again. She's as fit as they come."

With a speed of 15 knots, the captain estimated travel time two weeks from Liverpool to Galveston. Couples kept together, and the entire Smaland group bunked in the same area, forming their own community among the 700 steerage passengers headed to Texas, including a large group of Jewish immigrants from Eastern Europe.

Among all the languages spoken, English was the least understood but the most studied. Immigrants made it a practice to talk among one another by selecting English words chosen from their pocket dictionaries.

Simon and his group settled into their bunks and agreed to take turns going to the top deck for strolls and fresh air, leaving a good number of their party behind to guard their possessions. The *Norna* handled the waves much better than the *Carlotta*, and the passengers found the rocking motion more tolerable. That said, within a day at sea, a good number still succumbed to seasickness.

The Lindberg group had barely left shore before conflicts arose between Alma and Brigitta. Alma was one of the first to fall ill with seasickness, and her usual dour temperament soured further. Brigitta asked Simon to help. "I've got my own child to tend to," she said, "and I don't need a petulant brat to take care of." She shook her head. "Alma demands attention all the time."

Many responsibilities were heaped on Simon as leader of the Lindberg Party, as they soon became known. Simon demanded his group stick together. He checked on their health every day, answered their questions, and acted as a go-between with the ship's crew when necessary. Simon insisted that parents closely guard the ten children, enforcing strict discipline.

"A child could easily fall overboard, never to be seen again," Simon said. "We've got to make sure the mothers never let their children out of their sight."

He headed off conflicts that might arise from mingling with other groups and cultures, not the least of these protecting themselves from illness. "We don't know what diseases these people might be carrying," he said. "I intend for every one of us to reach our destination alive and well."

Brigitta kept watch over the wives, alerting Simon of issues needing his attention. When Alma's health seemed to improve, Brigitta tried to enlist her help.

"You're not my mother!" Alma snapped. "I don't have to do anything you say."

Simon pulled Alma aside. "Your irritable behavior is unacceptable and you must promise to do better." He also urged Brigitta to be patient, confident that once ashore and at their final destination, Alma would adapt to her new life. Alma agreed to treat Brigitta better, but as soon as Simon was out of sight, she resumed her petulant ways.

Away from her mother's protective skirts, Alma soon learned that her budding beauty attracted attention from not just her group of travelers but the other groups on board as well. Her aloof, coquettish ways only added to her allure, and men flirted with her. Even the seamen saved the sunniest spots shielded from the wind for her. Men offered better portions at mealtimes or an unbruised apple for her dessert.

But to Liam Swenson, Alma's betrothed, she had only disdain, and she ignored him.

"Just look at how Alma behaves around other men while not giving me a single glance,"Liam complained to Simon. "I hope this game will stop once we are wed."

"I'll keep a close eye on Alma," Simon said, "and I appreciate your patience with her. You're a good match for her tempestuous nature."

Stella, on the other hand, was Alma's opposite. She compensated for Alma's lack of cooperation by helping Brigitta with the children and the cooking, never shirking a duty, and always pitching in.

"I'm excited about my future marriage to Noah Gustaffson," she told Brigitta one afternoon as they folded laundry.

"You treat your betrothed with respect and affection, and that's a nice quality in a wife, or a husband."

To Simon's watchful eyes, there seemed a disconnect in their natures. Brigitta had noticed it, too, and their pillow talk at night reflected on the potential unsuitability of this union. "Stella is obedient to Noah when they spend time together above decks," whispered Brigitta, "but he seems to lord his authority over her."

"Yes, and in front of others," said Simon, "He's made unkind remarks about her sturdy legs or her plain face."

"So you've observed that, too."

"My mother and father may have misjudged Noah," Simon whispered. "Stella is too nice a person to be treated so."

They continued to bicker about Alma. "You've got to take a heavier hand with her, Simon. If she's to make a good wife, she must accept her responsibilities."

The tight quarters onboard the *Norna* only increased the tension between the two women, and Simon thought, "I'll have no peace in my household until these two women are separated."

Onboard, the Lindberg Party used their time to speculate

about the coming landing, the journey inland, and what to expect when they arrived at their destination. More important, the group discussed how they would govern themselves in the new country. Coming from a culture where the government and the church held absolute control over their lives, the Swedes longed for the freedoms promised in America, but they were also accustomed to rules and lines of authority.

These conversations were invaluable to Simon as he observed who showed an ability to get along with others and who might be the naysayers found in any group of people. He encouraged the gathered immigrants to express their reservations about his role and offered to step aside if someone else wanted the position. Somewhat to his dismay, no one volunteered, and by unanimous consent, the Ljuders wanted Simon to remain as their leader.

"Very well, then. If I accept this role, I have some terms," said Simon. "As I see it, there are two main tasks ahead. The first is working together, solving problems, making decisions, and governing ourselves. The second task is the work of building our community when we arrive, both homesteads and shared structures, such as a school and a church."

He waited until almost everyone nodded.

"Until we see the land for ourselves, we don't know the extent of the work required of us, so I suggest we wait to establish our Building Committee. That gives us more time to know one another better and learn what skills each offers."

He held up his forefinger. "The first task, however, let's settle that now. I suggest four people, plus myself, develop our governing rules. We five will put it to the rest of you for a vote. We don't want the same autocratic rule we had in Sweden, where four people and the King ruled our lives. That's why we left Sweden. In America, each person—man and woman—will have a voice and a vote."

Murmurs of agreement floated through the crowd.

"But there still needs to be structure and guidance. When all voices have been heard, decisions must be made so we can move forward. We Swedes will argue till the cows come home, so there must be an end to discussion and a time for decision. On matters of importance to the whole community, we will vote; and in the event of a tie, as your chosen leader, I will have the deciding vote."

"Then what?" said one of the men.

"Then all must abide by the decision." Simon paused. "These are my terms for accepting leadership of this group. Do you agree to my terms?"

Their acceptance was unanimous and enthusiastic, and he became the official Lindberg Settlement leader, and they chose four others to work with him on governance.

"Humpf!" hissed Brigitta. "Of course they want you to lead them. Not a single one of them want the extra work you've taken on to lead this group of stubborn Swedes!"

After eight days of smooth sailing, the *Norna* cruised into the Caribbean, where the waters turned a beautiful aquamarine, and tropical sea breezes offset the searing sun. The tranquil seas lulled the passengers into a lazy comfort, at once shattered by a violent storm the likes of which they had never experienced.

Despite the ship's size, it pitched and rolled like a tiny toy. The captain instructed passengers to stay below decks, where they were thrown from their bunks and tossed side to side. The storm lasted through the night, terrifying the passengers that they might not see the next day, much less their new home.

Dawn did come, however, and the sea resumed its calm, almost flat surface. Once the ship entered the Gulf of Mexico, nearing the end of the journey, the water turned a darker, murky green. The sea then seemed to boil beneath them, tossing the ship up and down, side to side.

"Just another day or so," Simon said to his group. "We're almost there."

The ship's piercing whistles signaled to all the passengers that the destination was near, long before any of the passengers sighted land. Everyone lined up at the railings, eager for that first glimpse.

"Land Ho!" came the jubilant cry from a member of the crew, and an enormous cheer went throughout the entire ship. A gray hump on the horizon soon took on a more distinct shape and color, revealing the unmistakable coastline that stretched from one end of the horizon to the other.

Land! Simon exhaled a breath of relief, and his shoulders relaxed for the first time since leaving Ljuder almost a month before. All forty-six members of the Lindgren Party had survived the journey and were about to set foot on the land they would call home. The sky was blue, and the air was hot.

It was July 1909.

* * *

The New Land

"ALL PASSENGERS, SECURE YOUR belongings and prepare to disembark," came the captain's orders over loudspeakers. "Check your accommodations carefully and take your possessions with you. Wear your passenger manifest around your neck as you go through Immigration, including children. Your baggage and trunks will be unloaded in the rear of the ship and held in the baggage terminal until you clear Immigration."

The passenger manifest was a tag on a string of leather that included each person's name, occupation, marital status, country of origin, and destination once in the U.S. The children's tags included the names of the parents.

Simon organized the Smaland settlers into small groups, one person designated as head. He separated men and women, as required, to go through the lines at Immigrations. Inspectors looked for evidence of criminals or troublemakers, and doctors conducted cursory medical examinations for infectious diseases, such as smallpox, yellow fever, and tuberculosis. The exams were superficial and quick, not the least bit thorough.

"Stay together," Simon called out to the families. "Each of you must look out for the other. Constantly count and check that everyone in your group is with you, and no one is to wander away from their small group." He took a a moment to eye each group leader.

"Once each group has passed through Immigrations, we will reassemble just past that point." He pointed at a sign above an exit in the distance. "Look for me. We will wait until every group has completed Immigrations. Then all but the men I've chosen will go to the baggage terminal to collect our belongings."

Placing his hands on the shoulders of each family's leader, he said, "The head of each household will come with me to Mr. Berg's store in Galveston. There we will secure the wagons and horses he has for us, one wagon for each family, and return to you here. I don't know how long this will take. Wait in the terminal with our belongings until we return. Do not leave our belongings unprotected! Do not talk to strangers! No one is to wander off! Women and children, stay together and do not go off alone."

Some in the group had picked up a few English phrases, but none had command of the language yet. Simon feared the worst, should anyone get separated from the group.

Shuttling almost 1,000 disembarking immigrants through the Galveston immigration process was efficient, albeit stressful. Back in Sweden, they had heard frightening stories of immigrants who reached New York, only to be denied entry at Ellis Island because of disease or sickness. Then they were either quarantined in some dingy cell for an indefinite period or put back on a ship and returned to the same port they had left.

"Here in Galveston Harbor, the 'Ellis Island of the West,' conditions are much better," Berg had assured them. "We don't have the corruption or violence toward immigrants that happens in New York. Here, immigrants are welcomed. But you still must be cautious of charlatans and miscreants here whose livelihood is cheating and tricking immigrants out of their property. Never leave your belongings unattended, and women should stay with their menfolk at all times."

The gruffness of the inspectors, together with the illiterate Swedes, made the process unpleasant, and the busy docking area was confusing and intimidating. Simon stayed near the small groups in case an inspector's patience wore thin. The group didn't even have time to appreciate that they were on solid ground after two weeks at sea.

The eighteen men assigned to get the wagon teams were first to see and feel dry land. When they emerged from the shipping terminal, Simon scanned the dusty streets of Galveston and said to the others, "This hot, humid land is nothing like our native Sweden. Everything is covered in a dull coat of sand and salt, and where are the plants and grass? There's just those tall, spindly trees."

"Look at the people!" said Liam. "Their clothes are different. Their manners are different. Everything about them is different."

"And they walk so fast," said Simon. "They must have to get somewhere in a hurry."

"They're impatient with anyone who gets in their way," said Noah.

Joseph pointed toward the shore. "Look! There's the wall that seaman Basil told us about. It's massive! Imagine how many men it took to build that."

"It fits what we've heard about America," said Simon, "They are ingenious when it comes to building."

What also struck them was the newness of everything.

"All these buildings are still unpainted because of that hurricane," said Simon. "Strange how it's like the city has no history, but then, remember we're in the New World. Everything we will see is new compared to our Sweden."

With some effort, Simon and the others found Lucas Berg's store, an enormous warehouse of food, clothing, guns and ammunition, supplies, tools—everything needed for the journey inland. A line six deep of people, immigrants just like Simon and his group, waited their turn for the clerk's attention at a counter in the front of the store. Two hours later, longer than it took to go through Immigrations, their turn came. Simon provided the clerk with the document Mr. Berg had given them in Sweden, confirming an order for eighteen teams of wagons and horses.

The clerk chuckled at the word 'horses' and directed Simon to the livery at the back of the store. "We'll assemble the teams over there," he said. "Horace, come 'ere," the clerk shouted over the steady din in the store.

A young man, awkward-looking with stooped shoulders, came to the counter. His face was long and narrow, with a jaw that jutted out and a mouth full of teeth that pushed his lips forward, features that might have inspired his given name.

"This here's Horace Karlsson," said the clerk. "He works for the Berg Company and me. Horace, this here's your group of Swedes just off the *Norna*." The clerk pointed at Simon and the others. "Mr. Berg is sponsorin' 'em. I want you to get 'em to the campground for the night and stay with 'em, have supper with 'em, and give 'em what's what about livin' in Texas. Mr. Lindberg, Horace will be y'all's guide to your settlement. Anything you need to know, he'll tell ya."

Horace stepped forward and spoke to Simon and the others in their native Swedish with a strange accent and many new words they'd never heard.

"Welcome, new friends," he bellowed. "We been expectin' you, but y'all're a bit overdue. Musta' run into some bad weather on the crossin'. Mr. Berg figured out a long time ago that folks just gettin' here from the Old Country need to know what to expect, being's how y'all are brand new to Texas, and that things are a whole lot differ'nt than where you come from. No point in havin' folks dyin' just 'cause they don't know better. Now the first thang, tell all yer folks not to listen to nobody 'cept me here. My ma and pa came here from Sweden with Mr. Berg over 30 years ago when that crossin' took months! Lots of our people died on the trip, and others when they got here, of the fever, snakebite, and just plain ignorance. Galveston is full of thieves and con artists just dyin' to separate you from anythin' worth anythin' you got. Don't talk to 'em, don't listen to 'em. Do you understand me?"

Simon and his companions nodded, though a bit wide-eyed and dazed at the man's expressions.

"I was born here in Texas, and I speak the mother tongue plus Texican, so I will guide y'all to your new settlement in Manor and do my best to teach you how to survive here. I've never been to Sweden, but from what my folks told me, there's not much that's the same, especially the hot weather. It's my job to keep ya'll alive till you git to Manor."

Simon and his group now met an animal they had never before encountered—an American mule.

"No, sir," said Horace. "You don't get thirty-six horses; you get thirty-six mules. And y'all will be glad of it!"

It was almost dark when Simon and his party drove the mule teams to the baggage terminal, where the rest of their party had circled their trunks and belongings. They were hungry and irritable.

"Everyone, load your belongings in the wagon picked for your family," Simon said. "Be quick now. We'll make camp just outside town and have some food. Then we'll listen to Mr. Horace Karlsson, our guide, who will talk to us about Texas and where we are going. Tomorrow we'll come back into town and fully provision ourselves for the journey inland."

"Seems you ought to tell us how long it'll take to get there, Brother Simon," Noah Gustaffson called out, assuming the role of spokesman for the group.

"A quick answer is we head north to Manor, about 200 miles from here. We will start at first light two days from now. With luck, we'll be there in a week or more."

"Let me tell you this right now," shouted Horace over the restless crowd. "Your mules ain't your pets! They are slow but steady. They were born to pull wagons, plows, and carry ev'ry manner of heavy loads. Feed 'em, water 'em, hobble 'em; and they'll do the work you give 'em. But don't walk too close behind 'em or you'll feel a kick like a blast from a cannon."

After a supper of bacon, potatoes, and biscuits, the group gathered around a large campfire. Horace wasted no time getting into the "Lessons About Texas" handbook laid out by Lucas Berg for his Swedish settlers.

"The first thang, startin' right now, learn that campfire smoke is your friend. Git yourselves good'n covered with it before you settle down to sleep. It keeps the skeeters off'n ya. These varmints'll eat you alive 'less you got a good coatin' of wood smoke all over ya."

Several in the group looked sideways at each other, bewildered.

"That could be the most important lesson in this here book. Skeeters cause all manner of misery, includin' yella fever. Things are a lot better now than they used to be. In 1844, a third of Galveston died, and in 1867, yella fever killed another thousand people right here in Galveston. You folks are lucky. In 1900, a fella named Walter Reed discovered the cause of yella fever was skeeters, them kind that breed in still water and hot climates—like Galveston! So the idea is to keep 'em from bitin' ya. The skeeters are worse in summer. The cold winter kills 'em. Every evenin', put some green limbs and green wood on the fire to give off a lotta smoke. Then just bathe yourself in it."

He scanned the group to see who might have questions.

"That's enough for your first night. We'll talk ev'ry night till we reach Manor. Y'all be thinkin' of questions as we make our way inland. Save 'em for the campfire so that ever'body can learn together. Now y'all cover yourselves with smoke and git a good night's sleep."

On their second night, Horace gave another lesson. "I want you folks to recognize the kinda varmints that are harmless and the kinds that do ya mischief."

Horace gave vivid descriptions of stinging insects, the flying ones and the crawling ones, spiders to avoid, and snakes, the venomous ones and the good kind that keep rats out of barns. The four-legged creatures were too numerous to remember: skunks, opossums, raccoons, foxes, coyotes, wolves, mountain lions (also called panthers or jaguars), javelinas, wild hogs, bears, and all manner of deer.

"Many of these animals you hunt for food; others you avoid or kill if they come on your propity." He explained that some fowl were food sources—doves, ducks, geese, turkeys. Crows, however, were pests that could clean out a corn crop, while buzzards served as the carrion cleanup crew feasting on dead carcasses. "Some creatures, like buffalo, are farther north and west and no longer live in this part of the country."

On the third night, Horace focused on the two-legged humans who lived in Texas. By the late 1890s, hostile Indians ceased to be a concern, for the most part cleared out by the Texas Rangers. The government took land from the tribes to make room for the settlers and then forced the Indians to live on reservations.

"Mexican bandits, however, are still a problem, 'specially around the Texas-Mexico border, but not up around where you're headed," Horace said.

Slaves freed by the Civil War and their descendants still wandered from farm to farm, looking for plots of land to settle and "sharecrop." The Union government's pledge of "40 acres and a mule" proved an empty promise, as carpetbaggers and landowners made it all but impossible for former slaves to obtain clear title to land. To survive, they became sharecroppers for whites who did own land—in truth, slavery by another name.

"Be 'specially watchful for opportunities to make a deal with sharecroppers. You gotta dig wells, cultivate the land, plant crops. You can expand your farm production tenfold if ya gotta black fam'ly or two on your propity."

"Mr. Horace, we don't hold with slavery, and we'll have none on our farms," said Simon in a stern voice.

"This ain't slavery, Mr. Simon. It's good sense. The blacks git land, a roof over their heads, a garden patch, and a share of profits from the harvests. You give up an acre or two and git free labor."

"Cheap labor sounds good to me," Noah said with a smug grin. "If we can get the blacks to do the dirty work, that suits me just fine."

The closer the group got to their destination, the more concerns rose in Simon's mind about Noah. His swaggering, boastful manner just didn't sit well with Simon. Since Stella hadn't complained, he kept quiet.

"Water is always a concern in Texas. You either got a drought or floods to contend with," Horace said. "Ev'ry farm's gotta have wells and water reservoirs. We call 'em tanks in Texas. You'll get your water from Gilliland Creek, which runs through the area where y'all will settle. Just don't plant your crops too close to the creek bed or it'll wash 'em away when it floods."

During the voyage, Simon and the heads of each family had laid out a plan for their settlement. Each farming family set a goal of owning 200 acres in the next five to ten years, some even more than that. The tradesmen in the group had eyes on opening their businesses to capitalize on the area's exploding growth. The Anderssons in the group planned to open a bakery in Austin. The ironworker knew mules and horses would need shoeing and intended to open a farrier business, and a future blacksmith shop. Carpenters would find work everywhere.

Their trek north was on roads well-traveled. Each night Horace led them to a clear, flat patch where they circled their wagons and camped, and each night he conducted lessons about Texas and this strange, hard land.

"You know, you folks're lucky to have Mr. Berg sponsorin' you. He's got general stores in Elgin, Manor, and Austin, the state capital, selling whatever you need: lumber, tools, farming equipment, seed, home furnishings, clothing, food. His settlements have banks, mills, churches, schools, even doctors."

"But he's profiting off everything we buy, right?" said Noah.

"Sure, he got rich," said Horace, "but he's also created opportunities for folks like you to start fresh and get your own piece of the pie. If it weren't for him, you'd still be scratching out a livin' in Sweden, and likely starvin'."

With a frown directed at Noah, Horace added, "Tell me how else would you get a chance to own hundreds of acres outright and more if you have the stomach for it, for $1 an acre! That's the American way. He profits, but so do you!" He paused. "He's doing the same thing for ranchers. Those strong enough to take on the harsh prairies and hills git 4400-acre tracts with similar terms as you farmers."

"Please don't think we're not grateful, Horace," Simon said in an apologetic tone, as he glared at Noah. "All of us here appreciate what Mr. Berg has done for us."

The subject one night was about guns. "Where you come from," said Horace, "not all y'all had 'em. Here, you gotta have 'em! Not just for protection. The Texas Rangers and local sheriffs mostly keep a tight rein on bandits and such. But you need guns for huntin' and for killin' predators around your propity."

Horace held up two sidearms, a Colt and a Remington, both six-shooters.

"Now, either one of these'll work for you, but you need one or t'other. Each has six bullets. You wear it in your holster, but not when you're out plowin' your fields or doin' hard work around the farm. But if you're out in the brush or even just drivin' your wagon, wear it. Ya never know when you might need it. Your six-shooter is for close range, like shootin' a rattler or just by wearin' it, scarin' off a trespasser who looks up to no good."

He reholstered the handguns and picked up two other bigger weapons and held one aloft. "Then you need a rifle and a shotgun. This here's the Winchester repeater, 44 caliber. Good enough for the Texas Rangers, and it'll be good enough for you. You use it for huntin'."

Horace switched to the gun in his other hand. "This here's the double-barrel shotgun. It don't require careful aim like the rifle, and it'll do for bird huntin' and protection. It's short-range, and it'll hit just about anythin' you point at."

He set the guns down and gestured toward the listeners. "Your wimmen folk and your kids need to know how to shoot, same as you. What does your fam'ly do when you're off plowin' the field, and a coyote comes after your chickens? They need to know how to handle that shotgun and to shoot the varmint and not themselves! They just point and shoot, and this gun here will take care of whatever needs doin'."

Horace picked up one more implement. "The last weapon you need on you is a knife. These two here are called the Arkansas Toothpick and the Bowie knife. Either of 'em'll do. Around a farm, you'll always be in need of cuttin' somethin': rope, wire, birds' necks, skinnin' your deer, rabbits, or other critters you kilt and intend to eat. When we go to Austin, every fam'ly will need to git these weapons."

Horace set up a range with targets and gave the men their first shooting lesson. He showed them the safety features, then how to load and clean the weapons.

"Tomorrow before we sit down to supper, a few of us'll do a little huntin'. We'll do this every night till you folks feel comfortable handlin' these guns. They need to feel like a second skin to you. Simon, pick out two others. You'll go first."

That next night Horace took Simon, who invited Liam and Noah to join them. Simon wanted to spend time with both of his future brothers-in-law, especially Noah, to understand better their characters before they married his sisters.

Horace showed them that the best way to kill a deer was to find a watering hole, sit downwind, and just keep quiet and wait. They didn't see a deer that time, but they found deer tracks and wild hogs signs. On the way back to camp, Horace spotted something moving among some grass near a rock outcropping. He pulled his six-shooter, took careful aim, and fired. Then he unsheathed his knife and stabbed a still-writhing creature, pulling it up by the blade to show them.

"This here's one of them killers in Texas I hoped to show ya, a copperhead. The only way I knew he was here was 'cause the leaves were movin', but see how he looks just like the leaves? He's deadly poisonous. We'll take him back to camp to show the others. I hope we'll meet up with some other deadly vipers so you can see what they look like and how they hide."

As they got closer to their destination, Horace's lessons turned to what they needed to know when they arrived. "Where y'all are goin' is the best farmland in the whole state of Texas. Good black prairie land, nice'n flat. Crops'll grow tall as a man."

The journey was long and slow, sometimes making twenty miles in a day, others only ten, depending on weather and conditions of the wagon teams. The time allowed them to learn about the new land. They passed through coastal plains with unremarkable scenery, no mountains or forests, not even hills, which made easy work for the mules.

Nighttimes did indeed mean the invasion of the mosquitoes. Despite covering themselves with smoke from their fires, the bloodsuckers still found Swedish skin to bite. The travelers decided to add another layer of protection with axel grease, and that seemed to work, though being coated with the slimy stuff was unpleasant.

Their journey took them west and north, skirting the sprawling city of Houston, the largest city in the state. The landscape changed when they drew near the farming community of Brenham, the halfway mark, with gentle rolling hills and endless pastures of deep beautiful grasses feeding fat dairy cows. The Brazos River ran through the green hillsides.

Horace told them they were not far from the battleground where just 75 years ago Texas' ragtag army fought for Texas' independence from Mexico.

"If General Houston hadn't defeated Santa Ana, we'd be speakin'

Spanish right now," Horace said with a laugh, "but prob'ly you wouldn't be here at all."

Houses they passed stood in groves of trees, cooled by their shade. Even construction was different with homes made of wooden planks and painted white, instead of whole logs like their homes back in Sweden. Often, farm families would stop in their chores and wave to the passing wagons.

They spent their last night before reaching Manor in a pine forest with the blessed coolness of a tall tree canopy. They camped along a creek and set to work preparing the final supper of their long journey. Both Simon and Brigitta jumped at the sound of a terrible scream coming from the outskirts of the circled wagons, followed by a gunshot from Horace's six-shooter.

They raced to the sound and found Horace bent over a hysterical Stella, with Alma beside her wailing sister. Stella was cradling her right arm in her left hand, and Horace had his Bowie knife out. Brigitta and Simon rushed to Stella's side and gasped when they saw two distinct holes between the thumb and forefinger of her right hand.

Stella cried, "It hurts! It hurts!"

The remains of a rattlesnake lay near their feet, its head almost severed from its body by Horace's bullet. Horace held Stella's wrist in a tight grip and instructed both Brigitta and Alma to keep Stella still. He cut deep incisions in her hand, shaping an X across the bite marks. Then he bent over Stella's hand and sucked and spat, sucked and spat, sucked and spat, drawing the poison out of the incised bite mark. When he was satisfied he had removed enough poison, Horace made a sling for Stella's arm and carried her back to camp, the others trailing behind him.

"What happened?" Simon said to Alma.

"We were… collecting firewood," Alma said through her tears. "All of a sudden, Stella screamed. We never even saw… the snake. Stella reached to pick up a stick, but it was that snake, and it bit her."

"I told you to watch where you're stepping!" Noah scolded Stella. "Now you've gone and gotten yourself snakebit!"

"These snakes are ev'r'where," Horace said, in an effort to soothe Stella's rising panic. "They're next to impossible to see in the wild. They'll come in your henhouse, your corncrib, your barn. That's why you need your six-shooter with you at all times. At least these snakes will give you a warnin', 'less you come up on 'em too fast. It's best to make noises and bump things around when you're doing chores around your propity. That way, the snakes'll know you're around and slither away, or they'll shake their rattlers warnin' you. Thang is, they don't like you any more'n you like them. Stella just had the bad luck of trying to pick it up, thinkin' it was a stick of wood."

"What do we do for her?" Brigitta said.

"Stella'll either git well or she won't," Horace whispered to Simon and Brigitta. "I'll ride ahead to the next town and fetch a doctor. I hope I got enough of the poison out before it traveled through her blood. I was good'n' close when it happened and cut it open purty quick. She's lucky the bite is where there ain't major arteries. If we see swellin' goin' up her arm and turnin' red, then she's done for. If not, she should be all right. I'll be back quick as I can."

Hours later, Horace returned with a doctor who examined Stella and said Horace had done all that he could. The bite mark looked menacing, and the skin around it was darkening, but so far, he found no evidence of poison traveling up the arm, and the swelling had not increased.

"Keep her still and that arm still as well. Give her some of this medicine for the pain, the best we can do," the doctor said with a shrug. "We're lucky Horace was nearby and got most of the poison out. She'll be in pain, but she'll survive."

"How could this happen, so close to our final destination?" moaned Simon. "Until now, no one in our group has been seriously ill or injured."

The mood around camp that night was somber. This New World was so alien from their native Sweden, and they were just beginning to comprehend the dangers facing them.

Later that evening, Simon pulled Noah aside. "Noah, I've kept my eyes on you ever since we started our journey. As the family member responsible for my sister, I'm telling you that I'm displeased with your treatment of her. If she offers any objection to your planned marriage, I will end her betrothal to you."

"You can't do that, Simon! I've made this horrible journey with the promise she'd be my wife and give me children to help grow our farm in this godforsaken place!"

"Perhaps you should appreciate the qualities Stella will bring to your union instead of treating her so harshly. I worry what her life will be like if you are this way even before you're wed. I'll say no more of it now. Perhaps my words will impress upon you the need to mend your ways."

"You're not God!" shouted Noah. "I'll not be denied my rights! But we will talk again, Simon. She may not even be alive in the morning."

Stella spent a restless night and was in intense pain. At dawn, she was sitting up, drinking lots of cool water, and even asking for some food. Both Brigitta and Alma checked her bandaged hand often but saw no signs of swelling. A fever did take hold, but the site of the wound itself did not seem to worsen.

Horace examined her and nodded. "I think the worst has passed."

Simon decided Stella was safe to travel, so the group broke camp and embarked on the final miles to Manor. Leaving the forest, the group took a less traveled road due north. Now, at last, the relieved Swedes allowed themselves the luxury of expressing jubilation as each mile melted behind them.

* * *

Black Bottomland

ALL MR. BERG HAD told them was true. About 25 miles east of Austin, Elgin was a bustling town of 1,300 people nestled in the center of new farms. It was a prosperous agricultural center with two railroad lines passing through the center of town. Local farmers kept three cotton gins busy for the insatiable textile industry on the East Coast.

Manor was a much smaller town, just a few miles farther and twelve miles east of Austin. The Lindberg Settlement lay between Elgin and Manor.

Horace guided the wagons to a camping area that would be their temporary home for a few days. Simon and the owner of each tract went to the Austin Land Office to complete Berg's legal documents for 3,200 acres. Instead of farming, three families opted to start businesses in the towns, but Simon held onto their acres for future growth, while negotiating similar credit terms for those starting new businesses.

Each family head signed a contract to exchange work for two years with no wages and the right to then purchase that land with harvest profits. Berg provided lines of credit to buy building supplies, farming equipment, and provisions. Mr. Berg indeed held the fate of the farmers in his hands.

"How is this any better than what we had in Sweden?" Noah Gustafsson grumbled. "We're buried in debt to Berg."

"Because here we have a way of working out of our debt, and we will own our farm and leave something of worth to our children," Simon told him. "It will take time and hard work, but we are all young enough to build this future. In Sweden, we had no hope at all!"

The clerk at the Land Office gave them a map of their land, and Simon got another map of contiguous acres for any who aspired to more land in the future, including himself.

"I'm not about to repeat the problems in Sweden when the land is too small to support growing families."

Simon dreamed big. He set his sights on owning 500 acres with the work shared by the sons he and Brigitta hoped to have. His first son was now almost two years old and another baby on the way. Simon wanted a farm large enough for a large family.

Around the fireside one night, Simon vented his frustrations to the group. "I'm tired of having to explain over and over why we are here. The endless complaining has to stop, or I will no longer lead this stubborn group. And I need others to assume some responsibilities, because this takes too much time away from the work I need to do for my own family."

Liam spoke up first. "Simon, we are sorry we have burdened you, and we do not want to lose your leadership. It is not all among us who grumble and complain, just one or two. Perhaps now is the time to set up the Building Committee. Here in America, people elect their leaders. Let's do that."

They devised a plan that different ones would oversee specific tasks, such as digging wells and planting crops. Simon would continue as the liaison to deal with legal issues and community affairs with Mr. Berg's stores, the bank, and the Land Office. They appealed to Simon to continue as their spokesman and leader for the next two years. With reluctance, Simon accepted on the condition that others be held accountable for the duties they carried.

The settlers spent several days deciding how to divide the 3,200 acres among the farmers. Carving the land into fifteen plots was a difficult task resulting in heated disagreements. Of course, access to water was the highest priority for each claim.

They started in the center with the Gilleland Creek running through the tract, then parceled out tracts like spokes of a wagon wheel going out from the circle's center, with the creek's tributaries running through all parcels. They decided their homes would be built in the narrowest points of each spoke, so that the distance from one farmhouse to the next was walking distance. The houses would not encroach upon one another but be near enough for neighbors to help when needed.

The center of the circle, the wheel's hub, would be common ground for a church and school. Besides worship, weddings, baptisms, funerals, and community events, the church would serve as the meeting place when there was trouble.

Simon arranged for members of his Lindberg family to have their parcels adjacent to one another: Simon and Brigitta, Olga and Joseph, Stella and Noah, and Alma and Liam, thereby ensuring family continuity and shared work.

The entire community, in turn, would build each house. The initial plan was a simple and conservative design, two or three rooms, depending on the size of the family. Adding to the houses would come later; the goal was to get a roof over every family's head by winter. Families with expectant mothers took priority to give them suitable shelter during the fragile time of birth and infancy. For the others, families drew straws for their turns.

A dozen or more males tackled the construction of the houses while the women cared for the campsites and kept everyone fed. The fact that the houses all looked the same didn't matter, and repetition made it easier to replicate homes in quick order. During the dormant winter months, they would build barns, root cellars, pigpens, and chicken coops, all to be finished before spring planting.

Digging a well was as important as building the houses, and they attacked that task as a community. They agreed to share wells until each farm had its own well. Horace again proved his worth by introducing a water diviner who guided the settlers to underground sources closest to the surface, tracing Gilleland Creek's direction. However, he cautioned that houses could not be closer than 100 feet from the creek's highest point as protection from flooding. Soon multiple wells dotted the community.

The farmers bought milk cows, pigs, and chickens from nearby farms, and the community pooled funds to purchase a bull to build their dairy herds.

Back in Sweden, dogs and cats were considered unnecessary luxuries, as extra mouths to feed, but here these essential pets warded off unwelcome predators.

"No mice, no snakes," Horace told them. "A few barn house cats will keep 'em away."

They learned that well-trained dogs made excellent hunters as well as protectors of animals and children alike. Despite advice not to do so, the children made pets of the dogs and these intelligent, loyal animals became family members.

* * *

ON A TRIP TO the Land Office in Austin, Simon visited the Negro shantytown on the eastern side of town. Pulling his wagon under the shade of an oak tree, he beckoned the residents to gather.

"We are Swedish settlers, fifteen families, building farms on 3,200 acres in Manor. We're hoping to interest some black families to move there and become sharecroppers on our farms."

A few of the men drew closer, curious, but still kept a cautious distance away.

"We will set aside five acres for each family where you can build your own home, plant gardens, and have farm animals," he said. "In exchange, you will help us build our farms and grow our crops. You will get a share of profits from the crops at harvest time that will be your money, free and clear. We ask a fair day's work, six days a week, in exchange."

While Simon waited for a response, children ran helter-skelter through the dusty street that divided the town while the adults sat on porches attached to their shabby shacks. For what seemed forever, there was only silence, all eyes on Simon. At last, one man, built strong as a bull and skin as black as the soil in Simon's farm, stepped forward. He appeared to be in his early 30s, though Simon didn't know the Negro race well enough to guess their ages.

"We's free men," he said. "Our folks was slaves, but none of us be slaves no mo'."

"My people have never owned slaves, and we don't hold with it,"

Simon told the growing circle of men. "We're hard-working farmers starting new lives here in Texas. We learned that some folks like you might be looking to have some land of your own and are willing to help settlers like us grow and harvest our crops and share what we earn. I mean no disrespect to anyone here."

Several of the men cast wary glances at each other but stood still as statues.

"We have good bottom land in Manor that'll produce healthy cotton crops when we can get our fields cleared, plowed, and seeded. I'm told you people know how to do that. The land should produce enough for all of us willing to work it." He paused. "Think on it. If you're interested, come to Manor and ask for the Lindberg Settlement. You'll be welcome."

Simon doffed his hat, said goodbye, and pointed his wagon towards Manor. He smiled, content he had a knack for forging connections with the local community and its inhabitants. Besides that, he enjoyed getting away from the settlers. Their incessant squabbling and haggling gnawed at him.

When Simon returned to his semi-permanent tent, Brigitta and Stella were preparing the evening meal. Alma lay on her sleeping mat, complaining of a headache, Stella peeled potatoes, and little Simon scurried underfoot. The women were quiet, their usual chatter missing.

"I had an interesting visit with the black shantytown outside Austin," Simon said to the women. "I couldn't judge if they are interested in sharecropping with us, but at least we took the first step. These black folks are a sad lot, barefoot and wearing rags. How was your day?"

"Take a look at Stella's arm." Brigitta glared at Simon, hands on her hips.

Simon went to Stella's side and lifted her right hand. "Her hand and arm look fine to me." The snakebite would probably leave a permanent scar, but the wound was healing well enough.

"Not that arm. The other one," Brigitta snapped.

Simon took Stella's left wrist in his hand, and Stella winced. He pulled up her sleeve. A deep bruise covered the entire width of her wrist.

"What happened, Stella?" her brother said.

"I was helping with the well-digging and carrying a bucket of dirt from the well, but it was heavier than I thought, and I dropped it back down the well. Noah was below, and the bucket almost landed on him. He climbed out of the hole and grabbed my arm, and shouted at me for being so clumsy," cried Stella. "He was so angry! It was my fault. I should have been more careful."

Brigitta added, "The others said Noah called her a 'stupid, ignorant Swedish peasant'."

"This time, Noah has gone too far," Simon shouted, his face turning red. He stormed out of the tent, shouting, "Noah Gustafsson! Come and face me!"

Noah emerged from his tent, fists clenched, his face set as though he expected this confrontation. "She's to be my wife, and you're not to interfere with what goes on between a man and his woman. The clumsy cow almost killed me in that well hole!"

"You will not marry Stella!" Simon bellowed. "The engagement is off. You are not to come near my sister again. Is that understood?"

The two men glared at each other, the threat of violence just a breath away, depending on who blinked first.

Simon no longer cared if anyone heard him. The loud voices drew others from their tents. They had heard stories about Simon's temper, but nothing compared to seeing his rage against Noah.

"Fine," Noah spat out after a long pause. "Keep her. She's an ugly pig anyway, and I'm fed up with you and this whole bunch of ignorant peasants. I'm taking my stake and moving to Austin where I can find better company and prettier women."

Simon held back no longer. He pulled back a knotted fist, hardened by his many years of farm work, and hit Noah in the jaw, knocking him to the dirt. He loomed over Noah's sprawled body. "You are to gather your things and leave this community now. You are no longer welcome here," he growled through clenched teeth.

Simon became aware of the others standing nearby, watching, eyes wide and mouths agape. After apologizing for his behavior, he returned to his tent, his shoulders slumped in embarrassment. He felt guilty for ending Stella's engagement without at least talking to her first. The three women were waiting, having witnessed the furor with everyone else.

"Stella, I'm sorry," said Simon. I acted in haste and ended your promise to wed Noah. He is leaving."

"Thank God!" she cried as she hugged him. "I was so unhappy to have to spend my life with such a disagreeable and brutal man. Thank you for saving me. I don't care if I end up a spinster. I am so relieved to be free of him."

Tensions eased throughout the settlement with Noah's departure, like a thorn removed from a foot. The women congratulated Stella, sharing her relief that she was no longer promised to him.

People resumed their business of building their homes, and before winter, new wooden houses, each like the other, were finished in time to welcome three babies into the world, the first American-born citizens to the Lindberg settlers. Simon and Brigitta were blessed with another son. Olga and her husband Joseph followed with a daughter, and soon the third Smaland couple welcomed their first son.

Against his ferocious objections, Noah lost his rights to the land designated for him and Stella. Simon told him flat out to leave empty-handed, and then he reserved his sister's 200-acre tract until she married in the future. Always thinking ahead, Simon and the settlers built Stella's house so it would be ready for her when she did wed, with no notion yet of a prospective husband for her.

Not long after Noah's expulsion from the community, Horace approached Simon, requesting a private conversation.

"Simon," he said in an uncharacteristic formal tone. "I'm here on serious business. Your sister, Stella, and I... I've had high admiration for her since first layin' eyes on her in Galveston. Her bein' promised, I didn't have no hope for the likes of me, but since that varmint's gone, and thank goodness he's gone. Shoot, many times I could'a lit into him for the way he treated Stella. Well, anyway, I been sparkin' Stella. Turns out, she kinda likes me, too. What I'm sayin' is, what we both wanna do is, well, we'd like your permission to git married."

Simon thought he had kept his eyes on everything and everyone. He admitted to himself that with Noah gone, he hadn't paid close attention to his sister. He had seen Horace with Stella and assumed Horace was doing his usual teaching and guiding, as he always did with the group. But Stella and Horace marrying? His mouth dropped open!

"You're a traveling man, Horace. I'm surprised you haven't already returned to Galveston."

"Simon, your group was the last one Mr. Berg is bringin' over from the Old Country. So my job was gonna end after gittin' you folks here. Meetin' Stella and seein' how settlin' here looks mighty fine... It's all good fortune for me. I'd rather live in this part of Texas anyway than Galveston with its storms and skeeters. And I gotta tell you, Simon, seein' how that young lady come through that snake bite as she did, I couldn't imagine anyone braver than her. She's a hard worker and, by all accounts, an even-tempered, all-around pleasant person. She'll make a fine wife."

"I... I... I must first speak with Stella," Simon said.

"A' course." Horace nodded. "You know where to find me."

After Horace left, Simon found Stella within earshot of the whole conversation and shaking with anticipation.

"Stella, is this what you want?" He put one arm around her shoulders. "Is this your choice?"

"It is!" she gushed. "Horace is the kind of husband I want, and I know I will always be safe with him and cherished by him. I couldn't ask for a better person to be my husband."

"Then you have my blessing!" Simon said. "You're of age now, and our community deserves a happy occasion after our long journey and all our hard work. Let's finish the houses and set a wedding date right after."

* * *

SEVERAL BLACK FAMILIES showed up one day, walking barefoot from Austin with their belongings strapped to their backs and heads, one mule for the lot of them. They were ready to accept Simon's offer of five acres. The man who spoke first was the same one who had addressed Simon that day he had visited their shantytown, and he seemed to be their leader.

"Mr. Simon, my name's Mo Brown. This here's my wife, Effie, and these are my chillen, Rayfort, Clarice, and Tom."

The others took turns introducing themselves to the farmers, five families in all.

"More fam'lies are coming," said Mo.

Simon learned that each farm could expect all the help they needed for the heavy work ahead. He invited Mo's family to become part of his farm, and they climbed into his wagon to see his land and the site set aside for the sharecroppers. Simon had chosen a generous plot of land a distance away from the settlers' homes, a little valley adjacent to the railroad tracks bordering the Settlement. The area was too hilly for crops, so he thought the sharecropper dwellings would suit the land.

Mo expressed concern about the lack of a breeze through the valley to ease the summer heat. Effie, however, said the tree cover would make up for it, and her excitement about having their place was evident. One landlord owned the rundown shacks in Austin, and their meager earnings as day laborers barely covered the rent. Effie said owning the land and their house outright would be a tremendous improvement in their financial circumstances.

The Negroes possessed immense agricultural knowledge of cotton farming, while the Swedes knew nothing about growing it, so the black families were a welcome addition to the Lindberg Settlement.

Language, of course, was the first obstacle. The Swedes picked up English words and phrases as fast as they could, but when in their own group, they conversed in the native tongue. The black people spoke a dialect that was often incomprehensible to others.

Horace proved his worth time and again, often stepping in to translate.

"I am lucky to have Horace in the family," said Simon.

Simon placed Stella's track next to his to have ready access to Horace's vast Texas knowledge and interpretation skills.

* * *

Cotton is King

MO AND THE NEGRO sharecroppers proved to be a godsend to the Swedish settlers, acting as teachers and laborers.

"You pro'bly heard that here in Texas 'cotton is king'," Mo said. "Well, tha's right, I reckon, right now. But you never know about cotton. One year you have a great harvest, and the next year you have a drought and git nothin' for your hard work. And what price you git for your crop 'pends on what's goin' on in the world."

"Tell me, more, Mo. We need to learn everything you know," said Simon, soaking in every word.

"Right now there's a war goin' on in Europe, so the mills up north need all the cotton they can git to make uniforms."

"How long do you think we will have this strong demand?"

"When this war is over, prices'll drop faster than sundown. You gotta make hay when times are good, and be ready to sit it out when times are bad."

"Do your people resent working for farmers like us, Mo?"

"It's a little diff'rent from when my folks was slaves. The white man owned us and made us work for free, sunup to sundown, growin' cotton for Europeans. Now, we ain't slaves, we's free men, but seems like sharecroppin' is just another word for it. We's still po'."

After a couple of successful harvests, Simon invested in a new plow that cut through the thick black sod like butter, producing 500-pound bales of cotton per acre from his farm. Though cotton prices fluctuated, Simon and the other farmers made money.

Simon told his neighbors, "I've done the numbers again and again. With the sharecroppers' help and two harvests a year, we will see a profit in the second year. At these prices, there's no reason we can't pay our debts and own our land in the third or fourth year."

The booming Elgin town provided whatever they needed for farm and home, and townsfolk, many earlier immigrants themselves, were eager to coach the newcomers on the cash crop. The 'old timers' taught the settlers to plant corn and maize to provide animal feed for cows, pigs, and chickens. Simon and the other farmers also decided to raise dairy cows. Every family had a home garden providing all the vegetables a family needed.

As far as Simon could see, their future in Texas was bright.

For the next twenty years, the Lindberg Settlement enjoyed uninterrupted growth and prosperity. Profits from harvests were more than sufficient to pay Berg for the land and to repay their loans. They invested in additional land and new farming equipment. The Swedes established a reputation in the Elgin and Manor townships for being honest, frugal, church-going, hard-working farmers. Best of all, they were good investments!

* * *

Alma and Liam

SIMON ASKED ALMA TO sit at their dining table, then took a seat across from her. "Alma, you're eighteen now, and it's time you're wed to Liam Swenson," he told her. He and Brigitta had endured Alma's petulant behavior for three long years, and time had done little to improve her temperament.

"Why do I have to marry Liam Swenson? I don't want to marry

him or anyone for that matter."

"Our parents promised you to Liam, and you will honor that promise."

"I never wanted to come to America in the first place. You made me come here with you. You didn't make Stella marry Noah Gustafsson. Why are you forcing me to marry Liam?"

"Noah was a bad man, and praise God we saw that before she married him. Now Stella is married to Horace, a good, God-fearing man who works hard on his farm and cares tenderly for his wife. And they are expecting their first child. Stella is honoring her duty as a farm wife."

Alma stuck out her lower lip. "America is supposed to be a free country. I want to stay free and marry no one."

"It is God's will that women marry and bring children into the world! Brigitta and I have children of our own, and it is not our responsibility to provide for you all your life. It is time you recognize your obligations. Perhaps marriage will help you accept that you are no longer a child, and you must do your share as a wife and partner to your husband. I will say no more about it."

Simon left the planning details to Brigitta. "Please, Brigitta, do the best you can to prepare Alma for her duties as a wife, especially the marriage bed."

Liam, on the other hand, was happy that the date was set, and at last he would take his place in the community as head of his household and farm. He was ready for a wife.

"With a wife," Liam whispered to himself, "someone'll share the work in building the farm. Alma will manage the household and keep food on the table so I can be free to work the land."

Still, he wondered about Alma's reticence toward him and her troubling frailness. She was so thin. "Marriage will help Alma. She has been lonesome for her mother back in Sweden," he thought, "but when we have children of our own, she will find meaning and joy in having her own family here in America. She will become strong in time; she just needs time learning how to be a wife."

It was a joyless wedding, and Alma looked like she was at a funeral instead of her wedding. They were married by the local pastor in the aptly named New Sweden Lutheran Church. Their first night in the marriage bed was a disaster! Alma cried and cried in agony. Liam felt it was his duty to perform the act of husband, but he had hoped it would be a happy event for them both. Afterwards, he was miserable, and for days Alma was the coldest to him she had ever been, as though he had committed a terrible offense.

These were their first months. When Liam felt enough time had passed, he approached her again, driven by his own needs and his sense of obligation as a husband to sire a family.

"Alma, it is our duty as husband and wife to create children," Liam said, "and you must submit to me so that God's will be done between us,"

From time to time, Alma relented and surrendered her body to Liam.

"I thought this act between husband and wife was supposed to be pleasing," Liam thought to himself. "It's not! It's distasteful for us both. Alma is not getting stronger, and she's growing more sickly by the day."

The burdens of daily housework and cooking were too stressful for Alma. Liam engaged the services of Clarice, Mo Brown's daughter, to perform the household chores that Alma found too tasking. Then, at least, Liam had a clean house and a hot meal waiting for him at suppertime.

The years passed, and still no children for Liam and Alma. Liam threw himself into his work on the farm. His sharecropping family made it possible for Liam to manage the farm. Among Jacob and Mae Jefferson's five children were three strapping, strong boys who worked as hard as full-grown men.

Liam set his mind to cultivating as many fields as he could. War was again brewing in Europe, and clothing manufacturers could not keep up with the demand for military uniforms. "Now is the time to take advantage of these prices," Liam said. "The fabric industry on the East Coast will buy as much cotton as we can grow."

Besides cotton, Liam developed a healthy herd of dairy cows and provided milk for customers as far away as Austin. With the help of Jacob and his sons, Liam built barns, sheds, henhouses, and a water storage tank for his dairy cows. He tried raising pigs but gave it up because Alma complained of the terrible stink when the wind blew toward the house.

Sunday was reserved for worship at the New Sweden Lutheran Church. Sometimes, Alma accompanied Liam to church, but often she felt too poorly and stayed home. Liam often invited Alma's family to Sunday dinner, which they accepted.

"I know Alma is a trying person," Simon said to Liam. "We want to help."

Ever hopeful for his own children, Liam had expanded the original two-room house to include four bedrooms in all, a living room and formal dining room. The front featured a veranda wrapping around two sides of the house, and the back included a screened-in porch that admitted breezes but kept out mosquitoes. Sometimes, the whole Lindberg family would stay for the weekend—Simon and Brigitta and their children, Olga, her husband Joseph, and their three children, Stella, Horace, and their daughter. When the children squabbled over who could sleep on the screened porch, Uncle Simon settled it. "Draw straws. Short straws sleep on the porch; long ones sleep in the house."

Trees around the home provided shade from the relentless Texas sun. Liam's kitchen had a new gas stove and oven that Clarice treated as her own, turning out delicious meals, bread, cakes, pies, and cookies.

Americans were mad for machines, and Liam was the first in the settlement to get his own automobile. He was eager for the newest contraptions, going to Elgin and Austin as often as he could to see the latest inventions showing up in stores and showrooms. Often he convinced his brother-in-law to tag along. "Simon, we still have to rely on mules and wagons to get our cotton and hay to market, but look at the newfangled plowing and threshing equipment that will make us even more efficient and productive."

* * *

A War Hits Home

"THE WAR TO END all wars."

Simon read the headlines to a number of the farmers gathered after church. Though Germany posed no direct threat to America's shores, war fever infected the country, and thousands of young men volunteered to fight the Kaiser in France.

"No men from our Settlement are getting involved in this," Simon said, expressing the age-old Swedish position of neutrality in wars. The Swedes living in the Elgin and Manor farmlands considered the Great War none of their business, but the war meant another cotton boom for the Swedish settlers. East Coast manufacturers couldn't keep up with the demands for the war effort. Cotton prices were higher than ever, and the U.S. government paid top dollar for their cotton.

The Lindberg Settlement was realizing the American dream. They were living in *high cotton*.

As Mo predicted, however, when the war ended, prices hit rock bottom. All at once the farmers found themselves with a product no one needed.

Returning injured and sick soldiers brought back more than their broken bodies. The Spanish Flu followed them and spread through military hospitals, infecting doctors, nurses, volunteers, and nearby communities. The epidemic raced through populations around the world, claiming 50 million lives worldwide, killing more than all the bullets of World War I.

The Lindberg Settlement lost two children to the disease. One day Alma suddenly collapsed and was bedridden with a raging fever.

Both Brigitta and Stella took turns caring for her, applying cold cloths to her fevered brow, and plying her with chicken soup and water. Her family feared she would not live through the night.

After a week, Alma's fever miraculously broke. She recovered, but the disease left her frail body even weaker than before.

* * *

The Chosen One

LIAM GAVE UP HOPE of Alma having children. Her frailness and ill temperament were a permanent condition. When Liam performed his marital duties on occasion, not relishing the experience, Alma submitted to her obligation without any tenderness or affection.

But one day Alma announced to him, "I'm pregnant."

"At last!" Liam sang out. "A child will change everything. You will finally find a purpose in your life, and we can be a family."

The pregnancy was fraught with risks. The town doctor insisted Alma spend most of her pregnancy in bed to avoid losing the baby. Clarice's role in the household became even more essential, caring for both Alma and the household duties.

When the day arrived, Liam, Brigitta, Stella, and the town doctor were on hand during the long and difficult birth. At last, the welcomed cry of a newborn filled the house. A son was born.

As Alma cradled the new infant to her bosom, she announced to her husband, "You've got your son now. His name will be Oscar Nils, Oscar after my brother still in Sweden, and Nils after my father." Even now she defied her husband by flouting the Swedish tradition of naming the firstborn after the father's father.

Liam swallowed the insult and rejoiced that at last, he had a son! Now their lives would change for the better.

Alma had more to say. "I was forced to leave my mother. To leave my beloved Sweden and come to America. I was forced to marry you and to live on this farm among these black heathens." She glared at Liam. "Now I've given you a son. As far as I am concerned, my obligations as your wife are satisfied. From this day on, I will no longer be obliged to fulfill marriage duties to you."

Oscar Nils Swenson was born in 1922.

Alma kept Oscar to her breast well past the age of most babies. Even after he was weaned, he clung to his mother's skirts, rejecting Liam's attempts to introduce him to the farming life. After the baby's birth, Liam moved into one of the guest bedrooms; and Oscar shared the same bed with his mother until he was ten years old.

One day Liam came home from the fields and noticed Alma's hands shaking. "What's amiss, Alma?"

"I don't know. My hands just started shaking today, and I can't make them stop."

It didn't stop, and in fact, the condition worsened. Alma's already fragile frame grew even thinner, and the shaking condition affected her legs and her ability to walk. They sought help from Austin doctors, who diagnosed the disorder as a form of palsy, possibly caused by nerve damage from the Spanish Flu. The doctors told them no known cure was available, and Alma's condition would deteriorate over time. She could live indefinitely with her sickness, but her abilities to perform normal daily functions would be severely limited. In effect, she would be an invalid for the rest of her life.

Alma's emotional state grew worse as well. "As far as I am concerned," she told Liam, "you are the cause of all my misery. Our families arranged our marriage when I was still a young girl in Sweden, and you stuck us on this farm that I hate."

Alma blamed her ailments on Liam and his insistence on her having a child was the cause of the permanent damage her body suffered. Alma expressed her bitterness toward Liam in every conversation and action. Yet, she demanded her husband tend to her every need.

"Liam!" she often shouted at night, waking Liam to come to her bedroom and change her sleeping position. Or "Liam, prop my feet onto the stool." Or "Liam, help me walk to the kitchen."

Clarice tended to her more personal needs, such as bathing and dressing, but whenever Liam was inside the house, her demands for his attention never stopped.

The battles between Alma and Liam over their son Oscar continued unabated, centered around the father's attempts to teach his son about farming.

"My son is not going to be an ignorant dirt farmer. He's going to be someone important."

"Alma, you've got to stop coddling him," Liam begged. "One day Oscar will inherit the farm, and he needs to know how to run it."

Oscar resisted everything his father tried to teach him.

"My son is as rebellious as his mother," thought Liam. One day in complete frustration, Liam tied his son's hands to the plow handles to keep him from running off. "You will work this field," he yelled.

At day's end, Oscar ran to his mother. "Mom, Dad tied me to the plow," he wailed through tears.

Alma unleashed her fury upon Liam. In the end, Liam gave up trying to teach Oscar to farm.

* * *

ALTHOUGH ALMA AND LIAM lived in the same house, one may as well have still been in Sweden while the other lived on the Manor farm. Alma had no kind words for Liam, and Liam had no words at all. Alma lavished her attention on Oscar while Liam plowed his energies into the farm. Though they saw family and other neighbors in church and at occasional community events, Liam's closest associations were with the Jefferson family—and Clarice.

Liam lived his life in neutral. Rising before first light, he made a pot of coffee, a breakfast of eggs, bacon, and toast with lots of jam. He started his day at the kitchen table, making notes of the day's tasks, listing the highest priorities of the day's chores.

"Thank God for Jacob and his boys," Liam thought. "Without their help, and Clarice's, I could never get all the work done. Alma will never be a help, and Oscar fights me at every turn."

On Liam's list one day was a visit from the local veterinarian to dip his bull and cows in a parasite dip. The bull was peaceful enough and responded to harness, but corralling him through a narrow chute and into a trough of water filled with insecticide was another matter. It took four men to maneuver him through the water for his summer bath.

Liam's dairy herd had increased by a half dozen calves the past spring, and he would also ask the vet to see how they were developing.

The most exciting item on Liam's list was the delivery of a new tractor equipped with the latest harvesting device. At a recent farmers market, Liam had seen a demonstration of the tractor. The harvester could do the work of 40 laborers. In October, Liam planned to use his new machine to harvest the year's crop, which looked to be his best yet, and he grinned in anticipation. Renting the harvester to his neighbors would recoup his investment.

A forward thinker, Liam had his eyes on milking machines next. His dairy herd expanded faster than he had dared hope. "That bull is one of my best investments."

"It's ironic," he pondered aloud, "that it's getting harder to find laborers to do farming work. Without this equipment, I wouldn't be able to grow the farm as much as I want."

Yet he realized how dependent he had become on Jacob and his sons. Despite the evolution of mechanized farming equipment, they were essential in keeping up with all the work.

"There will never be a machine that can repair fences or paint a barn," Liam admitted to himself, "and how could I ever manage

Alma without Clarice?"

The last item on his list was a promised picnic for the Jefferson family, a sort of thank you from him for their hard work. Recent rains had filled his stock pond, and fishing for catfish would be a welcome respite from the day's toils, the worst of which was wrestling with the bull. Clarice prepared her famous fried chicken and apple pie. Liam had even gotten the recipe for Stella's Swedish sugar cookies, and Clarice baked batches for the picnic.

Late that afternoon, they sat on quilts under the shade and enjoyed Clarice's meal. After landing an impressive stringer of catfish, the Jeffersons cooled off by jumping in the pond. Liam stretched his lean frame on the blanket, looking up to the sky through the oak's branches. "Here, this moment, I am happy."

He looked at Clarice then, seeing her almost for the first time. She returned his gaze, and he stared into her deep brown eyes, set in her soft, round face. Her skin was the color of smooth chocolate milk. Liam's heart skipped a beat. A warmth surged through him that he had not felt for years, awakening a longing he believed was dead.

He found himself staring at Clarice and told himself he must stop the sensations coursing through his body. Instead, when he reached across the quilt and grazed her hand, she didn't pull away.

Liam now thought of little else than the next time he would see Clarice, be near her, and maybe touch her again. Clarice came to the Swenson household at eight each morning. By five o'clock, she finished her work and walked home.

Armed with full intentions to control the urges awakened within him, Liam had planned to be at work in the back of his barn when Clarice walked by.

When she saw him, she jumped. "Mr. Liam, you half scarit me to death. What'chu doin' out here?"

"Clarice, I can't lie to you. I've been waiting to see you," he said, almost whispering and surprising himself with the passion rising in his throat. "Please, can I talk to you?"

Glancing over her shoulder, Clarice followed him into the barn.

"Clarice," Liam said, "I must tell you how I feel, and I don't want you to be frightened. I cannot hide… my feelings any longer. Please, God… Clarice. I… I want you more than life."

Unable to contain himself a moment longer, he grabbed Clarice by both arms, pulled her to him, and kissed her.

"Mr. Liam," she cried in wide-eyed terror. "You know I can't be with you like this. Ms. Alma will boil me alive, she catch us doin' this."

Liam was past his power to restrain himself. He pushed her down onto a bed of hay, earlier tossed for the next day's feeding, and smothered Clarice in kisses. His hands roamed over her body, groping her ample breasts. He unbuttoned her dress, almost ripping it open in his eagerness to bury his face in her bosom. He pulled her erect nipples into his mouth.

The rough farmer's hands took on a life of their own, guided by male instinct as his fingers squeezed the soft flesh of her thighs that led to her moist womanhood. Then Liam felt Clarice's body melt and mold into his, her mouth responding to his, joining in a passionate union that Liam never knew existed. Their tongues twined together as if they could devour each other in pleasure. Clarice's hands unzipped his trousers, and she gripped his manhood, stroking and caressing at the same time.

Liam entered Clarice and in an instant exploded inside her, like water bursting through an overflowing dam. He felt an ecstasy he had only imagined but had been denied with Alma all the years of their marriage.

Shame overcame Liam as soon as he climaxed. "I'm sorry, Clarice. I didn't mean to force myself upon you. I couldn't stop myself. Please forgive me."

"Mr. Liam, what's gonna happen to me now?" Clarice said. "How's it gonna be with us?"

They scrambled to dress and tidy themselves, then sat in silence for a few minutes before Liam spoke.

"Clarice, there is no going back for me. I cannot bear to think of my life without you. I know this is wrong, but I can't help it."

"Mr. Liam, white folk and black folk ain't supposed to mix the way we done. It's against all the law."

"First, Clarice, please call me Liam. Second, we will find a way. This is my farm, my property, and my business. What people don't know doesn't matter. You leave it to me," he said. "I promise I will take care of you, and no harm will come to you."

They continued to meet each day after Clarice finished her work and the others had left for their homes. It was easy for Liam to claim to Alma and Oscar that extra farm work kept him until suppertime. But Liam wanted more than their secret visits in the barn. The double life he was building around himself was a strain, but the alternative of not having Clarice was unthinkable. His passion for Clarice deepened to genuine love.

Liam made a plan, and it started by talking to Clarice's father.

"Mo," he said. "I want you to know the truth, and I want to be open about my intentions with Clarice. You know how it is with my wife. I'm duty-bound to take care of her for life, but I'm not going to live without the love and affection that Clarice and I both feel for each other. I will build a house for Clarice, so she and I can see each other as much as we like. I promise to take care of Clarice for as long as she will have me. Will you give us your permission?"

"What about your wife, Mr. Liam? She gonna find out."

"I plan on telling Alma outright that I will have a life outside our marriage. Of course, Clarice will need to stop working in the house, and I'll find someone to take her place. Although we can't be together legally, Clarice is more wife to me than Alma ever was. My heart and soul belong to Clarice, and I will honor her in every way."

"Mr. Liam, I fear for my daughter. If folks find out, it could be real trouble for her." He shook his head. "Nothin' will happen to you; in fact, white bosses've had their way with our wimmen ever since our people done come here. How you gonna protect her?"

"As long as she lives on my farm, she is under my protection. No harm will come to her."

Mo frowned, thoughtful for several moments. "I don't feel I can refuse you, Mr. Liam, and Clarice already done talked to me and says she'll do whatever you say she do."

Liam then had Jacob and his sons build a new house for Clarice, one that was set apart from the other houses to provide privacy. He provided the lumber and materials to create a comfortable home.

The next step was confronting Alma. He picked his time when Oscar was out with his friends. Over the dirty dishes, Liam spoke the words that would define their marriage for the rest of their lives.

"Alma, for the past twenty years, you and I have been husband and wife, and for the past twenty years, you have denied me the love and affection a husband should expect from his wife. Our marriage has been a disappointment to us both. It's obvious you detest me, and you've done everything you can to punish me for marrying you against your will. You've even turned our son against me, and I think he hates me as much as you do."

He turned to face her. "I want you to know that I no longer will live without the happiness a man should expect in life. I accept my God-ordained duties and obligations to care and provide for you 'till death do us part.' But I'm telling you now that I will have a life outside the walls of the prison of this marriage. I will see that you're cared for, but beyond that, I will come and go as I please, and you are to have no say in this whatsoever."

He held up his palm. "You are not to discuss this arrangement with anyone else, including Oscar. If you want me to continue fulfilling my duties and obligations for the rest of your life, you must accept these terms and tell me now that you do."

Alma eyed Liam with the burning hatred she felt for him. "Do you think I am blind?" she seethed. "I may be broken in body, but I can see! Do you think I don't know what's happening in my own house with that black woman? You disgust me! You're breaking man's and God's law by lying with that woman!"

Liam stared out the kitchen window.

"But do you think I care?" Alma continued. "I welcome anything or anyone that keeps you away from me. I will not speak of the shame you're bringing upon us, not even to Oscar. But you get that woman out of my house! Today!"

Despite the harsh words between them, Liam heaved a sigh of relief. At last, all their unsaid feelings were in the open. There was no going back, but now Liam could look forward to the end of a hard day knowing that a kind and a loving person waited for him.

That was the truce Alma and Liam followed for the rest of their time on the Manor farm.

Oscar grew up pampered and protected by his mother and used the animosity between his parents to clear advantage. He went hunting and fishing with his friends whenever he wanted, and performed no chores around the farm. Oscar noticed how different his father acted when around the sharecroppers. Liam laughed, joked, talked, and treated them in a different manner than Oscar or his mother. Oscar also observed that every Saturday night, Liam showered, put on dress pants, shirt, and tie, and dashed himself with cologne before going out for the evening, sometimes not returning until the next morning. Oscar's curiosity got the better of him, and one night he hid in his father's pickup to see where Liam went.

His father drove to the sharecroppers' town and parked in front of a house bordered by a white picket fence. After Liam entered the house, Oscar jumped the fence and crouched below a window that had been left open to catch the evening breezes. He peeked over the sill and found his father and Clarice embracing and kissing.

Oscar gasped, crouching down. His father! With a Negro!

He raised on his haunches again and watched Liam and Clarice through the window. The dining table was set with fresh flowers, and the aromas of Clarice's famous cooking floated through the open window. Music played on a radio, and he watched his father dancing with a Negro. Dancing! A sinful act strictly forbidden in the Lutheran religion. He had never seen his father express emotions, much less physical affection with a woman, and a black woman to boot!

Oscar burned with rage. "What a hypocrite! Whites mixing with Negros goes against everything we believe, and it's even against the law!"

The words of one of his friends echoed in his mind. "Negroes are lazy, shiftless, untrustworthy, and a financial drain on America. Everyone knows blacks are inferior to whites, and blacks must be kept in their place."

In Oscar's white world, schools were segregated, and blacks were forbidden to share public places with whites. Signs identified "white only" water fountains and benches. Blacks were not allowed in white restaurants. "And here is my father, the great pious Liam, having an adulterous relationship with a Negro, while my mother suffers at home."

Oscar was so angry he didn't bother to sneak a ride back in his father's truck. Instead, he walked home. He never talked about what he saw that night; he was too ashamed.

From that time forward, Oscar's disrespect for his father turned to open defiance. He started drinking with his friends, coming home drunk every weekend. Liam's attempts to discipline his son fell on deaf ears.

"You can never again tell me what to do," Oscar said to his father.

* * *

The Great Depression

"MO IS WITHOUT A doubt the smartest man I know," thought Simon. "This cotton business is feast or famine. He was right that wartime means high demand for cotton, but when the war ends, so does the need for our cotton."

But collapse of cotton prices at the end of World War I paled in comparison to the effects of The Great Depression of 1929. It started with the crash of the stock market caused by over-speculation and people borrowing to buy stocks. The domino effect then took down factories, businesses and banks, putting millions of Americans out of work.

Banks foreclosed on loans that couldn't be paid, including farmers who owed money on their land. They were forced out of their homes, and caravans of unemployed, homeless Americans took to the roads, looking for work in the cities and standing in bread lines for food.

"We will be all right," Simon told his people gathered in his living room. All were worried about the terrifying news day after day as the Depression crept closer to home. "The people who are hurt most are those who still have outstanding loans at the bank for their land. We all own our land outright, and we have no debts. We will be okay."

"But what about our crops?" one farmer said. "No one is buying a single bale of cotton, much less a whole harvest."

"Yes, we will have lean years until this Depression is over." Simon nodded. "But in the meantime, we can take care of ourselves. We have gardens that give us all the vegetables we need, and our women keep the root cellars full of preserved fruits and vegetables to last the winter. Our livestock provides the meat we need, our cows for milk, chickens for eggs, and our ponds are full of fish. Even our sharecroppers are better off than itinerant farmers and wage-earning sharecroppers who migrate from one harvest to the next. These poor souls are just cast out. Our black families have gardens like we do, livestock, and they're debt free."

"What are we going to do for cash?" Joseph said. "We gotta have money for some things."

"Farming communities across the country are setting up farmers' markets in the towns and cities, selling food to city folk. We can do that, set up booths on the highway to Austin every weekend. And we can trade, too, when people don't have cash. Look, it won't be easy, but I promise you, we are in a much better position than just about anyone else I know."

The Lindberg Settlement, in fact, was a tiny oasis in the midst of the misery that affected most Americans.

"Thank God, Mo Brown taught us to plant sorghum and corn fields as well as cotton. We have plenty of animal feed. Most farmers and ranchers are killing their animals because they can't afford to feed them," Simon continued. "We'll be okay if we just stick together."

The resilient Swedes learned how to repair their own farm equipment and vehicles. When they couldn't find the parts they needed, they simply reverted to the old ways learned in Sweden; they got out the mule and the hand plow and kept going.

Texas Roots

"I hate farming," Gene McPherson said to himself, resenting the routine, dawn-to-dusk, never-ending chores and the predictable seasons that defined each day's tasks. "Where's the adventure? Where's the fun."

Even his father's conversations with other farmers had the same monotonous complaints: too much rain, not enough rain, too hot, too cold. Gene felt chained to the plows, the planting, the harvesting. At seventeen, the only thing he knew for sure was that he would not be a farmer.

Gene was born on the farm, same as his four sisters and brothers. His father had immigrated to America from Scotland as a boy, an indentured servant to a Pennsylvania landowner. When he completed his contract, he ventured west into the wilderness and claimed 100 acres of good bottomland along a Tennessee river. It was a decent farm that yielded enough to feed the McPherson family with five growing children.

But farming just wasn't for Gene. As the youngest, he stole away at every chance and disappeared into the mountains to hunt and fish. Or he sneaked into the closest alehouse and listened to the tales of mountain men and trappers.

"Why can't you do your share?" Gene's father said as he cuffed his ears for slacking off. Sometimes he took the strap to Gene when his disobedience was too rebellious.

Nothing worked. Gene stared at the mountains with longing and fed his imagination about freedom and adventure. He read all he could find about brave pioneers pushing West to tame new territories.

"That's the life for me," Gene said. "Davy Crockett and Jim Bowie were just like me once, young men who left home, craving adventure. I'm gonna do the same." Gene's favorite stories were about Texas, and his newfound hero was General Sam Houston.

Gene learned that Houston had left home when he was seventeen. For a year, he lived with the Cherokee Indians, and he fought in the War of 1812. He was even elected governor of the state of Tennessee. Houston's enduring legacy, however, was earned as the leader of the fight against Mexico to win Texas's independence.

One early morning in 1870, barely 17 years old with nothing more than a few belongings strapped to his back, Gene McPherson set his sights on Texas. He started on foot with no money in his pocket and food he squirreled away from the previous night's dinner.

"I'm a hard worker," he reasoned. "I'll find a wagon train heading west and hire on."

That was the extent of his plan, and he had no idea how long it would take him to reach his destination. He made it as far as Memphis when he had to accept work in a saloon, sweeping floors and cleaning out spittoons, just to get food in his belly and a place to sleep. It was a rough place, filled every night with even rougher characters.

"This is temporary," he told himself. "As soon as I get enough money in my pocket, I'll head west. Here, I'll keep my ears open till I hear of a wagon train, and I'll join 'em."

One night a group of men came into the saloon eager for whisky and cards. They were driving a herd to Texas, led by a Scotsman named Angus Murray, a specialist in cattle breeding.

Like most Scots, Angus was a natural storyteller and fond of drink. He intended to enjoy some whisky and spin some tales, possibly coming across prospects to join the drive.

Gene overheard the Scotsman's plan to cross-breed his prized Scottish shorthorn cows and his English Hereford bull with the rough, hump-backed brahman breed and the rangy Texas Longhorns. Angus was taking his herd to the Sweeney ranch in south Texas, the largest ranch in the country. They faced a drive of 2,000 miles, passing through hostile Indian territory and untamed frontier plagued by cattle rustlers and other dangers. Two of Angus' drovers had quit, and Murray was looking for replacements.

"This is music to my ears," Gene said. "This might be my chance."

Angus's thick Scottish accent became more pronounced with each drink. Two men had joined his table, feigning interest in his stories while plying him with whisky.

Gene had observed these two men before, and their game was to get a man drunk, then rob him when he left the saloon. Angus was falling into their trap. He approached Angus and said in Gaelic, "These bad men here are getting you drunk to rob you."

Angus, no stranger to trouble, sat up straight, eased his Colt 45 from his holster, and set it on the table, barrel pointed toward the men. He stared them down. "You men might want to get your skinny arses somewhere else!"

They scampered away, and Angus extended his hand to the young man. "Angus Murray! Thank you, sir. Please join me for a drink."

"I'd enjoy to, Mr. Murray, but I'd git fired for that."

"Well then, quit, come have a steak dinner with me, and let me tell you about an experience of a lifetime looking at you right now!"

In the most providential happenstance in his young life, Gene joined Angus Murray's crew to drive the rare cattle herd to Texas. His assigned task was keeping the bull tethered at all times and away from the Shorthorn cows.

"I've got other plans for that bull's romantic interests," said Angus, "as well as different plans for the cows, and I don't want calves between the two."

Gene was eager to please Angus. What he lacked in skill, he

made up in hard work. Angus, in the meantime, enjoyed the camaraderie of a fellow Scot, often lapsing into the heavy brogue of their homeland.

"Stick with me, lad, and you'll learn more in the next few months than you could learn in a lifetime," Angus said with a twinkle in his eye, as he slapped Gene across his back.

Once arriving at the Sweeney Ranch, Angus executed his breeding plan, siring the Shorthorn cows with Sweeney's brahman bulls. Murray's Hereford bull proved a prolific stud for Sweeney's existing Herefords, resulting in a hearty, meaty breed that Mr. Sweeney named the Santa Gertrudis.

"My Gertrudis steers are the best beef on the hoof," Sweeney bragged. "They tolerate the harsh Texas climate better than any other, and they guarantee me a superior price at market."

"Mr. Sweeney," said Angus, "our experiment worked. These are mighty fine cattle."

Gene hired on as a ranch hand, with Angus' high recommendation. "Gene, you're a good hand," Sweeney said. "You can stay on as long as you like. My boys will teach you everything you need to know about ranchin'."

For several years, Gene stayed on the Sweeney Ranch, learning the cowboy way of life and everything the vast Texas landscape could teach an impressionable young man. Taking herds from Texas to market in Kansas City became his primary duty. It was a rich but dangerous life, teaching Gene the lessons a man needed to survive. He learned well and gained a reputation among his fellow cowboys as one of the best horsemen and cattlemen in the state. He was also renowned for his humor and tall tales.

Gene enjoyed telling the story of driving a herd across the Red River bordering Texas and Oklahoma. The river was over its banks from recent torrential rains. The cowboys removed their clothing and stored them in the chuck wagon to keep them dry, wearing only their boots and sidearms. Gene lost hold of his horse's reins in white water and was swept downstream. Given up for drowned, the cowboys sat around the fire that night, commiserating about their friend. Then without warning, Gene walked into the light of the fire, still buck naked except for his guns and boots!

"We gave you up for dead!" the crew chorused. "How in the hell did you get out of that river alive?"

"Well," he said, "after gettin' washed downriver aways, I just let myself sink to the bottom with my pistols and boots holding me down. Once my feet touched the bottom of the river, I just walked out."

One day Sweeney asked Gene to accompany him for an important meeting with the legendary General Sam Houston in Huntsville, Texas. Sweeney wanted to update the General on his ranching success along the Rio Grande and seek additional land grants to increase his holdings. Gene seized the opportunity to meet his hero Sam Houston face-to-face, the man who inspired him to come to Texas in the first place.

Now much older, General Houston still commanded respect and admiration, and had become a gentleman rancher on a large spread near Brenham. The Texas Rangers, however, occupied most of his time. Houston recruited the toughest men he could find, skilled with rifles and pistols, men unafraid of chasing outlaws and renegades wherever the trails led. Their charge was to protect settlers and establish law and order throughout the territory. Their shoot-first-ask-questions-later reputation drove fear in the hearts of outlaws.

Houston said to Gene, "When you get your fill of pushing cows, join up with us, and you'll see some real adventure." He paused. "My Rangers' authority is unquestioned. They overrule the local sheriffs who are often on the payroll of the largest landowners. Texas Rangers can arrest, try, and hang a man on the spot, and few dare go against them. What do you think?"

"I'd like that, General Houston. I'd like that just fine!"

At 22 years of age, Gene joined the Texas Rangers and swore an oath to rid the frontier of roving Mexican bandits, Comanche renegades, cattle thieves, unscrupulous traders—the worst of humanity. His new family, his fellow Rangers, helped him grow into manhood in mind and body. His tall, lean frame was all sinewy muscle from many days in the saddle, chasing outlaws. Gene became one of their best marksmen and was as comfortable on horseback as walking. He grew a reputation as one of the toughest Rangers in Texas.

Gene loved his life of "rangerin'." The instant he showed his badge, men respected him, while outlaws feared him when he unholstered his pistol.

* * *

Awanita

AWANITA WANDERED A GOOD distance from her camp to check her snares. She and her small band of Delaware Indians had stopped their travels for a few days to rest and rebuild their strength. Only a dozen of them were left. Yellow fever along the journey claimed over half their number, yet somehow she survived. At seventeen, she was one of the ablest in the group, and her trapping skills kept the clan fed with rabbits and other small animals.

As Awanita searched the creek bed for tracks, her mind wandered, thinking about the harsh journey since their escape from the Oklahoma reservation in the dead of night, and losing her family to disease and hardship.

"My mother and father survived the Trail of Tears before I was born," she thought. "But this time, the yellow fever killed them and my brothers. I don't think we would've left the reservation if we knew it would be this hard."

Awanita's parents were among the thousands taken from their villages and relocated to Indian Territory in Oklahoma. It was President Andrew Jackson's campaign to remove Indian tribes by force from their ancestral lands and make the land available for white settlers. Choctaw, Chickasaw, Seminole, Creek, and Cherokee were also driven from the eastern United States.

Around campfires in Oklahoma, her father told stories about the Trail of Tears.

"We were sleeping in our beds," Awanita's father had told them, "almost 20 of us sharing our asi when the blue soldiers awakened us and forced us to come outside. It was a cold winter night, and the soldiers surrounded us, pointing their rifles and pistols at us."

Awanita and all the children sat still as they listened to the horrible story.

"We couldn't even gather our belongings. We were forced to march with the clothes on our backs."

As the tribe marched, always west, Indians from other tribes joined the march, swelling the ranks to thousands. Many died along the way, of whooping cough, typhus, dysentery, cholera, and starvation. They walked a thousand miles before arriving at a desolate, windswept prairie where they had been forced to live.

"Oklahoma was a bad place, but this Texas has not been better," Awanita said to herself. "Stories about Texas offering free land to those willing to settle must not be true. At least, not for my people."

Lost in her reverie, Awanita jerked upright when three white men emerged from the creek bank. She recognized the danger from the sneering faces of the men, and she turned and broke into a run.

The men surrounded her, cornering her against an embankment. They were dirty and smelly, with lumps of tobacco filling their cheeks and staining their teeth. One seized her wrists and wrenched her arms behind her back while another grabbed her buckskin dress and, with his knife, cut the leather straps tied at her shoulders. The leather skin fell to her waist, and the man put his filthy hands on her breasts.

"C'mon," one jeered to her. "We ain't gonna hurt ya that much."

She kicked him between the legs, and he doubled over. The third man stepped in and struck her, splitting her lip. She continued to fight, using all her strength to stay standing.

Gene had been hiding in some brush along the same creek bed, hunting a deer. He and his posse of Texas Rangers were camped nearby, on the trail of a band of Comancheros who had been stealing cattle and terrorizing settlers. A deer was in his sights when a ruckus behind him spooked the deer, and the animal bolted.

"Damn it!" Gene muttered.

He turned his attention toward a struggle coming from upstream, and he followed the sounds of men shouting and a woman screaming.

Gene sized up the situation. Three rough-looking characters, traders he guessed by their clothes, had trapped a young Indian woman, holding her against a scrub oak tree. She was naked to her waist, and her face bled from the blows by the men, but she was still putting up a brave fight.

"Now, hold on right there!" Gene McPherson shouted as he emerged from the brush. "Didn't your mama teach you that you never take a woman unless she asks you to?"

The attackers turned their heads in unison, staring at a well-armed stranger who stepped into the creek bed. They likewise analyzed Gene, saw he was alone, and measured his advantage. The men had stripped themselves of their side pistols in anticipation of pleasures ahead, not wanting their guns to get in the way. Gene was armed with a rifle and double-holstered sidearms, but then they numbered three and did have knives.

"Mind your own business," one of them snarled. "She's our'n, and you got no call buttin' in."

"Like I said, you don't force yourself on a woman who ain't asked for it," said Gene. "Now haul your skinny arses outta here before I git upset."

"Just who do you think you are anyway, gittin' 'tween a man and his personal business?" growled another.

One of the men sidled closer to the embankment where they had dropped their pistols. Gene drew his pistol and fired at the feet of the man, halting him at the edge.

"My name, gentlemen, is Captain Gene McPherson, Texas

Rangers. Now you can git outta here right now with no more bother from me, or you can keep on jawin', and I'll drop you where you stand, or I might arrest all three of you and take you to Pecos in front of Judge Roy Bean and hang you there. However, I got places to go, and so I'd rather not deal with the likes of you, keeping me from my official business—but if you insist…"

"Naw, heck. I'm not in the mood now anyway," the leader of the men said with a shrug. "She's just an Injun squaw and not worth tanglin' with the Rangers. You can have her. C'mon, boys. Let's git!"

Never turning his back, Gene watched them walk to where he suspected they had left their horses. Then he turned his attention to the young woman who had pulled the top of her dress to her neck and was scrambling up the embankment to make her getaway. Gene gripped her wrist, as tiny an arm as he could ever recall, and pulled her back.

Her first reaction was that maybe she stood a better chance, and perhaps she could fight off one man. To her, he was just another white man, and none of her people had fared well under their control.

"Don't be afraid, ma'am," said this new stranger. "Let me help you."

He dropped her wrist and raised his arms, palms opened, to show he meant no harm. He turned his back so she could tie the straps to her dress and cover her nakedness.

"Let's see to your face," Gene said as he removed his kerchief and splashed it with water from his canteen, then dabbed it on her bleeding lip and a blackening eye. "Where did you come from? Where are your people?"

Awanita studied the man. He wasn't handsome by Indian standards. His face was smooth except for the bushy hair under his nose shaped like a half moon. For living in the open, he was clean and groomed. He had the air of a warrior about him, straight-backed, alert, ready. His words spoke kindness, but she was wary.

Refusing to speak the little English she knew, Awanita answered his questions in her native tongue. Her people, a small band of Delawares, were camped nearby. The three white men attacked her as she was checking her snares.

Gene walked the woman back to her camp, his horse following, until they reached a gathering of a dozen or so Indians of mixed ages, a hardscrabble group, all skin and bones and clothed in tatters. An elder appeared to be their leader.

Speaking her dialect, Awanita explained what had happened and how this white man rescued her from three white attackers.

"Your deeds honor us. Sit. Talk. Eat with us," said the chief with body language as much as the spoken word in recognizable English.

Gene welcomed the opportunity to visit with a band of Indians he hadn't come across before. He had a knack for Indian languages and understood a good bit. Once when chasing a bad band of Comanches across the state line into New Mexico, he had been ambushed and wounded. Gene was left for dead in a dry ravine when some Navajos came upon him and took him unconscious to their lodges where they nursed him back to health. He stayed with them for six months. After he completed their sweat lodge initiation ceremony, he had been adopted into their tribe.

Gene was always curious to learn about different tribes and customs. Besides, this band was roasting several rabbits over a fire, and he was ravenous.

"Life in the Indian Territory is not good," the elder told him. "Our people are disappearing. We decided to try to find land of our own where we could live in peace away from the white man. We heard stories that Texas had land with no people, and we hope to find land here."

Gene didn't have the heart to tell him that white men will dominant any place they try to settle, and he doubted the little band would survive.

The chief told him the woman's name was Awanita, which means *fawn*. She was seventeen and the only surviving member of her family.

"By our customs," said the chief, "you have won Awanita. She is unmarried with no one to protect her. She needs a husband. She will go with you."

"Whoa!" said Gene. "I'm a travelin' man. I got no home and no need of a wife. I'm with my posse of Texas Rangers, and we're on the trail of some bad Comancheros who've been troublin' folks in this territory."

"Awanita is a tracker," the elder continued, with no trace of negotiation in his tone. "She can help you find the men you seek. She must go with you. My people will not accept her now. She belongs to you."

The chief then spoke to Awanita who, in total obedience to her chief, gathered her meager belongings, and stood next to Gene, ready to depart.

Conflicting emotions ripped through Gene as he realized the impact of his actions in protecting this Indian woman. He had lived a free and independent life ever since leaving his Tennessee home over ten years before. His life was on the trails, either traveling with rough men like himself or only his horse for company. He endured shootouts with outlaws, hanged men for horse theft, fought hostile Indians, drove cattle from the Rio Grande to Kansas, and chased badmen throughout the entire state. He was responsible for no one but himself, and never once had he considered settling down with a wife. Besides, Gene knew nothing about women, and the thought of marrying one terrified him.

Sure, the bordellos of the frontier towns tempted him with their offers of pleasures for a price. But he had heard about all the bad things that can happen to a man when he pulls down his britches in one of those places. He just felt it safer to keep to his life of solitude.

Now here he was, stuck with an Indian woman who refused to speak his language. His choice was either to take her with him or be responsible for her tribe casting her out.

When Gene returned to his camp with no game but a woman instead, his Ranger friends found his predicament hilarious. They teased him without mercy, taunting him about hunting deer and coming back with a wife! Gene also caught some of the men casting unwelcome stares at Awanita.

"I might have to fight off my own men," he thought.

From the first, Awanita behaved like a wife, following him around, cooking for him, waiting on him, and willing to share his blankets at night.

"Just hold on, Awanita," he said as he held up both hands. "If this is how it's gotta be, then let's git it done right. We'll have Judge Roy Bean wed us when we get to Pecos. Heaven knows what I'll do after that."

Judge Roy did more than marry Gene and Awanita. He reminded Gene that his years of service in the Texas Rangers earned him a land grant from Sam Houston, up to 4,400 acres of unsettled ranch land.

"General Houston will be happy to honor your request for a land grant, Gene, after your six years with the Rangers."

Gene studied the Judge's map, looking for a plot in his favorite part of Texas, what he called God's country, the Central Texas Hill Country. He found what he hoped was available, a considerable swath of unclaimed land west of Austin with the Colorado River running through it. He had traveled through there many times, driving herds from the Sweeney Ranch following the Chisholm Trail to Kansas.

To him, there wasn't any prettier land than the majestic Hill Country, with its purple crown glowing over the tree-covered hills, its valleys crisscrossed by many creeks. He favored the land around Cow Creek that flowed fresh most of the year. He already had in his mind just where he would build a house, atop a tall bluff overlooking a valley with Cow Creek below. He'd never have to worry about flooding during spring rains, and he could dig a well that reached the watershed, assuring him of water during droughts. In Texas, floods and droughts were a fact of life.

"Yes, sir! I can build a mighty fine ranch here."

The Chisholm Trail ran right through the area, and Gene could drive his herds or join other herds on the way to the Kansas rail yards.

Judge Roy drew up the papers and signed them right then and there. All Gene had to do to claim the title was file the documents in the capital city of Austin.

"General Houston will miss you, Gene," Judge Roy said, slapping Gene on the back, "but you've earned this. Best to quit now before your luck runs out and you stop a bullet."

At 28, Gene McPherson was now a settled man, a ranch owner, and a husband to a Delaware Indian woman named Awanita. Right there in Judge Roy Bean's saloon, Gene resigned from the Texas Rangers, collected his salary, and set his sights on Austin. Awanita traveled behind him on a pony her new husband bought her.

Now legally man and wife, Gene right away fell into the comforts of married life. What Gene didn't know about women, Awanita taught him. He took to calling her Nita for short, and she spoke enough English to converse about the essential things. Gene found her pleasant company, hard-working, and accepting of harsh conditions on the trail. He soon wondered why he had waited so long to take a wife, figuring he was reluctant to leave his boyhood behind, his wild and reckless ways, and grow into the kind of man who could handle the responsibilities of a family. Now enjoying the pleasures of being a husband, Gene accepted he was ready to settle down, build a ranch and home, and yes, even have some kids.

Awanita didn't disappoint. She got pregnant soon after they married. As Gene staked out his land and started work on their home, Awanita's body bloomed right before his eyes.

"I'm gonna have to hurry and git this house built. That young'n'll be here before I know it."

His first son was born, barely a month before the two-room house was ready. The "shotgun-style" house was typical of Texas frontier homes. A breezeway separated the living space from the kitchen, providing a comfortable, covered area to sit and avoid the hot sun. The simple design made it easy to add rooms as the family grew. And it did. Nita delivered ten more sons and daughters before their family was complete. Gene had plenty of sons to work the ranch, while the daughters tended the gardens, chickens, and other house animals, and prepared meals for the hungry family of thirteen.

Besides the land grant through Sam Houston's good graces, Gene was gifted some brood cows from Mr. Sweeney's Santa Gertrudis and Hereford herds and from each breed a male calf with promising virility. On the drive to his new ranch, he gathered a sizable number of wild longhorns lost from trail drives throughout the years. In a few short years, Gene grew three sizable herds of each breed, which he kept separated on different pastures.

Nita was a hard-working partner with Gene and a good wife. She maintained the house, raised the children, kept his bed warm at night, and never complained. When he drove herds to Kansas, Gene was absent from the ranch for long stretches. At first, Gene worried about leaving her and the kids alone, but he soon learned she could manage without him.

From time to time, roving bands of Indians came through their property. Most settlers feared them, but Nita was hospitable, feeding them beans and cornbread. As a result, Indians knew they could travel in peace through Gene's ranch, every now and then taking a steer for food, which Gene never minded.

One trip, they presented Nita with a fine paint colt in thanks for her kindness. Nita loved that pony. Then during a frigid winter, the Indians came through again and took the pony back, killed it for food, and warmed their hands in the horse's body.

"It's all right, husband," Nita said. "My people don't own property like the white man. They simply let me have the pony for a while, and took it back when they needed it again. It is our way."

Nita did nothing to hide her Indian heritage. She wore tanned leathers for clothing and her hair in one long braid, and her body grew rounder after each birth.

Their neighbors didn't accept them.

"I don't trust any redskin," one rancher confided to others. "They're just a bunch of thieves and murderers, and I'm keeping my kids away from theirs."

Behind their backs, locals called the McPherson children half-breeds, and many bare-knuckle fights broke out when any of the boys heard it.

Skinny, rangy, gangly, their skin was the color of coffee, inherited from their Indian mother, and the rest a testament to the intense Texas sun. Ranching was their religion, from sunup to sundown. As soon as a boy was walking, Gene had him on horseback. By the time a son was six years old, he was herding cows.

The brothers were inseparable—rough, rowdy, hungry for adventure. As they grew toward manhood, they possessed the confidence and cockiness that hard living produces, eager to prove their prowess over friend and foe alike.

* * *

Sam and His Doll

GENE AND NITA'S youngest son was named Sam, after Sam Houston. To live up to the legacy of his famous Texas Ranger father and for his standing in the family, Sam fought hardest. When the McPherson boys weren't ranching, they competed in rodeo events, each one vying for bragging rights around the supper table.

They wore holstered sidearms over their chaps and were outstanding marksmen, again competing with one another. Sam distinguished himself by his skill in rodeoing. He competed in all the events—bareback and saddle bronc riding, steer wrestling, steer roping, and bull riding. Sam had the same lean, muscular frame as his father with the perfect agility and quickness suited for a rodeo cowboy.

One weekend three of the brothers, Jess, Walter and Sam, were headed home from a rodeo. They had some pocket money from their winnings and decided to stop at a saloon for a game of cards. At a table in the center of the room, three tough-looking vaqueros sat playing poker and downing tequila. The Mexicans invited the McPherson boys to join the game, and luck turned the gringos' way. Losing their money to the Texicans, the three angry vaqueros stormed out of the saloon.

Soon after, Sam and his brothers pocketed their winnings and finished their beers. As they came out the doors of the saloon and headed toward their horses, gunfire erupted from all around them.

"Ambush!" Jess yelled. They dived for whatever cover they could find while drawing their pistols. "These damned Meskins surrounded us. I'll take the left, Walter, you take the middle, and Sam, you got the right."

Deadshots all, the three McPherson boys emptied their pistols in the direction of the gunfire, and the violent shootout was over almost as soon as it had started. When the smoke cleared, all three Mexicans were dead.

"We gotta git outta here," Walter shouted. "We could hang for this."

"Why?" Sam said. "It was self-defense."

"Well, I ain't waiting around to be sure of that. Sheriff Polk's no friend of our'n," said Jess.

Well known by local authorities, this wasn't the first time the McPherson boys had tested the limits of the law. They decided to split up, leaving that night with no word to their family. Walter headed east to Florida, where he joined friends and hired on at a ranch there. Jess went to California to prospect for gold. Sam, just 15 years old, left Texas for New Mexico.

He was miserable and homesick in New Mexico, and the desert didn't suit him. After less than a year, Sam returned home.

"Where the hell have you been?" his father demanded when his youngest showed up.

"New Mexico." Sam hung his head. "I'm hopin' the law's tired of lookin' for me, and maybe I can come home now."

"The sheriff came here after you and your brothers kilt those Meskins. They were wanted for murder, dead or alive, and there was a reward for 'em."

"Well, can I have my share of the reward then?" Sam said.

"Hell, no. You cowards lit out, so your mother and I spent it."

Walter and Jess never returned, establishing homes and families in Florida and California. Sam picked up where he left off, spending several years working the ranch and riding rodeo. He resumed driving herds to Kansas, earning a reputation as a good hand.

On one drive up the Chisholm Trail, the drovers crossed a swollen river, its banks flooded from recent heavy rains. It was a tricky crossing with the currents and debris. The horses panicked and were determined to swim the shortest distance, which was also the river's deepest and most treacherous part. The riders couldn't get the horses to follow their lead.

"Try this trick," Sam called to the other drovers. "Just reach over and splash water into the horse's eye and he'll swim the other direction."

The crew tried it and the horses accepted their lead. All crossed safely.

On another drive, Sam was driving a herd near the Texas-Oklahoma border. The crew boss was a stubborn man and distrustful of Indians. A small band approached the herd and asked for a few cows in exchange for crossing their territory. The trail boss pulled his pistol and waved the Indians away, warning them not to come back.

"Boss, just give 'em a few head, some of those wild steers or the sickly ones," Sam said, remembering how his parents had taught him to work with the Indians and show them respect. "It's a small price to pay to pass through without trouble."

"I'm not encouraging thievery and begging," said the trail boss.

The following day the trail boss and a young cook's assistant struck out toward the nearest town to stock up on supplies, about a two-hour ride west of the herd. "We'll be back by supper," the boss told the crew. "Sam's in charge till I git back."

They didn't return that night and still had not showed up by midday. Sam halted the drive and organized a search. They found their bodies in a ravine about halfway between the campsite and town, their skin peeled and their heads scalped.

"Let this be a lesson, boys," Sam said. "All this could'a been avoided if the boss just worked with the Indians a little."

The drovers buried the bodies in unmarked graves in Montague County, a desolate part of Texas, and finished the drive to Kansas.

"What a waste of life," Sam told his companions. "Now they'll lie here forever, forgotten."

As Sam grew into manhood, his restlessness made him eager to make his way, just as his father had done. He and his brothers would inherit the ranch one day, but Sam wanted a place of his own, and he wanted it now. By competing in rodeo events and winning, Sam earned money for a down payment on a loan to buy some land. It was small, but it was a start, and he was confident he could build just as fine a ranch as his father's.

Near the McPherson ranch was a prosperous stretch of land owned by Jack Ford, who lived with his wife and eleven daughters. The Ford ranch straddled rich river-bottom land that was never short of good grazing and fresh water. Their herds were the largest and fattest, and they commanded top dollar at market. Mr. Ford hired ranch hands since his eleven daughters couldn't do all the work, especially roundups and trail drives.

Sam hired on to add to his savings for his own ranch. Driving a herd north to the Kansas railways paid fifty dollars, a tidy sum. He no longer wasted a cent on gambling or drinking. He worked hard and distinguished himself among the bunkhouse crew.

"That McPherson boy is the best hand I've got," Old Man Ford said to his crew boss. "There ain't nothin' he don't know about cows or horses."

Roundup in springtime was one of the busiest times in the life of a cowboy, and Sam's favorite time of the year. Following each winter, herds were full of bawling new calves that needed branding. One day, the foreman called Sam over. "Pick out a steer and take it to the Ford house for slaughter."

When Sam rode up to the Ford house with a steer in tow, Doll, one of Ford's daughters, was feeding chickens. Short and chubby, Doll stood out from the other daughters with her curly blond hair and bright blue eyes. They locked eyes from the first.

What struck Sam was how different Doll looked from his mother. Sam hated to admit how much it bothered him by the way the townspeople treated Nita and his sisters. Sam didn't care that much how the men treated him and his brothers; they could take care of themselves. It was different for men. Respect was earned by how hard you worked, handled a gun, or stood up in a fight. But women couldn't fight back. They had to accept their lot. As far as anyone could tell, the gossip and rejection didn't appear to bother Nita. She never talked about it. But it bothered Sam.

Maybe that's what attracted Sam to Doll. Her skin was pale white, and her hair was so blond, it was almost white. She had a daintiness about her, suggesting she was spared from heavy chores. Sam imagined the kind of family he would have with a woman like Doll.

"The neighbors and townspeople will respect her," he thought, "and our kids will be accepted. Not like it is with my mother and brothers and sisters."

Old Man Ford was sitting on his porch, squinting as he watched that brief exchange between Doll and the drover. "You stay away from those McPherson boys," he warned her later. "They're good-for-nothing, half-breed cowboys without a nickel to their names and will never amount to anything." He then spoke louder so all his daughters would hear. "Any McPherson boy who comes around here will find their butts full of my buckshot."

That didn't stop Sam. He found ways to deliver messages and trinkets and flowers where Doll would find them. He enticed her to meet him in secret at a swimming hole where Hickory Creek cascaded down a small bluff, creating a waterfall and a deep pool. The cool oasis became their special place. They fell in love, and Sam felt he could not live without her. He was 18, and Doll 16. Sam proposed.

"Papa will never consent," Doll said to Sam, weeping.

"Then we'll sneak off."

One morning before dawn, Sam crept beneath Doll's second-floor bedroom window, set a ladder, and she climbed down it, clutching a small bundle of clothing. They rode double into the new day and for the next several days, as far as El Paso. A mission priest married them. Sam knew he would lose his job working for his new father-in-law, so he planned to start married life on land Sam had purchased with his rodeo earnings and live in a tiny cabin he had built.

They sent word to both sets of parents. Gene and Nita gave their blessings but were concerned about the rough start facing them. Mr. Ford, on the other hand, had a different, but not unexpected, reaction.

"No McPherson is allowed on my property!" he shouted.

Little good it did him. Before long, two other McPherson boys had "culled his herd," running off with two more Ford daughters!

One day Gene found his wife of 38 years slumped in a chair, her body worn out. "I never knew she felt poorly. She never complained."

He wanted to bury her in the community's cemetery, but the townspeople wouldn't hear of it. It was a Christian cemetery, and no heathens were allowed.

"They won't stop me," Gene said.

Despite their objections and under cover of darkness, Gene, his sons, and daughters buried Awanita in the town cemetery in an unmarked grave. After her death, Gene surrendered to old age, allowing his sons to run the ranch while he awaited his own death.

* * *

THE ROARING TWENTIES ushered in good times for Sam and his family. The war in Europe fighting the German Kaiser raised the demand for beef, and cattle prices skyrocketed. Sam's ranch was along a tributary of Cow Creek, not far from the secret waterfall where he had courted Doll. He was well on his way to making his dream come true, confident his ranch would succeed, with his devoted wife by his side.

Over the next ten years, Sam and Doll enjoyed a time of prosperity. Doll gave birth every other year, five children in all, three boys and two girls. Sam grew his herd bit by bit, reinvesting profits into buying more land.

Doll didn't have an ounce of parental discipline or domestic skills in her. She left all decisions up to Sam, content to keep him happy. The rest was just not important to her.

The children were required to work the ranch and go to school, but they still had plenty of time to swim in the falls at Hickory Creek, ride bareback through their property, fish in Cow Creek, and run wild and free.

Sam worked his cattle and drove them to market, enjoying top prices for beef purchased by the government. He borrowed more money to build a sturdy, large house for his family, a barn, and a feed shed.

Around the table at night, the family would devour Doll's chicken and dumplings, her one specialty, as though it was their last meal. Doll served herself last and insisted the neck was her favorite piece of chicken.

"Kids, pay attention," Sam said. "Only a mother would deny herself a good, fatty piece of chicken and choose the bony, scrawny neck for herself, saving the best pieces for her family. Always treat your mother with the respect she deserves."

"Oh, Daddy, you treat Mama like a queen," his daughter, Beth, said.

"I learned from my own daddy to honor my wife above all others. Doll fills me with pride. I like to fret over her, and I intend to make her life as easy as possible."

The family had plenty to eat, and Sam and Doll were good, loving parents. Sam was strict but fair, taking a disobedient child to the woodshed if necessary. All the boys were required to work the ranch with their father while the two girls assumed the domestic duties ignored by Doll. The kids attended school regularly, usually barefoot, and often riding three to a horse to the one-room schoolhouse a few miles away.

Though poor, they were happy, unaware that their entire world was about to collapse.

* * *

Itinerants

WHEN THE STOCK MARKET crashed in 1929, ranchers like Sam didn't think it would affect him. Indeed, he didn't own stocks or bonds; all his money was tied up in his land and cattle.

"What's happenin' with rich folks Up East ain't got nothin' to do with us. I got my land and cattle, and whatever my family needs, I can provide with my own two hands. We'll weather the storm."

What Sam didn't figure, nor could anyone else at the time have imagined, was the impact the crash would have on every aspect of American life, including farming and ranching. When the Great War ended, the demand for cattle and cotton, Texas' two major industries, evaporated.

Yet farmers and ranchers continued to grow more cotton than the world needed and raise more cattle than the markets would buy. Factories closed, and businesses went bankrupt. The country found itself with an overabundance of crops and livestock and no buyers.

Prices tumbled, and ranchers couldn't sell their cattle for what it cost to feed them. No one was buying beef, and stockyards were bursting.

"People are starvin', Doll," Sam said to his wife, "and the

government wants us to stop raisin' cattle! Are they crazy? There are bread lines all across the country with out-of-work folks looking for soup and a slice of bread." He paced, his voice growing louder. "Yet, thanks to the government, I can't raise cattle, and I can't sell them. How are we supposed to pay the loan on this ranch if we can't ranch?"

Sam had about 1,000 head of cattle at the time. The government sent men with rifles to shoot them and used bulldozers to push the carcasses into a hollowed ditch, paying him rock bottom prices. Unable to pay his loans, the bank foreclosed on Sam's land, and the McPherson family was forced out of their house.

"We got no choice, Doll, We gotta find work somewhere."

Sam loaded his wife, five children, and belongings onto a mule-driven wagon and joined thousands of other Americans on a nomadic way of life, going from job to job.

As sharecroppers, Sam and four of his children picked cotton for daily wages, dragging long canvas bags behind them. Each picker had to turn in at least 300 pounds of cotton at the end of each day, requiring them to fill the bag multiple times.

Doll and the two youngest children stayed in their rented cropper's cabin. Sam made breakfast each morning, packing up leftover biscuits and sausage as lunch for the McPhersons working in the fields. Each day Doll prepared a meager supper for them when they returned, their hands raw and bloody from the thorny points of the cotton bolls. They soaked their hands at night in warm saltwater so the cuts could heal by morning.

Beth, the middle child, was old enough to work the fields and joined her father and two brothers in the backbreaking work. They all hated it, but Beth hated the cotton worms most. These annoying, sticky creatures feasted on the leaves of the plants and found their way onto the pickers' clothing. The kids took turns pulling the worms off. When Beth fell into an exhausted sleep, she suffered nightmares about the worms covering her body.

As the demand for cotton production slowed and pickers were no longer needed, Sam worked as a "cedar chopper," cutting cedars from ranch land. An even worse job was clearing cactus for cattle feed. On top of everything else, the country was experiencing a prolonged drought. Sam plowed cactus patches while Beth and her brothers gathered the pears onto piles. Then they set them on fire just long enough to scorch off the thorns. Then the cows chewed the burnt pears for moisture within the plant.

Whatever odd job Sam found, the children were required to put in a day's work. It always seemed to be hot work, too. Beth was the hardest worker who won praise from her father for her work ethic. Her two older brothers, however, dodged work as much as they could. Beth complained to her father, but Sam felt times were hard enough without coming down on the boys, irritating Beth at her unfair treatment.

The Great Depression brought the family low. Their fall from grace moved them from self-sufficient landowners to itinerant workers, migrating from one odd job to the next. Sam did his best to keep the family's spirits high. He was their backbone, and he believed things would improve in time.

"We just have to stick together and get through these times," he assured his family. "The Depression can't last forever."

At last, the Depression released its chokehold on the country and necks of the poor. Just one generation after the last "war to end all wars," the world was on yet another war footing. Adolf Hitler brainwashed the German citizens to take revenge for their humiliation of losing the Great War by declaring war on all of Europe. He convinced his followers that it was Germany's destiny to dominate the world. Germany gobbled up one European country after another and set its gun sights on the United Kingdom with the intent to bomb the British into submission.

"America ain't joining in the fight," Sam said to Doll. "This war is just what's gonna save us. Imagine all the people who'll have to find jobs in factories just to provide weapons and such for the military. And food, too, not to mention uniforms!"

She leaned over his shoulder to read the headline aloud. "War

Demand For Gasoline Fuels the Oil Industry."

"They've got to keep those war machines moving." Sam grinned. "And imagine how much 'Texas tea' this state can produce. Drilling rigs are springing up everywhere."

"Maybe you can find a good-paying job in the oil fields," Doll said as she patted his shoulder. "1939 has been another tough year for us."

* * *

"I GOT IT, Doll, steady work!" Sam said one day, coming home jubilant. "I got hired on as a roughneck for an oil company. Pack up! We're headed for Houston."

A quick learner, Sam picked up the trade fast. The family settled in a rented house, the kids started back to school, and for several years life returned to a normal routine.

Sam was part of a four-man crew. One day they were tasked with unplugging a well, using a pipe as leverage on the chain tong. It required the strength of all four men. One of them was known as a slacker, shirking his fair share of the work. Another worker took exception to the lazy fellow.

"Pull harder, fatty."

The slacker said with a sneer, "Hell with it. I'm not breakin' my back," and he let go.

The pipe recoiled with a murderous velocity. The other two men scrambled out of the way, but Sam was caught off guard, and the pipe struck him in the head, crushing his skull.

Doll, who had never held a job nor made any major decision in her life, was now a widow with five children. She received a small "death benefit" from the drilling company, the only money she had to her name. Adrift and alone, Doll reached out to her estranged family who still lived on their ranch in the Hill Country.

"You made your bed," her father said, still bitter because of her elopement, "and you just gotta sleep in it."

Mrs. Ford appealed to her husband to offer some help, and he gave in, sending Doll a little money, with the enclosed note: "You can't come home. You left here, and you aren't welcome back, but we'll help you and the kids get settled in Austin."

The three oldest children, Alvin, Marvin and Beth, loaded Doll, the two younger children, and their meager belongings onto the wagon once more and moved the family into a house their grandparents had rented for them.

Alvin, Marvin, and Beth had to quit school and get jobs to support Doll and the two younger kids. Alvin, the oldest, left home as soon as he could, taking his chances on the open road, and the family never heard from him again. That left 16-year-old Marvin and 14-year-old Beth as wage earners. Marvin found work as a ranch hand, and Beth worked in the local Five and Dime at the soda fountain. Between the two of them, they barely made ends meet.

Doll surrendered to her grief, often unable to get out of bed. She fell into a deep depression and relied on her children to carry the burden of the family.

Beth seethed in bitterness. She had adored her father, who made her feel special and safe.

"Why do I have to do everything?" Beth said to her mom. "I had to quit school and get a job. I have to do the cooking and cleaning. Why can't you help out, Mom?"

"I don't know what to do," Doll said. "Your father took care of everything. Beth, you and Marvin just have to take care of us now."

With Sam and Alvin gone, the McPherson family of five was again struggling to survive, and Beth's anger increased day by day.

* * *

Another World War

"THIS IS MY TICKET out of here, Sis," Marvin said to Beth. He showed her the newspaper. As the war engulfed Europe and Asia,

America could no longer sit on the sidelines. "I'm joining up."

"You can't leave me here alone," Beth wailed. "You gotta help me with Mom and the kids."

"I can't help it, Beth. I hate ranch work, and I'm always hungry. At least, in the Army I get three squares a day and a bed."

It was early in 1941, and the U.S. was recruiting volunteers for the war against Hitler in Europe. It was before the attack on Pearl Harbor. Marvin lied about his age and enlisted in the army. Beth was now the only wage earner for her mother, younger brother, and sister. She was stuck. Her bitterness so filled her that she thought she would choke.

Beth watched her brother leave. "But what about me?"

The Swedish Farmer and the Car Hop

When Beth heard that sexy waitresses earned more than clerks at the five-and-dime, she got a job wearing short skirts and roller skates at a drive-in burger joint. Tips were good, and she found herself on the receiving end of compliments from young men, many who were soldiers in uniform. She was flattered.

One day a group of rowdy young men, out for fun in the pickup truck of someone's father, came to the restaurant. All the girls blushed and gushed over the men who flirted with the waitresses.

"I kinda like that somber-faced redhead with the pale blue eyes," Beth said to her co-workers. "He's got a nice swagger about him." She raced the other waitresses to the truck, taking their orders for beers and burgers, when the redheaded man spoke up.

"Hey, gorgeous. How about ignoring these other ignoramuses and just talk to me?" he said.

He was not that tall but had a muscular build. His physicality was poignant as he shoved his buddies out of the way to talk to Beth. When she returned with their order, he flirted with her again, a new experience she enjoyed. No one had paid attention to her since her father was alive.

"My name's Oscar Swenson, and I see your name is Beth. How about going out with me sometime?"

Beth was too shy to give him an answer, and just skated away as though serving the next customer was her only concern. The truth was she felt too awkward to talk to him.

"Why am I so ugly!" Beth said to herself. "I'm clumsy. My hair is plain and stringy. I'm just so unattractive." But, Beth admitted, having the attention of a handsome young man aroused her emotions and awakened her hopes.

"Anyway," she said, "after the way I acted, I'll never see him again."

The next night, however, he was back, this time without his friends. Another waitress went to his truck to wait on him, but he asked for Beth.

Beth skated over to his truck.

"Remember me? Oscar Swenson. You want to go to the movies with me?"

Beth was again tongue-tied and couldn't look him in the face. "I'll have to ask my mother."

"Well, let me take you home after work, and we'll ask her together! What time do you get off?"

They drove to Doll's house, and Beth stumbled through the introductions. Oscar took the helm and, using his characteristic charm, swept Doll off her feet. He had Doll chuckling at his jokes, and she was putty in his hands.

"What do you do, Oscar?" Doll said.

"I'm a farmer, ma'am, though right now I'm working as a carpenter. My folks have a few hundred acres of good bottomland in Manor, and we grow cotton and corn. We've got a herd of dairy cows and a vegetable garden that would feed the U.S. Army!"

Doll's eyebrows raised at this, and she asked him about his family.

"My folks immigrated from Sweden in 1909 and settled with aunts and uncles throughout Manor and Elgin. I was born on the farm," he said with obvious pride.

"Do you have brothers and sisters who help?" Doll said.

"Nope, just me. My mother is poorly, never has had good health, so it's just my father and me. We have sharecroppers living on the property who help with the hard work."

Not only did Doll approve of this young man, but she envisioned a potential husband and provider for her daughter. Beth stood to one side, observing the interaction between her mother and this gregarious young man, and learned more about Oscar than from their brief conversations. For the most part, she had just taken his orders for burgers and fries and cold beers.

Their first date was to the movies, and they dated only each other after that. Beth fell head over heels for her handsome, blue-eyed, red-haired Swede. Their passions and the raging hormones ruled them both. They made love on their second date in the pickup truck Oscar borrowed from his father. Their dating routine was nights in honky-tonks for drinking and dancing and stopping somewhere to make love in the truck or private places they might find like the drive-in movie theater. Most nights, Oscar was roaring drunk by the time he headed for home.

When Beth announced she was pregnant, Oscar shouted he wasn't ready to be married and have kids. After he cooled down, he said, "Well, okay, let's get married."

Oscar could put it off no longer. It was time to introduce Beth to his mother and father.

Alma made no attempt to hide her dislike of Beth. "My son is not ready to take a wife, especially someone like you. He's going places, and his plans do not include marrying someone beneath him."

"Mom," Oscar said, "whether or not you like it, we're gonna get married. And you might as well get used to the idea 'cause we're having a baby."

Alma was so upset that she insisted Oscar help her to her room and bed. Liam Swenson, on the other hand, was kind and gentle with Beth. Their conversation was formal and polite, and Liam did not mention Alma's illness or her treatment of Beth. While Oscar settled his mother into her bed, Liam showed Beth the family farm. He drove her in the same pickup truck where Oscar and Beth made love on many occasions.

As with rushed marriages of young people, Oscar and Beth had not thought too far ahead about where they would live and how they would support themselves. Beth was so enamored with Oscar that she gave him total authority over her. Oscar quite enjoyed that power, a welcome departure from the unspoken disapproval of his father and the smothering control of his mother.

They were married by a Justice of the Peace and returned to the Manor farm with their suitcases. Without asking permission, they moved into Oscar's room.

It was an uneasy household. Oscar continued his habit of drinking every night after work, coming home drunk. He was fired from his carpentry job, showing up too often late and hungover. As Beth's pregnancy advanced, she no longer accompanied him to the beer joints.

Alma criticized everything Beth did, and Beth had no clue how to behave or perform in the strict, immaculate household. She tried to help with preparing meals, but most of them were either burnt or inedible. Since her family had lived an itinerant life, crowded in rented cabins filled with someone else's furniture, there just didn't seem to be a point to being tidy.

Alma was jealous of her son's attention to his wife. The couple had no privacy. On many occasions, when Oscar and Beth were making love in their bedroom, Alma eavesdropped outside their bedroom door and shouted, "There will be no obscene behavior in my house!"

"Why have you settled for this white trash, Oscar?" Alma whined. "You deserve much better! I've taught you better than this. And now you move her into our house!"

"You just need to give her a chance, Mother," Oscar growled, "and stop harping on it."

To escape the bickering, Oscar fled to the beer joint, returning late at night. When drunk, he yelled at Beth about how worthless she was, how he should never have married her, and that she was holding him back. Beth's tears angered him even more.

Out of the blue, he pulled his arm back, hand doubled in a fist, and struck Beth across the face, catching her under her eye. She fell onto their bed, and didn't speak. She curled into a ball, whimpering, more convinced than ever that she was no good. It had to be her fault. She couldn't please him now that she was fat and ugly, and even his mother hated her. A familiar feeling returned to her: she felt trapped and powerless.

The following day Oscar, now sober and shamefaced, begged Beth to forgive him. He chipped some ice from the icebox and treated Beth like an injured bird. Beth's face sported an unmistakable black eye, and Oscar begged her to forgive him.

Neither Alma nor Liam said a word about Beth's black eye. A veil of silence fell upon the four of them, as if nothing had happened.

A few days later, Beth went into labor, and Oscar drove her to the hospital in Austin. She returned a few days later, without a baby. The infant hadn't survived.

* * *

Draft Dodger

"MY SON IS NOT fighting in this war!" Alma cried aloud, as she shook her finger in Oscar's face. "I don't care about Pearl Harbor. Millions of others have already volunteered to fight Germany and Japan. Let everyone else get killed. They cannot have my son, and you will not join!"

The war dragged on. As Germany's and Japan's resolve remained unabated and casualties mounted, the United States realized many more men were needed than those who volunteered in 1941. Congress enacted the Selective Services law, granting the government authority to draft eligible men into the military to replace the thousands lost in both the European and Pacific campaigns.

Oscar succeeded in dodging the draft as long as possible, but in November 1944, his *Greetings* letter caught up with him, ordering him to report for induction into the U.S. Army. He had no intention of reporting for duty and simply didn't show up, hiding out at his parents' farm. So the U.S. Army dispatched two Military Police to bring him in.

"Oscar, the MPs are at the door," Alma whispered as she shook him awake. "Go out the back and hide under the house. I'll tell them you're not here."

The MPs weren't so easily dispatched. They searched the premises and found him crouched under the house. They dragged him out, kicking and screaming, handcuffed him, and threw him into their jeep. Oscar hurled insults, arguing they had no right to take him. Despite the crying Swenson women, the MPs drove away, escorting Oscar to Fort Sam Houston for basic training.

Because of his experience and hunting skills, the U.S. Army trained Oscar in carpentry and rifle marksmanship, specializing as a radio operator and a scout. After boot training, Oscar returned to the Manor farm for a two-week leave, handsome, yet surly, in his uniform. Oscar embraced his mother first, then his wife. He pushed away, a sudden look of shock on his face, and cast his eyes down, toward Beth's belly.

"What?" he said through clenched teeth. "Again?" He looked at the baby bump pushing through Beth's cotton dress."

"I found out just after you left for basic training. I'm sorry, Oscar. I didn't mean it to happen."

"Your timing is terrible," he stormed at Beth. "I'm shipping out to Japan."

The dreaded invasion of Japan had begun. Despite suffering heavy losses, Hirohito and his generals refused to surrender, even as the United States military reclaimed one heavily fortified island after another throughout the Pacific atoll. A massive American armada was steaming across the Pacific, bearing thousands of American soldiers for the land invasion.

Among them was the reluctant warrior, Oscar Swenson.

Oscar and his battalion were taking their turn top deck when

Japanese Zero fighters attacked the fleet. Launched from aircraft carriers, American fighters engaged the enemy in ferocious aerial combat. One by one, the Zeros dropped like stones into the ocean. One kamikaze pilot, however, managed to get through the defenses and aimed his plane at a troop ship, crashing midsection into the ship, causing tremendous damage.

"Damn!" was all Oscar could say.

The Japanese air force and its naval fleet were destroyed. America now controlled the skies, and B52s bombed the Japanese mainland every day, without mercy, as the land invasion fleet steadily made its way to the Land of the Rising Sun.

"Every family with a son, brother, or father is terrified about the Japanese invasion," Beth said, reading the headlines to Alma and Liam. "These newspaper stories say that Hirohito has ordered every man, woman, and child to arm themselves with whatever farm tools they have as weapons against our soldiers." She crinkled the pages together in her lap and closed her eyes. "They're predicting a bloodbath when our GIs come ashore."

August 6th and August 9th, 1945: "The United States drops atomic bombs on Nagasaki and Hiroshima." Thousands of Japanese civilians were killed in an instant as the fireballs flattened both cities. Warned that Tokyo was next, Hirohito, at last, capitulated and accepted General MacArthur's unconditional surrender.

A cheer went up on Oscar's ship as the soldiers heard news, realizing that their lives were spared. Oscar celebrated with the thousands of GIs onboard, "I didn't even have to fire a shot!" he said to his bunkmates.

Back home on the Manor farm, Shannon felt a sharp pain in her lower abdomen. Later that day, Beth gave birth to a daughter in the same month that the costliest war in world history came to an end.

Beth named her Shannon.

* * *

OSCAR MISSED THE fighting. Instead of invading Japan, he was part of General Douglas MacArthur's occupational forces, enforcing the terms of surrender, and keeping a boot on the necks of the defeated Japanese.

Like thousands of other GIs, Oscar was stationed on one of the many army bases erected throughout the defeated nation. Soldiers rebuilt infrastructure destroyed by the bombing, and Oscar worked as a carpenter.

At night, though, he sneaked off base, disguising himself as a Japanese peasant in pajama-like pants and a pointed straw hat. He searched out the sake bars with their prostitutes. Oscar enjoyed the power the conquering soldiers had over the Japanese citizens. He even commandeered the Japanese home of one of his ladies of the night, often sleeping between the girl and her mother in their post-war shanty. At dawn, he'd don his disguise and sneak back onto the base.

The MPs kept busy chasing AWOL soldiers like Oscar and escorting them back to their quarters, but for the most part, a war-weary army just left the soldiers alone, marking time until they were shipped back to the States.

Oscar collected Japanese souvenirs: a Japanese saber, the Rising Sun flag, ladies' combs and scarves, wooden carvings, and jewelry. When he returned home that November, he brought a chest full of booty, proof of his Army service, including his Army bolt-action rifle.

Oscar called and told Beth he would be discharged soon and home for good.

"I've got a joke for you, honey," he said:

'What are you going to do when you get home?' the soldier asks his friend.
'Make love to my wife!'
'Then what are you going to do?'

'Take off my pack and make love to her again!'
"So get ready! I'm coming home!"

The end of World War II and the return of soldiers from Europe and the Pacific heralded a period of growth and prosperity as the government eagerly got its veterans back to work. Americans rushed to put war and death behind them, and veterans took advantage of opportunities offered to the returning heroes. GIs received generous loans to go back to school and to buy homes.

That optimism and prosperity skipped Oscar and Beth.

Shannon was a year old when she met her father for the first time. Oscar resumed life as he had left it, living with his parents in their home. The household had been a cold and hostile one while Oscar was away, with Alma and Beth avoiding one another as much as possible. Beth had delivered her baby alone at an Austin hospital, and Liam brought mother and daughter back to the farm where the tensions between Alma and Beth remained. When Oscar returned, the hostilities increased. Liam retreated to Clarice's, staying most nights there. Oscar shouted at both his mother and his wife and paid little notice to his daughter.

Then one day the farmhouse mysteriously burned to the ground. It happened when Oscar, Beth, and Shannon were in Austin visiting Beth's mother, Doll. Liam was with Clarice. Alma had been home alone.

Neighbors sounded the alarm to the Elgin volunteer fire department, but they arrived too late. They found Alma sitting outside, saying not a word. Mo Brown alerted Liam, who rushed back to the farm to find his home in ashes and his wife sitting under the shade of an oak tree, silent.

"Why, Alma?" was all Liam could say.

At last Alma spoke. "We will sell this farm now and move to a new house in Austin. It's time Oscar and that wife of his got their own place. Liam, you'll get a job with my cousin in his bakery; I've already arranged it."

She glared at him. "Now it won't be so easy for you to see your black mistress, and I never want to set foot on this place again."

When Oscar and his family returned from their Austin visit, only the blackened skeleton of the house remained. Beth wandered through the ashes, looking for anything to salvage. A stack of dishes seemed to be unblemished by the fire. She stooped to pick up one of the plates, only to have it crumble in her hands. Nothing survived the fire.

And that was the end of life on the Swenson farm.

III. DESCENDANT

From birth, Shannon was different. Independent. Defiant. Fearless. At an early age, she stamped her feet, hands on her hips, and shouted, "No!" when her mother told her to do something. However, Shannon followed her father like a puppy, jumping into his lap whenever she could.

"She's a difficult child," Beth whined to Oscar.

"I don't have a problem with her."

"She knows she's the apple of your eye and does no wrong where you're concerned."

"You just don't know how to handle her," Oscar admonished.

"But you're spoiling her," Beth said. "Shannon needs to know she just can't do whatever she wants and get away with it. The world doesn't work that way, at least not for women."

* * *

Lasting Impressions

AT THE TIME OF the fire, Shannon was just a baby and had no memory of the farm. She did remember their first house, a shack in East Austin. The house had doors but no windows, just unfinished open spaces. Her other early memories were of a loud house, full of shouting and crying. She remembered she stayed with relatives when she was three years old while her mother went to the hospital to deliver a baby. After a few days, her mother came home, again without a baby.

"Mom, when will I have a baby brother or sister?" Shannon asked.

Her mother's eyes filled with tears but she gave no reply.

Oscar resumed work as a carpenter. He bought his first pickup truck, a 1947 Chevrolet, his pride and joy. He built a cover for the back where Shannon rode. Oscar wasn't always a terrible father in the early years, and he taught daughter about the outdoors. They enjoyed family vacations to the Texas coast, a different fishing village each time, often including trips into Mexico for bullfights and souvenir shopping in the border towns.

The family camped on beaches or stayed in fishing cabins. When it came to the outdoors, Oscar was fearless. One trip, Oscar pulled a shark parallel to the boat and stabbed it in the head with his knife, breaking it off at the hilt. The shark, as long as the fourteen-foot boat, was towed back to shore, and Oscar hauled it onto the beach by hand.

Sometimes other families vacationed with the Swensons, working or drinking friends of Oscar's. One summer, the men went surf fishing while the wives and kids played in the sand and swam in the waves. Oscar's friend, Jack, hooked a magnificent tarpon, a rare event in Texas' shallow surf. The fish breached the waves with his sharp, silver nose pointed skyward. A crowd gathered on the beach, wondering if Jack would be able to land his prize.

"Jack, where's your gaff hook?" Oscar shouted.

"I didn't think I'd need it for beach fishing," Jack shouted back.

"That fish is gonna get off the hook," Oscar said as he waded out toward the fish. When the tarpon made one of its spectacular aerial jumps, Oscar grabbed him! He somehow held onto the quivering, muscular creature and waded back to shore.

"Did you see that?" spectators on the shore said to one another. "How did that man have the strength—and courage—to catch that fish in midair?"

To Shannon, her father was invincible, and to Oscar, Shannon was his precious daughter, He pampered her, and Shannon learned how to handle him and avoid his wrath.

The days after beatings were peaceful times in the Swenson home because Oscar was attentive to Beth and Shannon, and often took them on overnight deer hunting or fishing trips. That, Shannon grew to understand, was to allow Beth's bruises time to heal.

"Mom, why are you holding that raw steak over your eye?" Shannon said once.

"They say the cold from it helps a black eye."

"Looks to me like you're wasting a good steak."

Since the Swensons no longer owned their farm, they often visited Aunt Stella's and Uncle Horace's farm. Oscar hunted doves or raccoons with his dogs, while Shannon roamed the fields. In the summertime, she spent an entire week there. Aunt Stella was kind and welcoming. She taught Shannon how to make her delicious Swedish angel sugar cookies, and Uncle Horace let her drive his tractor. She shot rats in the barn with her BB gun, caught catfish in the pond, fed chickens, and worked in the garden.

Their farmhouse boasted an expansive veranda, wrapping around two sides of the house and shaded by stately oak trees. Shannon played scenes from *Gone With the Wind*, pretending to be Scarlett O'Hara. She persuaded Mo Brown, who still worked on the farm, to be her plantation slave. He agreed because no one could resist the little tow-haired girl who convinced people to play along.

"Mo, how old are you?" Shannon said one day as they sat on a row of plowed, black dirt.

"I don't rightly know, Miz Shannon."

"Where are you from?"

"Why, here, mostly, Miz Shannon. I been here most my life."

"Were you born here?"

"Naw. I come to Mr. Horace and Miz Stella when I was full growed with my wife and four chillen."

"Where were you before that?"

"In Austin. Your Uncle Simon drive up in his wagon one day and asked us to come sharecrop on farms here 'bouts. I been here ever since."

"Where were you before Austin?"

"My folks come here when I was a kid from East Texas. Times

was hard on black folks there. My fam'ly thought we'd be safer in Austin."

"Safer from what?" said Shannon, frowning.

"My folks was slaves. After the Lincoln war, black folks was freed, but life was still hard. Lotsa white folks hated us blacks and would do harm to us, 'specially the menfolk. Here, with Mr. Horace and Miz Stella, we be safe. Always plenty to eat, a roof over our heads, land we own, no white folks botherin' us. We don't bother nobody, and nobody bother us."

"I wish I could live here, Mo. Uncle Horace and Aunt Stella are so nice to me. It's not the same at home. Mom and Dad fight a lot. I love my Grandma, but I don't think she likes me. She's always so cross. Grandpa doesn't talk much, but he's real nice to me."

"All fam'lies got they own ways, Miz Shannon. You just gotta decide what way you gonna be, don't matter what other folks do. You be awright, I reckon," Mo said to her with a nod.

Shannon roamed the Karlsson farm, exploring at will. Once, she wandered to the farthest part of the farm, where the sharecroppers' homes were clustered next to the railroad tracks. One house stood out, painted white and with a picket fence border. A family gathered on the front porch, a mother and several children running about.

The woman in the rocking chair said, "You must be Shannon. Com'on in, chile. I'm Clarice. These are my babies, Liam, Margie, and William."

When Shannon came inside, Clarice offered her a glass of lemonade, leaving her in the living room while she went to the kitchen. Curious as usual, Shannon studied everything in the tidy house, especially the collection of framed photographs on tables and shelves.

Her back stiffened when a familiar white face stared back at her. It was her grandfather, Liam, posing with Clarice and three black children, a proud smile across his face. Something inside told Shannon not to talk to her parents or anyone else about what she had seen, and she never did.

Shannon spent a lot of time with her grandparents in the new Austin home. Alma's palsy had ended her mobility. Whether sitting or lying, she needed assistance getting up and down and required someone to walk alongside her, holding her elbow. She shouted at Liam, day or night, to move her or change her position, and as far as Shannon could tell, he never lost his patience. Shannon helped in these tasks while Liam was at work.

Liam's job at the nearby bakery allowed him to come home for lunch as well as his two coffee breaks so he could check on Alma. A creature of habit, he brought fresh Danish for his morning break, poured coffee into a saucer to cool it, and sipped from the plate. He ate cake or cookies with his lunch, and ice cream or sherbet accompanied his afternoon coffee—a sweet at every meal.

Shannon loved Liam's Model A Ford. She watched for her grandpa to come home, and he paused at the beginning of the driveway as she jumped onto the running board to ride the short distance to the garage.

Though Grandpa Liam didn't talk to her much, she loved his quiet, gentle presence. Every Saturday, he went out, and Shannon watched his deliberate routine of getting ready for his evening. After his shower and shave, Liam donned dress pants and polished shoes, and a fresh white undershirt.

He always tipped a bottle of Evening in Paris onto his undershirt, dabbing two spots near his heart. Over time, his undershirts bore two holes from the cologne. When the delicate sapphire-colored bottles were empty, he gave them to Shannon.

Grandpa Liam then put on a clean white shirt, which he had ironed, a tie, and left, not returning until everyone else was in bed asleep, or even the following day. Liam never said where he was going, and Alma never asked, but her mood on Saturday was more sour than usual.

Shannon wanted to ask her grandfather about the photos she saw in Clarice's living room, but her instinct warned her against it.

By the time Shannon started school, Beth went back to work to support the family. Oscar spent most of his earnings as a carpenter on his drinking, never leaving enough for rent and other expenses. Beth attended beauty school and earned her hairdresser's license. With Beth working, the family moved into nicer rental houses. The first one after the shack was a two-bedroom duplex built over garages in a black neighborhood. One of Shannon's playmates, a young black boy, drank from a fountain with a "Whites only" sign above it.

"Git outta here, boy! Cain't you read?" yelled the store proprietor as he chased the boy down the sidewalk.

"He's too young to read, mister," said Shannon.

"That's no excuse. You keep him away from here."

It was the same with benches at bus stops, seats on the bus, pools, not to mention schools themselves. Though Oscar's own family was at the bottom of the white social ladder, "poor white trash" by any definition, Oscar considered himself far superior to blacks.

When Shannon was still in elementary school, Beth brought home another baby. This boy survived birth but was born with severe disabilities, having what was then called 'water on the brain'. His head was too large for his body. He must have been in pain, for he cried all the time.

One night Oscar, home late and drunk, slammed his fist against the wall at the baby's constant crying. After grabbing him from his crib, Oscar clutched the baby to his chest, squeezing him hard.

"Oscar, leave him alone. Put him back in his crib," Beth pleaded, but he wouldn't.

When Shannon awoke the next morning, the baby was no longer crying. "Mom, where's Timmy?" she said, after she found the crib empty.

"Go to your room," she shouted, "and don't come out till we tell you."

Shannon learned Timmy had died. She turned to her father. "Where did Timmy go?"

Oscar wouldn't look at her. "Don't ever ask about him again," he growled.

The beatings were regular as rent. Screaming and shouting came first, then Oscar's fists to win the argument. At this stage of their marriage, Beth no longer whimpered in the corner but met his fire with her own. Their fights were epic, and the house roared every night.

As Shannon grew older, she grew to understand something was wrong with her family. One day after a drunken fight the previous night, Shannon said to her mother, "If I were married to a man like that, I'd divorce him!"

"Where on earth did you ever hear that word?" Beth cried.

Somewhere amidst the chaos of the dysfunctional Swenson family, Shannon acquired the art of pretense. She pretended she was someone else, someplace else. She created beauty and perfection in her imaginary world: harmonious families gathered around the dinner table, no ugliness, or shouting, or fighting. Homes were clean and comfortable, and families loved one another.

Grace Kelly, Audrey Hepburn, and Jacqueline Kennedy were her role models for their grace, beauty, and self-control. Shannon emulated them—the way they dressed, walked, and talked, and most of all, their steely self-control. Observing her mother and father railing against one another, she promised herself, "Someone's got to be in control! That will be me!"

"Stop acting like you're better than us," Beth barked at her daughter. "You're not! Day-dreaming will just get you disappointed."

Shannon was awakened one night by a fight just outside her bedroom door. Unable to bear the sounds any longer, Shannon went into the hallway and stepped between them, breaking them apart, yelling at her father to leave her mother alone. Enraged further, Oscar's hands went around Shannon's neck, strangling her.

Shannon tried to wrench his hands from her neck, but his grip was too tight. She couldn't breathe. He was strong as a bull.

Beth pulled at his arms, "Oscar, let her go, let her go."

Oscar released his hold just long enough for Shannon to bolt, grab her mother's car keys, and run out the front door to go for help. Shannon still did not know how to drive.

"Oscar, I've got to stop Shannon. Let me go get her," Beth wailed.

He stood still, staring down at his hands. Outside, Beth found Shannon behind the steering wheel of the car, hands shaking, trying to figure out how to start the engine.

"Come back inside," Beth said. "It's okay. Your father has stopped."

When Beth and Shannon returned, Oscar glared at them from the hallway. Shannon's eyes met his. She walked over to him and put her index finger right under his nose, stretching up as tall as her five-foot frame allowed. "If you ever lay a hand on my mother or me again, I'll call the cops on you!"

As she spoke, a sensation of a steel rod ran through her spine. She felt no fear of her father, and a voice inside said she would never fear any man. The father-daughter relationship was forever broken after that night. Shannon now saw her father as a drunken, abusive failure, and Oscar knew his daughter was lost to him.

The beatings continued. True to her word, Shannon called the cops, who only scolded Oscar. The police as a rule didn't intervene in domestic disputes.

At long last, when Shannon was sixteen, Beth divorced Oscar, and he disappeared from their lives.

* * *

SHANNON'S PARENTS HAD never stepped into a church unless it was to attend a wedding or funeral. Every so often, Shannon attended a fundamentalist church with her grandmother, Doll. She liked the pulpit's messages, as well as the structure religion imposed. The rules were clear, with the 'do's and don'ts' taught with no room for doubt. The dictates to live a righteous life, obey God's laws, and commit no sin fit her idealistic views for herself. It was all part of her plan to live a perfect life—to be better than her parents.

Left to her immature conscience, Shannon deduced that sex outside of marriage was a sin. Yet sex within marriage, learned from watching her mother and father, trapped a woman forever. Neither choice suited Shannon.

"Never trust a boy," Beth told her. "They only want one thing." She pointed her index finger at Shannon. "Once you give them what they want, they'll want nothing more to do with you." She shook her head. "You'll be a tramp if you have sex. You'll get pregnant and end up like me."

With Shannon's abusive father out of the picture, she imagined their house would know peace. But Beth's anger and bitterness persisted. Now a single mother with the entire burden of supporting the family, she worked hard and long hours to make ends meet. Her unhappiness poured onto Shannon, a strong-willed, rebellious teenager. The battle between Beth and Oscar shifted to mother and daughter.

Shannon fantasized about her escape. As soon as high school rules allowed, she got a job, dividing her school day in half to work as a junior secretary. She equipped herself with superior typing and shorthand. For her, working in an office was easy.

Beth expected Shannon to help with expenses, and Shannon agreed to a point, but she also wanted to save money for college. She gave her mother half.

"You always think you're better than the rest of us. People like us don't go to college, and the sooner you learn your place, the better," Beth yelled. "As long as you're living under my roof, you'll obey my rules, and until you're eighteen, you will do what I say."

In secret, Shannon saved to purchase her first car and pay her first semester's tuition. She turned 18 on a Wednesday, a workday. That Saturday, Shannon stuffed all her belongings into her battered 1954 Chevrolet and left home, never to return.

* * *

The Cost of Freedom

Shannon didn't look back. She had not a single regret as she left her home in the rearview mirror. She didn't have a place to live yet, but with a full-time job, she was brimming with confidence.

"At last, I am on my own, free to make my own decisions."

Her first stop was the Dean of Women's Office at the University of Texas to find approved housing, required for entering freshmen. The dean showed Shannon a list, the expensive sororities at the top to cheapest at the bottom. The last listing was a boarding house for girls, $245 a month, including utilities. That became Shannon's home for the next several years.

College was intoxicating, and the freedom exhilarating. Eight girls shared the boarding house, two to a room, and as they became friends, they traded food, clothes, boyfriends, and their stories. These girls came from low-income families, too, and Shannon learned she wasn't the only one coming from messed-up families. Shannon grew close to her housemates, in particular her roommate, Marjorie, a drama major.

Shannon's side of the room was neat and orderly; Marjorie's looked like a bomb had exploded. While the room provided a bureau and closet, Marjorie chose to shove everything beneath her bed, including uneaten pizza and dirty dishes. Whenever the kitchen ran low on plates or utensils, the girls raided Marjorie's room, zeroing in on the space under her bed, to reclaim whatever was needed.

Shannon had never known anyone like Marjorie. She bounded

from subject to subject, and her exuberance was contagious. Her stories of onstage acting roles were a continuous fascination and a happy substitute for the unhappy home Shannon left behind.

"This is what I hoped life could be like," Shannon thought. "Marjorie has no limits to her imagination. She's a free spirit."

The campus teemed with students of every socio-economic background. Among the masses of students, Shannon found groups where she fit in. Her family background and financial status didn't matter, and high school triviality was a thing of the past.

Shannon excelled in some courses and struggled in others. Freshman English was reputed to be the hardest for new students, but Shannon aced that course, even garnering encouragement from the professor to pursue writing in her future.

"Imagine that! Encouragement from a professor!" thought Shannon.

She chose as her two majors English and Business Administration. Shannon loved the study of literature and the use of language. Because of her logical, problem-solving mind, she excelled in business courses.

Classes were just a part of what was going on. The war in Viet Nam and the Civil Rights Movement brought passionate debates all around campus. Students for a Democratic Society recruited eager followers, as did the NAACP and the Black Panthers fighting for justice and equality. The women's liberation movement launched. Shannon possessed a self-righteous indignation at injustices forced onto the less fortunate. As her impressionable mind absorbed student wisdom shouted from outdoor pulpits, her opinions grew more assertive.

James Baldwin visited the campus when Shannon was a sophomore. She was one of the thousands who listened to his lectures on his bestselling essay, "Notes of a Native Son." Having seen her father's shameless racism throughout her life, Shannon learned about the more subtle forms of racism pervasive throughout American society. She saw parallels to discrimination women experienced in the workplace and social norms dictated by the white, male-dominated society. Feminism took root, and Shannon determined that sexism would not get in her way.

"I won't allow any man to dominate me, in marriage or my career," she promised herself.

Shannon pursued freelance writing opportunities to earn extra income, writing articles for publications that paid by the word, even a fashion column in a local weekly magazine.

She had no time for boys and dating. Besides, the boys she met seemed immature and shallow.

"Why is taking a girl out to dinner 'code' for having sex? That's a pretty bad exchange, if you ask me," she thought. She enjoyed intense conversations with men about politics, religion, race relations, social injustice, books, and movies, but sooner or later every man interpreted her interest as a prelude to sex.

"Why can't a woman have friendships with men without feeling obligated to have sex with them?" she fumed.

Then she met Josh.

Josh was a teaching assistant in one of her English Literature classes, a few years older than Shannon, and on track toward professorship. He was attractive, intelligent, and passionate about contemporary American writers such as Ernest Hemingway, F. Scott Fitzgerald, and Tom Wolfe.

Shannon had written an essay comparing the writing styles of successful American writers with their English contemporaries. Josh gave her high marks and asked her to schedule a session with him in his office to discuss her paper in depth. Shannon was flattered and booked an appointment for later that same week.

"I'm intrigued by the stark differences you point out, not just in writing styles but in the psychological makeup and cultural biases you suggest beyond the written words," Josh said. "Could you explain that further?"

Shannon thought a bit before answering. "I find it fascinating that in person, the English have perfected the art of restraint and understatement, yet their written works are the opposite. Their thoughts express a profusion of images and complexity of phrasing. On the other hand, American writers demonstrate our inclination for bluntness, directness, and a rush to get to the bone marrow of the situation as fast as possible. It's so illustrative of our very natures, the English and the American."

They talked for an hour before another student knocked on his door for the next meeting.

"Shannon, I'd like to talk with you more about your ideas on writing and your perspectives. Would you consider having dinner with me so we can talk longer and uninterrupted?"

She wondered about the wisdom of accepting his invitation. Still, she enjoyed their conversation so much that she said yes.

They met at a popular outdoor restaurant near campus, a favorite watering hole for students and staff. Over margaritas and enchiladas, they talked for hours. During the meal, Josh reached across the table and held Shannon's hand, and she let him. They met a second time for a movie and dinner, and Josh held her hand through the entire feature.

Like a deer in headlights, Shannon was infatuated with Josh, his intelligence and good looks, his sophistication, and how attentive he was towards her. She lowered her guard. He invited her to his apartment for drinks, and she accepted. Within moments they shared passionate embraces and kisses. Shannon experienced new emotions. She desired Josh.

But as he groped her body and fumbled with her clothing, she pulled away. "No, Josh. Not that." Up to that point, Shannon's experience with boys had been necking in parked cars.

He smirked at her objection and reached behind her back to unhook her bra.

"No, Josh," she said in a stronger voice and tried to pull away.

But he had her locked in his arms and backed against a wall. The bra proved no match for his nimble fingers, and he was soon clutching at her breasts with one hand while the other went under her skirt, pulling at her panties.

"Stop!" she said louder, panic taking hold of her.

"You can't tease me this way, Shannon, and then deny me," he said with a voice husky with lust.

She tried to push him away with all her strength. He pulled back his right arm, made a fist, and struck her, hard, across the face, just below her eye. He then grabbed her blouse with both hands and ripped it open, buttons skittering across the floor. He tore her panties off, shredding them as they fell onto the floor. Before she could react, his pants were unbuckled and unzipped.

With one hand on her chest pressing her against the wall, he positioned himself. He entered her, searing her insides with his violent attack. Then he pushed her down on the floor, one arm pinning her, the other grasping at her breasts and forcing kisses all over her face and neck. At the same time, he rammed her without mercy until he climaxed and spilled his seed inside her.

Lying with his total weight upon her, Josh fell into a semiconscious slumber while Shannon, struggling to breathe, closed her eyes, unable to move.

"What has just happened, in the short space of a few minutes?" she thought, in shock.

She edged out from under him while he lay still, oblivious to her movements. Putting on the torn panties was pointless. She hooked her bra and wrapped the blouse around her, tying the hem into a knot to keep it somewhat closed. She pulled her skirt over her scraped and bruised legs, slipped on her shoes, and grabbed one of Josh's sweaters to cover her body the best she could. She tiptoed out of the apartment without a word.

When she returned to the boarding house, Marjorie was still up, book in her lap, studying for an exam. Marjorie took one look at Shannon and gasped, "My God, Shannon! What happened?"

"Josh raped me," she said, her voice flat.

Marjorie jumped up and put her arm around Shannon. "Do you want to go to the hospital? You've got to press charges against him."

"No! No. I'm all right. Just bruised and so ashamed. How could I let this happen? Me! Of all people!" Shannon said, shaking with both anger and shame. "I always said I'd never let a man lay hands on me or abuse me the way he did. I'm no different from my mother or any other woman."

"Shannon, you can't blame yourself for this. He's a monster for what he did, and you can't let him get away with it," Marjorie said.

"So what do I do, Marjorie? I tell the campus cops that we went to a movie, had dinner, drank margaritas, and then went to his apartment—but I didn't want sex? They'd laugh me out of the station."

Shannon skipped classes for the next three days and called in sick at work. She needed time for the swollen cheek and bruise to fade. Lucky for her, her eye didn't blacken, which would have taken longer to heal. When she looked in the mirror, her mother's face stared back, mocking her.

The hardest part was returning to Josh's class. She was determined not to let him scare or intimidate her. Neither of them made eye contact or spoke, and he showed no signs of remorse or even recognition. He resumed his pattern of flirting with female members of his class, soon picking out a favorite who, like Shannon, hung on his every word.

Shannon made a decision, and she shared it with her roommate. "I've learned something, Marjorie. A woman is not safe with a man, any man. You can't trust them. Never again. Never again."

Time does heal. One day yielded to the next, then a week, then months. Then the semester was over. She saw Josh in class, but they never spoke. After a few months, he seemed to settle on one girl, and Shannon heard from other students that they were engaged. Shannon still couldn't understand what it was in her that Josh targeted, possessed, and discarded. She couldn't escape feeling it had to do with her inadequacies as a woman.

Then one day, out of the blue, Josh called almost a year after that night. "Shannon, I want to see you again. I've missed you."

She suppressed a gasp, then paused. "Let's see if I can get this out the way I want to, but first, let me ask you a question. Why?" "I've been having a rough time. That night, I wanted you so desperately I just couldn't stop myself. After that night, I thought you were the only one for me. So I blocked you out and deliberately put other women in the way. You're the kind of girl I want to be with, but I didn't want to be in a serious relationship. I was scared. I'm so sorry, Shannon. Please let me make it up to you."

"And your engagement?"

"It's finished. She's like a child who wants someone to take care of her, and she's not mature and resilient like you. I ended it."

"I see. Well, then, Josh, let me suggest you take that oversized ego of yours and that penis you can't keep zipped and go fuck yourself. If you ever call me again, I will go to the campus authorities and expose you for the rapist you are. You may or may not go to jail for it, but your career and reputation will be ruined. Don't tempt me."

She hung up.

When she graduated, she elected to receive her dual degree parchments through the mail, too busy at her job to take time off for graduation ceremonies. Besides, since no family would be attending, she saw no purpose in observing the tradition.

"It's time to put these degrees to work!"

* * *

Dr. Ross

SHANNON LANDED A JOB coordinating a symposium attended by intellectuals from throughout the world to discuss "the twenty-first century." The idea of mingling with accomplished, famous people was irresistible. Shannon assisted the executive director, Dr. Howard, in gathering scholars to present their predictions of the major issues confronting the new 21st century. Guests included scientists, anthropologists, philosophers, writers, orchestral composers, economists, and sociologists from the United States, Europe, Iron Curtain countries, Africa, and the Caribbean.

Shannon was in her twenties, single, and attractive with long, blonde locks. Her Texas charm and infectious enthusiasm impressed the attendees, and her organizational skills were flawless. Dr. Howard's authoritarian style confounded Shannon. He tried to keep her in check, to make sure she sat in a row in the back, not have a front row seat. It wasn't what he said or did outright as much as it was his manner and reactions. When Shannon gave a weekly report on the conference's progress in characteristic excitement, her co-workers smiled with her. Dr. Howard only glared.

One of her co-workers whispered, "Hey, Shannon. Better back off a bit. Dr. Howard thinks you're too forward with the attendees."

"Back off? Ha! Just watch!"

Shannon did her thing, caring for the attendees with flawless efficiency and courtesy. To Dr. Howard's obvious chagrin, they sang her praises to him.

An older, elegant Black man from the Caribbean was among the conference participants who represented the Third World. A Marxist, Dr. Finlay Ross had lived his entire life advocating for socialism and racial justice. He had published several books on the Black experience, from the slave revolt in the Caribbean in the 1700s to the civil rights struggles of the present day. He was tall and soft-spoken, deferential to the other participants, choosing to stay in the background.

One morning Dr. Ross commented to Shannon how much he disliked the Continental breakfast served each morning. "I require a full, hot breakfast to start my day. Do you know a nearby restaurant where I can go?"

"I'll take you to a diner just down the block," she said.

Each morning she accompanied Dr. Ross and an anthropologist from Zambia, who also didn't care for sweet rolls, to the restaurant. They ordered a complete English breakfast of eggs, sausages, beans, tomatoes, toast, and copious amounts of coffee. As she got to know the professor better, she asked why he had not yet spoken up at the conference. The Eastern and Western powers dominated the conversation, the dialogue stuck on the Cold War, and the subject of the emerging Third World had not come up.

Dr. Ross promised Shannon he would do so soon.

True to his word, at a general session, Dr. Ross stood to be recognized by the chair. He then gave an oblique, abstract interpretation of the emerging Third World and how he believed it would reset global priorities. When he finished speaking, he sat down, and the whole room was silent. Even Shannon admitted to herself that she didn't quite understand all he said. The commentary returned to the struggles of East vs. West debated by the big guns from both sides of the Iron Curtain. Dr. Ross' observations went undiscussed.

Over breakfast, Shannon asked him what he thought of the Civil Rights movement in the U. S. and apartheid in South Africa, both struggles capturing headlines throughout the world. Dr. Ross referenced his talk from the previous day, saying that people of color around the globe will soon rise up, no longer accepting white domination.

"South Africa is the beginning. In time, the forced separation of races will be a thing of the past, and nonwhites will insist on economic and social equality."

"I want to go to South Africa and help end apartheid," Shannon said, "and I want to write about the struggle."

"You?" He laughed. "What can you do? You are a young, naïve, American white woman! Not even. Girl! You have no idea how dangerous South Africa is, and you must not think of this!" He shook his head. "Tell me. Where have you traveled?"

"Nowhere yet," she said, casting her eyes down and feeling a bit embarrassed and silly.

"And where is the first place you want to go?"

"Paris!"

"Then you shall," he said with a grin.

At the closing dinner, everyone raised their glasses for the customary toasts. One of the distinguished guests raised his glass to Shannon, asking how he should address her, as Miss or Mrs?

Without skipping a beat, Shannon called out, "Ms!"

From the corner of her eye, she spotted Dr. Howard glowering at her.

For all its hype of gathering intellectuals and thought leaders to discuss the future, the symposium turned out to be futile. The participants couldn't even agree on the agenda. The conference ended, and all the participants returned to their parts of the world.

Two days later, Shannon received a special delivery letter. Inside was an open round trip plane ticket, first-class, to Paris, with a note scrawled from Dr. Ross. "You must see Paris, and Paris must see you!"

Shannon's jaw dropped open at the incredible, generous gift. In her excitement she rushed to the main office and showed her co-workers the ticket and Dr. Ross' letter. Dr. Howard stood at the door to his office, glaring at Shannon. Then, without a word, he turned and closed the door.

As she reflected on Dr. Ross' gift, Shannon's cautious nature asserted itself. She returned the ticket with a letter to Dr. Ross, thanking him for his generous gift while refusing to accept it.

"I'm preparing for my trip to South Africa," she wrote him. "I'm saving money and arranging my travel documents. I've found out there are limited but acceptable accommodations on freight ships, very cheap, and I'm looking into that as a way to get there."

He wrote her again. "Don't do anything yet. Let me come back to Austin, and we will talk about this. Make me a hotel reservation, and I will be there over the next weekend."

After Dr. Ross arrived, Shannon met him in the hotel restaurant, where they spent hours talking about what was happening on the ground in South Africa and the dangers.

"South Africa is a cauldron right now. The repressive white Afrikaner regime doesn't want the truth to get out, and they hide their savagery from the world. As a woman journalist, both blacks and whites would set upon you. Your being American won't protect you once you're in-country. At a minimum, you'd be raped and beaten, but more likely you'd be killed and never heard from again. I mean this most sincerely. Put this out of your mind."

While he paused, Shannon squirmed.

"You know nothing yet of the world, Shannon. First, learn. Read James Baldwin's essays. There's Donald Woods' book, *Cry Freedom*, about the South African activist Steven Biko, and many other worthy books written about apartheid. Read my books. I brought you copies."

They talked about the differences between socialism and capitalism. Dr. Ross had devoted his entire life to fighting for the freedoms and rights Americans take for granted.

"You, my dear, are a capitalist. It's who you are, where you were born, how you think. There's nothing wrong with that, except it will get in the way of your understanding the struggles going on in countries where people are fighting for equality and freedom."

A battle waged within Shannon, her self-righteous nature to fight injustice struggling against the idea that she might not be up to the task. She bit back her inner turmoil and listened.

"Arm yourself with information, knowledge, facts," he continued. "Then, maybe then, and only then, will you be in a position to write about their struggles."

"How long will such an education take?" she wondered.

"Do me the honor of keeping the plane ticket. Hold it until you're ready. Paris is as good a place as any to start your education. There's no more beautiful place in the world than the City of Lights, and I want to imagine you in Paris for the first time."

When Dr. Ross left, Shannon felt a bit defeated but also a bit wiser. She accepted how little she knew and how foolish she must have seemed to him.

"If I want to make an impact in the world, I must learn about it! He's right. All I would accomplish is getting in the way."

She also appreciated that Dr. Ross never said anything

inappropriate or suggestive. He made no advances at all, and she sighed in relief that perhaps she had achieved a wholly intellectual and platonic interaction with a man.

* * *

Pushy Broad

WHEN SHANNON COMPLETED her role coordinating the symposium, she accepted a job, replacing a retiring secretary in a lobbying organization, a small office of three men and three secretaries. During the first half of the day, the lobbyists were at the state capitol—the Hill," they called it—influencing the passage or prevention of legislation that would affect their industry.

Shannon stayed at the office from 9 AM until 1 PM while her boss was on the Hill, but she could do whatever she wanted in the afternoons when he was on the golf course. That's what attracted Shannon to the job. She could take classes in the afternoons and pursue her freelance writing. Besides that, the pay was her highest earnings yet.

There was one major flaw, however. The association produced a quarterly newsletter mailed to over 100,000 members. Although the publication was printed offsite, one of the secretaries maintained the massive mailing list in-house on an old linotype machine. She had developed a nervous disorder, probably from operating this ancient machine, and Shannon was assigned to take over the task.

On the surface, it seemed a no-brainer. However, Shannon learned each keystroke made a delayed sound after being struck. Shannon was a fast typist, but she had to slow down before entering the next keystroke.

"No wonder the woman's nerves are shot!" Shannon thought. "This just won't do."

With her problem-solving skills, Shannon broke the task into its parts. She learned about new technology that could manage the list offsite by a company that would print and mail the newsletter, eliminating the cumbersome linotype function. She had to prove it would be a more economical approach. Shannon developed a cost analysis that demonstrated savings by eliminating the extra office space for the in-house function and reducing staff by one person. On paper, the savings were substantial.

Shannon presented her proposal to the director, whose jaw dropped a bit. He told her he would review the proposal and slid it into his top desk drawer.

A short time later, two suited executives strode into the office with no appointment and demanded to see the director. They were representatives of the board of directors who had oversight responsibility of the lobbying organization and authority over the director.

Sitting just outside her boss' office and with a clear view, Shannon overheard both executives complain about the office's high costs while the country was experiencing a bad recession. Standing and speaking in a loud voice, one of the executives said, "Just what are you going to do to reduce overhead?"

To her surprise, the director pulled Shannon's proposal from the desk drawer and handed it to his superiors. The executive sat down, reviewed the proposal, and then, in a much calmer voice, one of them said, "We compliment you on your foresight in addressing this situation. We approve the plan and insist it be implemented without delay."

Shannon was charged with executing the cost savings strategy, although her boss handled the layoff of the secretary. Shannon celebrated in seeing her goal attained and felt no guilt for the secretary who lost her job, a middle-aged, disabled woman.

Shannon experienced love-hate relationships with her superiors in her career. She scored high marks and success when a boss gave her free rein with minimal oversight. Yet under micromanagers, Shannon conflicted head-on with authority, sometimes resulting in failure. She felt equal to any male worker, often superior, in terms of job performance. But she learned she would have to fight for equality in the workplace; nothing would be given to her.

In another position, Shannon attained an executive position and prepared for her annual performance review by finding out what her male counterparts were earning. The review took place in her boss' office, and he seated them on adjoining corners of two couches. The manager gave her an excellent written review, almost perfect, but she frowned to hear her salary increase was lower than she expected.

"With your raise, your earnings match the top five percent of women in your field in the whole state!" he said, defending the monetary increase, while reaching across and touching a bangle bracelet Shannon was wearing, spinning it around her wrist as he talked.

Shannon withdrew her arm. "When I'm in the top five percent of *all* workers in my field, male *and* female, then I'll be satisfied." She stood and walked out of his office, shutting the door behind her.

She knew that this general manager was weak in his job performance—and vulnerable. He had an outsized ego and was disloyal to his bosses, the owners. He managed the business as though it was his personal fiefdom, and he was running it into the ground. The business was failing.

Over the next two months, Shannon developed a plan demonstrating how a new business model would reduce costs while increasing revenue. She laid out the new positioning in the marketplace, sales and marketing strategies, and complete financials that projected a profitable turnaround within three years.

Then she went to the manager and presented him with the plan. "If we execute this strategy, I think we can save the business. And I believe I am the right person to execute it."

Like her previous manager some years before, he opened his top desk drawer and dropped the plan into it.

"What was it that famous baseball player/philosopher Yogi Berra said?" thought Shannon. *'It's deja vu all over again.'"*

A corporate attorney representing the owners arrived

unannounced, informing everyone the owners had charged him to stop the bleeding. The manager couldn't hide how incensed he was that his authority was questioned, and he threw roadblocks in the way of the executive's discovery process, instructing employees not to talk to him.

But the lawyer made it his business to interview all mid-level managers and line employees. When it was Shannon's turn, he came loaded for bear. He demanded to know what she, as marketing director, was doing to improve business.

"Did the general manager show you my business plan?"

"What business plan?"

"The one in his desk." Then she opened her desk drawer and handed him a binder. "Here's my copy."

Within days, the owners fired the manager, but not just because of Shannon's actions. The manager was on the ropes for several offenses, and Shannon wasn't the only employee calling attention to his incompetence. But hers was the final nail in his coffin. Her business plan was approved, and she earned the trust and respect of the business's owners.

To male colleagues, Shannon had the reputation of "the lady with the iron fist in a velvet glove," or to those with less generous words, a "ball buster."

Shannon was driven to excel at everything she attempted, including looking her best. Hair, makeup, and clothing met rigid requirements for presenting a professional image. She was the first one to arrive at her office and the last to leave. She didn't hesitate to work weekends or holidays. She had a mind for business and organization.

Shannon was just as disciplined with her body. She maintained a yoga and stretching program, and took up running, jogging six miles a day. She played a good game of tennis, and golf became a passion.

She added bicycling to her regimen. One day she read an article about an upcoming triathlon in a nearby town. "That will force me to learn to swim," she told herself. She competed in four triathlons, once winning her age bracket.

It was this chapter in Shannon's life when she met Helen.

Helen had immigrated from South Africa and worked in the same company as Shannon. They met on a footbridge where Helen was enjoying a smoke. She was about the same size and stature as Shannon, blond and fit. Shannon loved her accent and her quick laugh, and their friendship was instant.

"How brave you are to leave your country and family and start a new life here," Shannon said.

"Leaving South Africa wasn't so hard. The politics there are unbearable, and I refused to live there any more. I tried England first, but it was too cold and wet." Then Helen seemed to recognize something about Shannon. "You're the one I've heard about," Helen added. "You're the one scaring all the men around here."

Shannon grinned and raised one eyebrow. "I like your sense of humor!"

"That's me. I look for fun in all places. I like people, except for the ones I don't, and I don't take things too seriously."

"I'm the opposite. I live for my work and success."

"Me? I'll take good company and conversation over work any time. We should get on just fine," said Helen. "A few of us meet for drinks after work. Why don't you join us?"

They discovered they shared some important common ground. Both their fathers were alcoholics. Both women were independent, adventurous, intelligent.

They shared another trait. Both Shannon and Helen enjoyed men, but they distrusted them. They were disdainful of women who considered a "good marriage" the ticket to a life of security. They were authentic women's libbers.

"Helen is the first person in my life I can trust completely," Shannon thought. "She doesn't judge me for my family, my past, or anything I say or do. She likes me for myself."

Helen became Shannon's touchstone.

Her Wall Crumbles

Helen phoned Shannon one day. "How's your tennis game lately?"

"Plateaued," Shannon said. "My serve wins some aces, and my forehand is reliable, but my backhand is still wimpy. Why do you ask?"

"Well, you know my job here at the club gives me some nice perks, and I get to hobnob with the best tennis players in the world."

"Yeah, you've got bragging rights for sure. So?"

"We've got a nice clinic coming up, and I thought you'd be interested. Some terrific touring pros are teaching, friends of mine from back home. Interested?"

"Heck, yes! When and where? I'll be there."

One of the pros at the clinic was Graeme Thorne, a handsome South African. Thorne's singles career was at its peak, sometimes succumbing to the up-and-coming younger bombers. However, he was still a formidable competitor on the doubles circuit.

Shannon signed up to focus on her backhand. It was a hot Texas summer day, and Shannon sweated bullets. Still, she pushed herself through each drill, followed instructions, focused on hitting the ball as instructed. She hadn't noticed the instructor until he came up to her after the clinic.

"You are a determined student!" the instructor said. "If you keep that up, you'll find your best game soon enough." He extended his hand. "My name's Graeme. What's yours?"

"Shannon Swenson. Thank you for the excellent clinic." She shook his hand.

"With a name like that, you must be Swedish," Graeme said with a grin.

"On my father's side. And you?"

"My father was born and raised in South Africa," he said. "My mother is German, but she's lived in South Africa most of her life." He glanced up at the sky. "It must be around noon. I'm famished. Would you care to join us in the club for lunch?"

"I'm hot, sweaty, and gross," Shannon said, grimacing, "and not suitable in close company with people trying to enjoy their food."

"Nonsense! We're all hot, sweaty, and gross, and we'll eat outside on the terrace. There! More comfortable?" He grinned. "All the teaching pros will be with us. So will your friend, Helen. Therefore, you'll be in good company."

"Well, all right. I am pretty hungry myself." She smiled, noting how disarming this man was.

Their lunch was at a table for two with the other pros nearby. With Shannon's consent, Graeme ordered a delicious trout filet, fresh vegetables, salad, and cold white wine.

Graeme shared his observations of her forehand but concentrated his comments on her backhand. The conversation moved to his tennis career, his next destination, and his schedule for the rest of the year. It was an exciting itinerary, and Shannon couldn't help imagining all the places he would go.

Helen popped by their table. "I'm glad you two are getting on. Graeme's a great teacher, isn't he?" She looked from one to the other. "Take good care of my friend, Graeme. Shannon, we'll catch up tomorrow."

They resumed their lively conversation, and Shannon learned that Graeme was the youngest of four sons in a traditional South African family.

"My father's ancestors were English who settled in the Cape Town province, then built a farm in the wine country. It's been in our family for generations."

Graeme talked about growing up, working in the vineyards and orchards by the time he was six years old. Their farm produced grapes for South African wines and fruit distributed throughout the country. Graeme and his brothers grew up playing tennis whenever they weren't working the farm.

"Since we lived too far from towns to participate in sporting activities, my parents built a tennis court near our house. They used the soil from a dormant anthill for the surface, making a fine claylike surface."

"So that's how you developed your tennis game."

"By the time I was ten, I was entering tournaments, and winning most of the time. As a teenager, my mother drove me to tournaments throughout Cape Town Province. When I turned seventeen, I entered the South African Open Championship and made it to the semifinals."

"Well, you went up through the ranks pretty fast!"

Graeme nodded. "I decided to turn professional. My mother homeschooled all of us, so my parents insisted I go to university first, and I played for the college team at South African University."

"What did you do after graduating, with what…?"

"With a degree in business. Then I joined the pro tour."

Shannon was fascinated by this handsome South African, listening to Graeme talk about his country. "One of my fantasies is to go on an African safari," she told him, then drilled Graeme for information about animals he had seen.

He laughed, telling her his region was famous for its springbok antelopes, and lions or the big animals associated with Africa rarely threatened them. He did tell her one exception, however.

"My grandfather, Pop, as we called him, went leopard hunting with one of the workers. The cat had become a nuisance on the farm, killing sheep. They both carried rifles. Pop rounded a bend along the trail he was following and walked under a tree where the leopard crouched in the branches. The cat leaped on him, and both Pop and the leopard tumbled down a hillside, wrestling all the way down."

Shannon sat still, holding her breath until Graeme continued.

"As luck would have it," he said with a chuckle, "the leopard hit his head on a rock at the bottom, which stunned him long enough for Pop to retrieve his rifle and shoot him. By this time, Pop's worker made it down the hill and found him pretty seriously mauled."

With a gasp, Shannon drew her fingertips to her mouth.

"He got Pop home, and they took him to the nearest hospital. Most of the injuries were claw marks all over his body except for a severe bite on his thigh. The doctor bandaged him up and sent him home with medicines for his wounds."

Graeme shook his head. "He recovered, but the wound in his leg never completely healed, always with a bad odor from infection left by the bacteria in the leopard's teeth."

"Wow! What a story."

Graeme asked Shannon about her history, parents, upbringing—all questions Shannon usually dodged. This time she found herself answering without hesitation. As she talked, Shannon watched for any hint of disapproval or judgment, but found none. Graeme put her at ease, and their conversations flowed without any effort.

Both Shannon and Graeme jerked upright when their waiter told them the dining terrace was closing.

"I had no idea it was after five o'clock in the afternoon, and here we are, both still in our same sweaty tennis clothes." Graeme looked around. "All the others have left."

"Good heavens!" She glanced at her watch. "I've got to get going."

"Not until you tell me when I can see you again," he said, holding her wrist. "I'm in town just a few more days before leaving for Paris. Will you have dinner with me tomorrow night?"

"Well, all right… but I'll meet you," said Shannon. "Where and when?"

"Seven o'clock. Right here. I'll make a reservation for the dining room inside."

"I'll see you then. Thanks for the nice lunch and a wonderful clinic," Shannon said, shaking his hand again, feeling awkward and stiff.

Shannon thought about this intriguing, considerate man that evening and through the next day. She rehashed their conversations and the peculiar, prickly sensations she felt as she pictured him and how comfortable she felt with him.

"He's very handsome," Shannon mused, "and with that perfect athletic body that tennis players acquire."

Shannon tried on three different outfits for their dinner date, settling on a short, form-fitting dress with just a touch of jewelry. She fussed over her hair until it was as perfect as she could manage and kept her makeup light. High-heeled, open-toed sandals set off her trim, muscled legs.

She arrived at the club just after seven, not wanting to appear too eager. The maitre d' escorted her to a linen-covered table for two next to a window overlooking the golf course. Graeme stood as she approached, dressed in nice slacks, an open collar white shirt, and a navy blue sports jacket. He took Shannon's hand, kissed her on each cheek in greeting, and seated her next to him.

"You look wonderful," he said.

"So do you." She couldn't help but notice how pleasant he smelled when he bent to kiss her.

"I've ordered a bottle of wine for us. I hope you like red. I found a nice one on the list."

Shannon again thought how refreshing it was to be with someone who is at ease with social graces.

"Tell me about your day," he said, "though I've had a hard time getting through my own because I couldn't wait to see you again."

"Me, too," Shannon said, then thought, "Did I just admit the same thing?"

Their evening seemed to race by as they enjoyed a nice steak, while the noise and activity of the restaurant fell away. They talked more about their families. It didn't escape her notice that when

Graeme described his home life, it was with tenderness and fond memories, while Shannon struggled to find happy times to share.

"I'm sorry to be so maudlin, but the simple fact is my family was pretty messed up, and I've spent the past ten years trying to build a life that's the opposite of all that. Frankly, I'd rather talk about my time after leaving home."

"I understand," Graeme said, his voice tender. "I don't mean to make it seem my growing up wasn't without its share of turmoil. My parents are very strict, especially my father. I outgrew his old-fashioned ideas. For me, getting away from home and going on tour has been perhaps what your leaving home has been for you. My father's views on life and the world are stifling and, quite frankly, just wrong. At least, for me. Let's do talk about happier times, but first, can you tell me how a beautiful woman like you has managed to stay single—assuming indeed you are."

"Well, I wondered the same about you!" Shannon said. "I can tell you I came close a couple of times but haven't found the right person. The men I've dated so far all ended up too small for me."

Graeme's eyes widened, and one side of his mouth curled up in a grin. "Oh, size is it! Are we talking about that?"

Shannon turned several shades of red as they both laughed. "No, no! I didn't mean that!"

They both paused to sip their wine while Shannon regained her equilibrium.

"What I mean is the men I've dated have small *thoughts*. They care about the space they occupy rather than the world beyond it. I felt confined, knowing there is much more to life than what I saw in any future I would have with them. It's pretty frustrating, actually, and many times I felt something was wrong with me, that I would never be satisfied or content with one person."

"I've been married before, Shannon," Graeme said, his voice turning quiet and serious. "A girl from back home. I have a daughter. Alexandra. We call her Alex. She's eight. She's been living with my mother and father for the past four years."

Graeme paused. "Cora and I divorced when Alex was just two years old. We met in college, had a thing, and she got pregnant. So we got married. It was doomed from the start."

"That's sad. Alex was so young."

"Cora resented my being on tour, but she hated going on the road with me. She toured with me for a short time but found being in different cities and hotels unsettling. Being surrounded by strangers was traumatic for her." He stared at the tabletop. "We couldn't make it work, and we grew to resent one another. Once Alex was born, it wasn't an option for her to travel with me. I wouldn't give up tennis. It's my life, and I love it. She gave me an ultimatum. Either quit tennis and settle in Johannesburg or divorce. So we divorced."

Shannon hung on every word, listening, and feeling sympathy for this nice man.

"One day I got a call from Cora's parents. She had been killed in an auto accident."

"What happened?"

"I'm still piecing things together, and some things, I'll probably never know. Alex doesn't talk about it. From what I learned after she died, Cora suffered from depression for much of her life and was taking antidepressants since her teen years. Cora never told me, and her parents kept it quiet, too. When we divorced, her depression got worse, and she relied on drugs to keep herself going. She became addicted to them. On top of that, she started drinking heavily. Her autopsy revealed she was way over the intoxication limit."

"How did she manage taking care of her daughter in that state?"

"That's the worst part," said Graeme. He took a deep breath. "When the accident happened, the police traced Cora to her parents, to give her the news about her death. They asked about Alex, and the police didn't know anything. They dispatched a team to Cora's apartment and conducted a search. They found Alex locked in a closet."

Shannon gasped, throwing both hands over her face. "No! No! That's horrible."

"The officers couldn't determine how long she had been in there. She was scared, crying, hungry. She had soiled herself several times over. It was dark in the closet… We never learned how long she was…" He sighed.

"Graeme, I can't imagine what she was feeling, what she went through."

"We didn't realize things were like this with Cora. Not her parents, and certainly not me. I have no idea what her life must have been like."

"What happened then?"

"The police took Alex into Child Protective Services. She was cleaned up, fed, and put to bed. They released her to Cora's parents until I could get there. I cancelled all my engagements and flew there the next day. As her father, I got immediate custody. I took her to my parents, and that's where she's been since this happened."

"How is she now?"

"It hasn't been easy for her. She withdrew into a shell. We got a counselor for her, but she was only four! There's just so much a counselor can learn from a four-year-old. I'll never forgive myself for leaving her in that situation."

"But you didn't realize how good Cora was at hiding her condition from everyone, even her own parents. How often do you see Alex?"

"Not as often as I like. I take at least one month each year, and on holidays."

"That's not much, is it?

"I'm developing business interests outside competitive tennis, so I have more control of my time and can build a future for myself and my daughter. For now, my mom has been a champion. She's given Alex a stable home, she surrounds her with love and attention. She home schools her, and Alex is doing quite well academically."

"I cannot comprehend what this young girl has endured," Shannon said again. "She needs all the love and security you can offer her, Graeme."

Graeme looked straight at Shannon for a moment. "Yes, you're right; and I realize that as a distant father, I'm falling far short of the mark. I don't know why I'm telling you all this. I just wanted you to know that part about me, and that I have a daughter who is the main focus of my life. Since my divorce, I haven't been involved with anyone, although I don't want you to think I'm a saint either!"

He smirked, a wry look on his face. "Let's just say that life on the road for a single guy offers plenty of temptations."

"And am I one of them?" Shannon blurted out.

Graeme jerked upright. "No! God, I hope I haven't given that impression. I certainly don't divulge my personal life to just anyone if all I'm interested in is a one-night stand!" He paused, took a sip of wine, and set the glass down. "Frankly, I'm a little hurt you think so, Shannon. I just felt you were someone I could talk to, and I wanted to be honest about my daughter."

"I apologize, Graeme. I have an automatic defense system that kicks in whenever someone is trying to get past my walls. I'm sorry I offended you."

"Am I wrong about you, Shannon? Are you someone I can trust and let down my own walls?"

"Graeme, I honestly don't know what kind of person I am. I haven't allowed anyone to get close to me. Sure, I've had boyfriends or casual flings, but after a disaster in my college days, I walk away when things get too close. I always feel I have to defend myself."

"Would you tell me what happened that made you shut down?" Graeme said.

"Not yet." Shannon shrugged. "Maybe one day. Maybe not."

"Well, that's honest enough, I guess. Maybe I'll be the person you can trust. Maybe not. But since our cards are on the table, will you let me see you again while I'm in town? I promise to be on my best behavior, but I'd like to see where this goes."

Graeme escorted Shannon to her car. "Will you have breakfast with me tomorrow?" he said. "I feel like this evening is ending too soon."

"Oh, I can't. I have an interview for an article I'm writing."

"Then how about lunch?"

"I won't be back in time. The interview is a bit out of town."

"Then dinner again tomorrow night? I'll keep asking until you say 'yes'."

"Okay. I'm not exactly sure what time I'll finish."

"Whenever you get back is fine with me, but not here again. Look, you know the area. Why don't you pick a place? Pick me up here, and we'll go to any restaurant you like."

"All right. Give me a phone number to reach you, and I'll call you when I leave my interview so we can reasonably predict when I'll be here."

This time Graeme bent his head and kissed Shannon on the lips, a sweet, lingering kiss, caressing her face between his hands. "Till tomorrow night then," he said as he turned and walked through the doors of the club.

Shannon's interview was in San Antonio, and she had difficulty paying attention, finding herself rushing through her questions, wanting plenty of time to get ready for her date with Graeme. She took the hour's drive home to decide on the restaurant. She settled on the famous Cliffside Cantina, a tourist trap with mediocre food, but the sunset views over Lake Travis made the restaurant a must-stop for Austin visitors. The sunset and the margaritas compensated for the lousy enchiladas.

Again, Shannon arrived at the country club's *porte cochere* at seven, and found Graeme waiting outside, this time wearing a nice pair of jeans, a short-sleeved shirt, and soft leather loafers with no socks.

"He looks good enough to eat," thought Shannon.

She had chosen a killer outfit that never failed to win compliments, a bright white summer dress, mid-thigh. It unbuttoned to the knees, showing off her legs, with a matching sleeveless top that accented her athletic arms, a bit of bosom exposed. High, bright yellow wedge sandals brought her five-foot-three height a good three inches taller, reaching Graeme's nose.

As she climbed out of the car, Graeme gave her an enthusiastic embrace. "I thought this day would never end," he said. "You look stunning! Do you want me to drive?"

"I'll get us there," she said, "I know the way. But I might ask you to drive back."

The restaurant was packed as usual, but Shannon had called ahead and persuaded the manager to reserve one of their best tables, breaking its "no reservations" policy. Even with a waiting line, their waiter escorted them right away to their table. As Graeme scanned the noisy, packed restaurant, she could tell he wasn't impressed and who could blame him.

"Not a fan of crowded restaurants?" she said.

"Well, I'm a bit surprised. Just not what I was expecting, I guess," Graeme said, replacing his frown with half a smile.

When the waiter guided them outside and onto the restaurant's massive tiered decking, threading his way among hundreds of customers, he seated them at an umbrella-covered table for two by the railing. A cliff dropped far below, disappearing into the hillsides and opening onto the lake's magnificent vista.

"Wow! What a view! No wonder so many people come here."

Not wanting them to wait for their first beverage, Shannon had used her powers of persuasion, with extra tips promised to the maitre 'd, and ordered frozen margaritas and nachos. Within minutes of being seated, their waiter brought two frozen goblets of the frothy drink and set the appetizers on the table.

"Have you ever had frozen margaritas?" she said to Graeme.

"No. I've heard of them, but this is a first for me."

"Well, I'm pleased to introduce a new experience to a man of the world." She held up her glass, and, laying on her thickest Texas drawl, said, "Here's your official welcome to Texas with the hope that ya'll come back real soon, hear?"

Graeme joined her in the toast and grinned at the refreshing, tangy sweetness of the drink. "I could get used to this."

Same as their first dinner together, the evening flowed as smoothly as the tequila drinks, though their conversation turned more personal, more intimate. They skipped dinner altogether, stuffing themselves on the nachos, queso, and guacamole, washed down with more margaritas.

The drinks hit them both, neither professing to be accomplished drinkers, and they rose from their table tipsy. "Would you let me order us a taxi," he said, "so neither of us is driving?"

"Graeme, that's smart. I'd hate for us to spend your last night in jail."

"I'll drop you off first, and take another taxi back to you tomorrow, then we'll come get your car. I have a business meeting first thing in the morning but am free after that. Would you spend the day with me and, of course, have dinner with me again tomorrow night?"

"Wow! Sure you won't get tired of me? I usually run someone off after a few hours," she said, grinning at him.

"I'll take my chances. I just want to spend as much time with you as possible before I leave. Why don't we drive into the country for lunch? Let me get behind the wheel this time, if you trust me with your car. I'm quite experienced at driving on the wrong side of the road."

The backseat of the cab was their first time in such close proximity. The electricity was unmistakable. Graeme reached across the seat and took hold of Shannon's hand, brought it to his lips, and kissed the back of her hand, then each finger and her palm. Their eyes met, and both inclined their heads toward each other and kissed. Graeme's arms enfolded Shannon, their kisses passionate, tongues touching, exploring.

They reached Shannon's apartment much faster than they wanted, and Graeme escorted her to her door while the taxi waited. He kissed her good night with exquisite tenderness and pulled away with obvious reluctance. "Sleep tight, Sweet Shannon. I'll see you tomorrow."

"Good night, Graeme. Thanks for a wonderful evening. Oh,

I've got an idea for our day tomorrow. Wear comfortable clothes and shoes, maybe even bring along a pair of hikers if you have them."

"Sounds fun," he said. "I'll have to stick with my tennis shoes, but if they keep me up on the courts, I should be able to manage a little hike." He returned for another kiss. "One for the road."

"The Texas Hill Country is known for its rolling hills covered with oaks and evergreens, lakes and rivers, and quaint towns that seem frozen in time," said Shannon, trying to sound like an official tour guide. "It's bound by the coastal plains south of the Colorado and Brazos Rivers and the oil-rich Permian Basin in the north. The rocky soil is unproductive for farming but ideal for ranching—and vineyards! Winemakers discovered the area in the 70s, and over fifty wineries weave through pastures of grazing cattle and horses."

Graeme laughed at her delivery. "Ah ha! Quite the expert, I see."

He piloted Shannon's standard shift Volvo with familiar ease, though every now and then he mistook the clutch for the brake until his muscle memory oriented to American driving.

Shannon directed him to a dumpy-looking outdoor restaurant with picnic tables set up under shady oaks. She ordered sliced brisket sandwiches with lots of barbecue sauce, potato salad on the side, and ice-cold Shiner beer in traditional Texas longneck bottles. Graeme loved it, and Shannon scored another first for her visiting South African friend.

Then she directed him to a famous landmark, Enchanted Rock, a state park with granite outcroppings dotting the hillsides with its centerpiece, a solid domed granite mountain. They hiked to the top for its sweeping 360-degree views.

"It's beautiful," Graeme said. "It actually reminds me of home. The same rolling hills, grasslands, and vistas as far as you can see."

It was a short drive to their next stop: Fredericksburg, a picturesque German town full of shops, restaurants, and bars along its main street. A motorcycle gang roared through town, capturing attention with their loud "choppers," leather jackets, and body tattoos.

Shannon and Graeme strolled the busy sidewalks, window shopping at Texas souvenir shops, first-rate art galleries, and chic jewelry stores. He asked permission to buy her a piece of jewelry as a memento, and they selected a simple turquoise ring with delicate swirls of silver. "It looks pretty on your small hand."

What they enjoyed most was sitting at a sidewalk cafe sipping Texas wines and watching the people.

On the drive back to Austin, they stopped at a few wineries. Graeme made mental notes, comparing the tasting rooms and overall ambiance with those in his country.

"These are nicely done, and I'm somewhat surprised," he said. "One day, our farm plans to produce its own label and open a winery. We've been talking about it for years. I like how these tasting rooms blend the cowboy history and ranch environment with a sophisticated, contemporary ambiance."

"You'll find the regions of Texas vary quite differently from one another," Shannon told him. "Austin is known for being liberal and intellectual, Houston is entrepreneurial and nouveau riche, and Dallas is old money and snobby."

Shannon made reservations at a South Congress tapas bar in Austin and chose light items after a day of eating and drinking. Sitting outside, Graeme enjoyed watching the customers come and go, men in their jeans and expensive Lucchese boots and women in sexy sundresses.

They sat quietly, holding hands across the table, enjoying the last of the wine Graeme selected.

Then, without warning, Graeme smacked the table. "Shannon! Come to Paris with me!"

"What?"

"Come with me! I'm leaving tomorrow. I don't know when or if I'll ever get back to Texas. Come with me."

Shannon sat up straight. "Whoa, Cowboy! You're moving way too fast here."

"But I can't bear the thought of not seeing you again."

"Graeme, we've only just met. I can't just up and leave and come with you to Paris." She shook her head. "I'm not that kind of person. Surely you know that by now."

"Shannon, you must realize that I am absolutely taken with you and have to see you again. I know this is fast, and I understand how crazy this sounds. Look, I've never asked a girl to come with me on tour before. Sure, I've had women in my life, some back home, some I've met in different cities, but no one that I've wanted to be with me, to travel with me. You've made me feel something I've never felt before, and I don't want to lose you."

"But we don't know each other well enough. Graeme, I've already told you how cautious I am. And I can't risk being stranded in another country, dependent on a man I've just met."

"Okay, consider this. Think about it tonight. Don't come tomorrow but follow me in a few days. I'll make two hotel reservations—you'll have your room. I'm playing in the tournament, and I have some business interests to tend to after. I'll extend the trip and show you around Paris." He shrugged. "After two weeks, you can decide if I'm worth the risk."

He paused, but when she didn't answer, he said, "I'm determined, Shannon. What's between us is different. It's not a fling for me, and I don't think it is for you either."

She looked him straight in the eyes as he took her hand. "Don't decide tonight. Think about it. We'll talk more in the morning on the way to the airport. Promise me you'll think about it."

"Okay, I promise I'll think about it, Graeme."

That night Shannon thought of nothing else.

"How can I possibly accept such an invitation?" she said to her reflection in the bathroom mirror. "I hardly know this man. I'll get over there and be stuck, relying on him for everything."

She climbed into bed, but spent hours tossing and turning. "He's a man! He'll expect sex. How do I say 'no' after going all the way to Paris to be with him?"

Then her other voice chimed in. "But he's different from any man I've ever met. He makes me feel wonderful when I'm with him. I may never meet anyone who makes me feel this way. Will I ever trust anyone?"

Shannon did what she often did in sticky situations. She called Helen, waking her from a sound sleep.

"I'm crazy about him, Helen," she said, "but I don't trust my judgment or instincts about men. What if I get to Paris and find out it's a mistake?"

"Why do you think I introduced you to him, Shannon?" Helen said. "I've watched you waffle around every man you meet. You're worse than I ever thought about being. Me, I don't carry around all that guilt like you do. But Graeme is not like any of those other guys you've dated. He's more than your match intellectually, he's successful—which is important to you—and he's not threatened by a woman with an independent streak a mile wide."

"I know. I've seen those traits the past few days, and Graeme is damned good looking besides."

"What do you want, Shannon? Jesus Christ himself!" Helen scoffed. "Come on! You won't gain anything by hiding out, and Graeme is the best chance yet for you to break out and find some real happiness. Someone your equal. Just give yourself a chance. And him!"

"Okay, I'll do it. But I'll go to Paris on my terms."

* * *

Paris At Last

ON THE DRIVE TO the airport, Graeme said, "Well… did you think about Paris?"

"Yes, Graeme, I was awake all night thinking about it. I don't know if I can ever be close to anyone or trust anyone, and I can't feel obligated. Being there puts me in that situation."

"Shannon, look, I've made a lot of money in my career and

business interests and sponsorships. It is no hardship for me to pay your expenses, and I know you can't afford it. Please let me do this for you. Please give us a chance to get to know one another and see where it goes. Give us two weeks. If, after two weeks, either of us feels differently, you come back to Austin with, I hope, wonderful memories of your first trip to Paris."

It dawned on her that this handsome tennis player was every bit as persuasive as she is. "I'll consider it on these terms." Shannon took a deep breath. "One, I will fly there on my own, with my ticket."

Shannon still had Dr. Ross' ticket tucked away.

"Two, I insist we have different rooms, and I will pay for my room. I hope you will choose an affordable hotel for me. Then if things don't work out, I can return home not feeling as if I had sold out." She looked him straight in the eyes. "Can you accept those terms?"

"I'll take any terms you offer," Graeme beamed, as though he'd just scored a match point. "When can you arrive? I'll take care of all the arrangements in Paris."

"All right, then!" Shannon grinned. "When will you be free after the French Open?"

"I'm playing next week, but it will be early enough in the draw that I have lots of downtime. Whenever I'm not required to be at Roland-Garros, I'll be free. If you want to wait until the tournament is over, then allow two weeks. Let's hope I'll play well and will move through the rounds. I'm playing singles and doubles both."

"Sounds good. What if I come in a week or so? That'll give me plenty of time to wrap up things here and organize myself to be away. If I'm lucky, maybe you'll still be playing, and I'll get to watch."

"Perfect. I'll arrange everything." Graeme grabbed her hand and kissed the back of it. "I'll pick you up when you arrive. I don't want to miss a moment of your visit to Paris!"

"Oh… uh, I have one other condition, Graeme. I'd like to arrive on my own before I see you, to get my sea legs and get acclimated."

"But then I'll miss seeing your first reactions."

"I promise not to do any sightseeing without you. By the time we see each other, I want to be comfortable and confident in my surroundings, not intimidated or overwhelmed in a foreign country with you. I know myself."

"You're the boss," Graeme said. "I told you I'd welcome you on any terms. I'm just thrilled you're coming! It's going to be a long two weeks ahead."

And it was for Shannon as well. It was easy enough to complete her current writing assignment, and she booked Dr. Ross' first-class ticket for a window seat.

She checked the weather for that time of year in France and what clothing was appropriate. She didn't want to stand out like a tourist, so she chose classic, simple styles for day and evening. Her frame fit a petite size four, right off the rack. Choosing shoes was more complicated. They would do a lot of walking, so comfortable shoes for daytime were essential—but not sneakers. Only American tourists, she read, wore sneakers when sightseeing. She opted for Italian Ferragamo shoes, pricey but comfortable and stylish.

For evening Shannon kept to simple, chic designs. When meeting Graeme's friends, she wanted him to be proud of her and not look like a Texas cowgirl!

She packed a raincoat and sweaters for the sudden Parisian showers and cold evenings. She filled her two-bag limit in no time. For carry-on, she selected a neutral Coach travel handbag with compartments for passport and French francs.

Her route would take her first to New York's JFK airport, then nonstop to Paris Orly.

On the way to the airport, she mailed a letter to Dr. Ross. "I'm finally on my way to see Paris! Thank you again for your generous gift, and I'll be thinking of you when I'm there."

When the flight touched down, it was early morning, Paris time.

"I feel and look like roadkill after that overnight flight, and I wouldn't want Graeme to see me looking like this. I can't wait to get to my hotel, have a shower, and enjoy my first café et croissant." She tapped the cover of the translation dictionary she had brought along.

Graeme had chosen the perfect hotel, tiny and very French, including the little elevator that barely held her, the bellman, and her luggage. Her charming room featured a window overlooking the terraced hotel cafe. A dozen roses were on the bureau with a note from Graeme: "I can't wait to see you! Rest up and get ready. In a couple of days, you'll be on a whirlwind tour."

She unpacked, showered, and changed into some comfortable clothes and walking shoes. Graeme had warned her against napping the first day. "Make yourself stay up to adjust to the time change. Then you'll crash the first night, sleep well, and wake up fresh and ready to go."

Shannon skipped the hotel's dining room. "I want to walk a bit and pick out a sidewalk cafe for breakfast." She chose a cafe on a corner with views of streets converging onto a busy boulevard. Perfect for people-watching. She ordered Café Américaine and, not one, but two croissants that melted in her mouth. She drank bottled water, "with gas," to replenish her dehydrated body after the long flight.

"It seems the world is walking by," she thought as she stared at the throngs of passersby.

Every type of person imaginable paraded the Paris streets: French nationals, Africans, Muslims, Asians, Americans, the last easy to identify in their shorts and sneakers. The many different languages were indecipherable to her. A Japanese group went by, following their guide in lockstep with cameras at the ready. Unescorted men cast admiring glances at Shannon, hoping for an inviting response, but wasted on Shannon.

Once refreshed and energized, Shannon paid her bill, agonized over how much to tip, and started her first French stroll. With no destination in mind, she wandered, stopping whenever she wanted, turning this way and that.

"I have no idea where I am," she thought, "but it doesn't matter." She felt quite at home, not walking at all but striding. "What a marvelous, wonderful feeling!"

The Parisian streets were everything she'd hoped for but beyond what she had imagined. Noisy, chaotic, crowded. Women walked arm in arm, and couples held hands. Conversations were animated and enthusiastic, leaving no doubt the ardor of each one's point of view.

She walked for hours, following the guidebook to the Champs Elysees, where she selected a bistro for a nice lunch and, of course, French wine. Eating inside for the whole restaurant experience, Shannon stuck to a safe menu of filet of sole, pomme frites, and cold white wine.

After lunch, Shannon felt quite drowsy and thought about returning to her hotel and the beckoning comfort of her bed. But remembering Graeme's warning, she browsed some art galleries and walked along the Seine. It was almost dark when she returned to her hotel, finding a nice bottle of rosé and another note from Graeme: "I hope you enjoyed your first day in Paris. Now you're ready for a nice glass of wine, a light supper, and a solid night's sleep. See you soon."

Shannon pulled the curtains closed so the morning light wouldn't wake her, and she slept like the dead a full nine hours.

"What am I going to do today?" she said to herself. There were many tempting things she wanted to see, but she promised Graeme she'd wait for him. "I wish I had only asked for one day to settle in, not two."

At that moment her room phone rang, and it was Graeme. "I hope I didn't wake you, but I just couldn't wait any longer to hear your voice."

"No, your timing is perfect. I got a great night's sleep, and I can't wait to see you."

"Then let's start tonight with dinner! I've got a match early this afternoon. Can I pick you up at seven?"

"I'll be ready."

"Wear something casual and comfortable."

At seven o'clock sharp, she took the tiny elevator downstairs. Graeme was already there, waiting for her, sitting on the round chaise. He sprang from his seat, ran to her, scooped her up in his arms, and twirled her around.

"At last," he whispered, his face buried in her hair. "You're here! I am so happy to see you. You look wonderful. Are you rested?" Words tumbled out in his excitement. "Tonight is officially your first night. I'm going to show you Paris, and let Paris see you! Come on. We're walking from here."

Taking Shannon's hand, he led her through the hotel's gold revolving doors into the early summer night. The streets were alive with people eager for their night out, restaurants and shops ablaze with sparkling white lights.

"Tell me about your match," Shannon said.

"For the first time in my life, I'm not sad and depressed that I lost! I made the quarter-finals but lost to my old nemesis. Now my schedule is easier. Except for the doubles, I'm free and all yours for the whole trip."

"I was hoping to see you play."

"Well, I do have a match tomorrow, and you can come watch. Doubles are different for me. It's more fun, and I don't take it as seriously. Lots less stress. Playing with a partner just seems to make the competitive part easier."

"That's so exciting. I can hardly wait. Tell me, where are we going right now?"

"For your first night, I thought we would go to a typical French brasserie that's usually packed and lively and everything French. From there, we'll stroll and take in the Parisian nightlife."

Right away they fell into the same comfortable pace Shannon so enjoyed when they were in Texas. The conversation was easy, and when their eyes met, it was hard for either to look away. After dinner, they walked the streets, holding hands just like the couples Shannon had admired the day before. From time to time, Graeme stopped, pulled her to him, and gave her a light kiss on the cheeks or lips, repeating how happy he was she was here in Paris—with him.

When the time came to return to her hotel, Graeme pulled her to him again, this time in a warm, firm embrace and a lingering kiss that made Shannon's blood run hot.

"About tomorrow. My match is at 2 in the afternoon. Could you get a taxi to Roland Garros and be there by 1 o'clock? I'll leave a ticket and pass for you at the Pickup Window. Come to the Players' Lounge after the match and wait for me at the VIP reception. I'll find you after I shower and change. Then we'll head out for an afternoon and evening of sightseeing and dinner."

"Sounds like a wonderful plan. I can't wait to see you play."

Shannon and Graeme strolled back to her hotel, and Graeme paused outside the revolving doors. He took her in his arms and kissed her, a long, passionate kiss, holding her body close to his.

"Good night, Sweet Shannon. Sleep well, and I will see you tomorrow afternoon." He then stepped into the street, hailed a taxi, and left her.

Shannon had an odd feeling as she watched him go. She was grateful he had not pressed her about coming upstairs to her room, yet she was sorry to see him go.

She had scanned magazines and looked at photos of what spectators wore to the French Open. She chose white pants, a perfect fit, topped with a tailored blue and white pinstripe shirt, collar upturned, and a navy blazer. Espadrilles gave her some height but were comfortable for walking. The leather Coach travel bag was large enough to stash a fold-up raincoat just in case.

Once arriving at Roland-Garros, she worried maybe she was a bit too conservative. Many women sported daring décolletage, wide-brimmed hats, and flashy jewelry. Shannon's conservative style won out. She always wanted to be seen for her own merits, not because of her clothing. Convinced she was suitable for the occasion, she found her seat in the VIP section, so close she could count the beads of sweat on the players' brows.

When Graeme came onto the court, he searched her out in the crowd and waved. She then settled in for a thrilling three-setter with Graeme and his partner just winning the determining final set in a tiebreaker. He waved again as he left the court, and Shannon made her way to the Players Lounge, where cocktails and canapés were served to guests wearing the same VIP badge.

He came out of the players' locker room much faster than she thought he would, all fresh and clean, his hair still wet from the shower. He was ebullient, though she didn't know if it was because of his win or seeing her again.

He put his hands around her waist and kissed her full on the lips. "I am so glad you're here. How did you like the match?"

"Graeme, it was thrilling! I should think you'd be exhausted. Those points went on forever, and I thought someone was going to be killed, all four of you at the net, hammering shots at each other."

"Well, the idea was to hit the shots away from the other players, but it's tough to do in this league. Come. I want to introduce you to some of my friends."

He took Shannon around the room and introduced her to the who's who of tennis. Shannon had to admit a bit of celebrity shyness in meeting some of her tennis idols. More than once, she heard phrases such as, "So you're the girl from Texas that Graeme's been talking about."

After they made the circuit around the room, Graeme whispered, "Let's get out of here."

With enough daylight left to do some sightseeing, they started at the Eiffel Tower, where they caught the sunset, bathing the city in a golden glow. Graeme pointed out Notre Dame Cathedral, the Champs Elysees crowned by the Arc de Triomphe, the Seine, Montmarte, the Louvre Musee, and other famous sites.

"We'll see them all," he said, "and more, and at our leisure with plenty of excellent restaurants and fine wine to keep us going."

Next, they boarded a riverboat that served dinner on the top deck.

"Now we're in a typical tourist trap, like the place you took me overlooking the lake in Austin," he said, "but every visitor to Paris must do this at least once. It's a great way to see the city from the water while sitting, enjoying wine and a meal, and talking."

The quiet dinner cruise was Shannon's first chance to ask Graeme about his daughter. "How's Alex?"

"I try to call her every day, and today she seemed in bright spirits. She and my mom are busy planning a birthday party for one of her cousins. I'm just so grateful for all Mom is doing for my daughter."

"How does Alex get on with your father?"

"Reasonably well. Dad is better with his grandchildren than with his sons. But he stays busy with the farm. Besides a morning pat on the head and a kiss on the cheek good night, he doesn't have much to do with Alex. She's a bit intimidated by him, as are most humans on the planet."

"When will you see her again?"

"Soon. I've got some things planned after the tournament and our time together. Then I'm headed home for a nice, long visit."

After their cruise of the Seine, they took a taxi to Shannon's hotel, where Graeme again escorted her to the hotel door.

"I'm afraid I can't see you until tomorrow evening. I've got a match in the morning, and you're welcome to come if you want, then some business meetings right after."

"I'd love to watch you play again."

"Okay. Same thing, then. I'll leave the tickets for you. Can you be there by 9:30?"

"I'll make it."

"My meetings are at the club right after my match, so I won't be able to see you until after. For tomorrow night, dress up! I'm taking you to one of Paris' most famous restaurants. I'll pick you up at 7."

The tennis was as exciting as the day before, but as fate would have it, Graeme and his partner lost. She wondered if his mood would be different when she saw him later. She made her way back to her hotel, determined to take a long nap to be rested before their night on the town.

She took extra pains to look her best, fussing to style her long hair. She selected a little black dress, quite short and flattering to her figure, set off with black high heels. Her jewelry was simple gold earrings and a gold chain necklace.

When she stepped off the elevator, Graeme was already waiting in the lobby. He rushed over, gathered her in his arms, and kissed her.

"Let me look at you. Wow! You've never looked more beautiful."

"Thank you. You look… pretty handsome… yourself." She was pleased as punch to see her dinner date was also in all black— trousers, collared shirt, and jacket, with Gucci loafers that looked buttery soft.

Her tone turned somber. "I'm sorry about your match. Do you feel up to a night on the town?"

"Are you kidding? Even my tennis partner commented on how distracted I was. Seeing you tonight was all I could think of. Hell yes, I'm ready for a night on the town—with you! And, Ms. Shannon, you're in for a real treat. By throwing my impressive weight around with the maitre' d, I was able to get a reservation at LaSalle, quite literally the most famous restaurant in all Paris."

Graeme hailed a taxi and, speaking fluent French, instructed him to head toward the Champs Elysees. The driver, of course, knew the route to LaSalle and dropped them in front of its glittering entrance.

"Welcome, Monsieur Thorne. Welcome back to LaSalle," said the tuxedoed maitre' d with a wave of his hand toward the dining room. "Your table is waiting. Your waiter will escort you."

The restaurant was already humming, and every table claimed. How glittering and bright everything was. The tables. The wall sconces. Even strips of floor lighting. As soon as they were seated, another waiter delivered chilled champagne and opened the bottle with its satisfying pop, not losing a drop. He filled their glasses before gliding away, all but unnoticed.

Graeme raised his glass. "To Shannon, the prettiest girl in the room. Welcome to Paris, your first of what I believe will be many trips here."

They sipped their champagne while Graeme gave her the replay of his match and why they lost, all in good humor. He also told her about his meeting with a group of Saudis interested in developing a tennis club in South Africa, hoping Graeme would be involved.

As if by magic the waiter reappeared when their glasses needed filling, then disappeared the same way. When they had almost emptied the bottle, the waiter delivered menus, in French, of course.

"Graeme, I haven't a clue about this menu and don't speak French. Can you help me?"

"*Oui, oui, mademoiselle.* Since you enjoyed a certain dish back in Texas, I've a particular one in mind for you as a starter. For entree, I'm recommending the Canard a' la orange for two. It's different, delicious, but not so utterly foreign and complicated to overwhelm you. Sometimes the French food can get too fussy, at least for my simple tastes."

Graeme placed the order in impeccable French, ordering a cabernet the waiter agreed was a perfect accompaniment for the duck.

Without warning, the lights dimmed, all but the table lights extinguished. The room hushed, and gasps went all around the room. Then the ceiling rolled open to reveal an incredible starlit Paris sky.

"You showed me a magnificent Texas sunset. I'm showing you Paris by starlight."

Shannon felt she was in a dream, a wonderland. "Graeme, it's beautiful."

The waiters brought their first course. Shannon was surprised to see slices of avocado fanning the entire plate, sliced almost paper-thin and topped with a delicate lemon sauce. The dish melted in her mouth.

"How thoughtful of you to remember I love avocado, but I've never tasted it like this," she said, while Graeme enjoyed his dish, a tart filled with carmelized beetroots, pears, and tiny greens.

Their omniscient waiter, still quiet as a church mouse, carved their duck entree at the table.

"Let's share a chocolate soufflé, shall we? I'm not sure we can each handle a dessert," said Graeme, ordering Café Americaine for Shannon and espresso for himself.

"Graeme, what a perfect evening. I could never have imagined anything as wonderful as tonight has been," Shannon said.

"We've got two whole weeks ahead of us. We're just getting started!"

They strolled the one block to the Champs Elysses, where they stopped at a sidewalk cafe and ordered two cognacs. They held hands across the table while watching the Paris nightlife.

"It's like the entire world is walking by us, yet we're the only two people on the planet," Shannon whispered.

"Do you like it, Shannon? Paris?"

"Like it? I love it!"

Again, Graeme escorted Shannon to her hotel, seeing her to the door. He embraced her and gave her a passionate kiss good night. Then, he turned on his heel and grabbed a cab, leaving Shannon feeling suspended in midair.

Their next few days and nights went as promised, filled with sightseeing and romantic dinners, including out-of-the-way places that only an experienced Parisian would know. One was at a family-owned restaurant that seated only twenty people a night, four nights a week. The owner and chef, a French woman in her mid-forties, served a fixed menu to everyone at shared tables. It was warm and friendly, like having dinner in a private home—a very unusual experience in a French restaurant. The food was unique, indescribable.

They spent an entire day in Montmartre, touring the domed Sacre Coeur, strolling the wide walking boulevards, exploring the artists' work, and sampling food from street vendors. They paid an artist to draw a pen-and-ink sketch of them, which turned out quite lovely.

One day Graeme asked Shannon if she would like to have lunch at his hotel, the first time he mentioned where he was staying.

"Yes, I've been curious about it."

They arrived at the famous George V Hotel. Graeme ushered her through the lobby and straight to the hotel's distinguished restaurant, where they ordered lunch. Graeme didn't mention his room upstairs. Shannon was curious to compare it to her own at her little room, but didn't dare ask. The elephant was still in the room.

"Shannon, tomorrow I have another meeting with that Saudi group, in a region called Chantilly, about an hour outside Paris. The meeting is being held in the Aga Khan's estate. The area is famous for its horse racing and breeding, owned by the Aga Khan. After our meeting, I'm invited to the races and to sit in the royal box. Will you come with me?"

"My goodness, Graeme. What a variety of experiences you've planned for us. I'd love to."

"I didn't plan this. It's a follow-up to that meeting at Roland Garros. They called today and asked if I would come out and talk more about their proposal. I was a little disappointed that it was interrupting our time together, but if you come with me, it could be a special experience for us both."

The next day, both their jaws dropped as they steered the rental car into the Aga Khan's magnificent estate. Beautiful thoroughbred horses grazed on emerald green pastures bordered by the Black Forest. The racetrack and clubhouse looked more like a luxurious palace than a sporting arena. They pulled into an expansive circular drive leading to the Khan's French-style chateau.

A uniformed attendant approached and opened their doors, then drove their car to an unseen parking place. A butler escorted

Graeme and Shannon through an expansive foyer to a book-lined study where four distinguished-looking men from Saudi Arabia, Iran, and Lebanon were seated. Graeme introduced Shannon, and a white-coated servant offered tea. They spoke for over an hour about the potential tennis club in Johannesburg and Graeme being a partner in the enterprise.

During the meeting, they never made eye contact with Shannon nor spoke directly to her. Once, Shannon attempted an observation about their vision for the South African club, and the men talked right over her, not even acknowledging she had spoken, as if she were invisible. Shannon struggled to hide her indignation, for Graeme's sake.

As they left the meeting, the Saudi host assured Graeme that arrangements had been made for the afternoon's races and to make himself comfortable in the club bar and dining room.

"The food there is excellent. We have a French chef who is quite good. Please be our guest, and bring your friend," the host offered, at last casting his eyes on Shannon with a lingering glance.

As soon as they were back in the car, Graeme turned to Shannon, who was frowning, staring straight ahead, arms crossed.

"I'm afraid I committed a social blunder. In the Muslim culture, women aren't welcome in business situations. I didn't think it through and was only willing to have this meeting if you came with me. It's my fault, and I'm sorry."

Fuming, she said, "I've never felt so out of place in my life! They were rude to me, and I am upset that you put me in that situation. You shouldn't have brought me along in the first place. I bet they thought I'm your mistress."

"Why do you care so much what other people think? What's important is what we think, you and me."

"Graeme, they looked at me as if I were nothing. It made me furious!"

"It's a cultural difference, Shannon. That's all. You're naïve to be so easily offended. Don't give it more importance than it deserves.

You've met a number of my friends and tennis colleagues. Has any of them treated you in any way but respectfully?"

"Well, no. They've been very kind."

"Yes, they'd better. They know this is the woman I'm falling in love with, and they'd better treat her right!"

Shannon sucked in a quick breath and was quiet a moment. Then, in almost a whisper, "What did you just say?"

"Well, I didn't mean it to come out in that kind of conversation, in an argument. Are we having our first argument, Shannon?"

"Damned straight!"

"Okay. I wondered how it would feel. Hurts, actually."

"Graeme, roll back a minute or two. What you said that you didn't mean to say?"

"You mean the part that I'm falling in love with you?"

"Yeah, that part."

After a pause, she said, "Why me, Graeme?" Shannon shook her head. "You're surrounded by beautiful women, wealth, a loving family, throngs of friends. Why me?"

"You mean besides your gorgeous face and this incredible body of yours?"

Seeing that Shannon didn't appreciate the humor in his wise crack, Graeme took his time and answered her question. "Beautiful women? Yes. You've seen them on tour. Many beautiful women pursue the players, looking for a one-night stand—not the other way around, mind you—and happy to talk about it on the cocktail circuit." He shrugged. "No, Shannon, I'm after something else, and I'm interested in you because *you* are something else. You have courage and strength. You fight for what you believe."

She took a deep breath, ready to answer, but he held up his palm. "Now, hold on. Hear me out."

He continued. "If you chose to, you could rely on your good looks and allow someone to swoop in and rescue you from your family history. You're idealistic beyond reason. Your passion and enthusiasm for life and everything new are barely kept in check by your reserve and caution to avoid falling off the cliff. You have a kind heart and are caring toward others, but you're afraid to show tenderness for fear someone will see it as weakness and take advantage."

She sat in silence, biting her lip.

"You're honest to a fault. It's not in you to lie. You're fearless when it comes to standing against injustice or unfairness. And you are so fiercely independent it scares me. It scares me that you'll never trust me or let me in. Never allow me to show you kindness and generosity that you've never had before. You won't trust yourself to let me love you—or trust yourself to love me back."

He clasped her by the shoulders and gazed into her eyes. "But I hope my determination and charm will eventually wear you down and you will accept the gift I'm offering you—free of charge." He took both her hands. "My love—and my name."

Gasping, Shannon said, "What? Are… are you… proposing to me?"

"Dammit, this isn't how I planned it, but yes! Yes, I am! I planned to propose on top of the Eiffel Tower or somewhere memorable and romantic, not parked on the side of the road in the heat of an argument. Shannon, I've loved you from the start. Your trip here has only confirmed it for me. I love you, Shannon, and I want you to be my wife. I want us to be together always. I want you to be a mother to my daughter and for us to have children. I never want us to be apart. Please, please, Shannon. Please marry me."

"But it's too soon," she said in a small voice. "We still don't know each other well enough to make that kind of commitment."

"Look, Shannon. I'm turning 43 next month; you're 30. I've been married, and I've known my share of women. You've known men, too. We know what we want and what we don't want. Do you seriously believe you will meet anyone else who will love you as I do? I know I won't! How many chances do you think either of us has to find 'the right person'?"

Shannon's eyes misted, her resistance evaporating.

"I'll never live up to that fantasy you have of what an ideal husband is supposed to be. But know this. I am determined. I don't care how hard you try to push me away. I will win this match!"

She laughed despite herself. "All right, Graeme, all right! I surrender. Graeme, yes, yes! I will marry you. I've loved you from the start, too, and everything I've learned about you on this trip just confirms that you are the kind of man I've been hoping for, the man I want for my husband."

"Good! Thank God that's settled!" Graeme sighed. "Tomorrow, let's find a ring. I'm sure somewhere in Paris, we can find the perfect ring."

They drove straight to the track and watched several races from the Aga Khan's royal box. Afterward, they toured the stables to see the magnificent horses, then went to the club for drinks and a sumptuous buffet set up for VIPs. On several occasions, people recognized Graeme, and conversations started. Each time, Graeme introduced Shannon as his fiancée.

On the drive back to Paris, they were both quiet, holding hands, relishing physical contact. As they entered the city limits, Shannon said, "Graeme, don't you think it's time I saw your room?"

"Are you sure?"

"Yes. I am more certain of it than anything I can remember."

They were tentative in their first night of lovemaking as they navigated around their inhibitions. Once that first time was behind them, their passion found free expression.

The two were inseparable after Graeme's proposal. Shannon checked out of her hotel and moved into the palatial George V, sharing Graeme's spacious suite.

Graeme was an attentive lover. He sensed Shannon's reserve and never pushed her, patient for her barriers to melt away, for her to welcome him into her body. Then it was as though neither of them could get enough of one another. For a week, they rarely left their hotel except to shop for a ring and to enjoy romantic dinners. They made love and talked, getting to know every detail about the other-about their friends, work, families, fears, hopes, and dreams.

In Paris' finest jewelry stores, Graeme steered Shannon toward the largest diamonds. Still, Shannon preferred something smaller, less ostentatious.

"My hands are small, Graeme, and big rings don't suit me. I want my ring to become part of my body, and a large stone just doesn't fit me. Besides, I don't want to draw attention."

They settled on a simple platinum gold band.

"My mother will give me a hard time, Shannon. 'Why didn't you get that girl a decent diamond ring?' she'll say. What am I going to tell her?"

"You'll tell her that we are going to have such an active and busy life that worrying about bumping a big piece of jewelry just wasn't going to work for us. Besides, I don't want to scratch our poor babies with a giant diamond."

At last, Shannon felt the time had come to unburden herself of the secrets she carried, starting with her darkest memory.

"When I was in college, Graeme, I became infatuated with a young teaching professor. He must have spotted me from the first as easy prey for him. On our second date, he raped me. It was so unexpected, and it was violent. I was so ashamed. After all I had seen in my own family, and the promises I made myself that a man would never lay a hand on me in violence…"

Graeme held her hands, but let her talk.

"After that, I just didn't trust myself with a man. And I distrusted every man. My father had been an abusive monster who treated my mother like his personal punching bag, and my mother suffered the consequences of his sexual control over her." Staring into space, she said, "Then one time, one time, I let my guard down with someone I liked, someone I trusted, and he turned out to be every bit the monster my father was."

She then asked no one in particular, "Do I have a sign on my forehead, red letters saying VICTIM, Come and Get Me? After that, I just shut down as far as men were concerned."

She swallowed hard. "I went through the 60s and 70s with that freedom and recklessness my generation pretended to enjoy, allowing myself occasional lapses with men who didn't mean anything to me. But I never got over the sense that I was letting myself down, that it was wrong for me. At last, I just shut down all the way. When a man his made moves, I just left. And I've lived that way for quite a while... until I met you."

Graeme watched Shannon a bit, wanting to be sure she had finished. "Helen explained a lot to me," he said. "After I met you in Austin, I had lunch with Helen and asked her to tell me everything she would about you. She told me you had a horrible childhood, a tough time putting yourself through school, financially on your own, and your deep distrust of men in general. So I had an idea of what I was getting into."

He gave her a wry half-smile. "We're not that different, Shannon. Cora got pregnant with Alex, and we married because of that. Neither of us loved the other. She insisted I do the 'right thing.' So we married, and you know how that ended."

Shannon nodded.

"Of course, having Alex as my daughter is the best thing that's happened to me—and meeting you. But my situation was different from yours in other ways. Both our families welcomed the marriage. Heck, they encouraged it. Our fathers considered it a merger with excellent business prospects, and my father thought I'd quit tennis and maybe take my place at the farm." He shook his head, sadness clouding his face.

"But your situation was much worse. You had no one supporting you, helping you. You must have felt so alone."

"I felt such a failure, Graeme," whispered Shannon through tears. "All my life, I told myself I was better than my mother. Yet, I was just like her, and I fell into the same trap she did. It's so unfair for women. A man can determine a woman's fate, and the consequences of bearing children seal her fate for life. At least now, women have some choices over their bodies. We have birth control and access to abortions, so we are not forced to bear children and sacrifice the chance to choose our path."

"You've really done everything on your own, haven't you?"

"At least I'm a bit more empathetic toward my mother. She didn't have a choice about getting pregnant, and she was a defeated woman who knew nothing but hard work and suffering her entire life."

"It's good you feel empathy for your mother. A ceasefire would be healthy for both of you, a reconciliation even better."

"That's a stretch at the moment," Shannon muttered. "Even if I'm open to it, Mom is still consumed with her suffering and unhappiness, being the victim. She lives from crisis to crisis, and Graeme, I refuse to get caught up in her whirlwind." She shrugged. "Maybe one day…"

"I hope I can help you stop seeing yourself as a failure. Far from it. You're the bravest, most resilient person I know, Shannon. And I'm glad you've unburdened your heart to me. Now I can better understand the harsh judgment you've imposed on yourself. No one gets through life unscarred, and we hope we learn from our experiences and become better for them. That idealized notion you've held onto for yourself is just not real, Shannon. It's an image, but we're both flesh and bone. To be as close as we want to be, as husband and wife, we must acknowledge those fault lines we try to hide."

He enfolded her in his arms. "This is the first time you've shown any vulnerability, Shannon. And thank you for trusting me. I want to do my best as your husband to protect you. At the same time, it won't always be possible, so it's reassuring to me, knowing how strong you are, that you can endure whatever you must. If anything, the failures you describe have only made you stronger. Perhaps in time, you'll learn to forgive, even your mother."

"Maybe… sometime."

"I've listened to you describe how you have admired successful, strong men, only to be disappointed when they show weakness. To me, it's proof we cannot put anyone on a pedestal. A person can't stay on a pedestal, even you, before getting knocked off, and when you think about it, it gets very lonely all by yourself up there. I refuse to let you put me on a pedestal—I won't let you. I've shown you my faults, especially my failure as Alex's father. I want you to know my faults and still love me."

"Graeme, every morning when I wake up, I realize I love you more today than the day before. Maybe we both had to go through our journeys to be ready for each other. God, I love you and want to be at your side for the rest of my life." Her eyes turned misty. "I love making love to you, with you. And to know I can surrender myself to someone I trust, who loves me and wants to be with me forever—I can't tell you how freeing that is."

"I feel the same way, Shannon. I feel I can trust you with my unvarnished self, not the man always competing, always out to prove himself. I can't tell you how many times on the road a woman offered herself to me just to say she had slept with a tennis pro. Those were some of the loneliest times of my life. It was just easier to walk away. How alike we are! Now we both are free to love one another, explore one another, and see where true surrender takes us."

The knock on the door told Graeme that their coffee and croissants had arrived.

"Here you are, my dear. Drink up while I tell you about a possibility before us, and you tell me what you think."

He opened the door and took the tray from the waiter's hands and set it on the coffee table. "You recall I told you I had something planned after our time here in Paris? It's a cruise of the French and Italian Rivieras with my closest friends. Rupert Reeves, a pal I've known since playing pro, has invited me to join him, his wife, and three other couples aboard a private yacht. He's made a fortune in tech stocks, and as a reward for a huge business deal he put together, he has the use of this yacht and crew for two weeks. We'll pull into different ports of call, spend a night or two seeing the local area, and then on to the next exotic harbor. They don't know yet about our engagement. Of course, I've told them about you, and they know we're together in Paris right now."

Shannon's eyes grew wide.

"I've known the guys my entire adult life and have become quite close to their wives as well. They treat me like a brother. Besides my family, these guys are the ones I want most for you to meet. They'll love you. They're always trying to set me up, to find someone and settle down. Now they'll be thrilled I'm finally doing just that."

He chuckled. "We won't be alone, that's the thing. But I'm confident the accommodations on board are very comfortable, and we will have our privacy when we want it."

"When do we... how do we?" Mouth open, she stared at him.

"What I propose is we get married first, a civil service here in Paris, to make everything official. That will remove any doubts about the seriousness of our relationship and take away any concerns you might have about being among married couples. It can be part of our honeymoon, if that's all right. What do you think?"

"Wonderful!" She squealed like a little girl. "It sounds like a once-in-a-lifetime trip. And I want to meet your friends. You've talked to me so much about them. But what about your going home and seeing Alex? Won't she be disappointed you're delayed even longer? And we haven't even told her about me."

"This trip has been scheduled for quite a while, so I'm not expected until after the cruise anyway. But you're right. I've talked to Mom about you. She knows we met in Texas, that I'm crazy about you, and you joined me in Paris. So she's aware something is up. I told her I was going to ask you to marry me, but she doesn't know yet you've accepted."

"How do you think Alex will react? I do so want her to like me."

"Let's talk to Mom first and get her advice about how to tell Alex. You and I have the next two weeks to talk it through."

"The one thing you don't want to do is surprise her with something this important. Perhaps you can introduce me to Alex on the phone, and we can break the ice before we meet face-to-face."

"That a good plan. Let's start the ball rolling tomorrow. And I'll confirm to Rupert that Mr. and Mrs. Thorne will be joining them for the cruise."

"Oh, my. I just realized, Graeme, I don't have suitable clothes for this kind of trip. Everything I brought was dressy and for colder weather in Paris."

"Same here," said Graeme. I've got my tennis togs and things to wear for dinner in the evenings. We both have some shopping to do."

Their itinerary would take them along the coastlines of France and Italy, warm sunshine during the day and cool, crisp evenings with breezes off the sea. So they needed adaptable clothing, but smart and chic. Daytimes, they would be sailing, and when in port, sightseeing. Evenings would be mixing with European society in glamorous Cote d' Azur casinos and restaurants.

Shannon had never been shopping with no limits on her spending. Graeme insisted on the best looks for them both. She was grateful his tastes ran the same as hers.

First things first, Shannon needed a wedding dress! Not the long, fluffy white kind but something classic and elegant for their appointment with the *mairie* for the marriage service. For Shannon, they picked a short, fitted white sheath with a princess neckline and a delicate lace hem. Graeme chose a creamy linen suit, white silk shirt, no tie, and brown Gucci loafers with no socks. Shannon wore her hair pulled back, hanging loose down her neck and a small wreath of fresh white gardenias. They were a splendid pair.

It was just the two of them, the *mairie* and witnesses for the service.

"Is this okay, Shannon?" Graeme said. "Would you like a formal wedding, maybe when we are in South Africa with my family and friends?"

"No, I don't need all the pomp and ceremony. I have what I want: you as my husband."

A photographer was on hand at the courthouse. Shannon and Graeme, as individuals, were very attractive people. Together, they were striking, compelling. A power couple.

Graeme called his mother the next day, and Shannon noticed he called when his father would have left the house for the day. He wanted the first conversation just with his mother.

"Mom, I have some exciting news to tell you. Shannon and I were married yesterday, here in Paris!"

Graeme held the phone away from his ear so Shannon could hear.

"What? So fast, Graeme? No wedding? I so wanted to be there."

"Neither of us wanted to wait or go through the fuss of a big wedding, and we were ready to start our lives as husband and wife. I can't wait for you to meet her."

"I'm sure she's lovely. From everything you've said, she seems a perfect match for you. You've waited long enough, and we all want to see you happy and settled."

"She's right here, Mom. She'd like to talk with you. Can I put us on speaker so we can both talk with you?"

"Of course. Let me meet my new daughter-in-law."

"Hello, Mrs. Thorne. This is Shannon. I guess we've surprised you. I'm so looking forward to meeting you soon."

"Please. Call me Charlotte. Everyone does. Now I must get busy and prepare for your visit in two weeks. We were, of course, looking forward to seeing Graeme, but now we must let everyone know he's bringing his new wife. Everyone will want to meet you."

"Mom, we wanted to talk to you about Alex, about how to break the news to her," Graeme said. "How is she doing?"

"Reasonably well, Graeme. She is so looking forward to your coming home. She doesn't talk much about her mother, just some occasional references. Her therapist thinks she's doing well under the circumstances. Her schoolwork is on par, in fact, quite excellent, considering. The cousins are a tonic for her. There's always something going on, and she's in all the shenanigans. She doesn't have time to mope around."

"How do you think she will react to my getting married again?" said Graeme.

"Graeme, she's pretty closed down. She's mostly happy here, and she and I have grown quite close. That said, there's a part that's missing. She misses a mother—and her father." She paused. "Now, I don't know, Shannon, if you are up for this or even fond of children—"

"Mom, you know how important Alex is to me, and anyone I would marry would welcome and care for my daughter as much as I do. Shannon is on board one hundred percent."

"Please, Charlotte, let me add my thoughts here," Shannon said. "Yes, Graeme has told me about Cora and Alex, and my heart goes out to his child. I can only imagine how difficult it has been to lose her mother and to have her father away so much. I will do everything in my power to fill the void she must feel. It will take time. Children don't trust instantly, especially if they've been hurt as Alex has. I'd like any advice you have on how I can become the person in her life she needs right now."

"You're right about the time. It took Alex a while to let me in, and now she's almost glued to my side. Graeme, how long can you stay this time?" said Charlotte.

"I'm taking a month off the tour. And if Alex needs more time, Shannon has agreed to stay longer. We haven't figured out yet where we're going to settle, and when we're there, we intend to make that decision. In any case, we want Alex to be with us wherever we call home."

"What do you think is the best way to break the news to Alex about us?" Shannon said.

"I like the idea of Shannon meeting Alex on the phone and then having a few conversations leading up to your visit, just like you're doing with me. My initial reaction was, 'Wow! So fast? Why no wedding? Etc.' Alex, no doubt, will have her own emotions when first hearing the news. But after talking, like we've done here, it settles in a bit. By the time you arrive, she will know more about you."

"Good. Settled," Graeme nodded. "How about you talking with Alex tonight and telling her about our marriage. Then we will call tomorrow, and she and Shannon can chat with one another. I'll also mail you a photo taken when we were married so she can begin to visualize her stepmother."

"Stepmother! Ugh!" said Shannon. "That's such a scary word. Let's avoid that if we can. Alex needs to know I want to be her friend, not replace her mother. That gives us space to create a relationship not constrained by that 'stepmother' tag and the negative baggage that comes with it."

The next night as scheduled, Graeme phoned home and spoke first to Alex. "Hi, angel. I'm so looking forward to seeing you in a couple of weeks, and I'll be able to stay a whole month. We'll have lots of time together. Has your grandmother told you the good news?"

"Yes," her voice a monotone.

"Shannon is eager to meet you, and I think you're going to like her a lot. She's here right and would like to talk to you. Can I put her on the phone?"

"Okay."

"Hi, Alex. My name's Shannon. Your dad is right, and I am so excited to meet you soon. He talks about you all the time, and you must be an incredible young lady."

No response.

"I met your father in Texas, where I live. He played a tennis tournament there, and I was a student in a clinic he was teaching. He's a great teacher, but you already know that. He tells me you're quite a promising player yourself."

Silence.

"You're probably wondering why we got married so quickly instead of waiting to meet you and the rest of the family."

"Are you pregnant?" Alex said.

Shannon laughed, a bit stunned that an eight-year-old would have the audacity to ask such a question. "No, heavens forbid. No, no, no! We just knew we wanted to start a life and home together, and we couldn't do that if we weren't married."

"What about my Dad being gone all the time?" Alex said. "Where will you live?"

"That's a lot of what we want to talk about when we're together in South Africa, because wherever we are, we want you to be there, too," said Shannon.

"And leave South Africa and Gram and all my cousins?"

"Baby, everything is on the table," Graeme said, "and we will talk about all of that when we're there. And you will be the most important part of any decision we make. I don't want to be apart from you any longer, and we want to make a home for all three of us."

"But you're still going to be playing tennis, right?" Alex's tone revealed an undercurrent of resentment.

"Less and less. You know, my competitive tennis days will end at some point, and I'm looking for other ways of making a living that won't involve as much travel. Our goal is to settle down and have a home, together, the three of us."

"That sounds good."

It was a beginning.

"That conversation was better than I hoped," said Shannon, after they hung up.

"What? She barely said anything." Graeme sighed.

"What she did say clearly revealed her concerns. She's very guarded, I can see. No telling what this child has gone through that we don't know about. She needs reassurance you won't be leaving her again because of me. At least she feels secure where she is now, and that's important. We must give her the time she needs."

* * *

Not in Texas Anymore

"MRS. THORNE, YOUR CAR is waiting," said the uniformed chauffeur as he took Shannon's elbow and guided her into a gleaming, black Rolls Royce, with Graeme stepping in just behind her.

"Graeme, what's going on?" She whispered in his ear as the driver loaded their luggage and took his place behind the steering wheel.

"Like I said, Mrs. Thorne, only the best for my beautiful wife. Just relax and enjoy the ride. And you don't have to whisper. He can't hear us through the glass."

The limousine took them to a private airport where they were escorted onto a private jet that flew them to Nice, and another chauffeur-driven Rolls Royce drove them to the marinas in Cannes. The car dropped them off at a berth where a 125-foot yacht was anchored, the *Princess Imagine*. A jovial group of passengers were on deck, drinking champagne, waiting for them.

"There they are!" shouted one.

"It's about time," chimed in another.

"Come aboard," called out a woman, her face was all but hidden under a magnificent white hat and dark sunglasses.

Shannon stood on the dock, transfixed, unable to move. She looked at the yacht, gleaming white, a stark contrast to the azure waters of the Mediterranean. She looked around her. Even larger yachts were docked in the harbor, dwarfing the *Princess*. These boats were equipped with private helicopters, jeeps, and vessels ready to ferry passengers to whatever was on the day's schedule.

"My God," she said. "Is this really happening? Am I dreaming?"

"If so, don't wake up just yet." Graeme laughed. "Now, come meet my friends."

Beaming with pride, Graeme introduced his bride to his best friends and their wives. They welcomed Shannon with open arms, toasting the newlyweds with chilled champagne. They were a diverse group: the hosts, an American couple who made a fortune in emerging tech stocks; Greg, another South African who had gone to university with Graeme, and his beautiful Australian wife, Sylvie; a wealthy, older British couple; and an Italian tennis player and his wife.

Shannon was the youngest among them, and she worried the women might resent an unsophisticated Texas girl. Yet they put her at ease right away and included her in their conversations. They joked that Graeme at last found someone to marry him, as if he were not one of the most eligible bachelors on the tour.

Their hosts, Rupert and Kathy, took Shannon under their wings and eased her into the group. They had heard quite a lot about her from Graeme and were eager to learn more about this woman who captured their friend's heart. Their questions were discrete. Shannon suspected that Graeme had warned them to stay off the subject of her family and upbringing. From the first day, Shannon loved their warmth and openness.

The Brits were the oldest couple, and the wife had a physical disability. Her husband was gregarious and friendly, while his wife was quiet and in the background. Despite her disability, she participated in everything, not letting her condition sideline her.

The Italian couple seemed as though they had stepped from a magazine cover. Franco looked like a Greek god, with sculpted muscles, tanned skin, dark hair and eyes, and a natural elegance that drew everyone's eyes to him when he entered a room. His wife, the woman under that big hat and the dark sunglasses, was a stunning professional model. Despite their show-stopping beauty, they were approachable and unassuming, as if they were oblivious to their physical beauty. Their self-deprecating manner even poked fun at themselves with quick humor and wit.

Graeme's South African friend, Greg Dawson, could have passed as a brother, and their good-natured repartee sounded like two sparring siblings. Greg was Graeme's business manager who oversaw his far-flung investments and partnerships. The trust between them was transparent. Shannon had learned that, without Greg's help, there was no way Graeme could stay on top of everything and continue to play competitive tennis.

"How dare you just hold a civil ceremony in Paris and deny me my right to be the best man at your wedding?" Greg poked his friend in the chest, teasing him. "You owe me! You and Shannon must have a formal wedding with all your friends and family. I deserve the honor of insulting you with the best man speech I've had in my head all these years."

"It's what we both wanted, Greg," said Graeme. "Neither of us wanted to go through all the folderol of a formal wedding. We just want to get on with our lives. You have plenty of opportunities to insult me without a wedding to do it."

Greg's wife, Sylvie, was the quintessential Aussie—fit, tan, and fun. She had a sense of humor that brought a cheerful atmosphere to the whole group, ensuring no one took things too seriously.

"No worries, mate," she said to Graeme. "I'll keep Greg in line. You and your missus just ignore him."

The cabins were spacious and elegant—and private. The crew of five included a chef who prepared their onboard meals and a young Swedish steward who performed his duties as though he had the best job in the world.

During the day, they sailed just offshore, going from port to port. They traced the French and Italian coastlines starting from Cannes, stopping in picture-postcard ports of call—Monte Carlo, St. Tropez, Portofino, St. Margherita, Magdalena. Then they sailed across the open sea to Sardinia and Corsica. At each stop, they went ashore to see the sights. They played the elegant casinos in Monte Carlo, went to the nude beaches on St. Tropez, toured medieval castles and churches in the hills overlooking the villages, and shopped at the trendy boutiques lining the main boulevards.

Shannon liked to watch the local fishermen mending their nets, and then treat herself to fresh pastries from local bakers. She continued her daily yoga routine on the yacht's top deck, enjoying incredible views of the shoreline on her left and the wide open Mediterranean on her right. They often swam in the sea, diving off the yacht's side.

Shannon noticed that the chef, who spoke passable English, left at dawn to shop for the day's meals, and she asked to accompany him. At the farmers' market, they went straight to the fish section where the catch of the day were still squirming on the tables.

"My goodness, that's the ugliest fish I've ever seen," Shannon said to the chef as she pointed to a spiny fish with a wide mouth full of teeth.

"Bon! Just what I'm looking for," said the chef. "That's the red racasse, the fish used in bouillabaisse, and I'm making it for lunch today. You have to take great care to get the white meat. The spines are very poisonous."

Shannon had an idea. "Bouillabaisse is one of my husband's favorite dishes, and today is his birthday. Would you go along and play a joke with me?"

They bought an extra fish and kept it alive in seawater. As they gathered around the table, the group sang happy birthday to Graeme, and the chef served him his "bouillabaisse," a clear bowl of seawater with the red rascasse swimming in it. They had a good laugh as the chef then tossed the live one back in the sea and served the real bouillabaisse for their lunch.

"Shannon, I know it's a bit crowded for a honeymoon," Graeme said to his new bride.

"Graeme, I really do feel like Cinderella, and my pumpkin is a floating carriage. I've always dreamed of traveling and seeing incredible places, but I never knew these places existed."
He clasped her hand and kissed it.

"Being with your friends helps me see you through their eyes, not just my own, and getting to know you from their perspectives," she said. "I like them, and it warms my heart to see how you're held in such high regard. I've never been happier, Graeme, and it's a perfect honeymoon."

"Shannon, this is our beginning. There is so much I want to show you, to share with you."

It was indeed just the beginning. Graeme didn't tell Shannon what else was in his head until the last day of their Mediterranean cruise.

"It's time you meet my family, especially Alex, and they are so eager to meet you. But after our visit there, I'd like to take you on a safari to Kenya and Tanzania. It could be an extension of our honeymoon."

"Graeme, that's been one of my dream trips. But we can't even think about that until we get with Alex and decide how and where we can put our family together. As wonderful as a safari sounds, let's please not even think of it until we've worked out where we're going to call home."

He smacked his forehead. "You're right. I'm anxious if the calendar isn't filled. You'll have to slow me down, Shannon."

"It seems, Mr. Thorne, that I'm also going to need a wardrobe for every occasion and every country," she said, teasing him and growing more comfortable with her new husband by the day. "I wonder if I'll ever be able to wear my cutoffs again!"

"What are cutoffs?"

"Never mind. I doubt you'll ever see them."

Thorneside

There are no quick ways to get to South Africa from Europe or the United States. Graeme and Shannon flew from Marseilles to London, spent the night at an airport hotel, and caught an early morning nonstop to Johannesburg, an 11-hour flight, before at last catching a shuttle to Cape Town—altogether a 16-hour ordeal.

When changing flights in Johannesburg, Shannon noticed the heavy military presence with armed soldiers throughout the airport. Going through customs was a bit intimidating as the agent, scowling, studied Shannon's American passport and her face.

"What is your business here?" he said to Shannon.

Graeme stepped forward. "This is my wife, and we're on our honeymoon and on our way to Cape Town to visit my family," he said, producing a copy of their marriage certificate.

The agent regarded Shannon with a menacing glare. "Do you plan to conduct any business while you are here, Mrs. Thorne?"

Again, Graeme spoke. "No, we are both on holiday, just visiting family."

With a grudging reluctance, he stamped both their passports and returned them to Graeme.

As they were only connecting to Cape Town, they didn't get into Johannesburg, and Shannon wondered aloud to Graeme what it must be like in the city. "Is that hostility throughout Johannesburg or just reserved for visiting Americans going through Customs? It's clear I am not welcome here."

"Try not to let it upset you. The authorities here are all pompous. Ignore them."

Upon their arrival in Cape Town, Graeme rented an open-top convertible for the 90-minute drive to his parent's home. Even though it was South Africa's winter, the days warmed to the 70s-80s.

Graeme, ever the tour guide, told Shannon, "You'll see lots of similarities between this part of South Africa and the South of France, especially the Provençale region. The climate is similar to the Mediterranean's, never too cold in winter and sometimes quite hot in summer. But the soil is ideal for vineyards and fruit orchards. The Eindeloos Rivier runs through our valley, and it's an endless water source that we access for irrigation. The Blou Berge surround us. That's Blue Mountains in Africaans."

"When are your parents expecting us?"

"In time for dinner. Mom says Alex is excited we're coming, though nervous about meeting you. She laid out all her best outfits to make a good impression. They know we've been traveling, so Mom and Dad will keep things easy tonight. Tomorrow expect a full house! My brothers, their wives, and all their children are coming."

"Should I be nervous?"

"Just be yourself. My family will love you. But I suggest you avoid talking about politics. Things are pretty sensitive these days, with the eyes of the world on us about our apartheid policies. South Africans resent Western attitudes and interference in our internal affairs. With your being a journalist, things could get out of hand pretty quickly."

"Aye, aye, Captain!" she said with a salute. "I promise to be on my best behavior. I want your family to like me, and I don't want to get off on the wrong foot, coming across as the ugly American."

"Good girl. While you're here, just suspend judgment of what's going on in the country and try to see my family as ordinary people who happen to be my parents."

"Got it!"

Cape Town itself was beautiful, and Shannon hoped they would get to spend some time there. The coastline was breathtaking. They headed north on the N1 highway and drove through ever-changing landscapes. Soon they crossed the Eindeloos River and entered South Africa's wine country. They then headed west, going through a valley bordered by the Blue River Mountains with vineyards in every direction. Roadsigns cropped up for Trelwyn when they veered off the main highway onto a smaller country road that ran alongside tributaries or canals of the river.

Not too far along, they made a right turn onto an unpaved, tree-lined driveway with vineyards on one side and fruit orchards on the other. The road wound toward the foot of the mountains, ending at the circular driveway of a magnificent, white, stucco home—in truth, a mansion. Graeme tooted the horn as he pulled in, and both Max and Charlotte Thorne came out onto their wide portico to greet them. Alex was tucked behind Charlotte.

Shannon's first impression of Alex was of a timid mouse trying to make herself invisible. She was smaller than Shannon pictured, very petite with delicate bones. She had her father's dark hair, which she wore long and down, shielding half her pretty face.

Unable to contain herself any longer, Alex raced into her father's arms while he spun her around and around.

"You're getting big, my girl! I almost didn't recognize you."

She buried her face in her father's neck and wouldn't let go.

"At last! You're here!" gushed Charlotte. She rushed to Graeme and gave him a huge hug, while Alex clutched her father's arm. Max waited a moment, then grasped both his son's hands in a firm handshake and clapped him across his shoulders.

"And tell us, who is this lovely creature?" cooed Graeme's mother.

"Mom, Dad, Alex, please allow me to introduce you to my wife, Shannon. Shannon, this is my daughter, Alex, and these are my parents, Charlotte and Max Thorne."

"Lovely to meet you, Shannon," boomed Max. "Welcome to Thorneside."

Shannon cast a glance at Graeme.

"I know." He rolled his eyes. "It's my Dad's sense of humor, naming the place Thorneside. He always said that raising grapes is like having a thorn in your side."

Shannon knelt to get eye-to-eye with Alex, taking both her hands in hers.

"You're even prettier than your pictures, Alex. I've been looking forward to meeting you, and I hope we'll become great friends." She stood up. "Charlotte and Max, lovely to meet you as well. Thanks for welcoming me to your home."

"Come inside." Charlotte led, with Alex now clinging to her father's hand. "Let's get you a refreshing drink."

Charlotte guided them through an open foyer with blinding white marble floors, past the giant, polished staircase, and onto an expansive terrace with views of the mountains. A servant brought a tray of fresh lemonade with Max's promise of their finest chilled white wine after they quenched their thirst. They settled onto comfy lounge chairs and began their first get-acquainted talk. Alex had not let go of her father's hand as she nestled next to him on the sofa. Shannon sat ramrod straight next to both of them, feeling a bit like a cat on a high wire.

"How was your flight? Were you at least comfortable for such a long journey?" Charlotte said, directing the first question to Shannon.

"Yes, ma'am," whispered Shannon.

Charlotte's eyebrows shot up, and she seemed to flinch. Shannon couldn't figure out what she had done wrong so soon.

Graeme jumped in. "Yes, it was fine. Long! But we look forward to a good night's sleep."

Max had already gone to the sidebar to pour the first glasses of wine and all but bellowed out, "Let's get this evening properly started. I'm going to give you a taste of South Africa's best white, Shannon, from our very own Thorneside grapes, and you tell me what you think of it."

The servant brought around a tray of canapés, and everyone dived in, for the distraction as much as hunger. Alex declined the food and sipped her lemonade. So far, she hadn't spoken.

The small talk soon turned toward Shannon. "Tell us, Shannon, about yourself," Charlotte said. "Tell us how you met, about your family, what you do."

Max interrupted her, sat up straight, and barked, "Give off, Old Girl. Don't give her the third degree so soon! She's only just arrived. How about you show them to their room first? Let them freshen up and change for dinner. We'll see you back downstairs in an hour. Does that give you enough time?"

"Of course! What am I thinking?" Charlotte said. "Come, my dears. Alex, let's you and me show them upstairs. Graeme, I've redecorated since you were here last and converted your old room into a guest room. I hope you don't mind, but it's more comfortable now. And you're right next to Alex's room."

As soon as they shut the door behind them, Shannon said to Graeme, "What did I do wrong? Did you see how your mother tightened up when I talked?"

Graeme hugged her. "It was you calling her 'ma'am.' That term is for older women, and she might have taken exception to your thinking of her as old."

"Oh my gosh, Graeme. I didn't mean it that way at all. In Texas, we address every adult as 'ma'am' and 'sir', and it's considered impolite not to. As kids, our parents punished us if we didn't say that, no matter their age."

"Ah. Learn something every day. Don't worry about it. Let's get unpacked, dressed, and back downstairs. I'm famished!"

Dinner was more formal than Shannon imagined. They sat around a gleaming dining table, and Alex was already seated next to her grandmother. A servant wearing white gloves served each course, starting with delicious tomato bisque. Enjoying the meal encouraged convivial conversation, and soon Max's attention turned to Graeme and his recent activities.

"I see you did well in doubles at the French Open," Max said in his characteristic loud voice.

Observing Max's manner and tone, Shannon thought to herself, "Max leaves no doubt who is in charge."

"Yes, I made it to the quarters, but I must admit, I was in a bit of a hurry to get through the rounds since Shannon came to Paris during the tournament. I'm afraid my concentration was elsewhere!" He smiled at Shannon and squeezed her hand.

"Graeme tells me that was your first trip to Paris, Shannon," said his mother. "Did you like the city? And how was the cruise?"

"I loved Paris! The hustle and bustle, the sights, the food. I really can't think of anything I didn't like, even the rain! Graeme has spent all our time together showing me sights I've never seen before, one amazing adventure after another." She went on, her enthusiasm bubbling over. "The cruise was wonderful, and Graeme's friends are terrific people. They were warm and welcoming, and I felt as though I had known them for a long time."

"And what are your first impressions of our country?" Charlotte said.

"I've just seen the bit between the Cape Town airport and here, but I'm surprised how what I've seen so far reminds me a lot of Texas. There are similarities in climate, vegetation, the expansive spaces. Texas is huge with an ocean, plains, mountains, desert, lakes, rivers. We, of course, have big cities like Houston and Dallas; Austin is quite small in comparison. But most of the state is agricultural, mainly cattle ranches."

"I've always heard about Texas," Max said. "I've read when visitors think of the United States, they think first of New York, then Florida because of Disneyland, California because of movie stars, and Texas for its cowboys. I'd love to see it someday. Is it true you ride your horses to work?"

Shannon and Graeme both laughed. "No, we typically leave our horses and boots at home when we go to work. But native Texans do come from that Western influence. My father's family were farmers, and my mother's were ranchers, so that life is certainly in our DNA." She glanced from Charlotte to Max and back again. "I'd love to show you Texas someday, and something tells me we might have that opportunity in the future."

With the ice broken, the conversation stayed on safe topics.

That night Graeme congratulated her on how she navigated her first night with his parents. "Dad is pretty intense, and Mom usually tries to counter him. But you've survived the first day. I think you've won them over."

"Alex barely spoke," said Shannon. "How do you think she feels so far?"

"I watched her, and her eyes stayed glued to you. She's trying to figure you out."

"What about your brothers?"

"Well, they might be a little tricky for you. All three are in the family business, and my oldest brother, Lucas, assumes the mantle of 'boss' over the rest of us. Two of my brothers are very involved in the politics of the country. They are quite militant about upholding our laws separating the races. Just steer away from those conversations."

"I'll do my best, Graeme, but you'll have to help me. If they ask me a direct question, I can't lie to them."

"I'll stay close," he said, hugging her.

The next day after breakfast, Max drove Shannon and Graeme through his impressive farming operation. Graeme sat in the front seat with his father while Shannon and Alex sat together in the back.

"Graeme said you were thinking about bottling your wine, too? Shannon said.

"No, I grow the grapes, and we ship them to the wineries to do that. It's such a separate business and highly competitive, plus it involves dealing with the public. I don't want the bother. We also import our fruit to distributors, which they get to the retailers."

"Sounds like quite an operation," she said. "I'm looking forward to seeing it firsthand."

"Lucas, who handles the vineyard production of our farm, wants to get into the winemaking business, but so far, I've held him off. He thinks a Thorneside wine label would be very successful. Maybe when it's his turn to make that decision, he will do it. Lucas and I plan to talk to Graeme, and we're hoping to convince him to take that on."

Graeme shifted in his seat.

"How many workers do you have?" Shannon said.

"Depending on the time of year, we have as few as twenty-five, and during harvest, we'll have as many as a hundred kafirs working."

That evening the pace picked up quite a bit when Graeme's three brothers and their wives arrived, with six children of all ages in tow. In their raucous greetings, all three brothers lifted Graeme off his feet. They were much heavier than Graeme, settling into their forties and fifties with a bit more around their middles than Graeme, with his disciplined, physically fit body. Their wives were a throwback to the 1950s, pleasant, traditional, a bit plump, and dressed in flowery cotton dresses and clunky shoes.

Alex disappeared in a swirl of cousins, who all made a quick getaway from the adults.

Lucas, the oldest and self-appointed leader of the Thorne clan, commanded the conversation. As the second oldest, Dexter was in charge of the family's fruit operation. Both Lucas and Dexter and their families lived in houses on other parts of the farm. Jude, the third in line, lived in Cape Town with his family and ran the distribution side of the company, shipping the produce from Thorneside.

"So, now that you're married, Graeme, when are you coming home and settling down here?" Lucas said.

"No plans yet, Lucas. Shannon and I haven't decided where we plan to live, and we have to make a decision soon. We've about worn out our suitcases."

"And you, Shannon, what do you think about bringing this wayward brother of ours home to South Africa?" said Lucas.

"Things have happened so fast for us, Lucas, but as Graeme

said, it's time for us to figure that out. We plan to talk with Alex about that while we're here." She gave a glance and a wink to Alex.

Charlotte arranged for the entire brood to have dinner on the outdoor terrace, all 20 of them. Even though the night air was crisp, the temperatures were mild. Men wore dinner jackets and the ladies a sweater or shawl. It was a delightful, joyous occasion, as one might expect from a family of four brothers who had not seen each other for a while. The wives peppered Shannon with questions. They wanted to know about her home, her work, and especially about plans for children of their own. None of the questions were invasive, however, and Shannon found it easy to answer them.

After dinner, the group retired to Max's study, where brandy and whisky removed any remaining inhibitions. Lucas said to Shannon, "What do people in your country think of what's going on here in South Africa?"

Prepared for just such a question, Shannon said, "I'm sorry, I am not current on the latest news. I'm so wrapped up in my personal life with Graeme that I'm out of touch."

"Well, to get you up to date, we in South Africa could care less what the world thinks of our internal affairs. As you can see from our farm, we are independent and self-reliant. We don't need help from the West to survive, and we damned sure don't need the West telling us how to live our lives."

"Lucas," Graeme held up both hands, cautioning his brother. "Shannon and I are here to be with family and for all of you to meet my wife. Nothing more, especially not to get involved in politics. So if you will kindly respect that, we will have a wonderful reunion."

"What's happening here is bigger than the two of you, Graeme," Lucas snapped, "and if you are a true South African, you will take your stand with us. It's up to us whites to support our government if we're going to hold onto what is ours. Besides, I understand Shannon is a journalist. She could be in a position to help us in the West, help diffuse the lies perpetuated by the terrorist blacks."

Max joined in. "South Africa is more developed and civilized than any other country on the whole continent," he said looking at Shannon, "because the whites are in charge. We've done that. This farm has been in my family for five generations. Before my great-great-grandfather settled here, it was dust. Through our hard work and hands, we've turned it into a paradise, a food basket for the entire country. That's what we will lose if the blacks take over. The country will go back to being a backwater desert of warring tribes."

"I'm not that kind of journalist," Shannon said, going against every instinct in her body to engage Lucas and Max, volley for volley. "I just write human interest stories, nothing political or important." She almost choked on her words.

"Lucas and Max, stop this right now," Charlotte said in her most diplomatic tone. "I will not have this evening with all my family gathered to meet Shannon spoiled by talk of politics."

In their room that night, Shannon's emotions erupted with Graeme. "I can't be silent if Lucas challenges me like that again, Graeme. What is happening here with apartheid and these inhuman separation laws is wrong and against everything I believe. Can't he see that the entire world is against these draconian laws and that eventually, South Africa must change?"

"It's complicated, Shannon. There are reasons why things are the way they are, and we cannot change them. We're not here to get into the middle of this struggle, rather to meet my family. I implore you to leave it alone. Don't take the bait."

"I'll try, but Lucas is making that very difficult."

"Your marriage to me, Shannon, has put you in a lifestyle where we will meet people from many different countries, cultures, races. Remember how you felt when you were in the meeting with the Saudis? You're no longer the inexperienced, unworldly girl from Texas. You cannot expect people to conform to what you know, to your way of life. Remember what you told me Dr. Ross taught you? Learn as much as you can, be informed if you want your actions to have an impact. Just reacting to what you perceive as injustice without knowing all the facts is reckless."

"But I have to be myself and call out injustice when I see it, Graeme."

"In this instance, no, you don't! And you must not! For my sake, if for no other reason. My brothers are who they are, and my parents are who they are. I told you I would likely never live in South Africa again because of their views, but they are still my family, and I love them. I want them to love you, too, and not resent you for political differences that could permanently damage how they feel about us."

He sighed as he shook his head. "Look. You've gotten a pretty good glimpse at my life these past few weeks and how many different circumstances I live in, move in. If I objected to every cultural bias or prejudice I encountered, I wouldn't be able to do business with any of them."

He held up his palm before she could answer. "Do you imagine the French aren't prejudiced? You should hear what the Parisians think of the French from the South. Or the Italians. Romans think they created art and culture and that every other Italian is beneath them. And don't get me started on the Brits!"

"So just where do you stand? When do you speak up against immorality or injustice? What do you believe?"

"I believe in you and me and my daughter and the life and family we will have together. Nothing else is important to me."

Stark differences lay between Graeme and Shannon, and if they allowed it, it could become a potential battleground between them.

That night Shannon did not sleep well. She sat a long time on the window bench that overlooked the vineyards. The night was quiet, with Graeme's soft snoring. She thought about what Dr. Ross had told her: "You know nothing of the world yet. First, learn all you can if you want to influence change." Shannon's instinct was to speak out against the injustices she saw in South Africa and the affluence that Max and Lucas believed was their inherited right. But her new husband, whom she adored, implored her not to react. She slept in fits and starts.

One by one, the family gathered around the breakfast table,

where Charlotte served up eggs and sausage. Max downed hot coffee, eating while standing up, and eager to begin his day at the farm. Lucas came in, had a cup, and discussed the day's tasks with his father.

"When can we get a day with you, Graeme, to show you around the farm and get you up to date on what's going on here?" said Lucas.

"How about tomorrow? Shannon can stay with Alex and Mom, and we can take the whole day. Today Alex and I are going to take Shannon to Trelwyn and give her a little tour of the area."

"Okay. Don't want to cut into your vacation," he said with a hint of sarcasm.

The nearby town of Trelwyn reminded Shannon of Fredericksburg, the little German town near Austin where she had taken Graeme. Strolling the sidewalks and window shopping, Alex sandwiched herself between her father and Shannon, holding onto both of their hands.

"We've just made a breakthrough," thought Shannon, feeling hopeful.

The day was a nice break from the tension she felt in the Thorne house at breakfast. Charlotte had planned another family dinner for that night, and Shannon was uneasy about it.

Dinner passed pleasantly enough, and after Dexter and Jude's families left, Max, Lucas and Graeme gathered in Max's massive study for drinks. Charlotte and Shannon soon joined them.

Max, now well into his second straight scotch, said, "So, Graeme, now that you're married, I hope you're ready to return home and take your place in the family business. We've still got that tract of land saved for you that would be a suitable place to build a home. You and Shannon will be starting a family soon, I expect, and jumping all over the world from place to place is not the way to raise a family. You've already had one failed marriage because you wouldn't stay put here."

"Dad, as I said, Shannon and I haven't decided yet. We plan to talk about that in great length and decide soon."

"What's to decide?" He bristled. "Your place is here. You can't be a tennis bum all your life, and you're no longer a contender in singles. It's simply a matter of time before that's all over."

"Actually, I'm doing quite well, Father. Besides playing competitive tennis, I'm working with several investors on setting up tennis clubs in different countries, and I'll run them. It will be a business that will provide for Shannon and me well past my playing years."

"Your place is here!" growled Max. "You're the only son not in the family business. If Lucas starts a wine business, he'll need help. Your fancy foreign friends would finally be worth something then."

"Max, don't press him," Charlotte said. "He and Shannon haven't talked about this yet. Give them time."

"Steady on, Woman! Am I talking to you?" Max stormed at Charlotte, striding across the room until his reddened face was just inches from hers. "This is men's talk and doesn't concern you. You've always protected Graeme and influenced him away from the farm. If I want your opinion, I'll ask for it!"

In an instant, Shannon saw it. Her childhood came flooding back to her, visions of her father, who visibly changed as one drink followed another. She knew a bully when she saw him, and she also recognized the defeated victim who cowered under the abuse. She now understood why Graeme often praised her independent nature and her ability to survive her abusive home.

Graeme's home had too many similarities to Shannon's. Maybe not the drunken brawls or poverty. but without doubt the verbal abuse was here, and she hoped the physical abuse was not. She at once saw Charlotte in a different light. This thin, frail woman with nerves taut as a bowstring, walked a tightrope, anxious to please the men in her family. A woman who put on a brave front. If Shannon had not just witnessed it, she might never have known.

Shannon learned from Graeme that Charlotte was German-born with family roots in the Alsace region of pre-WWI Germany.

Her mother had died in childbirth when Charlotte was just four years old.

Charlotte's father was a career military man and among the first called to arms when Germany declared war on Russia and the inevitable domino effect that embroiled the entire European continent. When he went off to war, he enrolled his daughters in an exclusive girls' boarding school while he fought in the trenches in France. He survived almost to the end of the war but was killed at the Somme when an artillery shell hit his underground bunker.

At the end of the war, Germany lay in economic ruin. The 1918 Versailles Treaty, with its harsh War Guilt clauses, smothered Germany in debt and despair. Boarding schools became holding pens for the country's thousands of orphans, Charlotte and Genevieve among them. The Catholic Church worked with outside nations to take in German children left without parents and destitute. The diocese in South Africa was one. Hundreds of German orphans were brought into the country, hopeful that homes could be found for them. Charlotte was one of them. Her one sister, Genevieve, three years younger, was sent to Australia, where a family adopted her.

At fourteen years of age, Charlotte was too old to be adopted, since families preferred much younger children. Hence, she spent the rest of her teen years in an orphanage in Johannesburg, attending school there and further indoctrinated into the Catholic faith.

When she turned 18, she left the orphanage and worked as a store clerk in a department store. Charlotte was quite pretty with typical Aryan looks of blond hair, blue eyes, and fair skin. She spoke passable English, though with a thick German accent.

One day a handsome South African man came into her store, right away noticing the lovely German girl. He introduced himself as Max Thorne and asked her out.

Charlotte had accepted and found herself swept away by Max's confident, take-charge swagger. He possessed the strength she remembered from her father, whose authority was unquestioned.

Max was from the Cape Town area and part of a farming family that grew grapes and fruit. A strapping Boer in his mid-twenties, Max needed a wife. The farm would be his one day, and he needed a woman who would give him children and perform the domestic duties of a wife. Charlotte fit the bill. Within a week of meeting Charlotte, he proposed. They married in a simple civil service, and Max brought his new wife to Thorneside.

Max was satisfied with his choice of wife. Charlotte had given him four sons, and she was, without fail, obedient to her husband. He let her run the household as she saw fit while he managed the farm. Still, there was never any doubt as to his authority over her and the entire family. He was every bit as domineering as Charlotte's father had been.

All these pieces fell together as Shannon watched the dynamics between Charlotte and Max. She felt compassion for her new mother-in-law.

The harsh exchange Max leveled at Charlotte left everyone in the room ill at ease. Graeme squirmed until, rising from his seat, he took Shannon by the elbow. "Mom, Dad, we'll say good night. It's late. We will see you in the morning."

"I expect I'll see you bright and early, Graeme," snarled Max. "We've got a full day ahead of us if you can tear yourself away from the womenfolk!"

Alone in their room, Shannon, near tears, said, "Graeme, why didn't you tell me?"

"Tell you what?"

Shannon could sense her husband was strung tighter than his rackets so she softened her tone. "That your father is abusive, especially to your mother."

"My father's just very strict and controlling," he said, his voice defensive. "He's never raised a hand to her. He's not like your father, and he's not drunk all the time. It's not the same."

"The abuse is. The hurt is. Those words your father used with you, and the way he put down your mother in the presence of her sons and her new daughter-in-law. Those are the acts of a cold-hearted bully."

"All families have their difficulties. My father has raised me and my brothers, sent us through university, and has provided livelihoods for three of his sons. He was raised in an old-fashioned, strict world where the man is head of the house, period! I don't want to talk about it tonight, Shannon."

He yanked the covers back. "Tomorrow, I'll be with Dad and Lucas. Can you keep yourself busy with Alex and Mom? I'll catch up with you at dinner. Now let's get some sleep."

* * *

BY THE TIME Shannon came downstairs for coffee, Graeme was already off with Max and Lucas. Alex sat at the table finishing a plate of Charlotte's pancakes.

"Did you sleep well, Shannon?" Charlotte said in her customary cheerful voice.

"Middling," Shannon said. "I guess I'm still a bit jetlagged. But I'm looking forward to spending the day with you two, and wondering, Alex, if you would show me around the farm? My legs could use a brisk walk. Maybe you would take me to those secret places where you and your cousins escape us grownups."

"Sure," she nodded.

After Shannon had fortified herself with more coffee and Charlotte's pancakes, she and Alex left for their walk. Now that it was just the two of them, the girl was more talkative and chatted away.

"Let's go to the barns first," she said, guiding Shannon to the outcroppings of buildings a short distance from the main house.

Several barns, warehouses, and sheds housed the heavy farming machinery and tools. There was a bunkhouse and kitchen where the farm's key workers lived. The farm manager lived in his own modest house, with his wife and four children. Even though it was a school day, the children were all home.

Charlotte homeschooled Alex and was on "school holiday" for as long as her father was home.

"Shannon, this is Gramp's farm manager, Joseph. Joseph, this is my stepmother, Shannon. Joseph lives here all the time, and Grams lets me play with his kids a lot, especially when my cousins aren't here. We like to go fishing in the creek nearby."

"Hello, Joseph. I'm pleased to meet you," Shannon said, extending her hand.

Joseph hesitated, then stretched out his own. "Pleasure to meet you too, Missus."

They wandered about the farm, not paying much attention to where they were going but rather walking at a leisurely pace with Alex talking nonstop. She spoke about how easy her courses were, and wondered aloud if her grandmother expected enough of her. Alex didn't want to fall behind other students her age. But when she compared herself to her cousins who went to the local public school, it seemed she was ahead of the work they were doing.

No mention was made of her mother, although Alex spoke in loving terms of her Gram and how close the two were.

Alex led Shannon to a thick grove of eucalyptus trees and down a foot-trodden path to a broad, rushing creek. They followed along the creek awhile until they came to a small waterfall that emptied into a pool below.

"This is where we come to swim. It's deep enough to dive from the top."

"Can you swim, Alex?"

"My cousins taught me."

"You're lucky to have learned at such a young age. I only learned to swim just a few years ago," and Shannon told her the story of signing up for triathlons to force herself to learn to swim.

"Wow, you'd swim a mile?" Alex said.

"Well, it was always in a pool. If I ever got in any trouble, all I had to do was get to the side of the pool or just stand up. I was afraid to compete in triathlons in open water like the ocean or a lake. But once I learned the breathing rhythm, I was surprised how easy swimming is and how long you could do it. I've been a runner for a long time, and of course, anyone can bike."

"I haven't learned how to bike yet, but I'd like to," Alex said.

"That is going to be easy to remedy, young lady. When we are settled, wherever that is, I promise you're getting a bicycle, and we'll both go on biking adventures."

"Oh, I'd love that. Where do you think we will settle?"

"Alex, I don't know. Your father and I plan to spend a lot of time talking about that with you. We want to make sure it's the best place for all of us. As much as he still must travel, it needs to be a place with an international airport and access to major cities around the world."

They followed the creek a little farther, Alex pointing out the best fishing spots.

"That's another love of mine, Alex. Fishing! There's something else we can do together if you'd like." Shannon paused. "Hey, this talk of fishing has made me hungry. How about we head back to the house for a snack and a cold lemonade? Your father should be home soon."

Graeme returned home in quite a state. She could tell from his face that his day had not gone well. Later, in the privacy of their room, he told Shannon what happened.

"Shannon, Dad and I can't have a civil conversation on any subject. It takes every bit of my self-control to hold my temper. It's not restricted to politics either. We are just not made the same. Let's the three of us drive to Cape Town tomorrow and see my brother, Jude. I'd like to get away from here for the day."

"I'm for that. Alex and I are making such progress, but a day together, just the three of us, would do us good. I know Alex wants to spend more time with you, Graeme."

It was another mild winter day for the drive to Cape Town, and they drove with the top down. Once they entered the city, however, they felt an eerie silence. The streets were almost empty, and no blacks were in sight. As at the Johannesburg airport, however, armed white South African soldiers stood in groups on every corner.

They pulled up at the distribution center, a mammoth concrete structure without windows. They walked into the building, expecting to see a bustling workplace with men and women sorting produce onto conveyor belts for loading onto delivery trucks for shipment. Instead, none of the equipment was operating, and not a worker was in sight.

They headed to the office, where Jude and his shop manager were in the midst of in a heated discussion.

"Hey, Jude!" Graeme bellowed out in a poor attempt at the Beatles song, an old family joke. "What's going on?"

"Welcome, Shannon, Alex, and Graeme. Please meet Mr. Viktor Behoort, my plant manager? Viktor, this is my youngest brother, Graeme, his new bride Shannon, and my niece, Alex."

"Pleasure to meet you." Mr. Behoort gave a courteous bow.

"Viktor, carry on. We'll meet again at the end of the day to review any updates. You guys, come in, sit. Can I offer you some coffee or tea?"

"Whatever you have that's handy is fine," Graeme said, "but tell me, what's going on? Where are all the workers?"

"There was an incident in one of the townships near Johannesburg two days ago, a riot led by some terrorist troublemakers, according to reports I've heard. The police put it down quite severely and arrested hundreds of people. News of it is spreading through the black population, and they're calling for mass strikes throughout the country. None of my black workers showed up this morning."

"Has this ever happened before?" Graeme said.

"Not on this scale. Quite often, we hear of labor strikes or refusals to carry pass cards or something of the like, but it's all been around the Johannesburg area, nothing this far south. So far, we haven't suffered any significant disruptions."

Jude glanced at Shannon before he continued. "I try to treat our workers fairly and navigate through the government's latest crackdowns the best I can. Generally, my workers respect the bubble I've put around our operation, the workers, and government policies."

"Have you talked with any of your workers about this latest episode?"

"I've tried. I was waiting for you and thought we might drive out to the home of my floor supervisor and see if he'll tell me what's going on."

"Let's go," Graeme said.

"The black township is on the outskirts of Cape Town. So far, we've not followed the rest of the country and created a Bantustan like Johannesburg, Pretoria, and northern parts of the country."

"What's a Bantustan?" said Shannon.

"It's one of the Land Acts where blacks are resettled onto designated areas called Homelands. It's another severe step in separating the races by geography, and I expect Botha will do one here soon."

The paved road ended onto a dusty one as they neared the black community. A police roadblock stopped their car before entering the town.

"What's your business here?" barked the officer as several other heavily armed policemen surrounded the car, peering inside.

Jude produced his identification. "I own a warehouse distribution center in Cape Town, and none of my workers showed up this morning. I'm on my way to see my floor supervisor and find out what's going on."

"We can't let you pass, Mr. Thorne. Trouble's been brewing in one of the townships around Johannesburg, and we have reason to believe that terrorist leaders are organizing mass strikes and possibly violent actions against the country."

"Well, that horse left the barn," snapped Jude. "They've already struck my plant. Not a worker is there, and my fruit is going to rot if we don't get it packaged and shipped."

"Sorry, sir. I've got my orders. No whites are allowed past. You must turn your vehicle around and go back."

"Can I at least just get word to my man so he can contact me?"

"Nothing doing, Mr. Thorne. We've got orders to keep the blacks in their communities until we can apprehend the leaders of this current trouble. Shouldn't take long, sir. The police are on top of it and rounding up the instigators as we speak."

Jude turned the car around and headed back to the city.

"There must be some way you can talk to your workers and find out what's going on," Graeme said.

"Let's head to my home. We have a maid who is married to one of my workers. Let's see if we can find out anything from her." Jude turned the car toward his residence.

"She's not here," said Margaret, Jude's wife. "She just didn't show up, and with the birthday party coming up for Justin. Terrible timing! I need her today."

Graeme took Jude by the elbow. "Jude, I think it's time you told me what's going on. It looks like things have gotten much worse than I imagined."

His brother heaved a big sigh. "People like our father and Lucas are refusing to see how the Nationalist Party's policies toward coloreds are destroying the country instead of protecting it. The Boer government just comes up with one act after another to further divide the races and isolate the blacks from white society. Botha fails to realize that his government punishes the blacks so severely that it's making it impossible for them to work and live."

"Have you tried talking to Dad and Lucas about it?"

"Of course, I've tried telling them that South Africa must adapt to the times to survive, that 9% of the population cannot sit on the necks of the other 91%. They're convinced, as all of Botha's thugs are, that by pulling the noose tighter and tighter, the blacks will have no way to fight back. Sooner or later, though, we'll have a revolution on our hands and a bloody war."

"The tension is palpable," said Graeme. "South Africa feels like a time bomb about to explode."

"They even limit education in their schools by allowing them to learn only what the government decides they need to know to be laborers, workers, or servants. They call it the Bantu Education. They've clamped down on any news getting outside the country, and there's severe censorship to prevent anyone daring to speak against the government and the apartheid policies."

"Can't they see it's not working?" Shannon said.

"They listen only to their own voices. But look at my operation, for example. I depend on my African workers. Without them, I'm out of business. So why can't we work with them to get what we both need?"

"What about Dexter? Where does he fit into all of this?" Graeme said.

"Dexter goes along with whatever Lucas says. He thinks if we mind our own business, we can continue as we always have. But if we can't move our products, what good does it do to grow our crops?"

"I knew it was bad but didn't know it had gotten this bad. I spent the whole of yesterday with Dad and Lucas, and they didn't say a word about this. Instead, both of them tried to browbeat me into moving back to South Africa and coming into the business."

"He and Lucas are some of Botha's strongest supporters. I've tried talking to them both, but you know how stubborn they both are. Change is just not in their nature."

Graeme turned to Shannon. "Honey, I'm sorry, but under these circumstances, maybe we should head on back to the farm. On the way, I'll drive you along the coastline to show you how beautiful this area is, and the three of us can have a nice lunch at a restaurant I know. It overlooks the ocean and has spectacular views. Is that okay with you both? Brother, do you mind if we don't stay?"

"It's best. I've got to see what I can do about this situation. I'll probably call around and see if some of the other business owners can meet with me. Maybe someone knows more than I do."

In the car, Shannon put her hand on Graeme's shoulder. "What are you going to do?"

"Not much we can do. Even though I'm from here, I'm considered an outsider. I just want my family to be safe."

He drove along the famous Cape coastline, showing Shannon magnificent views. They arrived at the farm after dark and raided the refrigerator for a light supper. Shannon put Alex to bed. Then, exhausted, she and her husband fell into a dead sleep.

The following day Shannon awoke before Graeme, her body clock still scrambled. She felt desperate for a cup of coffee and wandered into the kitchen, interrupting a heated discussion with Max, Lucas, and Dexter.

"I'm sorry. I didn't mean to intrude. I'll grab a quick cup of coffee and head back upstairs."

"No worries, no worries," said Max. "Just family business and going over today's workload."

"Graeme will be down in a few," she said as she turned to leave the kitchen.

"Okay," said Max, "and I think it would be a good idea if you and Graeme stayed around the farm for a day or so, not go driving about. There has been some trouble up north and rumors that there might be organized protests around the country. Best to be safe till the police have gotten things buttoned up again. I'd just feel better if you stayed close to the house."

Graeme was dressing when Shannon returned to their room.

"I promised Dad I'd spend the day with him again and resume our conversations. I want to talk with him about what's going on, but on my own. It will be a difficult enough conversation without adding you into the mix," Graeme said. "Do you think you and Alex will be all right staying here with Mom?"

"Yes, I believe so," she said. "Alex and I might just walk to the barns and back for a little exercise. Alex is warming up to me, and I want to encourage her to keep talking to me."

"I agree. I'm not surprised she's warming up to you. I knew she would like you. That will make it easier for us to take Alex away from her grandmother and the farm."

"It sounds as if you've decided on not settling in South Africa," Shannon said.

"I wouldn't say 'decided' exactly, and I won't make decisions without you and Alex. A part of me wishes it could happen. I love my country, and it would be nice to be close to family again, especially Mom. But after my time with Dad yesterday… It seems we butt heads on everything. Today will probably determine if it's even a possibility. Right now, I'm inclined to get the heck away from here."

Since the men were already fed and out to their chores for the day, the three Thorne women shared a late breakfast. They sat on the terrace, enjoying coffee and the soft morning sunshine. Whenever Alex was with her Gram, she seemed at ease. Charlotte had done an excellent job of gifting Alex with a love of reading, and she sat on the sofa, engrossed in a book.

Shannon and Charlotte both started the same conversation at the same time.

"Shannon, about the other night…."

"Charlotte, I'm sorry about…."

"You go first, Charlotte."

"That outburst the other night. Please think nothing of it. Sometimes when Max drinks too much, he gets louder and lets his temper get the better of him. Things have always been tense between Max and Graeme, and Max feels I protected and spoiled Graeme as a child, him being the youngest. It's just that Graeme always had his mind set somewhere else, outside the farm. He's never taken an interest in it. The other three just assumed he would work in the family business, but Graeme had other ideas. When he excelled in tennis, he saw that as his ticket out. I encouraged it because his kind, gentle spirit just doesn't fit with Max's rough ways."

"Thanks for telling me that, Charlotte. Graeme hasn't said anything negative about his family, and he has always spoken of you with love and affection."

"That's true, Shannon. We do love one another, and despite Max's gruffness, he loves Graeme, too."

"Charlotte, Max did frighten me the other night when he spoke to you the way he did. The words he used with Graeme were unkind and hurtful, suggesting he is a 'tennis bum' who doesn't make a decent living. He even blamed him for his 'failed marriage' because of his chosen career."

"Yes, Max hates that Graeme chose tennis over the farm, and he resents that Graeme travels all over the world with his 'fancy friends', as he calls them. He hopes to take advantage of your visit to persuade Graeme to give up tennis and come back to the farm."

"Charlotte, I don't mean to pry, but please let me ask you. Has Max ever hit you when he gets angry?"

Charlotte recoiled at the question, pulled both her hands to her mouth, then put both hands over her eyes, trying to push back tears.

Alex looked up from her book.

Shannon went to sit beside Charlotte and wrapped her arms around her mother-in-law, holding her as she sobbed.

"Please, Shannon. Don't say anything to Graeme or the boys. They have no idea. They've never seen their father strike me, and it would cause such trouble if they knew."

"Charlotte, let me tell you about myself, the truth about myself that I wanted to keep from all of you."

Shannon then shared her own story about her abusive father, her victimized mother, and Shannon's abrupt and complete break from her family.

"I haven't seen my mother in almost ten years because I'm terrified of being pulled back into a toxic environment that might trap me. It has mostly been by luck, Charlotte, that I was able to break free. Now I understand one of the reasons Graeme is drawn to me. He knows from personal experience how hard it is on family members to live in a hostile home."

"But most of the time, Shannon, we are quite civil and happy."

"I'm guessing, Charlotte, that's because you go along with whatever Max wants."

"Things are different here, Shannon, than in the United States. Here, wives obey husbands. My sister Genevieve writes me that women in the U. S. are gaining more rights every day—owning property, equal pay, and even protection in the courts from bad marriages. But not here. Once married, always married, and obedient to their husbands. It's the way I was brought up and what the church teaches."

Shannon patted Charlotte's arm. "You help me understand Graeme more and love him even more. My experiences with my father taught me one thing that has stayed with me: not to be afraid of a bully!"

Charlotte sniffled and smiled at her new daughter-in-law.

"You're very courageous, Charlotte, to stay the way you have, for the sake of your family. That takes more courage than I can imagine. Please know this. You have a friend in me, someone who understands what you're going through and who is willing to listen and help any way I can. You'll always have a place with us for as long as you want."

Out of the corner of her eye, Shannon caught Alex's smile.

Shannon felt a profound respect for Charlotte and a distinct dislike for her father-in-law.

When Charlotte regained her usual regal composure, Shannon looked at Alex and said, "Come on, kid. Let's go for our walk."

On the way to the barns, Shannon started the conversation she planned to have with her stepdaughter. "Alex, I am so sorry about your losing your mother. Please know I never intend to take your mother's place. I hope to be your very best friend. If you ever want to talk to me about your mother, you can. You can trust me."

"I'm forgetting what she looked like," Alex said in almost a whisper, surprising Shannon with her candor. "She was pretty, but I can't see her face anymore."

"Do you want to talk about your life with your mother, before the accident?"

"Mom was real moody. She hated my father for leaving us, and she talked bad about him all the time. Sometimes she wouldn't get out of bed, or she'd sleep on the couch for a long time, and I couldn't wake her up. But the worst was when she'd lock me in the closet, or disappear for a long time."

Unable to stop herself now, Alex continued her heartbreaking story. "Then Mom would appear all of a sudden and wonder why I was in the closet. She'd get angry that I'd messed my pants, but then she'd bathe me and feed me like nothing had happened. Lots of times, we didn't have much food in the house. I'd eat cereal without milk 'cause the milk was sour. Mostly I'd eat bread and jam."

"I can't imagine how difficult that must have been for you."

"Then it would happen all over again. She'd lock me in the closet and go away. Sometimes I liked being in the closet, 'cause at least I felt safe. It was better than when she left me in the whole house by myself. Then I'd get really scared. I hid some food in the closet so I wouldn't get hungry."

"Did you see anyone else from your family?"

"Grandma and Grandpa visited sometimes, and Gram and Gramps. They'd bring me treats and new dresses and be real nice to me. Mom would act just fine when they were there, but when they left, it would be just me and Mom again."

Alex paused, as if she remembered something else. "One day, these strangers came to the house, a policeman and some other people. They unlocked the closet and let me out. They took me to a place where they gave me some clothes and food and asked me a bunch of questions. I spent the night there, and the next day my Dad came and got me. He brought me here to Gram's. Then he just left again."

"Did you miss your father?"

"I just got used to him not being there. He'd call on the phone, but that's not the same as being with a person. He's more like a stranger than a father. When I see him, it's okay. But I always know he's gonna leave again, so…"

Shannon's heart broke as the little girl unburdened herself, imagining how alone she must have felt. "Alex, I am so sorry you have gone through all that, through very difficult times alone. You're such a brave girl to still be the sweet, kind person you are. When parents divorce, it's hard on the children, and the child lives with one parent and visits the other. Because your dad's job requires him to travel, the court decided you would live with your mother."

"But that's not fair, Shannon."

"No, it isn't. But no one knew, including your father, that your mother was so ill, and no one knew what you were going through." Shannon stopped walking, bent down, and looked Alex in her big, beautiful, brown eyes. "I understand now why you're angry with your father. I hope in time you will forgive him. But please know that your father and I agree that we will never leave you alone again."

"I believe you, Shannon. I didn't at first. I thought you'd leave me with Gram so you could travel with Dad. It's not like that much has changed with him. He's still gonna be gone most of the time." She squeezed Shannon's hand. "But now, I don't think both you guys will leave me again."

"I promise, Alex! We will never leave you alone again.! How many girls your age have gone through what you have? You're an incredible survivor. I am amazed and proud of how strong you are."

Walking hand in hand, they reached the barn, and Alex wanted to go to Joseph's house to see if his children were around. They passed by the bunkhouse first and came upon a few workers finishing their morning tasks and on their lunch break. They greeted Shannon and Alex, friendly enough but avoided making eye contact.

Alex spied Joseph's children and dashed over to see them. Some women were setting up a lunch of cold meats, fruit, and water.

As Shannon walked to the table to greet them, she noticed a newspaper. Not having seen one since their Mediterranean cruise, she scooped it up to catch the headlines.

A photo on the front page caught her attention, shocking her to her core. A terrified, teenaged boy was carrying the lifeless body of a younger boy, and a girl was running alongside him, hysterical, crying, waving her arms.

June 16, 1976

"Police fire into protesting children in Soweto. Hundreds killed."

The headlines and photos were glaring, grotesque.

Shannon kept reading: Fluctuating crowd estimates reported 3,000-10,000 middle school children flooded the township's streets, carrying posters and singing songs to demonstrate against a law requiring their classes be taught in Afrikaans instead of their native languages. Their destination was the local soccer stadium, but heavily armed police and military vehicles blocked their way while helicopters circled overhead.

At first, police fired tear gas into the crowd. Then they opened fire, shooting live bullets into thousands of school children.

The newspaper, a black African daily called *The World*, estimated the death toll at 700 children.

Shannon gasped. "No doubt, this is what Max, Lucas, and Dexter were discussing in the kitchen when I came downstairs yesterday, and it explains why Max cautioned us not to venture from the farm." She turned to the workers, who stared at her. Shannon wanted to show the newspaper to Graeme but realized the workers might get in trouble for having it in the first place.

She put it down and whispered, careful not to let Alex hear her, "I am so sorry. Please don't worry. I won't say anything to Mr. Thorne about seeing the newspaper."

She retrieved Alex and led her away, hurrying out of the bunkhouse. When they reached the house, Charlotte met her.

"Shannon, there's a phone call for you from the United States. The phone is in the hallway."

"Who on earth could be calling me from the U.S.?" She picked up the receiver. "Hello, Shannon here."

"Shannon, I'm sorry to interrupt your honeymoon. Robert Aldrin in New York. I want to ask you a favor."

Aldrin was Shannon's editor for a publication that often ran her stories. "I heard you're in South Africa at the moment. We're aware of a massacre of school children at a black township near Johannesburg. And a photographer at the scene has sent wire photos. Horrendous. It's on all the wires, and the whole world has seen them. Everybody is clamoring for news about this. Since you're there, would you do a piece and get it to us as soon as possible?"

Shannon took a deep breath before answering. "Robert, I just learned about the Soweto massacre by accident when I came across a black newspaper. I'm at my in-law's farm outside Cape Town. We are a considerable distance from Johannesburg. I had no idea how repressive this government was until I got here. Censorship is absolute; no stories by foreign press are getting out. Americans are distrusted, and white women cannot go about freely. If that weren't enough, Graeme would forbid it. I don't see how I could do a story for you."

"Well, think about it. I'll try to find someone else, but you were top of mind since you're there. It's major headline stuff right now. What the heck is going on in that country?"

"It's worse than my husband imagined. I'll think about doing a story and talk to Graeme, but I highly doubt I can do it."

Around cocktail time, Graeme arrived home with his father, covered in dust from his day's inspections. His mood was even worse than the day before. Their talks had not gone well.

"Graeme, have you heard about Soweto?" Shannon said when they were alone.

Graeme's eyebrows shot up. "What do you know about Soweto?"

"You first."

"Dad says there was a riot in one of the townships near Johannesburg, and the police intervened. Some people were killed, others arrested. Now, your turn."

"I came across a black African newspaper by accident today when exploring the farm. The 'riot,' as your father called it, was a demonstration by thousands of school children protesting the law that their curriculum must be taught in Afrikaans. The police opened fire on them, killing maybe as many as 700 children. Graeme, there are photos!"

Shannon gathered her courage and broached the subject, anticipating Graeme's reaction. "Then my New York editor called. He wants me to do a story on the 'Soweto massacre.' He said the story and photos are all over the wires, and the entire world is going crazy trying to find out what's going on."

Graeme sat down in a chair by the window, put his head in his hands, and was very quiet. Steadying himself, he said, "I hope you told him an emphatic 'no!'."

"I told him I'd think about it and talk to you."

"What you don't see, Shannon, is things are not just black and white. This apartheid situation has evolved over a hundred years. South Africa stands head and shoulders over other African countries for its prosperity and development. Look at all the other countries on the African continent. It's one brutal war after another, tribe against tribe, slaughtering each other so some new potentate can sit on a throne. And behind every one of these coups is the West, secretly providing funds and weapons so they can get their hands on whatever resources that country has to offer. Oil, gold, diamonds."

Graeme stood up to face her, the light from the window framing him. "No, Shannon. I won't allow it. I absolutely forbid you to get involved in this."

"Graeme, you know how those words affect me! And I cannot believe you are defending this regime and its brutal policies. You sound like your father talking."

"This isn't about your journalistic instincts or your need to fight injustice. This is about my family! It's a life-or-death matter. Whites aren't even allowed near these townships, not to mention a woman. You'd be arrested on the spot and, as a foreigner, suspected of inciting sedition and rebellion. That's an imprisonable offense, probably torture. There's no way I can allow you to go anywhere near this."

"Are you saying we do nothing?" She stood as well, squaring off, and faced him, struggling to keep her voice calm.

"I'm booking our flights out of here as soon as I can get reservations."

"Graeme, I won't fight you on this. I recognize this is way over my head."

"Thank you, Shannon," he sighed with relief. "Oh, thank God, thank you!" He gripped both her shoulders. "Things here are much worse than I realized. South Africa is a powder keg, and this Soweto incident might provide the match."

Shannon tried to squelch her inner voice shouting at her to take action, until she came upon an idea. "Graeme, listen to me for a moment."

Graeme dropped his hands and looked in his wife's face.

"Just please hear me out. What if I develop a story about how apartheid affects the whites living in the country, not the blacks? And I won't write the story until I'm back in the States."

Shannon saw Graeme's face change in an instant, now contorted in anger. "What is it you don't understand! Out of the question! Word would get back to the police here and could put my family in jeopardy."

"I'd write under my maiden name, not Thorne. They'd never know."

"What you don't grasp is that South Africa is a police state. People inform on one another. Whites who sympathize with the blacks or who oppose apartheid are then subject to house arrest, at a minimum, imprisonment, even exile."

He paced across the room, then spun around and faced Shannon, his hands on his hips. "Just how do you think we would even get out of the country? All it takes is one informer to put the secret police on our tail, and they'll watch our every move, tap the phones…"

"I didn't realize that."

"I'd probably get my passport yanked and be under suspicion for sedition. Either I'd never be able to leave the country or get back in. And my family? As soon as the police linked you to me, my family would be targeted, and they'd be ruined. You don't live here, Shannon, but they do."

"Of course." She swallowed hard.

"Oh, Shannon. Your naïveté is reckless and dangerous. South Africans have to solve the problems of South Africa, not some starry-eyed, aspiring American journalist. Your chasing a big story could destroy my family. How can you even think of it?"

He bit back his anger and softened his tone. "Look, I'm getting our reservations out of here tomorrow, and that's the end of it."

She was torn, between her love for her husband and her compulsion to do what she thought was right. Her stomach in knots, she barely made it to the bathroom in time, heaving and crying at the same time. She barely slept that night.

She awakened before Graeme and the rest of the house and crept downstairs to call Dr. Ross in the States, relieved when he answered. She relayed what had happened and how conflicted she was.

He was quiet for several minutes, considering his response, then he said to her, "Knowing when not to do something requires wisdom. Shannon, I have fought racial prejudice my whole life, but I've also lived with one foot in each camp. I live among whites while trying to improve the conditions of my people. My wife is white. Did you know that?"

"No… I didn't."

"I have children who are half white and half black. My work heading up Caribbean Studies at this university is a tiny part here. I must understand both sides if I am to make persuasive arguments for black freedom and equality.

"I'm listening."

"Your experiences in South Africa will stay with you; you won't lose them. In time, you will know when it is right to bring them into your work. Examine your drive to do something big. It's valuable to do small things as well. If you read the books I left you, you will recall that my historical works stretched back 200 years. The people I wrote about were dead; I could do them no harm."

"Yes, I read them and remember that time span."

"When you or I take up the pen and write something that others will read, we assume the authority of a teacher." He paused. "You know I'm a Socialist, but do you know I am also Christian? The ancient Bible contains more wisdom than all texts combined. In the Bible, God warns us about taking on the role of teacher, that we must be very cautious of what we speak. Do you claim to understand the plight of black South Africans, the agenda of the ruling white Boer government, and the whites caught in the middle? Enough to tell their story?"

"Not really."

"You must examine yourself, your motives. Is your ego driving you? Is your sense of injustice so strong that you would imperil your husband and his family? It's essential for you, right now, to do no harm."

"But what do I do? It seems wrong to just sit by without doing anything."

"Your husband has given you good advice, Shannon. Sometimes doing nothing is the hardest. Let South Africans solve the problems of South Africa."

"They've been fighting this injustice for years, and it's only gotten worse."

"Change takes time, and the unwise are impatient for change. Yet that impatience matters not a bit. Change comes in its own time, and South Africa is on the path of change. Nothing will stop that now."

That was a hard lesson for Shannon—to do nothing. Yet, Dr. Ross caused her to reflect on the times in her life when she had reacted with righteous indignation, certain that she was right and others wrong, when she showed no regard for how her actions might hurt others.

Shannon recalled the middle-aged secretary who lost her job because she didn't want to operate a linotype. One of her bosses was fired from his job, partly because he didn't give her the raise she expected and had offended her sense of propriety. How many times had she acted out of her selfish interests, heedless of damage to others?

She could now see that her strong will and independence masked an arrogance, which led to some of her worst regrets. She was shocked at herself, at how close she came to perhaps doing irreparable harm to her husband, his family, and her marriage.

When Graeme was awake, Shannon apologized to him. "I am so sorry. I wasn't thinking clearly. I'd never want to harm your family or you. Please forgive me. I'm so ashamed."

"Thank you, Shannon. I'm relieved. I want to get us out of this country while we still can. Who knows when this government might close the airports. They're desperate to keep the world ignorant of what's going on here."

"Do you think the government suspects a person as well-known as you?"

"As a public figure, I haven't voiced my views about South Africa's apartheid policies. I can't take the risk of harming my family. The government probably suspects I'm in opposition, but I haven't advertised the fact. I may be on their list, anyway, especially now that I'm married to an American woman."

"What's next?"

"Let's get with Alex today and talk about where we're going to live. I'm leaning toward New York."

"Well, that would suit me!" Shannon smiled. "About Alex. She's angry with you for leaving her with her mother and even deserting her here at Thorneside. She's worried you'll leave her again, but this time with me. She feels you abandon her over and over."

"I sense it, Shannon, but what can I do? My work requires me to travel, and I can't change that. I hope to slow it down. But it will always be a part of what I do."

"Then perhaps you can involve her in that. Take her with you sometimes, let her see what you do, show her some great sights, and spend quality time together, just the two of you. You see how she loved our days together in Trelwyn and Cape Town."

"You're right. Let's the three of us talk privately after breakfast. It's time we settled things."

* * *

"ALEX, WHAT WOULD you think about living in New York?"

"Why can't we stay here on the farm with Gram?" Alex whined.

"It's your home, too, and Gramps wants you to stay here and work with him and Uncle Lucas on the farm."

Her voice turned cheerful. "Then we wouldn't have to move, and you wouldn't have to travel."

Graeme put his hand on her shoulder. "You make a pretty good argument for an eight-year-old. But South Africa is on the brink of civil war, Alex. The signs and dangers are everywhere. It will be a very different country for white people soon, and maybe not safe. And frankly, I disagree with how South Africa treats its black people. So does Shannon. We would be on opposite sides with Gramps, Lucas, and many others we know."

"But how can you leave your family?"

"Gramps and I just don't get along, and we don't work well together. It would be an unhappy situation for all of us." He turned to take her chin in his hand. "Tennis is my life, Alex, and my livelihood, and I love it. It's what I do, and I do it damned well!" He let his hand drop to his side. "But I am working on projects that won't require me to travel as much as playing the pro circuit does. I just need time to get some deals done. Then my goal is to be with you and Shannon and not be gone as much as I am now. I want to be with you both, to take care of you and protect you."

"But that's not true, is it, Dad?" Alex blurted out. She stood and glared at Graeme through eyes now blazing with an anger she had never expressed. "You left me for years with my mother when you were on tour, and you weren't there to protect me. You left me with Gram for the past four years and stayed gone most of the time, and you haven't been here to protect me."

Alex's voice faded into sobs. "And you'll leave me again with Shannon when you go back on tour. You can't say you'll protect me because it's just not true."

Graeme's eyes teared up from this unexpected onslaught from his daughter. "You're right, Alex, I have been gone for most of your life, and it pains me that you have endured so much on your own. I am so sorry for all that. I love you more than my own life, but how can you know or believe that when I haven't been there for you?"

He hugged her, then leaned back to look into her eyes. "I promise I'm doing everything I can to change how it was for you in the past."

"How are you going to do that?"

"What would you think about sometimes traveling with me?" He grinned at her. "Come on the road and see what I do. I'll show you some sights you've never seen, and we'll spend time together, just the two of us. The rest of the time, we'll be a family, and when you're not traveling with me, you'll be with Shannon. We promise, both of us—you'll never be left alone again."

Her anger spent, Alex surrendered to tears she had buried for years. Graeme engulfed his daughter with his arms and held her tight while she buried her face in his chest.

"Just go ahead and cry, my angel. Go ahead and cry," he told his daughter as he gazed at his wife, his own eyes misty, and silently mouthed the words, "Thank you, Shannon,"

After a few minutes and her tears had subsided, Alex said, "I'm okay with New York if that's what you decide. Just promise you won't ever leave me alone again."

"I promise, Alex. Never again," he said, and held her again in a tight embrace.

* * *

"DAD, WE'VE DECIDED we're going to settle in New York," Graeme said to Max. "With things as they are here, we are leaving in the morning."

"You're turning your back on your own family for what?" Max yelled, exploding in anger. "A new American wife who twists your thinking with Western propaganda? Foreigners who don't give a damn about you? Still chasing a childish dream of forever playing tennis for a living?"

"Dad, it's more than one thing." Graeme shook his head. "I didn't realize how bad things have deteriorated in South Africa. This regime is getting more brutal by the day. How can anyone of good conscience accept what Botha and his thugs are doing to anyone of color here?"

"If we don't keep our feet on their necks," Max said as he jabbed Graeme's chest, "this country will go back to the wasteland it was when we came here hundreds of years ago. We've created a paradise in what was once just dust and primitive tribes living in dung huts, me and my father, and his before him, and even before him. Generations of Thornes. And now me. I've done that with my bare hands, with my sons at my side—except for you! Do you think we're just going to give it back to the blacks and let the country dissolve into chaos like the rest of Africa?"

Graeme took a step backward. "I don't expect us to agree on this, Dad, but neither can you expect me to ignore my conscience and sit idly by. The South African government is on the wrong side of history, Dad. Time has run out. If whites don't work out a peaceful sharing of power and give these people the freedom they deserve, then all-out war is the only outcome."

"So let it be war, then," stormed Max. "We're ready for them, and we'll beat them back into the bushes they came from. But you, turning your back on your flesh and blood. You care more for your new American wife and your fancy Euro-trash friends than you do your own family. She's turned you against us, hasn't she?"

"No, Dad." Graeme held up his hands, palms forward. "No, she hasn't."

He rested his hands on his hips. "If anything, I've defended you and asked her not to voice her views. I didn't want her to hear the things you've just said. The truth is, Dad, it's not just the politics in the country. You and I are further apart than we've ever been. Yes, being in the world has changed me, knowing other people, cultures, and countries. But I hope for the better. You're a perfect reflection of this country. You're like a mirror of what white South Africa stands for, and frankly, Dad, I detest it. There is just no way you and I can work together, or that I could make a home for myself and my family here."

"Then get out! Leave! But once you go out that door, don't ever think of coming back. As far as I'm concerned, you're dead to me. You are no longer my son!"

The next morning, Graeme, Shannon and Alex joined Charlotte in the kitchen for coffee. They didn't see Max, and Shannon guessed that he had left at sunrise while the household was still sleeping, unable or unwilling to face his youngest son. Charlotte alone saw them off, forcing a thin smile until farewell hugs dissolved them all in ragged sobs.

"You must promise to visit us in New York soon," Shannon whispered in Charlotte's ear.

The tires of their rented car crackled on the gravel as they drove off, leaving Charlotte rooted in the same spot, waving goodbye.

"Try not to be too sad, Alex," Shannon said as they both looked back and waved until the house, and Charlotte, were no longer in sight. "Your grandmother will visit us as soon as we're settled, and she plans to visit every year. She knows she has a home with us for as long as she wants to stay."

The three of them rode to Cape Town in silence, filled with despair, worry, and guilt. Despair for the violent upheaval the country was facing. Worry for Graeme's family and how they would fare in the difficult times ahead. And guilt for leaving Charlotte, without knowing when or if they would ever be able to return to South Africa.

None of them realized they were at the historical turning point that marked the beginning of the end for apartheid. Sam Nzima's photo of the three children, one of them shot and killed, had run on every front page throughout the globe. That photo became one of Time magazine's most influential photos of all time. Worldwide public opinion now condemned South Africa's apartheid policies.

At last, voices within and without the country were heard, led by the Anti-Apartheid Movement of exiled South Africans to the internal African National Congress, the official voice of black South Africa. In time, Graeme added his voice, at last speaking out against apartheid when he had the opportunity, and Shannon was free to write about the repression and fears she witnessed when a visitor in the country.

The Soweto incident resulted in mass protests throughout the country led not by adults but by their youth who, in one voice, protested apartheid and demanded a better future. Even white South Africans dared to speak in public against Prime Minister Botha's crushing police actions.

Following the news after Soweto, Shannon learned that the United Nations denounced apartheid and placed an arms embargo on South Africa, crippling its ability to wage war against neighboring Nigeria. The United States and the United Kingdom followed with harsh economic sanctions.

Yet, the country endured another decade of brutal police suppression.

"How much longer will the people suffer?" Shannon wondered.

* * *

A Home in New York

THEY NEEDED TIME to decompress, all three of them. Graeme's visit to Thorneside had lasted less than two weeks, far shorter than he planned. The country on the verge of civil war, the conflict in the Thorne home, tearing Alex away from her beloved Gram—it was altogether overwhelming.

That awful fight with his father left Graeme sad and distressed over the awful last words with his father. He wasn't sure he would ever be able to forgive Max, and both had said things they could not retract. Shannon lost sleep over the tension in the Thorne household and the horrifying realities of apartheid. As for Alex, the scars of her tumultuous eight years were laid bare.

All in all, they were a mess.

Shannon and Graeme decided to live outside New York City, preferring something quieter than the bustling city. They found an older home in a tiny hamlet at the base of the Passaic Mountains, yet just an hour from Manhattan and the major airports. The neighborhood was forested and teeming with wildlife. It wasn't like the farm in South Africa, of course, but for New York, it felt like the country.

For Graeme and Shannon, it was their first time as adults to live in a house instead of rented apartments. Shannon threw herself into remodeling their home, and Alex decorated her bedroom the way she wanted with splashes of pink and butterflies.

True to her word, Shannon presented Alex with a new bicycle. And she bought one for Graeme and herself as well. She taught Alex to ride, an easy task, since the girl was a natural athlete. Soon the two of them were going for bike rides through the neighborhood. When Graeme was home, Shannon planned weekend getaways, loading all three bikes onto the car's bike rack. They headed north to country roads in Vermont and New Hampshire where they biked all day and at night stayed in quaint bed-and-breakfast inns.

They got a dog! A first for Shannon and Graeme and a delight for Alex. Shannon chose a purebred Shetland Sheepdog puppy from a breeder, and they named her Shy Ann. Shannon put herself and the puppy through dog training and found the dog intelligent and responsive. Obeying the typical commands of sit, stay, down, and come took only a few weeks to master. Over time Shannon taught her to retrieve her leash for walks and even bring Shannon's walking shoes.

Alex and Shannon hiked in the Passaic Mountains, Shy Ann following, tail wagging with excitement at the excursion. They picnicked beside a pristine lake with no one around for miles.

Alex and Shy Ann were inseparable, and the dog seemed to provide just the tonic Alex needed to help her heal. One of the repercussions from Alex's traumatic years with Cora was fear of a dark room. When Shy Ann slept in Alex's room, her nightmares lessened and her fears subsided.

Graeme's investments and projects quite overwhelmed him, although his friend Greg kept abreast of the business ventures, and Shannon organized his travel. Shannon's writing pursuits shifted to the back burner, applying her time and energy to Graeme's career, Alex's care, and their home.

As promised, Graeme took Alex on some trips to famous cities during her school breaks. She enjoyed the adventure of sightseeing in new places and relished having her father to herself. When Graeme attended business meetings, Alex sat reading a book, watching him out of the corner of her eyes and listening to every word.

Alex grinned with pride to learn her father was admired and trusted by his fellow players and tournament organizers. She overheard him described as intelligent, articulate, and sophisticated, and the sports press sought him for interviews whenever tennis was in the news.

Alex saw how hard her father worked for his family. She realized the toll it took on him, being on the road so much, living in hotels, eating in restaurants, and being away from his family. Alex knew he missed Shannon and imagined he must have felt that way when he was separated from his daughter. Alex also saw how much she and her father both relied on Shannon. She was their anchor.

On one of Graeme's return trips from France, Shannon and Alex, now nine years old, greeted him with a candlelit dinner, serving his favorite dishes.

"Wow! What have I done to deserve this?" he said.

"Can't we just plan a special dinner for our main man without needing a reason?" Shannon said.

"Yes, but… I've gotten to know you, wife, and you usually have a reason for the things you do. But if this is just a welcome home, that's fine with me!"

"Humpf," she sniffed, "you do seem to know me better than I know myself. There is a reason for this little celebration we've planned for you, and, yes, we have some news."

"Oh," he wondered aloud as he winked at Alex, "you've got a new writing assignment? Somebody ace an exam?"

"We are fortunate to live in a spacious house, where we can laze about, watch TV, paint the walls any color we like," Shannon said as she swept the room with a broad gesture, "mow our lawn, plant flowers, and plenty of rooms to do… whatever."

"Hummm," said Graeme. "Sometimes I worry if we haven't bitten off more than we can chew, or if this house is too much for you. I'm away so much, leaving you and Alex here to take care of everything."

"It's not too big at all," she said. "I bet we can fill every inch."

"What are you talking about, Shannon? Am I missing something here?"

"Graeme, Alex is going to be a sister! You're going to be a father! I'm going to be a mother! We're having a baby!"

The instant look of shock changed to a huge smile and a loud "Woo hoo!" that all the neighbors must have heard. "Are you sure? When?" He jumped from his chair and rushed to surround Shannon in a giant bear hug, lifting her off her feet.

"Yes, I'm sure. I took a positive home test and backed it up with an OB appointment. She confirmed I'm pregnant and now a good eight weeks along. I wanted to wait until you were home to tell you."

"And how are you feeling? Is this why you were nauseous in South Africa? What does the doctor say?"

"That I'm made for babies!" She beamed at him. "Everything is great. Seven months from now, the next Thorne baby will be born."

Now that Graeme knew, Shannon got on the phone with Helen. She hadn't told anyone else, and now she couldn't wait to share the news with her best friend.

"Guess what, Helen! I'm pregnant!"

"Fantastic! Guess what? So am I!"

"Wh… what? How? Who?" Shannon said. "I didn't know you were even seeing anyone."

"I'm not."

"But I don't get it. How can you be… Who is the—"

"No one you know. I was seeing someone for a while; then I wasn't. Now I'm pregnant, and I'm thrilled. End of story."

"My goodness, Helen. That's very bold of you. I mean, I've got Graeme. How will you manage?"

"One major leap at a time," Helen said in her matter-of-fact voice. "I'll manage. You know I've always wanted a child but never dated anyone I wanted to marry. I'm 34, and you're 31. It's not like we have all the time in the world."

"Well, then. Our children will have a brother or sister growing up together, won't they?" Shannon said. "How could they not be best of friends?"

Though they were many miles apart, Shannon and Helen compared their pregnancies over the phone, replaying doctors' visits, setting up their nurseries. Both were strong, healthy women, and their pregnancies advanced with no difficulties. They were obsessed with eating right, exercising, and preparing for their babies' births.

Helen's baby came first, a textbook delivery of a beautiful girl she named Cecelia, or Cece for short.

Graeme cleared his calendar to spend Shannon's ninth month at home. One morning about 5 AM, Shannon woke with a sudden pain in her lower abdomen. At once alert, she lay still a while, waiting to see what happened next. Five minutes later, a second pain gripped her, same as the first.

She shook Graeme awake. "I think it's started."

He bolted upright and reached for his watch, ready to time the cramps. After a few minutes, he said, "Let's take a short walk to make sure it's not false labor."

Before they were halfway around the block, Shannon suggested they go back.

"I feel a lot of pressure, and the pains are coming faster. This isn't false labor."

Graeme gathered Shannon's things, and got Alex ready to stay with a school friend. Shannon, in the meantime, immersed herself in a hot bath. When Graeme came in to ask if she was ready, he found her shaving her legs.

"What in bloody hell are you doing?"

"I'm not about to check myself into the hospital ungroomed."

Graeme drove as fast as he thought safe while Shannon spent the hour with her eyes squeezed shut, trying to squelch nausea as Graeme navigated curves in the road. When they arrived at the hospital's maternity ward, the charge nurse said, "Get her right to delivery. This baby is coming."

Two hours later, their son was born.

Gabriel was the name they chose. Graeme was giddy with happiness over his son, and Alex fell into her Big Sister role with total devotion, gentle and soothing when she held the baby. Alex helped during Shannon's early days of recovery, bringing her teas, soups, and nutritious meals to rebuild her strength.

Charlotte, who had waited by the phone, booked her flight the moment she hung up from Graeme's call. She came for an extended visit and helped Shannon through the early weeks, happy to spend time with her new grandson and her beloved granddaughter. Shannon fell into her role of mother as though born to it, surprising herself, astonished by the powerful love she felt for her baby son.

"Don't you want your mother here, Shannon? It's such a wonderful time to share," Charlotte murmured in a careful tone.

"Mom is into her new marriage now, Charlotte, and I doubt she'd want to take time away. Besides, we're still distant from one another. She hasn't even met Graeme. He wants to meet her, but I just haven't felt it 'safe' yet. We talk on the phone every now and then, or I get one of her long letters full of remorse and accusations. It sets me back all over again. She's an unhappy woman, Charlotte, and it's contagious."

Charlotte nodded. "Someday, perhaps. It's just not good to leave wounds open. I can't imagine being away from my grandchild at a time like this. Maybe one day you'll find it in your heart to forgive both your mother and father."

"That's what I hope, Charlotte. So far, whenever I think of them, only the bad memories flood back. I'm so happy with Graeme, Alex, and now Gabriel. I don't want anything to spoil it."

Gabriel's baby stage brought the usual stresses: colicky crying, car drives to soothe him to sleep, and late-night feedings. But the baby stage went by too soon. In the blink of an eye, it seemed, he was crawling, then toddling, then starting school.

Gabriel was the spitting image of his father. He possessed Graeme's natural charm and made friends with everyone he met. Many children Gabriel's age lived in their neighborhood, and the house hummed with children coming and going.

Graeme's business activities increased, as well as his travel schedule. When he was home, he devoted his time to Shannon, Alex, and Gabriel. Still, Shannon could see he was worried about his business ventures. He tried to get tennis clubs into his newly formed management company, especially ones in the United States, but things were going much slower than he had hoped, and he was forced to rely on playing competitive doubles tennis to keep everything afloat. Now in his mid-forties, he worried how much longer he could continue.

Helen and Shannon alternated visits, getting the children together at least twice a year. Helen often spent the holidays in New York. Christmas was Shannon's favorite season. She went all out, decorating her home with a giant Christmas tree and presents for everyone. They took the kids to Rockefeller Center to see the tree and the lights in Manhattan. Shannon hosted an annual Christmas party for family and friends, a highly anticipated event for everyone.

Charlotte's visits were often over the holidays, too. "I'm happy Graeme chose New York. Since we are living in fearful times in South Africa, I want at least one of my sons to live abroad. The United States offers the most security and opportunity, and my visits bolster my strength for the challenges back home."

Every now and then, Max came, too, and those visits were tense, with everyone on edge. He would stay only a week, insisting his farm could not be without his attention longer than that. Charlotte retreated into the acquiescent wife Shannon remembered when first meeting her. Father and son fell into their pattern of offense-defense in their conversations. Max lobbed innuendoes and downright insults that Graeme deflected or ignored until a comment hit its mark, with both erupting in anger.

"No doubt this is how Graeme honed his upbeat, enthusiastic personality that he exhibits to everyone," thought Shannon, "to counter his father's mean spirit. I suppose I should thank Max for inadvertently making my husband the pleasant, considerate person he became."

"I hope you've given up your roving ways, Graeme," his father once slurred after a few drinks, Shannon within obvious earshot. "With a wife and two children to support, you should be past chasing tail all the time."

Graeme took that bait. It was more insult than he could accept. "You're right about one thing, Dad. Shannon is the wife of my dreams and fulfills every part of me. I hoped you would see that for yourself and not feel the need to be crude and cruel in my wife's presence! You've always been a brute and a bully to my mom and to all your sons. But you're a role model to me, Dad, for what not to do as a husband or a father. I'll never disgrace or abuse my wife as you have my mother, and my children will never have reason to fear or hate me."

Max left for South Africa the day after that awful exchange. As soon as he was gone, the household resumed its companionable harmony.

"Charlotte, I don't know how you can stay with Max," said Shannon. "We worry about you, and you know, you're always welcome to come live with us."

"It's all I know, Shannon. South Africa is different from the United States. Women are not considered equal to men."

"It hasn't been that long that women here have won some rights. Most of our progress has come about as recently as the 60s with the Women's Movement. I've faced sexual harassment, male dominance, and wage discrimination in almost every job. When it was a choice to accept or confront it, I've confronted it every time."

"That's one of the things I like most about you, Shannon. You stand up for things you believe in."

"It's not bravery at all, Charlotte. It just made me so mad when I did the same or better work than a man and earned less. My pride just won't accept that." Shannon paused. "What about Dexter and Jude? Are they abusive with their wives?"

"My other daughters-in-law are like me," Charlotte said. "They submit to their husbands' authority and accept their lot in life. I'm afraid Lucas is severe with his wife and children, if not physically, then certainly verbally. He is a mirror image of his father. Even as a boy, Lucas bullied his brothers. Instead of being a big brother and looking out for his brothers, he ordered them around, just like his father. He never hesitated to smack them if they didn't toe the line."

She heaved a great sigh. "The other two, Dexter and Jude, I'm not so sure, but I hope not. They both want to please their father and are always trying to gain his approval. Their wives are quiet and retiring, never daring to disrespect or disobey outside their home. Jude and his wife don't come around often. Maybe they are uncomfortable being in our home or even being with Lucas."

"What about Graeme?"

"Graeme was always different. As a small boy, he would stand up for me, even once talking back to his father when Max shouted at me. Max gave him a good hiding, I'm afraid, and I was powerless to stop him. But that didn't prevent Graeme from speaking against his father when he mistreated me. That's why he wanted so badly to get away from the farm. He hated seeing how his father behaved toward me, but he couldn't stop it."

During that conversation, it dawned on Shannon that maybe she owed her father a debt of thanks.

"My father's treatment of my mother is what caused me to make a conscious choice never to fear bullies and to stand up against them," Shannon thought. "I hadn't realized before, but Graeme and I have that in common. Both our fathers were bullies, our mothers badly treated, and we rebelled against that. We chose a different way for ourselves, to stand up for people who couldn't or wouldn't stand up for themselves." She nodded. "Maybe that's why I have such a self-righteous streak and hate injustice."

Mo's voice came back to her when she was a little girl. "All fam'lies got they own ways, Miz Shannon. You just gotta decide what way you gonna be, don't matter what other folks do."

"When I'm with you, Shannon, in your home with you and Graeme," Charlotte said, "I'm the person I want to be. I can't talk openly with my sons' wives or anyone else back home like I can with you. Hard to explain, but it's like the political situation has invaded our private thoughts. We are all on guard, careful not to say or do the wrong thing to attract attention. We keep a low profile and just hope the problems of the country will not reach us here."

Her thoughts seemed to float across the seas, back to her home at

Thorneside. "But South Africa is my home. There I'm the mother of three other sons and grandmother to six. Max is not always so bad, just when he drinks too much. I feel my children and grandchildren need me. I couldn't leave them to Max."

Shannon and Charlotte exchanged many conversations during her visits that bonded them tighter. Charlotte became the mother she never had.

"Shannon, don't be so hard on your mother. Remember, she was trapped in her marriage, not so different from me. She did the best she could under her circumstances. The longer you persist in distancing yourself from her, the more harm you do yourself as well as Gabriel, her grandson. Give her a chance. She may surprise you. This bitterness of the past will poison your heart."

Charlotte could travel safely to the United States, but there was no way Graeme could visit South Africa now. Conditions in the country had deteriorated since the Soweto massacre, and the country had erupted in open conflict. President Botha and his Boer government cracked down on all forms of protest. Police rounded up leaders and sent them to prisons, like the infamous Robben Island that held Nelson Mandela and other black leaders.

Shannon and Charlotte talked often by phone, each sharing what they knew.

Smuggled film footage leaked out of South Africa showed military raids of black townships, people pulled from their homes, mostly young black men. The world watched as people were thrown into police vans and taken away.

"They're even taking children as young as ten or eleven years old," Charlotte said, ignoring risks of government wire tapping. "Families go to the police stations looking for husbands and sons, and often they are told that their loved one has died "falling down stairs," or "committed suicide" in their cells. Most are never seen again."

"We see TV coverage showing the crackdowns in the townships, people beaten, shot."

"Here at the farm," Charlotte continued, "most of the young

men are gone. We don't know where. Max has loaded guns all around the house, and he's afraid we might be attacked in our beds, our throats cut. Our workers have never shown any hint of violence towards us," she said, "but we've heard stories where workers have turned on the white farmers."

"There are demonstrations everyday on American college campuses," Shannon told her, "demanding our government do something. The only action I've seen is public outcry against companies that invest in South Africa. It's becoming political suicide for any company to do business there. *The New York Times* calls the South African regime 'a rogue regional terrorist organization without good standing among the community of nations.' "

"What we feel here at the farm is fear and distrust everywhere. Max doesn't trust any of our black workers, including Joseph. I can only imagine how much worse it must be in the cities. I am so afraid for our country, and I don't see the end in sight."

From prison, Mandela smuggled out a message to South African blacks: "Unite! Mobilise! Fight on! Between the anvil of united mass action and the hammer of the armed struggle, we shall crush apartheid!" He abandoned his previous strategy of peaceful resistance and advocated violence as the only way to break the backs of the apartheid regime.

Graeme was no longer silent. After Soweto, he made his choice. Whenever the press interviewed him, the questions gravitated to South Africa and apartheid. Graeme used the platform to denounce Botha and his policies. He had no illusions about how the ruling government viewed Graeme Thorne. If he tried to visit South Africa now, he was confident the government would seize his passport and imprison him.

Graeme's opposition drove yet another wedge between him and his father.

* * *

SHANNON AND ALEX were inseparable. She gave Alex the space to grow at her own pace, though always nearby whenever Alex wanted help or to talk. Alex sought her when she had something on her mind, often while Shannon was preparing a meal. Alex liked to sit at the counter and just talk, with no specific direction or topic in mind. Alex shared stories about how much her father was respected, and she understood how hard he worked to provide for his family.

"Travel isn't all it's cranked up to be," she said one evening. "We get up early to catch a flight, then sit around the airport because the plane is late. We eat in restaurants all the time or grab icky food when running to catch a flight. Then when we get there, Dad has to go right to the tennis courts."

"Not as glamorous as it seemed, is it?"

"The hotels are beautiful, except they aren't home, and I miss my own bed. But Dad has to be nice all the time, no matter how tired he is, hungry or irritated. People always expect him to answer their questions, and say what he thinks about everything, and what they should do about their problems."

"Interviews can be so exhausting," Shannon said.

"I asked him if he likes being on the road, and he said he'd rather be at home with his family. I'm glad he took me with him some times. I got to see Paris, London, and some other places in Europe. But I prefer home, too."

Shannon was relieved that their relationship seemed to skip the typical mother-daughter tensions. She let Alex be herself, and Alex was grateful for the love and warmth offered by her stepmother. Their enjoyment of one another's company was genuine.

One day Alex surprised Shannon with a request. "Shannon, what do you think about adopting me? Legally, I mean."

"Wow!" said Shannon. "I would love nothing better! I mean, I feel like you're my daughter anyway, but what makes you want to take that step?"

"You've been more of a mother to me than my natural mother ever was, and besides, you're my best friend. I hate telling people you're my stepmother. I'd just like to do away with that word."

"I have to agree with you there, Alex. Every time I say 'stepdaughter,' the word sticks in my throat. I'm sure your Dad would be happy for us to become mother and daughter legally. What would you like to call me?"

"Well, 'Shannon' still sounds best to me. We're so used to that, but whenever anyone asks, I'll be able to say you're my mother." She paused. "There's another reason, too. If anything ever happens to Dad, I'd just like to know you're my mother and nothing can change that."

* * *

SHANNON FELT HER life was as blessed and any life could be. Graeme was a generous and thoughtful husband, and he liked to surprise her.

One day he said, "You're getting something for your birthday that's on your bucket list. Ten days away from your responsibilities here and a trip to one of those Tuscany cooking schools you're always talking about. For you and Helen. I've already cleared it with her. She's practically packed."

"But I can't leave you and the kids for ten days. Gabriel is still so young and—"

"Alex and I can look after Gabriel. I'm not completely helpless, you know. And Helen is going to leave Cece with us. We'll take care of them both. Neither of you has an excuse. Look, I'm gone so much, and you never complain about staying here and keeping the home fires burning. It's your turn. Go! Enjoy yourselves. And come back ready to impress your husband with some new recipes."

Their trip started in Florence, staying at a moderate little hotel with a lovely rooftop bar for cocktails. Then they roamed the streets to pick a restaurant for dinner. One night, irresistible aromas lured them to a restaurant where the special of the evening was pasta with freshly grated truffles. The dish melted in their mouths. During the day, they were typical tourists seeing the sights and marveling at Da Vinci's *David*.

After a few days, they drove their rental car into the countryside to a beautiful villa hidden in the hills. The villa offered a dozen comfortable guest rooms very well appointed and detached from the separate building that housed the immense kitchen and dining room.

A vivacious Italian chef conducted cooking lessons for ten students, mostly women. Every day they prepared lunch and dinner, following the chef's fabulous menus. Nothing was too ambitious for their teacher, who challenged them to make homemade pasta, crusted sea bass, paella, and tiramisu. They enjoyed their lunches al fresco, served under a canopy of grapevines and accompanied by perfectly paired wines. Staff served the dinners, prepared by the students, in the candlelit dining room. The table groaned under many bottles of wine and after-dinner liqueurs enjoyed late into the evenings.

It was just the tonic Shannon needed, a reset, reminding her how good it felt to be in the world. She wondered if there was yet an unfulfilled purpose left in her life. She pushed aside the thoughts, content knowing she was happier than she had ever been.

"If there is something in the future, then eventually it will show itself."

One late afternoon she and Helen were lounging by the pool before dressing for dinner.

"We can do this, you know." Helen sat up straight.

"What?" Shannon murmured, stretching her hand over her shades to blot out the sunlight.

"Have our own B&B and cooking school, just like we talked about in our younger years."

"Helen, that was another life ago, before marriage and kids and mortgages. I don't see that happening now."

"I know," said Helen. "But can you imagine having a place like this? We would kick ass!"

Happiness Has a Shelf-Life

Alex graduated from high school with honors and started university at an Ivy League school on the East Coast, preferring to stay close to home.

Graeme's travel schedule remained intense. He seldom played competitive doubles, rather exhibition matches or clinics at locations for future tennis clubs. Graeme loved that the house was full of children and, when home, taught tennis clinics for the neighborhood kids on their community court.

As soon as Gabriel was old enough, Graeme took his family on their long-awaited safari to Africa. He even paid for Helen and Cece to come, and Charlotte joined them in Nairobi. They spent two weeks seeing every animal on Shannon's list while staying at luxurious lodges that rivaled the best European hotels.

One of their stays was in a tented camp rung with electric wires to discourage wild animals from roaming the grounds. Shannon felt alive in a way she had never felt before—adrenaline rushes in seeing the wild game, kinship with the Masai tribesmen, and comfort in the limitless landscapes.

"Can you smell that?" she said to the others.

"What?"

"That wonderful musty smell. The earth."

"I don't smell anything," they all said.

"It's just that wild imagination of yours, Shannon," Helen teased.

"It's there! she said. 'The smells of Africa,' just like Ernest

Hemingway described in his novels. It fills my head."

She was surprised at how aroused she felt at night when she snuggled close Graeme in their tent, listening to the lions roar and the elephants trumpet just outside their compound. They made passionate love with the chorus of wild animals around them.

"I don't know why," she said to Graeme, "but I feel so at home in Africa. Like I belong here. I've never been so happy."

A few weeks after returning from their safari, Graeme, Shannon and Gabriel had gathered around the table. Gabriel was grinning from ear to ear.

"What?" Graeme said, eyebrows raised. "Has someone gotten some good grades at school?"

Unable to contain himself, Gabriel blurted out, "Mom's going to have a baby!"

Graeme picked Shannon up and twirled her around the room. "That's wonderful news! Gabriel, you're going to have a new brother or sister."

Then with a sudden knowing and a twinkle in his eye, he whispered to Shannon, "Do you realize both our children were conceived in Africa. I don't know what that means, especially. Just an observation from a very interested and willing participant."

* * *

A BLIZZARD PILED snow several feet deep, with no sign of letting up. As the winds howled, the temperature plummeted to near zero. The long Christmas holiday had begun, so Alex was home for the next several weeks. Shannon expected Graeme home that night, and she was relieved Gabriel's school declared a snow day, so both Alex and Gabriel were safe at home.

"I'd hate to get stuck on the road picking him up from school," she said, her pregnancy now in its fifth month, and second-trimester discomforts settling in. She expected Graeme's flight might be canceled and waited for him to call with that news. Her doorbell rang, and she opened the front door to two police officers.

"Mrs. Thorne?" said one of the policemen.

"Yes. What is it?" Shannon said, wrapping both arms across her expanding belly to shield herself.

"May we come in?"

"Yes, of course. Tell me. What's going on?"

"Please, is anyone else home with you?"

"My husband's away. He's due back tonight. It's just me and my children home. Please, tell me why you're here."

"I'm afraid there has been an accident, a plane crash. A flight from London to New York was diverted to Atlanta because of the blizzard. Something happened while the flight was still in the air. The plane crashed over the Atlantic, and the word we have is— there are no survivors. Your husband's name was on the manifest. I'm so sorry to bring you this news. Is there someone you can call? Someone who can be here with you now?"

Everything after that was a blur. Shannon moved as though drugged. She called her dear friends, Ruth and Adam, from across the street, who came over right away. They took the children in tow and called Shannon's physician, who recommended a safe sedative and bed rest as a precaution.

Ruth made the critical phone calls to Charlotte in South Africa, Greg in London, and Helen in Austin, who said she would take the first available flight. Charlotte began the horrible task of notifying friends and family.

The first face Shannon saw when she came out of her sedated haze was another shock. "Mom, is that you? Am I dreaming?" Shannon asked through her fog.

"It is me, Shannon. Helen and I are both here. I'm here to help, Shannon, if you'll let me."

"Oh, Mom!" Shannon wrapped her arms around her mother, squeezing for dear life, as she dissolved into heart-wrenching, body-wracking sobs.

"You just go ahead and cry your eyes out, Shannon. We're here."

"Where are Alex and Gabriel?" she said through her tears. "Where's Helen?"

"Shannon, I'm right here beside you with your mom. Cece is here, and she's with Gabriel and Alex; they're keeping each other occupied. Alex knows what happened and is being strong for Gabriel. He suspects something terrible has happened and is desperate to see you."

"Oh, yes. Give me a few minutes to compose myself. I don't want them to see me like this. Is there any news? Is there any hope at all? Does anyone know what happened?"

Helen spoke. "The most we've gathered is that the plane had some midair malfunction when it was over the Atlantic. It just went off the radar. They've spotted some signs of wreckage, but until they recover the black box, they won't know what happened. There were no warnings on the ground."

Shannon pulled the sheet over her head.

"I've talked to Charlotte and Max," Helen continued. "They're notifying family and friends and waiting to hear from you to make plans to come over. Greg is on his way. He was in London with Graeme, and he's booking a flight. The storm is over, thank God, so he should be here tomorrow."

Shannon got herself up and went into the bathroom. Splashing cold water on her face helped revive her, though her reflection in the mirror spoke volumes. She wanted to be in control for the children's sake, and she needed to think through how she would tell Gabriel. Now ten years old, Gabriel was devoted to his father. And Alex. She's lost both her parents now. What must she be feeling?

After returning to her bedroom, she looked again at her mother, a woman she had not seen for twenty years. Beth had aged a bit. Her hair was dyed red, which looked quite good on her. She put on a little weight but otherwise appeared the same.

"Mom, I… can't believe you're here. How—"

"Helen called. She planned to come as soon as she heard, with Cece. But with school, they can't stay long. She knew you would never ask for my help on your own, so she picked up the phone and called me. Shannon, I'm here as long as you need me."

"But what about your husband?"

"He can look after himself for a while. He understands this is where I want to be right now."

"Now is not the time to be proud, Shannon," Helen said. "You need your mother's help, and she's right; you'd never have asked for it yourself. Now is the time to surround yourself with family and friends—that's us!"

"Graeme is dead," Shannon said in a monotone. "I'll never see him again." Her gaze bounced from one face to the other and back. "He'll never meet our unborn child. How do I go on without him?"

There was no body to bury. No trace was found of the passengers. The authorities believed the plane suffered a catastrophic mechanical failure that resulted in a midair explosion. Shannon, Max, and Charlotte settled on a memorial service in New York and a second one for the family at Thorneside Farms in South Africa.

Shannon fell into her strong woman mode, taking charge of what needed to be done. Her main concern was the children. Gabriel was so shaken by the loss of his father that he stuck close to his mother. Alex retreated into her shell, reminding Shannon of the fragile, young girl she first met.

"We promised Alex we would never leave her, and now her father is gone, too," Shannon muttered to her mother and her friend.

"But you're here, Shannon," said Beth. "She's not alone. Give her time, and she will come to see that."

Many in the sports world, not just tennis, attended the memorial in New York, as well as Graeme's friends and business associates. Sports press covered his passing, many in attendance, and expressed their high regard for the articulate, intelligent South African athlete.

The neighbors pitched in and brought food to last a month, a big help for out-of-town visitors who accepted Shannon's invitation to stay at the house. Shannon wanted to be as distracted as possible, encouraging guests to stay.

One evening the house was empty of all guests except Greg. Beth had returned to Austin after the memorial service, and Alex had coaxed Gabriel to bed early so Shannon and Greg could talk. They settled in the living room over a glass of wine for him and juice for Shannon.

"Shannon," he said, "Maybe it's too early, but I feel we must go over Graeme's business ventures and where we stand."

"I'm ready, Greg. I need to know, and now is as good a time as any."

"Well, Graeme had a will and left all his assets to you. With South Africa's policy of not allowing South Africans to take wealth out of the country, Graeme kept his money in bank accounts in the UK, Switzerland, and the U.S. His investments in the markets have held up pretty well."

"Yes, I know all that. We get the statements here, and I see them every month."

"Yes, good. I thought you were up to speed on all that. Graeme had a life insurance policy worth $100,000." He set his glass down. "What we must talk about are the business ventures Graeme had been working on these past few years as he left the tour."

"Go on."

"For the last number of years, Graeme's focus has been developing tennis clubs in the U.S. and Europe, as you know. Unfortunately, all the deals depended on Graeme running these clubs—his name, personality... the person, if you would. I was to be the business administration partner, but the investors were buying Graeme's name and reputation."

"I see," said Shannon, imagining worse news to come.

"Now, I'm afraid, all the investors have pulled out. They paid hefty consultancy fees for Graeme's and my involvement to this point. Without Graeme, there are no deals to be done."

He sighed. "I've reread all the contracts. Specific language says if Graeme is unable or unwilling to perform his role as agreed, the contracts are null and void."

"So that's it?"

"I'm afraid we're out. We received our consultancy fees, so you've got whatever remains in the bank accounts. This house, of course, goes to you; but I understand you have a considerable mortgage on it. You don't have excessive debts, thanks to your keeping on top of that side of things. But I'm afraid you can't count on any of the business ventures that Graeme and I had been developing."

"I see." Her voice was numb.

"Graeme knew it was himself he was selling. Time had run out for him to compete on tour. He hoped to get a few deals on the ground, make the projects successful, and negotiate actual ownership in the properties. That was his financial plan for the future. It was a good one, and it's a whole lot more than most tennis professionals have going for them. Being in his early 50s, he was banking on having the time to make his plan work. He just needed more time, and that was taken from him."

"What about any money he put into the deals?" Shannon said.

"Graeme's investment was risk capital, I'm afraid, his way of buying equity into the deals. I'm afraid it's gone."

"What about Graeme's share in his family's business?" Desperation had found its way into her voice.

"You probably know more about that than I do. Graeme told me his father excluded him from any shared interest in the family business, once he declined to be involved in it and moved to America. His father is pretty bitter that Graeme turned his back on the farm and left South Africa."

"They left things between them on very bad terms. Max disinherited Graeme altogether."

"Even if there were assets intended for Graeme, those wouldn't be available until after they died. Then there's still the problem of getting it out of the country. South Africa does not allow ex-pats to take wealth out. If you and your children moved to South Africa, then in time, you might inherit Graeme's share. That seems a remote possibility and quite a long time in the distant future before you'd see any of that."

Shannon threw aside her prenatal rules and poured herself a glass of wine, took a long drink, and sat back. After a minute, she said, "So, it sounds like I've got some latitude but not forever. I've got enough time for the baby to be born and a year or two. After that, I'll need to go back to work."

* * *

Return to Texas

AFTER THINKING THINGS through and running the numbers, Shannon decided to return to Texas, at least until the baby was born. It was both a practical and emotional decision. She needed family around her now, going through the last of her pregnancy and the baby's birth.

With Graeme gone, Helen was her closest friend in the whole world. She didn't think she could face the next few months in New York alone. She could rent the New York house for now and decide later about a permanent place to live.

During Beth's visit, mother and daughter did a lot of healing. In the years they had been apart, Beth had mellowed. That daily struggle for survival with Shannon's father had at last worked its way out of her system. Her new marriage had its challenges, but in general, they both seemed to care for one another, and the marriage was as good as most.

Beth had taken up golf and was passionate about it. She played every day and competed in tournaments throughout the state, winning more than her share. Golf changed Beth's outlook. No longer was she the angry, bitter person Shannon remembered, but one who laughed and enjoyed life.

During Beth's time in New York, she had gone out of her way to show how much she loved her daughter and wanted to be part of her life. She adored Gabriel, who soon became attached to his newly-discovered grandmother, and she welcomed Alex as her own granddaughter.

Beth heaped praises on her daughter, often telling her how proud she was of her. Shannon never heard those words growing up, ones she had always longed to hear.

"My heart first thawed, then healed," she said to Helen, "and I have you to thank for that."

"You've taken a huge step, Shannon. You've chosen to forgive your mother."

"I don't want to lose her again. And Alex is taking the next semester off from university to help me with the baby and be available for Gabriel."

"Truth be told, you both need each other. Neither of you wants to be apart while your grief is so raw."

"I plan to be in Texas before the baby is born, Helen. I'll rent us an apartment for a while, someplace near Mom. Get Gabriel in school…"

"Then what?"

"After the baby is born, I'll have to figure out what to do. Graeme's estate isn't going to last forever, not with three children to support and educate."

"One step at a time, Shannon. Things will work out. You just have to give yourself time. Right now, the most important consideration is that you and this baby get the rest and care you need."

"I'm sure you're right."

"Cece will be so excited! You know, Gabriel is her best friend, and the two of them are thick as thieves. And of course, I will be glad to have you back—finally. You've been gone a long time."

Shannon rented a house near Beth, who promised to help Shannon with the coming birth and the early weeks after. Gabriel had grown quiet and moody since Graeme's death, preferring to stay in his room and read rather than play with his friends.

"Cece is just the tonic he needs," she told her mother, "and she takes his mind off the loss of his father."

The emerging relationship between Shannon and Beth blossomed. However, Shannon knew there were conversations she and her mother would never have, and she accepted that.

Charlotte's words of wisdom came back to her. "Beth did the best she could in a situation that would break any ordinary woman. Beth hadn't meant to direct her anger onto you. She just recognized her own lost youth in her daughter."

Shannon now saw a woman who was a loyal and sensitive human being, who loved easily and wholly, and who blamed herself whenever anything went wrong. She had loved Oscar and still felt her marriage failed because of her failures as a wife. Whenever she spoke of Oscar, she did so with affection.

Shannon wished she could talk to her mother about those difficult years, but she dared not tread on the fragile foundation the two were building.

"Maybe one day…" she thought, feeling a wistful tug at her heart.

* * *

The Swedish Farmer and the Car Hop
Final Chapter

IN SHANNON'S SEVENTH month, a disturbing phone call came from a distant relative.

"Shannon, this is Ludvig Johnson, a cousin of your father, Oscar. Excuse me for calling you. I've gotten word that your father is near death and that the next of kin should know."

In the back of her mind, Shannon always expected a call like this might come one day. Over the twenty years since she had last seen her father, Shannon looked at homeless men on the streets, half expecting that some day she would find her father among them.

"Where is he?" she said.

"In New Orleans. Right now, he's living in the back of an old car in a junkyard. The junkyard owner is the one who called me, and he got my name from Oscar and tracked me down. He says your father is not eating and is skin and bones. He hasn't come out of that old car in days."

As it happened, Beth was visiting Shannon when the phone call came.

"You guys want to take a road trip to New Orleans? Dad's there, and they say he's dying. I'm going to see about him."

"Yes, we'll go with you."

Shannon shifted into her driver mode. First, she called the Veterans Administration to locate Oscar's military service records to confirm that her father was entitled to medical benefits. Shannon arranged for Oscar's admission to the Veterans Hospital in New Orleans, assuming she could get him there. Then she alerted New Orleans police and asked for their help in bringing her father to the VA Hospital, fearing he would not agree to go.

Early the next day, the four of them drove eight hours to New Orleans. Their first stop was the VA to sign admissions paperwork and name Shannon as legal guardian over her father. They found the junkyard, and a policeman was waiting for them. The owner directed Shannon to the vehicle where Oscar was camped while Beth stayed behind with Alex and Gabriel.

"Dad?" Shannon called out a few times. "Can you come out of the car and talk to me?"

Oscar worked his way out of the back seat of the dilapidated vehicle, holding a quart of warm milk in his hands.

"I got an upset stomach, and that good ole boy who lets me stay here gave me this milk."

Shannon could not have prepared herself for what she saw. Oscar's hair had thinned considerably, no longer red but white and grown to his shoulders. His scraggly beard reached his chest. His fingernails were so long, they curled at the ends. He wore ragged pants and a dingy, stained shirt. His shoes caught Shannon's attention—rubber work shoes with no socks and tied with wires instead of shoelaces.

"Dad, we got a call that you were very sick and needed help."

Oscar looked at Shannon, no recognition registering in his face. "No, no. I'm fine. Just an upset stomach is all."

"How are you doing?" said Shannon, struggling to make conversation.

Oscar rambled about living in New Orleans and his wife and his daughter back in Texas.

"Dad, do you know who I am?"

"Well, you do kinda look familiar," he said through rheumy blue eyes.

"I'm your daughter. Shannon."

Oscar's eyes clouded, and big tears fell down his grimy face. He reached out and put both his arms around Shannon, embracing her in a shaky hug, yielding to sobs, gibbering incoherent words.

Shannon bent down, awkward and difficult, considering her advanced pregnancy, and removed the wires from her father's shoes, replacing them with the laces from her sneakers. Then, taking his elbow, she led him to the police cruiser.

"Dad, we're taking you to get some help. You need to go to the hospital so they can get you well."

"Okay," he said in a meek tone. "I think that's a good idea."

"Dad, this nice policeman is going to take us to the hospital. I'll ride with you if that's all right." Looking at Beth, Shannon said, "Mom, will you guys follow in my car?"

Oscar looked at Beth with no flicker of recognition.

As they got him settled into a room, Oscar was gentle as a lamb and cooperated with nurses and staff. The hospital communicated with Shannon every week on Oscar's recovery. To their amazement, he soon bounced back. Regular meals and no alcohol restored his body to a healthy pink complexion, and his characteristic sense of humor returned. In two weeks, the hospital was ready to discharge him to Shannon.

On their return trip from New Orleans, they stopped at a

restaurant for dinner. Oscar had no teeth and gummed his food, lower lip touching his nose as he chewed. It was both comical and sad. While sitting at their table, Oscar stuffed his pockets with packets of salt and pepper, sugar, catsup, crackers, napkins, straws— anything lying on the table.

"Dad, what are you doing?"

"You never know when you might need this stuff."

"You don't need to do that anymore, Dad. When we get to Austin, you'll be in a nice home with a warm bed and your meals provided. On weekends you can say with me. How does that sound?"

Oscar nodded.

"You'll get to know your grandchildren. As long as you stay off the booze, Dad, you can be part of our family."

Their weekends together were pleasant. Oscar regaled her with his stories. Shannon enjoyed preparing healthy meals for him, and he put on weight. Shannon took Oscar places she thought he would like to see again. The lakes where they spent many family outings. An outdoor watermelon place where they enjoyed cold slices on hot afternoons. He reminded Shannon about long gone days when watermelons floated in huge ice water tanks and customers picked their watermelon.

"The owner cut a plug out of the heart of the melon to let you taste it and decide if it was sweet and ripe before you even bought it," said Oscar.

Sandy's Hamburgers was another familiar family haunt where they stopped for burgers and ice cream.

In the evenings, Oscar and Shannon often played dominoes. During one game, Shannon drew the perfect hand. She held every domino with the number five, and it was her turn to go first. She played the double-five, blocking her father from any moves.

He went to the boneyard over and over, muttering "Sheeut!" after each draw. Toward the end of the game, he held every ivory in his hand, yet could not play a single domino. They both laughed, with Shannon winning the whole game on a single hand.

They also had long talks. Oscar rambled about his marriage to Beth, stories that over time had morphed into his version of reality, altogether different from Shannon's memory.

Unable to keep silent, Shannon told her father, "Dad, you forget. I was there! I remember what happened, the beatings, the fighting."

Anger found its way in her voice as she let out feelings trapped for too long. "I remember all the miscarriages and the stillborn babies, Dad. And I saw you hitting Mom in the stomach when she was pregnant. I think the only reason I survived to be born is because you were away in the Army the whole time Mom was pregnant with me."

As if in explanation, Oscar mumbled, in almost a whisper, "Beth got pregnant every time I hung up my pants! I told her I didn't want kids."

Their conversations allowed Shannon to confront her father about those terrible years and speak her truth to him. His conversations contained not a whit of empathy or sentiment toward anyone else.

Yet those talks freed her. She saw her father, not as the monster she remembered, but a terribly flawed human being. His life had been one of endless failures, rejection, and loneliness. She pitied him, but she no longer felt shame. For better or worse, he was her father, but his sins were not her sins, his failures were not her failures.

Before long, Oscar's compulsion to drink returned, and the nursing home complained about his behavior. Then one day, the facility called to say that Oscar had left and hadn't come back.

A few weeks later, Shannon received a call from a Houston hospital saying her father was there. Now in her ninth month, she visited Oscar in the hospital. "Dad, if you'll agree to get help and stop drinking, you can be part of our family. But if you don't, then I'll walk out this door and have nothing more to do with you."

Oscar told her he had a friend who would let him live at his place, and gave her the address. "I won't go back to that nursing home," he said. "I just can't be locked up."

Shannon turned her back on her father, walked out of the room, and never saw him again.

Shannon's second son was born, and she named him Nathan. The birth was almost identical to Gabriel's, yet there was a tremendous difference. Shannon, of course, loved her little boy, but the delivery was overshadowed by sadness that Graeme wasn't there and that her son would never know his father.

Alex and Beth surrounded Shannon and put on happy faces to welcome the new infant. Still, Shannon fell into a depression that cut into the joy a new mother should feel. Her body knew it, too; her milk dried up after a few weeks, and the baby had to be bottle-fed.

Beth helped Shannon heal and get back on her feet. When Shannon was curled in a fetal position for days at a time, Beth took charge. Alex took Gabriel in tow while Beth took on the night shifts.

Alex had never seen her stepmother be anything but a rock, and Shannon's weakened state was a shock. She became a surrogate mother for Nathan. Between Alex and Beth, they provided the strength that Shannon didn't have it. They got Gabriel off to school and made sure the family was fed, including Shannon, who would not have eaten without Beth's insistence.

During the day, Beth put Nathan in the bed with Shannon so the baby would know his mother and to help Shannon out of the dark corner where she had retreated. Despite everything, Nathan thrived; and in time, Shannon came around.

When the baby was six weeks old, Shannon answered a knock on her door to find two uniformed police officers standing on her porch.

"Mrs. Shannon Thorne?" one said.

"Yes?" Shannon said, sucking in a giant breath, memories racing through her of that day officers delivered the tragic news of Graeme's death.

"We are sorry to inform you, but your father has passed away.

His body was found in an old shack somewhere in Houston, and he apparently died of heat exposure and a heart attack. He had no identification on him, just this birth announcement from you, and that's how we were able to find you."

The police handed Shannon the few possessions found on her father's body. Gabriel's birth announcement was still in the envelope with her return address in the corner. A worn newspaper article featured a photo of a pretty blond woman where Oscar had drawn a circle around the image and scrawled, "My daughter, Shannon."

Shannon reflected on the miracle that had occurred. Finding her emaciated father in the back of a junked car after decades of living on the streets. Spending time with him, sober, and talking about those years when they were a family. Losing him again to the streets but finding him through her baby's birth announcement. Death and life, connected, a miracle.

Oscar was no longer lost and alone. Shannon arranged for his remains to be brought home, cremated, and laid to rest next to his mother and father in the family plot, burying the last of her bitterness along with his ashes.

In a cruel irony, Beth's health went into a steep decline not long after Oscar's death. Beth's husband called Shannon to say she had suffered a severe heart attack.

Unknown until now, x-rays revealed that Beth's heart had suffered damage in her youth, perhaps from rheumatic fever. The cardiologist diagnosed chronic heart failure. "There's no cure for it. The heart will continue to weaken until another attack, or the heart just stops beating."

As Beth's condition worsened, she lost strength and was unable to get around unaided. Shannon, the grandchildren, and Beth's husband surrounded her with love and attention.

On Easter Sunday, Shannon spent the day with her mother, helping Beth to the couch where they sat and talked. At one point, Shannon put her head in Beth's lap, hugging her mother's knees, crying, while Beth stroked her hair.

"I'm not ready, Mom. We've found each other again, and I want more of you. I'm not ready for you to go."

Beth crawled into to her bed and stayed there. Family and friends came one at a time and said goodbye.

"I'm ready to go," she said to Shannon. "Take care of the little ones."

With her last breath, she said, "I love you." Then she was gone.

* * *

Back to Work

GABRIEL SETTLED WELL enough in the Texas elementary school near their rented house, the same school as Cece. With Cece's help, he gradually returned to his former self.

Alex resumed college at Skidmore University in Upstate New York, where she was enrolled in a dual degree program studying Business and International Affairs.

Shannon spent Nathan's first year at home with him and welcomed Gabriel when he got home from school. She felt it was vital for the three of them to stick close, to take their time, and find a way forward.

When Nathan turned two, Shannon faced the reality that she had to go back to work.

"I've got to find a way to earn enough to support these two boys and make sure they go to whatever university they choose. Alex has a long way to go, with her hopes set on law school. That won't be cheap, and Graeme's money isn't going to stretch that far."

She put out feelers to see what might be possible.

* * *

SHANNON SAT IN THE Dallas executive offices of a former employer from earlier career days.

"I'm glad you reached out, Shannon," said Ivan Hart. "We just might have something to talk about."

"You were at the top of my list when I started my job search," Shannon said.

"Well, you helped save one of my failing companies from bankruptcy. I appreciated your initiative, and I'm glad we stayed in touch over the years."

"Ivan, my life is quite different from the last time I worked for you," Shannon said. "I'm a widow now with three children, one just off to college and two young boys. I'm their sole support, and I've got to find something that allows me to earn a good income, yet still be able to raise my children."

"Yes, I know about Graeme's death, and I was sad to hear it."

"Thank you. I remember your card, which I appreciated."

"I knew Graeme. He was highly regarded in the tennis world," Ivan said, "and later in his career, well-respected as a businessman. He distinguished himself as an eloquent and intelligent spokesman for the growth of the tennis business. His views outside tennis mattered as well, like the political situation in South Africa." He paused. "Yes, Shannon, I'm very aware of your family situation, what's ahead of you… It won't be easy."

"I know, Ivan, but I have no other choice. When Graeme died, he left enough to provide for us for a few years, but not indefinitely. I don't want to wait until the money's gone before I start working again."

Shannon trusted Ivan. Despite the fact he was among one of the country's wealthiest businessmen, Ivan was always down to earth. He related well to other people, regardless of their economic situation.

"Let's jump in," he said. "I have an idea we might have something suitable for you. As you probably know, one of my business entities is a small hotel company, Hart Hotels. We're just in the United States right now, with eight properties so far. But I'd like to expand the brand into Europe. I think it would do well there. I've got people scouting locations now."

"Yes, I know about your hotel company, but Europe? How would I fit in, given my situation?"

"Hear me out. The company's headquarters are in New York. When I heard from you, I could see you filling an important role during a property's ramp-up years. Once we've secured a location, I see you developing the preopening plans, creating a sales and marketing approach, building the sales team, planning the grand opening events. After we open the hotel, you move on to the next one."

She nodded. "Go on."

"I understand you still have your New York house, and that's ideal because you'd have to be based there. You could work from home half of the time, attend meetings in the New York office, and travel to Europe at least a week a month, sometimes more often."

"Wow! That's quite a job description and an exciting one! Why do you think I could do this job?"

"Because I know the quality of your work. You require minimal supervision, take initiative, have a thorough approach to projects with exquisite attention to detail, you're creative and resourceful—and you're loyal. That counts for a lot in my company."

"But Ivan, I've got small children at home," said Shannon.

"That's what nannies are for, Shannon!" He pointed at her. "Look, Shannon, this job comes as close to your needs as anything you'll find. The money will be commensurate with your skills and contribution, and you know we take good care of our people. At year's end, a nice incentive is awarded based on performance. And of course, you'll have the company's insurance plan, very important for you and the children."

He shrugged. "No doubt there will be sacrifices, and it'll be hard work. You know the kind of company we are. We believe in loyalty, and we believe in family. But we all put in the time, and we all rack up the frequent flyer miles."

"How long do you visualize this position would last?"

"Our European expansion plan is projected over the next five years. We'll take things one year at a time, reviewing deals in the pipeline to see where we go the following year."

Ivan wrote some numbers on a piece of paper and passed it across his desk to Shannon. Her eyebrows shot up.

* * *

New York Without Graeme

IVAN'S FIVE-YEAR GIG flew by and stretched another three years, consuming Shannon in the aggressive European expansion. Lucky for her, the New York house was vacated before their return from Texas. Her tenants, who had purchased a home in Westchester County, left the house in immaculate condition, showing little wear and tear for the past two years.

Shannon decided to renovate anyway. She wanted to remove painful reminders of her previous life there, with Graeme. "I don't think I can live in this house again if I see Graeme in every room." She started with her bedroom—new furniture, fresh paint, new hardwood flooring. The downstairs den became her office, fully appointed with the communications technology required for the job. The boys and Alex each had their rooms, and she converted the spare room into a comfortable space for the new nanny.

The most important decision she would ever make was hiring the right person to watch over her two sons when she was away. She placed local advertisements and held lengthy phone conversations with candidates before agreeing to face-to-face interviews. Once someone scaled those hurdles, Shannon conducted extensive interviews with all their references, even checking the references' references. Using the company's resources, she had thorough background checks conducted on the final candidates.

She narrowed the search to a lovely English woman who lived not far away, a retired, married lady who needed extra income to help her two grown sons. To verify what the woman said in the interviews, Shannon drove to the woman's address, a tidy house in a very respectable neighborhood. She knocked on the door unannounced, and her husband answered the door. He welcomed Shannon into their spotless home, and invited her for tea.

"Terry, I'd like to offer you the job," Shannon said, now convinced she had vetted this lady in every way possible. "I spoke with all your references and confirmed everything you said in the interviews."

"Well, guess what? said Terry's husband. "I've visited your neighborhood as well and watched the comings and goings at your house. I wanted to be sure what kind of neighborhood you lived in and see for myself what my wife was getting into."

Later Shannon told the boys, her excitement spilling over, "You're going to have an English nanny, just like Mary Poppins!"

Her family settled and secure, Shannon threw herself into her work with the ferocity she had shown before meeting Graeme. She became two people: a driven, goal-focused executive at work and a dedicated mother at home.

Ivan's development team succeeded in securing two locations, one outside Paris and the other in The Netherlands. Her first European trip took place just over a month after moving back to the New York home.

Her approach was typical of Shannon overdrive. Before arriving at the hotel's site, she conducted thorough research of the area to learn about potential markets and competition. She developed relationships with local authorities and resources. By the time she arrived, she had meetings scheduled with advertising and public relations agencies and recruitment firms. Candidates for hire were lined up, waiting for interviews.

Shannon knew what she wanted in employees—hard work ethic, integrity, adaptability, and willingness to work with different nationalities, including Americans! During her travels with Graeme, she learned about the deeply-held prejudices from one country to the next that erupted into open hostilities.

"Two world wars did not happen in a vacuum!" she reminded herself.

Ivan established Shannon's authority "across the pond," and the male executives in Europe respected her as the "American lady with an iron fist in a velvet glove."

"That's fine by me," Shannon told herself. "I'm not here to make friends."

Shannon melded into the different cultures with no trouble—English, Spanish, French, Dutch, German—and established trust with co-workers. But huge inequalities existed between male and female workers. Shannon was keen to establish equal opportunities for women in the workforce, a novel concept in the European hospitality industry, and she was intolerant toward discriminatory practices based on gender.

"I'll have none of that under my watch," she told herself.

She mentored female employees in their confidence and self-esteem and looked for ways to promote them through the ranks. Whenever possible, she brought promising women into management roles.

On one occasion, Shannon convened a meeting of the sales teams from six different countries. Her role was to facilitate the integration of the teams into the company's culture and to observe the new head of European operations, Lars Groot, who would conduct the meeting. Lars was a tall, handsome Dutchman with an authoritative management style. Françoise Laurent, a delicate, reserved young woman Shannon had hired for the French property, was quite intimidated by Lars' aggressive manner.

About two hours into the meeting, Lars admonished the team in his loud voice, standing and pointing with forceful jabs of his finger. Françoise jumped up and left the meeting in tears.

After asking Lars to call a break in the meeting, Shannon followed Françoise to the outside patio, where she had fled.

"I quit!" Françoise stormed. "I refuse to work for that man."

Shannon talked her from the edge and assured the woman of her value to the company. Her confidence restored, Françoise agreed to return to the meeting, but not before Shannon met privately with Lars.

"That woman is an emotional weakling," barked Lars, wagging his finger in Shannon's face.

Shannon bit his finger. Hard.

"You bit me!"

"Well, Lars, if your finger had not been so close to my face, I wouldn't have been able to bite it, would I? Do you have any idea what that action means to the person on the other end of that finger?"

He crossed his arms and glared down at her.

"With your stature and loud voice, coupled with your position as her boss, it's no wonder she doesn't want to work for you. You intimidate her. But it's your job to make her feel safe and comfortable with you—not feel threatened. For you, it's easy. For her, it's hard. If you want her, or anyone else for that matter, to be successful, you've got to meet them where they are and bring them up. You owe her an apology, and I expect you to fix this."

He did.

But Lars was not a co-worker Shannon disliked. Quite the opposite.

"I hold him in high regard," she told Ivan. "He's got boundless enthusiasm, and he's a born hotelier. Properties under his management reflect the local culture, are exquisitely appointed, and offer guests impeccable service."

"If you think he can deliver the product that Hart Hotels demands, then I support your observation," Ivan said. "We're going to put him in place to run our new property in Germany."

However, when Lars was appointed the transitional general manager at the German hotel, huge problems developed. Reports filtered to the home office about high employee turnover, dislike for the manager, a threatened strike, even sabotage.

"We're sending you to evaluate the situation and resolve it," Ivan said.

Shannon met with senior and mid-level managers, even with the front office, restaurant, and housekeeping staff. She soon sorted out three bad apples were conspiring to get the Dutch interloper fired and bring back their former German manager.

"I found out what's happened" she reported to Ivan by phone. "There are a few workers here who are undermining Lars, gossiping about him, complaining about the new ownership, and spreading discontent. It's a simple case of cultural prejudice."

"What are you doing about it?"

"I fired all three of them."

Despite their protests that German laws protected employees from being fired, Ivan's lawyers determined that their behavior met the "cause" guidelines for termination, so Shannon had legal cover. She and Lars hired some new blood, and he built a robust, successful team.

Back home was a constant juggling act, managing work and raising a family, absences from home eating away at Shannon.

Charlotte visited every year, and Alex, now in law school, spent her holidays and summers at home. Alex dated but found one reason or another to break off any budding relationships.

"She's a 'mini-me,' " Shannon murmured. "Like I'm looking in a mirror."

Alex eclipsed Shannon by a good three inches. She had grown into a striking woman, tall, lithe, dark hair, so much like her father. But her personality was like Shannon's. Even Charlotte recognized it.

"Shannon, none of my dates has inspired me," Alex said. "They are such small thinkers, and if I'm going to be with a man, I want him to at least see the whole world, not just the tiny part he knows."

Shannon almost choked on her coffee when Alex told her this, recalling that same conversation with Graeme when they first met.

"In time," Shannon said. "One day, I promise, it will happen, as it did for me. Just hold true to yourself, and don't be pressured to be or do anything that isn't what you want."

Shannon enrolled the boys in karate classes, baseball, and other sports that offered male role models.

"The boys can't grow up surrounded only by women," Shannon told the nanny.

Nathan differed from Gabriel, who had the advantage of knowing his father for the first ten years of his life. Nathan lacked Gabriel's confidence. He worked hard at pleasing everyone and tried to live up to what he thought others expected of him. Nathan was sensitive and caring. His teachers placed him with rowdy students for the calming influence he had on other students.

One evening Shannon overheard Gabriel and Nathan talking about their father.

"What was Dad really like?" Nathan said.

Gabriel was silent a moment. "Dad was kind to everyone he met. Not just important people, but ordinary people as well. Cab drivers, the garbage man, neighbors."

He looked up, staring at nothing, remembering and choosing his words. "Dad was a kid at heart and joked around a lot. He taught the neighbor kids to play tennis, and coached my little league team. He travelled a lot, but you could tell, he liked being home with his family most."

"What did he think about Mom having another baby?"

"I was the one who told him! We were sitting around the table. Mom was building up to telling him she was pregnant when I just shouted it out! Dad was so excited."

Shannon was gratified to witness an undeniable love between them and a big brother tone from Gabriel, as if to say, "Don't worry, Nathan. I've got your back."

Terry confided to Shannon that Nathan retreated to his room when she was away on her trips and seemed depressed.

"How long can I continue this pace and this work?" Shannon wondered. "I'm doing everything I can to provide for the boys and ensure their future, but I'm missing so much."

She liked the generous income her job provided, and the healthy year-end incentives went straight into college funds that were building up nicely.

"It's the long game I've got to keep my eyes on, and we have to make sacrifices to get there."

IV. LEGACY

Charlotte confided to Shannon that conditions were the worst they'd ever been in South Africa. A desperate President Botha enacted his 1985 State of Emergency Act. No persons of color could mix—white, black, Asian, Indian. All press was censored. Freedom of speech was nonexistent. Police watched everyone. Suspicions of sedition meant incarceration without trial.

"Shannon, even Max admits that Botha has gone too far. The whites have had enough, and the mood in the country is that both races need each other."

"Here in the U.S.," Shannon told Charlotte, "we're reading that the economic sanctions are responsible for devaluing your Rand and the cause of your double-digit inflation. Bit by bit, the South African government is being strangled. Surely, Botha can't hold on much longer."

At long last, in 1986, Shannon read the welcome headlines: "Botha resigns and his repressive government has collapsed."

With his resignation, apartheid began to unwind from the country's soul. F. W. de Klerk was elected president, a moderate with plans to unravel the apartheid laws and bring the races together, to end the hostilities, and to reinstate rights to blacks. Soon, South African ex-pats returned and visited families for the first time in many years, or reclaimed their abandoned homes.

After a decade of violent upheaval, civil unrest, police brutality, and a crushed economy, the country as a whole, white and black, was ready to accept change and face an uncertain future.

"How will these changes affect Graeme's family?" Shannon wondered.

* * *

A New South Africa

SHANNON THOUGHT THAT maybe the time had come to take the children to South Africa and see where their father was born and raised. Neither Gabriel nor Nathan had been to South Africa, and Alex had not been back since she was eight years old. She discussed it with Max and Charlotte.

"Yes. We think it's safe for you to travel here now. Visitors, including Americans, are returning and free to move about."

They made their plans for the kids' summer break. Shannon's business was in a lull, and Alex took a leave of absence from her clerking job at a New York law firm.

Max, Charlotte, and Lucas greeted them at the airport, after arriving in their spacious Range Rovers big enough for all of them and their luggage. Lucas brought along two of his grown children to reconnect with Alex. Shannon was determined to be on her best behavior and not let either Max or Lucas provoke her. Still, she was relieved not to ride to Thornside with Lucas.

Max and Charlotte lavished attention on Gabriel and young Nathan, eager to show their grandchildren around Thorneside. Alex felt at home right away and rushed straight upstairs to her old bedroom, finding everything as she had left it.

Charlotte planned an elaborate dinner on the terrace for the whole family. Lucas, Dexter, Jude, their wives, and their children joined them, and Shannon was delighted to meet the new ones born since her last visit. All told, they numbered twenty-three with the last name, Thorne—minus one.

Graeme's absence sliced through them all, especially Shannon and Charlotte. Conversation tiptoed around his death, but when the brothers reminisced about their childhood days, growing up at Thorneside, Shannon could sense that Graeme was in their thoughts.

Gabriel's curiosity about his father was insatiable, listening whenever his uncles mentioned Graeme, and he bombarded them with questions. Nathan was quiet, absorbing stories about the father he never knew.

The next day Max and Charlotte loaded their daughter-in-law and three grandchildren into their car to tour Thorneside, with Max giving his best tour guide spiel.

"He's not given up the fight," Shannon thought. "He's hoping for a convert still, if not from Graeme, then maybe one of his children."

Fourteen years had passed since Shannon's last visit to Thorneside. Things were different as they drove through the farm. She remembered the farm being in spotless condition, maintained by workers everywhere she looked. But with many fewer workers now, the farming equipment sat idle in the barns instead of working in the fields.

From Max's monologue, nothing had changed, and everything was still in his complete control. Some dormant fields were "resting," he said. "We rotate crops every seventh year so that fields are not overworked and the earth can regenerate itself."

"Wow!" said Gabriel. "You own all of this, Gramps?"

"Yes, Thorneside covers some 10,000 acres,"

Rising early while the house still slept, Shannon embarked on a walk, retracing the path she took on her first visit. She walked straight to the barns, where a white man directed the black workers. The men stopped and looked at her with curiosity, especially the Boer manager. They exchanged polite nods, and she continued her walk toward Joseph's hut, the farm manager when she was last here. There he was, sitting outside his hut, white-headed now with grandchildren scurrying about, enjoying the sunrise with a mug of hot Rooibos tea.

"Joseph, do you remember me? My name's Shannon. I was married to Graeme."

"Of course I 'member you, Miz Shannon. I'm happy to see you again, and so sorry about your husband's death. We were very fond of Mr. Graeme. He was a kind man."

"Thank you. Yes, Graeme was a remarkable human being. We had two sons together, and of course, Alex is with me. I've been raising all three of Graeme's children. We're living in New York now."

"I'm glad you took that young girl to America. This country is a hard place for young people, especially young women, white or black."

"How are things now, Joseph? When I was here last, the Soweto massacre had just happened."

"Let's go inside and talk, Miz Shannon. It wouldn't help for the Boss Man to see us talking. I'll make you a cup of Rooibos. I have a few minutes before I report to work."

"Are you still manager of the farm?" Shannon said as she held her steaming mug.

"No, no. Just a field worker, although the Boss expects me to keep everyone in line when we're working. That's why he still lets me live here. Mr. Max don't trust us blacks to be in charge. A lot of workers left for the bigger cities to get involved in the movement, including my two boys. The only ones left around here are the older folks like me and the married ones with kids."

"That means a lot of work for you, doesn't it?"

Joseph nodded. "There's more work here than those of us left can do, but Mr. Max don't let no one on his property he don't know. There was some trouble at one or two farms. Some blacks burned farmhouses and run the whites off. The police rounded up every black man in the area, and their families never heard from them again."

"That's awful."

"We're being very careful and trying to stay out of trouble."

"Just in case you don't know," Shannon whispered, "the world is applauding the changes happening."

"Things are changing, Miz Shannon, finally! Even inside the country, many whites are against the old laws. We don't have to carry pass cards no more, and our children get a better education. The whites realize they need us as much as we need them, and if they want their houses cleaned and their crops tended, they know they have to pay us and let us move about free."

"Those are good changes. Long overdue."

"But, Miz Shannon, we'd best stop talking now. I don't want to start trouble for you or me, and I must get to work now."

"I'll go, Joseph. Thank you for the tea and for talking with me. Good luck. I'm praying for you, your people, and your country to at last put this whole nightmare behind you."

"We're close, Miz Shannon. Everyone can see the end coming, and I just hope I live long enough to see it."

Max let Gabriel and Nathan drive his tractors and even his Land Rover on their private roads. He took Alex fishing in the same creek she had loved as a child, catching enough fish for supper. In the evenings, he was calm, drinking in moderation, and muted in his conversations.

One night Max took advantage of a quiet, private moment when Shannon stood on the terrace, watching the sun set and sipping a brandy.

"Shannon, I have some things I need to say to you... Must say to you."

He paused. "I loved Graeme, too. We fought all the time. He was determined to go his own separate way and wanted nothing to do with the legacy I'm trying to leave to my sons and grandchildren. It broke my heart, but I know I hurt him, too. I miss him, and I am sorry he's gone and for your loss, yours and the kids."

Max lowered his head. "You're doing a fantastic job with them, and I admire you for it. Even taking in Alex the way you have, it's clear she looks to you as the mother she never had."

Shannon stared at him and said nothing.

"I told Graeme I was taking him out of my will," he said, now looking at Shannon, "but his share of Thorneside will be passed to his children when I die."

He leaned on the railing and stared into the distance. "You've also provided Charlotte a safe place where she can visit outside the farm. When she returns, she's lighter somehow, happier, and our lives have been easier. The truth is we're closer than we've been our entire marriage. She's more confident, more outspoken. More than once, she's taken me down a few notches and didn't bat an eye."

He shook his head. "I didn't know she had it in her. You helped her find that strength. We're more like partners now, equals. And that works just fine for me."

Max took both of Shannon's hands in his. "I'm grateful to you, Shannon."

She tilted her head to one side and gave him a sad smile. "If only Graeme could have heard you say those words. He so wanted your love and your approval. But thank you for saying it to me. It means a lot."

She slid her hands from his grasp. " I couldn't have been your first choice as a wife for your son, someone from thousands of miles away and with strong opinions so contrary to your own. I loved Graeme with all my heart, and his kids are all I have left of him. As long as I have his children, I'll always have Graeme with me."

Thorneside Farms Winery

Shannon couldn't sleep that night. She spent hours sitting on the same window box overlooking the vineyard, reminded of that sleepless night a lifetime ago when her instincts screamed at her to write about the Soweto massacre, and her husband begged her to squelch those impulses for the safety of his family.

She sat here again, hearing voices from her past.

"Let South Africans solve the problems of South Africa."

"Change takes time, and the unwise are impatient for change. Yet that impatience matters not a bit. Change comes in its own time."

And now a new echo: "…the legacy I'm trying to leave my sons and grandchildren."

When she settled back into her bed, her head was clear. She must talk to her father-in-law first thing in the morning.

Shannon was up early, dressed and waiting in the kitchen, mugs of hot coffee poured.

"Max, may I join you on your rounds this morning? I want to talk with you… privately."

"That sounds ominous, Shannon."

She imagined the hairs on his skin must be standing on end, his defense responses at the ready.

"I said everything last night, and it was one of the hardest things I've ever done."

"It's because of what you said, Max. Please, it's not an ambush. I have no harsh words in me. It's just a crazy idea that for some reason seems possible to me, even in the cold light of day."

"Okay. Let's take our coffee with us and get started. I have a full day ahead. What about the rest of the family?"

"I left a note for Alex to look after Nathan and Gabriel while I'm with you."

As Max's noisy work truck started down the gravel drive, Shannon jumped right in. "Max, something you said hit me like a ton of bricks. You talked about the legacy you're trying to build and leave for your sons and grandchildren. When Graeme and I were here fourteen years ago, you wanted so badly for him to settle here and build a house on land you had set aside for him."

Max nodded as he steered around ruts in the road.

"Is that land still available?"

"Yes, it is," said Max. "I never had the heart to do anything else with it. I've always thought of it as Graeme's, and I guess I just wanted to preserve it for some reason, maybe for his kids one day."

"Max, here's the idea I had last night. I haven't discussed it yet with anyone else, because you're the person to talk to first. Look, I know you and I are worlds apart on so many things, especially the politics here in South Africa. But besides your son, another wise person in my life told me that change takes time and that South Africans are the ones who must change things in South Africa."

He glanced at her, his curiosity aroused.

"I see two huge changes here, right now. One, can you tell me, is apartheid really on its way out? Is your country going to bring the races together? I've got to have your honest opinion about that."

He didn't answer.

"The second change I see is sitting right here beside me. You're not the same Max. You're more tolerant, even kinder than I remember. You're amazing with the children, and I even see how you are different with Charlotte. You're gentler and, I could even go so far to say, more considerate. Your words last night were words of a humbled man."

"A lot has changed, Shannon," said Max. "Losing Graeme was

a gutshot, I don't mind telling you. All I could see were the years we fought and the last conversations we had. Graeme and I both said terrible things to each other, and I regret every mean-spirited thing I uttered. I realize now I drove him away. Because he didn't want to stay here and farm with his brothers and me, I turned my back on him."

"Yes, you did."

"Graeme's death made me realize how easily I could lose Charlotte, too. She's a wonderful wife and mother. You know that. But I've never been the husband she deserves. If I lost her...." Max's voice thickened as his throat tightened and tears welled in his eyes.

"I decided that with the time I have left in this life, I'm going to treat my wife the way she deserves. Hell, I'm going to try to treat everyone the way they deserve, even the blacks! I saw the bully I became, especially to Charlotte and Graeme, and I want nothing more to do with that man."

"I see that change. It's astonishing to see."

"As far as what's happening in the country, Shannon, it's beyond me. This race business—apartheid—it's all I've ever known, how I've lived, my father before me and his before him. But even I didn't want it to go as far as it did. We just let it happen because, as whites, we had the better end of the stick."

He gestured toward the empty pastures. "But, heck, I've had great workers here for years. Take Joseph, for example. I need him. Depend on him. But these politics have just gotten in the way of everything. We can't even talk to each other without suspicion and distrust. I'm ready for it to be over, whatever happens next. It can't be worse than what we've had the past ten years."

"Max, here's my idea, and please be honest with me about what you think." She paused. "I've lost those closest to me, except my children. I lost my husband, who was the most wonderful man I've ever known. Recently both my mother and father died. Thank God, I have three beautiful children, but without their father, I'm on my own again, the way I was when I met Graeme."

"You're one tough lady, that's for certain."

"I have a job, a great job, that pays me well and allows me to set aside money for the boys' educations. But it forces me to be away from the kids too much. The price we are paying for my job is very high."

"So what do you want to do?"

"What if we took that land, built a house on it, and made a home here?"

Max's bushy eyebrows shot up as he twisted to face her.

"You just knew me as a journalist. But I have a head for business and marketing, and I'm so organized that I drive everyone around me crazy."

"I can just picture that," he said with a snicker.

"My idea is that, with your help, I will develop Thorneside Farms Winery!"

Max's jaw dropped. "You? How…. What…"

"It's what you wanted Graeme to do. What if his wife does it instead? With his daughter, Alex. We'll need a good corporate lawyer, and, look, we now have a lawyer in the family! I'm confident Alex can get licensed to practice here in South Africa, and she might love to come back. To come home."

"To come home," Max echoed.

"With your help, I'd build the winery here at Thorneside, complete with a wine-tasting room open to the public. Graeme and I visited many of them, and he imagined one here. I'm antsy to work on something I'm passionate about, something for the kids and me. I could do this, Max, and it would connect the kids, all three of them, to you and Charlotte and their part of the heritage you want to leave your grandchildren."

"That's an incredible vision, Shannon."

"We'd have to work out lots of details, of course. The political differences, for one, will require us both to set some pretty strong boundaries. I'm thinking more about Lucas than anyone. And I'm still the opinionated, liberal woman from the U.S. that you and Lucas detested. For this to work, we'd all need to agree to respect each other's differences."

Max pulled his truck over to the side of the roadway and sat in silence.

"Say something, Max. Anything," Shannon said.

"Like you," he whispered, "I never had a thought even close to what you've just described. The distance, our dislike for one another, even just the safety for Americans in this country. I resolved that I'd probably never see any of you again."

He let go of the steering wheel. "But what you've described, Shannon…. I can see it. It fits. Despite our differences, I've always known you were smarter than a tree full of owls. I have no doubt you'd be successful at this. And to have my grandchildren here, Alex back, making a home on Graeme's land…."

This time he didn't even try to hold back the tears. He wept for the son he lost and for the hope of his son's family making a home on the farm and being a part of the Thorneside legacy that was so important to him. He wrapped Shannon in a big bear hug, his work-hardened hands gripping her shoulders as he released feelings he'd held back for years.

"I don't know how we resolve everything, only that we will, as long as you and I have the same vision. I'll handle my boys, and don't worry about Lucas. I'll keep him in line. Whites here have learned to eat some humble pie. We just have to practice new ways. It won't be easy, but nothing worthwhile ever is."

He grinned at her. "What was it your friend said? 'Change takes time?' Then let's not waste any more of it. I'm on board, Shannon. 100%!"

* * *

"MOVE BACK TO the farm?" Alex said, gasping at the suggestion. "I thought you hated it here, and hated Gramps, too!"

"So much has changed, Alex," Shannon said. "The politics. Your grandfather. Until now, it wouldn't even be possible for us to consider moving here. But Botha is out. A new government is committed to ending conflicts between the races. There's no going back. South Africa is on the threshold of an exciting, new future."

"What about Gramps?"

"As for Max, I admit I couldn't stand being in the same room with him. But he has changed so much. I just wish your father could see him now, sit with him and talk with him, about all that stood between them as father and son."

"But Africa? C'mon, Shannon. You love Texas, and you love New York."

"I love Africa, too! I've fantasized and imagined Africa all my life, and each time I've come here, I love it even more. It's a land where, for some strange reason, I feel at home, as if I belong here."

"But what about your differences with Gramps and Lucas and how women are treated? Everything you stand for, in fact?"

"I've mellowed, Alex. I'm not that naïve, self-righteous, judgmental girl I was fourteen years ago."

Alex stared at her.

"Here's my idea, Alex. We—you and I—build the winery using Thorneside grapes, label it, and sell it throughout the country. In time, even export it. With the contacts Graeme and I made over the years, we can put together the right people to help us do this."

"You and I? You, maybe. But where do I fit in?"

"You'd be our corporate attorney. We're going to need one to build the wine business and our brand."

"Even if my U.S. license was accepted, I'd have to go to university here and get a South African law degree. With apartheid laws being rescinded and so many new laws replacing them, things must be a mess. I'd need to know the laws inside and out, and be prepared to confront the old establishment here who, I'm sure, won't welcome us with open arms."

Shannon gripped her daughter's arm. "Excellent thinking, Alex. We'll build a legacy in your father's name, here at Thorneside, that is the birthright for you and your brothers. Rather than you and me struggling in some job or business in the U.S., why not invest our efforts right here, in land we own and a future that belongs to us?"

"Shannon, you've left out one small detail. We don't know the first thing about making wine!"

"Not yet. But we'll learn! While you're getting your South African law license, I'll go to wine school! Before we dare break ground, we'll have the most knowledgeable people helping us. I'm confident we can find a vintner who will make fabulous Thorneside Farms wines." She waited. "What do you say?"

"It is exciting, Shannon. I admit the idea of moving back to the farm, being close to Gram and Gramps again... I love the idea. And it would be wonderful to build something in memory of Dad, something that will last. I say, 'let's do it!' Where do we start?"

* * *

It Fits

THAT START WAS a family meeting with Max and Charlotte, Shannon, Alex, Gabriel, and Nathan. Shannon outlined her vision for them to live at Thorneside and develop the winery. Max confirmed the land held for Graeme was still available and assured everyone the site was more than adequate.

"Since it's near the road, it will be easy to build an access drive to the property," Max said. "The tract is sizable enough for what Shannon thinks the winery will need without infringing on your private home. Plenty of space. It can work."

"This is a good idea for so many reasons," Alex chimed in. "For me, of course, it's coming home and being with Gram and Gramps again and all the other family. But I like the idea of building something in memory of my father, so Gabriel and Nathan will have a real sense of what he meant to all of us. I don't know everything that has to happen, but as Shannon and Gramps said, it fits for us to do this."

"Shannon, are you sure?" said Charlotte. "I mean, I would love it for myself and Max. But this is a lifetime decision. It's not something you can undo in a few years and go back to the U.S. without losing everything you've invested here."

"You're right, Charlotte. I must think through all the implications and what it will require. If we are agreed, my next step is talking to Greg, Graeme's business partner. He's experienced in international business. Look at all he and Graeme were involved with before Graeme's death. If he can't answer our questions, then he will know who can."

"That's a reasonable next move," said Charlotte.

"I've got to make sure it pencils out before making the decision. I've done many business plans in my career, so it will be second nature for me to put a plan together."

"Charlotte is right, Shannon," Max said. "This shouldn't be a quick decision on your part. It might be impossible to reverse it. The wine-making process itself is a long-term deal. Even after you do all the production steps, the aging process means it will be years before you can open a single bottle. It's one of the reasons I never pursued it."

"You're both right. Nathan will be in high school before we uncork the first bottle. We'd always face the risk of the whole enterprise failing, and I must be very thorough in determining if this is the right decision for us. I mean, it's our lives!"

"But the opportunities are real, aren't they?" said Charlotte.

Shannon smiled at her mother-in-law. "The best advantage is the vineyards are already mature and producing wine-quality grapes, and we have the site and location."

"The downside," said Max, "is it could be years before the business yields a return."

"But let's look at the alternative," said Shannon. "My job in the States requires me to be away from the family too much, and though I'm making good money, it's not a long-term future for us. To me, it seems the long-term investment here is more promising than what I can accomplish there."

She turned to face her father-in-law. "Max, can you put together the costs for building our house? I'll provide some design specifications. I hope what we get from selling the New York house will cover construction costs. Graeme told me they are considerably less here."

"We built this house and Lucas' and Dexter's," Max said, "not to mention all the farm's structures. We have a pretty good handle on the construction part. What are you thinking in terms of timing, Shannon?"

"After talking to Greg on the feasibility of this plan, I need to understand what's involved in getting passports and residency permits for us. I'm assuming Alex is considered a South African citizen still, so no issue there. With Gabriel just graduated from high school, he'll be entering university soon, too."

"What about you?" said Charlotte.

"It will take me some time to do my side of things. I need to spend some time in Europe, visit vineyards there, learn the steps in converting grapes into delicious wines carrying the Thorneside Farms label. And search for the right vintner! That person is the key. Without a vintner to move here and oversee the wine production, it's a nonstarter."

Shannon paused as she looked from face to face. "Gabriel, we haven't heard from you. What do you think about this?"

"I like being close to Gram and Gramps, and in a way, close to Dad," Gabriel said. "We don't really have family there since Grandma Beth died. But, Mom, what about Helen and Cece?"

"I know, Gabriel," Shannon said. "Leaving Helen and Cece is the worst part of my plan, and it will knock a big hole in our lives to put such distance between us."

"Alex, can you get more time off from your job? How do you feel about a road trip?"

"I'm just a lowly law clerk, Shannon," said Alex, "and the menial tasks I do certainly aren't mission-critical. That said, I also don't have privileges and perks, and I'm afraid if I ask for the extra time, they'll tell me to take all the time I want—and be unemployed by them! So, for me, it would be a decision to resign and commit to our new plan. It's a much bigger decision for you, since you're the breadwinner for the family."

"You're right. I'll call Greg in the morning." Then Shannon frowned. "Max, I've got to talk to Lucas before taking another step. He and I must have a frank conversation with one another."

"Let me talk to him first thing in the morning," Max said, "when we're in the fields together. Maybe you and he can go to dinner together tomorrow night. Trelwyn now has several. nice restaurants since you were here last.

* * *

"LUCAS, MAX SAYS you two had a thorough conversation about the idea of the kids and me moving to South Africa," Shannon said. "What do you think about me, with your help, developing the Thorneside Farms wine business?"

They had placed their order and were nursing their beverages, Shannon sipping her lemonade and Lucas a cold tap beer.

"You're biting off more than you can chew, Shannon, and I told Dad so. He's all excited about the possibility of you and the kids moving here, taking an interest in the farm. So is Mom. But can it work? I doubt it."

"Why not?"

"You're doing this on your own; Graeme isn't here to help. You and Alex? Come on! Neither of you has wine-making experience, and two women trying to establish a wine business in South Africa is ludicrous."

"What makes you say that?"

"Because it's a tough business. Lots of competition. I know these guys. They're my customers, and I see them all the time. They buy my grapes. They're years ahead of you with established processes and labels. They'll eat you alive."

"Because we're women?" she said, fighting her impulse to take the bait and jump into a war of words.

"Well, yes, to be perfectly honest. Look, I'd love for it to work. If Graeme were sitting here talking to me about it, I'd jump at it. I've wanted to get into the wine business for years but just haven't had the time or resources to do it on my own. But you? You're not even South African! And Alex is just out of law school. She's just a kid with no experience."

"Lucas, I'm glad you're honest with me, though I suspect Max asked you to be supportive. Your reasons are why I wanted us to talk, just the two of us."

Shannon set down her glass and sat up straighter. "All my life and my career, men have told me what I could and could not do because it's a man's world and women aren't capable or strong enough. Time and again, I proved them wrong. Once I commit to something, however, I do whatever is necessary to get it done. Graeme knew this about me but loved me anyway. In fact, my aggressiveness and determination amused him, and he wasn't intimidated by it at all."

Lucas sat back, crossed his arms across his chest, his face stern.

"I'm going to take some time, some intense deliberation before making this decision. Once I do, if I do, nothing will stop me." She paused. "But I can't do it without your help, and I won't do it unless you and I respect our differences and give each other the space to be ourselves."

Squaring her shoulders, Shannon got to the point. "Lucas, you will not be my boss, and you cannot bully me. We cannot repeat those horrible confrontations that happened when Graeme brought me here fourteen years ago."

He stared at her, redness creeping up his neck.

"All that said, I'm not the same naïve girl I was then, and my rough edges have softened a bit. We don't have to agree with one another or believe in the same things. I fully intend to respect your views, and I expect you to respect mine."

She tightened her right hand into a fist. "But I will not change who I am to conform to your notion of womanhood or who you think I should or should not be."

Then she tamped down the adrenaline coursing through her. "You and I need each other to make the wine business successful. I need your grapes, your know-how, your relationships. The wine will carry your family name, and our success will benefit every member of this family." She paused again. "Are we on the same page?"

"Not yet," Lucas growled. "I'm not even sure how our family going into the wine production business will affect our current customers. We will compete with them, so potentially this could hurt our family business instead of helping it."

"That's a good point," Shannon said, "and I'm sure you thought of that all these years you've wanted to start a winery. What concerns you now that didn't before?"

"I just saw it then as an extension of what we did and not a threat," Lucas said.

"So, what's different? Because it's me doing it? Or a woman doing it? Instead of you or a Thorne son?"

"Something like that," he said.

"Are you capable of accepting the working relationship I've described? I can be a great partner or an annoying adversary," Shannon said. "I won't make this decision and invest all our savings and my children's futures unless you and I have an understanding. The winery will be my deal, and I will not tolerate interference or bullying from you."

"A woman has never talked this way to me before, Shannon, and I don't like it one bit! The tips of his ears reddened. "Do you expect me not to have an opinion or voice in it?" he said, his words turning harsh, combative.

"Not at all. Max and I discussed a plan to set up a board of directors among family members who will have a voice in the business's success. But there is a professional, appropriate way to express that voice, not through interference and second-guessing."

Lucas' face now turned beet red. "You come here with your American know-it-all, your Western solutions for our country, spouting all feminist and anti-racist crap—hell, you're not even really family, not anymore. You made it clear over the years how much you dislike me and my father and our beliefs. Now you want to move in here, take over a part of our business, our name! How do you think I feel?" he snarled. "I don't know if I can change how I feel or even if I want to. Graeme and I disagreed on just about everything, but at least he was blood."

Then, after regaining control, he added, "I just need time to think about this."

"Fine. I understand that, Lucas. At least we've taken the first step to be bone honest with each other. I must do what I think is right for my children and me, for Graeme's children. Neither one of us will be happy starting this venture if we cross swords at every turn. I've said what I require to have a cordial working relationship."

"My God, you are tedious!" Lucas barked, unable to hold back any longer. "Don't you get exhausted carrying that huge chip on your shoulder? Saint Shannon. Self-Righteous Shannon. Judge Shannon. You honestly think, like all Americans, you have the answers to everyone's problems, don't you, including us ignorant, brutish South Africans? Do you hate all men, Shannon? Especially us white South African men? Do you ever put yourself in anyone else's shoes? If you would just come down off your high horse and, as you say, meet us where we are, then maybe you'd understand why things are done the way they are here."

"Wow!" said Shannon, leaning back in her chair. "You've certainly given me an earful."

Pausing a bit, Lucas took some deep breaths. Shannon could detect his struggle to compose himself.

"I always have to protect my backside when I'm around you. I have to defend my way of life and my beliefs, even my manhood."

Shannon bit her tongue and kept silent.

"We've been through hell here the past ten years, Shannon, and we've seen everything we've known completely flipped on its ass. Things have to change, because this separation of the races has gone too far. I mean, my God, they outnumber us ten-to-one, yet we're trying to control every aspect of their lives. We can't run this farm without the blacks."

Lucas then spoke in a conciliatory tone she had never heard from him before. "I'm coming around, Shannon. But Rome wasn't built in a day, and I don't want you to shove it in my face every time we talk."

"Lucas, there's truth in what you say about me. Graeme and a dear friend of mine back in the States often reminded me of the same blind spots."

When he opened his mouth to speak, she held up her palm. "Not in those words, of course, but the message is the same. It's been a long time since anyone has taken me down like that, at least not since Graeme died. I promise to reflect on what you've said, and I appreciate your honesty."

"I need to think, too, Shannon," Lucas said in a much calmer tone. "I might have some conditions of my own, but they won't be unreasonable."

* * *

THE FOLLOWING DAY Max and Lucas were waiting for Shannon to come downstairs and join them for coffee on the terrace.

Lucas started. "Shannon, I'm not the same person I was either. The last ten years have been tough on all of us in South Africa, and the whites especially have had to accept change or lose everything. Things are going to be different, whether we like it or not."

He glanced at his father. "Mom and Dad want this to work. Even I do. I mean, there's no reason Thorneside shouldn't have a wine lable; we've been saying that for years. And if we are frank with each other, if you don't do it, Shannon, probably no one will."

"Does that mean—"

"I'm willing to do my part." He heaved a great sigh. "Hell, I don't want to bully anybody. It's just my manner is too gruff sometimes. I learned it from the best, by the way." He cast a glance at his father. "But the 'rules of engagement' as you Yanks like to call them, are okay with me. As long as the family has a voice and share in the success, I agree. After all, as you said, it's our land, our grapes, and our name. I won't be a silent partner, but I will be a civil one. Can you live with that?"

"Yes, I can, Lucas." Shannon said, nodding as she stared into space. "No one could ask more of you. And perhaps, once we're into the thick of it, we'll work together as a team. Who knows? Miracles do happen. Look, the way I see it, we want the same thing, and we are family after all—even me."

* * *

SHANNON PHONED GREG to outline the winery scheme.

"What you're talking about is pretty daunting," Greg said. "What do you want from me?"

"Greg, I need your help to tell us the pitfalls, what to look for, what to avoid. And I want you to introduce us to Europeans you and Graeme met in the wine business and people in South Africa who can help us."

"I can see why you think it's a good idea because it does fit, in many respects. My first reaction is it will take a lot of money to get it started, and you won't see a penny for a long time. That doesn't mean it can't work, just that there are lots of risks."

He was silent a few moments. "Give me a few days to think about it. In the meantime, I'll contact a good friend who owns a vineyard in France. Through the years, Graeme and I put away enough of his wine to bankroll a winery! I'll set up a meeting. I'm sure he will share what he knows. You and Alex get yourselves to Provence."

Shannon and Alex flew to Marseilles. They rented a sporty

convertible for the two-hour drive through the magnificent Provençale countryside. Shannon remembered the area's beauty from her honeymoon cruise years before, but now she saw rural France up close.

"No wonder Cézanne and Van Gogh were so inspired by this place, It's beautiful," said Alex.

The majestic Provence Alps spilled into the hilly terrain leading to a coastline dotted with seaside villages with endless vistas of vineyards interspersed with lush fields of lavender and sunflowers. In the distance stood palatial villas nestled among olive orchards and the mountainside fortresses of Le Castellet and La Cadiere, built centuries ago to repel Nordic invaders.

Their journey ended when a discreet sign signaled the entrance to Lavande sur Mer, and Shannon turned onto a narrow gravel road bordered by vineyards on both sides. The security gate opened onto a car park set among olive trees, and the footpath led to an open terrace with a breathtaking view of the golf course winnowing its way through vineyards and, on the horizon, the Mediterranean.

The hotel resembled an expansive villa with white, red, and blue stucco condominiums carved into the hillsides. Shannon and Alex were speechless, gawking like regular tourists. They stood at the terrace wall, breathing the sea air, committing the view and the moment to memory.

A waiter carrying a silver tray interrupted their reverie. He offered a glass of chilled rosé, a welcome refreshment from the Lavande vineyards.

"Welcome, madame and mademoiselle," said the waiter in his heavily-accented English. "Monsieur Moreau sends his welcome and says he will join you in the lobby after you are settled. He reserved a table in our restaurant for dinner at 8 o'clock. Will that be sufficient time for you?"

Their room offered the same views from their private terrace. The unusual bathroom featured a small circular window that swung open to the outside, inviting one and all to look out or look in!

Traditional Provençale colors on the draperies and furnishings complemented the warm terra cotta tile floors. If they hadn't been eager to see the hotel, they would have sat on their terrace and enjoyed the chilled bottle of white wine left for them from Monsieur Moreau.

Refreshed after a bath and wearing light summer dresses, Shannon and Alex strolled through the hotel, marveling at the architecture and beautiful Provençale appointments. Perfect June weather and a light sea breeze floated lovely fragrances of the countryside, including the scent of nearby lavender fields, ablaze in blue. The timing of their visit avoided the July and August hordes who jammed the French coastlines for their annual vacations.

Andre Moreau, their host, was waiting for them, looking very French in black slacks, an open collar shirt with an ascot around his neck, and a dinner jacket. Shannon recalled her first date in Texas with Graeme, who had the appropriate attire for every occasion, every season, every country. God, how she missed him!

"Shannon, welcome to Lavande sur Mer! You are as beautiful as Graeme described," said Andre, taking her hand and kissing the back of her wrist in the formal European manner. "Of course, you must be Alex. Welcome as well. Your husband and your father," he said as he glanced at them in turn, "was a good friend. I am glad to help his wife and daughter in any way I can."

They lingered over dinner, enjoying the chef's specialties as Andre paired wines with each course. Throughout the evening, Andre shared delightful anecdotes of his friendship with Greg and Graeme.

"We met at the French Open. I'm more a golfer, but Roland Garros is a highlight of the year for any Frenchman who enjoys sport, and I met Graeme at a reception after winning a match. He was in high spirits. We had the most interesting conversation about the immigration situation in Europe, especially along the coastal areas that are overrun with people leaving North African countries. Most cocktail conversations are trivial, but not Graeme's! He delved passionately into any topic, but he was an intense listener as well. He wanted to learn before forming an opinion."

"That sounds familiar," thought Shannon. "How many times did Graeme and Dr. Ross tell me to do the same?"

"We became good friends," continued Andre, "and Graeme visited here from time to time to play golf, drink wine, and smoke cigars long into the night." He tilted his head toward Shannon. "Now, how can I be of help?"

Shannon and Alex both laid out the vision they had for Thorneside Farms Winery.

"What we have going for us is mature vineyards that are already producing grapes for South African wines," said Shannon. "We want to create our label and market it throughout the country."

"Our problem is we don't know the first thing about making wine!" said Alex with a laugh.

"We will start here," Andre said. "Tomorrow, I will take you on a yeoman's tour of Lavende sur Mer. I've arranged for our vintner, Monsieur Lyon, to take you through the steps, from grape harvesting to bottling. He's a bit abrupt, like many Frenchmen, but he's one of the best winemakers in the country. He has, as we say, 'the nose.' I am lucky to have him."

"Sounds perfect," said Shannon. "We can't wait to get started."

"After you've seen Lavande, I've arranged visits with colleagues in other parts of Europe who produce different wines but go through the same steps. You'll see operations in Northern France, Germany, Switzerland and finish up in The Netherlands. It's, as you call it, a 'whirlwind tour,' but in the end, you'll have a good idea of what you're facing. You will at least know enough to decide if this is what you want to do." Then he cautioned them. "You are contemplating a lifetime commitment."

For the next two weeks, Shannon and Alex drove throughout Europe from one vineyard to the next. Andre opened doors for them, and as a courtesy to him, the vintners gave them a detailed immersion into the art of making wine. The regions were different, the people vastly different, but the steps were the same.

Shannon categorized the risks of every step. The most daunting to her was the length of time wine had to age in each cask and bottle, from the youngest to the most aged.

Shannon knew what they would name their best bottle. It would be called Graeme's Reserve, a bold red reminiscent of the favorites she and Graeme enjoyed. Whenever they found a perfect wine, they had lingered over it, allowing its aromas and tastes to make their way through their senses. It was a spiritual experience for them both and always led to a night of passionate lovemaking.

On their last tour of a vineyard in The Netherlands, a particular young lady caught their eye. She was working as an unpaid internist for the head vintner at a respectable vineyard in the southern Limburg region. Her boss was an intimidating Dutchman who yelled at everybody. Most workers quivered in his wake, but this young woman was unflappable. She worked circles around everyone else with efficiency and poise, and she managed a smile, no matter how tense the situation.

"What an impressive young woman," Shannon thought.

Shannon asked her host, Lars Van Dijik, about her.

"Oh, Isabel? She's an intern. I don't even pay her. But she's the hardest and best worker I have. She's just out of university and thinks she wants to be a vintner, but no grower will ever hire a woman for that job! I've told her, too, many times, but she's stubborn, that one. Suits me, though. I get more than a day's work from her, and it costs me nothing."

"How can she afford to work for free?" Shannon said.

"Universities here have intern programs that help graduates master the skills they will need in their careers. It's a great program. The university pays them small stipends, and companies like ours have the benefit of their work. We provide her a free room in our employee housing complex, and she gets her meals in our cafeteria."

Isabel sported a mass of dark hair that fell in haphazard curls around her pleasant face, always in a smile. Shannon learned Isabel was half Dutch and half Jordanian.

"Alex, take a look at that young woman there," Shannon whispered to her daughter. "Watch her for a while and tell me your impressions. I'm curious about her. Let's see if she might like to join us for dinner, away from here. I'd like to get to know her a bit."

"I want to be a vintner," Isabel told them later over dinner, between bites of pasta. "Everyone tells me no one will ever accept a female vintner, but sooner or later…"

Isabel enchanted Shannon with her lively conversation and worldly sophistication. Her Catholic family immigrated to The Netherlands from Jordan. With limited opportunities in the dominant Muslim culture for a Westernized Jordanian man married to a Dutch woman, they left the country just ahead of a civil war that engulfed the whole region. Her father established a business in Amsterdam as a tailor, his wife as a seamstress. Isabel was off-the-charts brilliant, excelling in all her classes and mastering several languages. She was fluent in both her parents' languages as well as English, French, and Italian.

Over dessert, Shannon told Isabel about their vision to develop a wine label in South Africa. Alex, being as discrete as possible, studied Isabel's reactions.

"That's exciting!" said Isabel. "Two women developing a wine label in a country as male elitist as it gets! You are incredibly brave."

"Brave, yes. Experienced, no, I'm afraid," said Shannon. "We're in Europe now, touring wineries to get a quick education of what's involved before we make our go-no-go decision. We at least realize we must have someone on the team who knows what they're doing."

Isabel's eyes widened, now aware of the purpose for this dinner. "I could be that person!" she said, her voice bold and direct, brimming with confidence. "I've been studying winemaking for years, and I've worked at several wineries, learning hands-on what's involved. Are you possibly thinking about me for your winery?"

"Don't get too excited, Isabel!" said Shannon. "Alex and I know just enough to be dangerous. Everyone advises this is a high-risk endeavor. Some even predict there's no way we can succeed in such a male-dominated business."

"But you're serious, right?"

"Yes, we're serious about exploring what's involved and making an informed decision before committing our lives and life savings into it."

Isabel nodded.

"Let me be honest with you. I watched you work and how you handle the stresses and pressures of a challenging work environment with Mr. Van Dijk. I'm sure you realize South Africa is behind the rest of the world in its treatment of women as well as its black citizens. Frankly, the fact you are female is not what drew me to you. If anything, it sides more in the 'negative' column because it adds another risk to those we already face, three women going against the norm. But I'm intrigued by the potential marketing power of it. Just imagine if three women could pull this off! We'd make history!"

Shannon laughed as her eyes swept from Alex to Isabel. "But I'm getting ahead of myself. Alex and I are in our exploratory phase and must stay open to the possibility that our idea is impossible. Fact-finding missions are supposed to be objective, and we're trying to be."

"Oookaaaay," hummed Isabel.

"That said, we wonder if you are intrigued enough to consider visiting us in South Africa. Check out the mature vineyards at Thorneside that have produced grapes for wineries for years. Learn about the competition there, what wines are successful and why. Imagine yourself living there, too. South Africa isn't the most enlightened place in the world, especially for single female entrepreneurs. Spend a week with us, or as long as you need, and make your independent assessment. It's in your best interests and ours to be as objective as possible. Failure would hurt you as much as us."

Isabel looked straight at Alex, "I have a few questions for you, Alex. You and I are quite close in age. What do you think about all this, and what is your role?"

Alex leaned toward Isabel. "Though Shannon isn't my birth mother, I consider her my mother in every sense of the word. She has raised me since I was eight. After my father died when I was eighteen, she has had the sole parental responsibilities for my two younger brothers and me. Shannon has been my rock most of my life."

She smiled across the table at Shannon. "To answer your question about my role in the winery, you must understand the place Thorneside has in my history, in our history. I was born in South Africa and spent several years living there with my grandmother and grandfather after my mother died. The farm has been in our family for five generations before me. My father's legacy and inheritance pass to my brothers and me."

Alex held up her hand, illustrating as she touched her fingertips, one by one. "My grandfather and three uncles run the farm now. First, there's Gramps, the overseer. Next, my Uncle Lucas who manages the vineyards. Third, Uncle Dexter manages the fruit orchards. And fourth is Uncle Jude who distributes our products throughout South Africa."

"Sounds like quite a family operation," said Isabel.

"The notion of having a Thorneside Farms wine label has been under consideration for many years. Gramps hoped my father would return to the farm after his tennis career to make that happen. Unfortunately, that wasn't to be. Gramps and my father didn't get along well at all, and even if Dad had lived, I don't think he would have done it."

Isabel rolled her eyes. "Ah. Families. Sounds familiar."

"There is no way my uncles can pull this off themselves! They are the stereotypical South African males, particularly Lucas. They don't deal well with the public, especially marketing a product to men and women. In their minds, problems are solved by bossing workers into submission or sharing beers in the local tavern."

"Aren't things changing down there now?"

"Yes, South Africa will be a different country, now that apartheid is on the way out. We'd never consider living in South Africa under the old regime, but change is happening."

"For everyone?"

Alex nodded. "It isn't just the blacks who have been at the bottom of the social ladder in South Africa, but women as well. The country is at least fifty years behind the United States."

"Same where I came from, except worse. Hundreds of years, maybe."

Alex nodded at Shannon. "Partly because of my mother, I'm very interested in pursuing women's rights, especially as it relates to the law. I specialized in international law but also women's property rights. I'll get my license to practice in South Africa and learn all the legal requirements for our company, as well as the pitfalls. As our corporate attorney, I must prepare us for the inevitable barriers to entry, not the least of those, because we are women."

"Hooray for you!"

"To me, it is an opportunity to be a part of positive change in South Africa, to pursue my passion for the law but as it applies to our own business. Most important to me, we will create a lasting legacy honoring my father and protecting my birthright."

Alex locked eyes with Isabel, as if she were making her closing arguments before a jury. "You're right, Isabel. You and I are contemporaries and just starting our careers. Yes, it's a huge challenge for me and Shannon. But I believe the fact that we are women gives us an edge. We are both persistent, determined, and stubborn! And we could use another strong woman just like you!"

Shannon beamed at her daughter.

"How soon can I come?" Isabel said. "I'm intrigued."

* * *

GREG PUT TOGETHER the bones of a business plan. He also gathered an impressive list of contacts that he and Graeme had developed over time who would be valuable assets in the years to come.

"I've pulled some numbers together, but I'd like to go over them with you, face-to-face. What do you say if Sylvie and I visit you at Thorneside?" he said. "We'll bring Michael so he can hang out with Gabriel and Nathan."

"Greg, that would be wonderful," Shannon said. "You'd be welcome, Max and Charlotte would love to have you. There's someone I'd like you to meet. We may have found our vintner."

While in their hotel rooms at night, Shannon sketched the house she wanted. She drew the house in a U-shape with rooms and a balcony facing east to get the sunrise over the mountains, and ceiling-high windows facing west to catch the sunsets overlooking the vineyards. She wanted five bedrooms on the second level with French doors opening onto a shared balcony, her bedroom on one end, the children's rooms in the middle, and a guest room on the opposite end.

Downstairs she sketched an oversized chef's kitchen, casual and formal dining areas, a comfy den where the family would spend much of its time, a game room for the boys, and maid's quarters. The centerpiece of the downstairs would be an expansive outdoor terrace, not as massive as Charlotte's but large enough to host family and guests.

She outlined plans for a separate guest house, detached from the main house. Thorneside is not close to a major city, and Trelwyn didn't offer acceptable accommodations for visitors. She anticipated there would be frequent overnight guests related to the wine business, and didn't want her private residence to serve as an inn.

Her head was spinning.

She left it to Max to work out the details, with Charlotte's critical eye for good taste.

* * *

GREG GATHERED THE TEAM in the den: Shannon, Alex, Max, Charlotte, Isabel, and even Lucas. Expecting him to be the contrarian, Shannon's instinct to invite him to the meeting was spot-on. To her surprise, Lucas was open and cordial, and she could tell he appreciated being included.

"Shannon," Greg said, "everything I've researched confirms you're looking at three years before you uncork your youngest bottle, five to six years for your premium labels. We all recognize our greatest asset is that our mature vineyards already produce wine-quality grapes for several varietals. But it will still take years for the grapes to age in the casks and bottles. Once bottled, we have the job of getting people to try it, and that's a straight-up marketing task. It will require an ongoing promotional campaign to woo buyers and build customers. And that's assuming no missteps in quality, that we don't lose an entire bottling year in a vintage turned to vinegar."

Shannon squirmed in her seat and scanned the faces of the family members for their reactions.

"What concerns me is not your commitment but the years before earning a single Rand!" Greg tapped his finger on the stack of papers in front of him. "We'll need a capital loan for the construction and equipment, but also for operating overhead before product reaches the market." He paused. "I'd like you to consider me as a partner and investor. Sylvie and I have discussed it, and we'd like to help. We believe in what you're doing. Your highest risk is being under-capitalized, not having the funds to cover overhead until you're producing a return."

"Well, let's have a look at those numbers," said Shannon.

"Here are some spreadsheets that illustrate what I'm talking about." He passed around pages for them to follow. "There's a huge upfront investment in the equipment itself. And operational overhead and wages to pay for several years before sales kick in. The promotional campaign alone will be a fulltime job for you, Shannon. If I had my way, you'd be on the road nonstop, soliciting investors and promoting the brand. My best estimates suggest it will take five or more years before you break even."

"Greg, you've done some incredible work here, and I wish I could argue with your conclusions—but I can't." Shannon sat up straight. "What makes me uncomfortable is having outside investors who will dilute the family's ownership in the winery. I'd rather see what we could borrow and repay over time than surrender ownership shares to outsiders. In my corporate career, I learned firsthand how those outside investors assert control and pressure. In the end, you're working for the investors instead of yourselves."

Max spoke up. "We don't like outsiders in our business. We've built what we have by our own hands, bit by bit. It might take longer, but we're not going anywhere, and I say it takes as long as it takes."

Lucas chimed in. "I agree with Dad. No outside investors."

"The proceeds from selling the New York house will pay the cost of our new house here," said Shannon, "and we have some savings from Graeme's estate to cover the kids and me for a while, but not five years! I don't have to draw a salary, but I have to cover my costs. All that travel will be pretty expensive."

Charlotte jumped in the conversation. "Why can't I home school Nathan for a few years, just like I did Alex. That will save on that private school tuition, Shannon. Universities here in South Africa are a lot less than in the U.S., and you've been saving for those high-cost tuitions in the States. We are so used to being self-sufficient here on the farm, and it will be business as usual when you and the children become part of our lifestyle."

"All that will be very helpful," said Greg, "but it doesn't solve the problem of covering overhead for five years or more before seeing a return. Without outside money, I don't see how you can stay afloat."

"Let's all sleep on it," Shannon said. "We'll have clearer heads in the morning."

* * *

Three For One

THAT NIGHT SHANNON called her friend, Helen, back in the States.

Hello, Shannon. What's up?" said Helen. "I'm at work. Everything okay?"

"Helen, I've got so much to tell you. It's all positive, but the ground is moving under my feet. You're not going to believe what I'm about to ask you." She swallowed hard. "How would you feel about moving back to South Africa?"

Helen closed her office door and signaled to the receptionist outside to hold her calls. Shannon spent the better part of an hour telling Helen about her wild scheme.

"Remember our trip to Tuscany, to the cooking school? Remember how we talked about having our bed-and-breakfast and cooking school? What if we did that here at Thorneside? And you would run it?"

"First, you're crazy!" Helen said in that logical tone of hers. "You're talking about uprooting your family and moving to a country that has been one of the most despicable places on the planet for years. Second, you're talking about investing all your money and your children's futures, starting not one business, but three! Third, you're talking about taking Cece and me down with you! As I said, you're crazy!"

"Yeah, but other than that, what would you think about moving back to South Africa and running the B&B and cooking school here, like you suggested when we were in Tuscany?"

"Why in the world would I uproot Cece and me, quit a job I love, leave the United States which I love, and move back to a broken country I left long ago?"

"Because you said you love South Africa, just not its government politics. But that's all changing. Apartheid is on its way out, and the future here is exciting. You and I could be a part of the future. And because you have family here… and me. And you'd be running a business where you have ownership, where you would build a future for yourself and Cece."

The debate continued until Shannon said, "Look, let me send you something in writing that outlines what we're talking about. You'll see how the three businesses support one another. The B&B and cooking school generate income until our wines are ready for market. Just read it. I'll call again in a week."

"When are you coming back here? I mean coming *home*?"

"We're returning to the States soon to put the house on the market and begin our immigration process. We'll get together and talk about this face-to-face. It's wacky enough, Helen, that it could work."

"Well, it won't hurt to talk. Maybe you'll have come to your senses by then."

Bright and early the next day, over coffee, Shannon outlined her new idea to the team. "We could have the B&B up and running within a year and the cooking school the following year. Both could produce revenue as soon as we open, though I'd be conservative on the occupancy projections, Greg, and ramp up slowly."

Shannon's enthusiasm came through her voice. "We're building a guest house anyway. Let's expand that concept for maybe 15 guest suites, with the cooking school separate but linked. The kitchen can also serve the B&B, and we could have an area for catered events. We could even do weddings." Talking faster as her excitement grew, she concluded, "It's a complete package that would generate revenue year-round with more immediate returns than we will see from the winery."

"That's certainly a far-reaching idea, but how would you run all three?" said Greg, eyes widened.

"I wouldn't attempt it if Helen weren't involved, and she can definitely run the B&B. As for the cooking school, I'd need to find our head chef, probably Italian or French."

She turned to Greg. "We'd lean on you, Greg, for your financial skills to keep all three balls in the air. It's a larger upfront investment, but it's more feasible when you look at a whole package. The very diversity of income streams mitigates some of the risks. If one piece falters, we'll dial up the other two to offset."

Shannon looked at the others, trying to gauge their reactions. "The three businesses would share the brand, Thorneside Farms, each entity adding to brand awareness, each playing off the other. People would come for the B&B experience only, a charming, romantic getaway located within vineyards. The cooking school would attract an international audience who would stay in the B&B. And all guests would be exposed to Thorneside wines, even before bottles reach the table."

Max and Lucas seemed in shock, their jaws open.

"You're talking about car parks, security, staff housing, public intrusions… It's just more outside exposure of Thorneside than I'd considered," Max said. "We'd have strangers running all over the place."

"The winery was going to open that door anyway, Max," said Shannon. "The difference, as I see it, is scale. We could design it for a maximum of 50 people onsite at a time. When the B&B is full capacity, it would be 15 couples at the most. The cooking school would be 10 to 12 people, using that many guest rooms. Catering could be limited to 50 or less. I doubt the winery will have drop-in guests of more than a few dozen on weekends. Each business is quite intimate and limited in size, and we would control that."

"And after that, Shannon," Lucas tossed in sarcastically, "are you going to want to build a shopping center?"

Expressionless, she held Lucas's gaze without blinking. "We need to generate revenue before our wines are ready to sell. These businesses support one another. And this way, we generate a return in one to two years, not five."

Looking at everyone in the room, one at a time, she said, "The way we left it last night was pretty bleak. We were looking at huge losses for five years. The three businesses lessen that time and diversify our risk."

As if handing out assignments, Shannon said, "Greg, can you run some forecasts based on the three businesses?"

To Max, she said, "I don't see any reason why you can't proceed with plans and designs for the house. We will send you specs as soon as we have them for the three entities, so you can study the site and pace it out. You can confirm if this concept fits the land you've designated for us, while maintaining the integrity and privacy of the rest of the farm."

"But I… I can't commit… not yet," said Max.

"We're still in research mode. The only commitment thus far is Alex, Gabriel, Nathan, and I will move here and start the winery. One way or another, we will make that work. It's a question, I guess, of how long it will take for the wine business to make money."

"What do we do next, Shannon?" said Alex.

"We go back to the States to put things in motion there—sell the New York house and start our immigration process. You will be the first to relocate and get yourself enrolled in September. While all this is going on, Greg and I—if you're willing, Greg—will continue to plot and plan and crunch the numbers."

Isabel said nothing as she observed the proceedings.

"Isabel," said Shannon, "you've got the big picture of what's going on here, but of course, you don't know enough to make an informed decision. We will keep you in the loop."

They all sat in stunned silence, taking in what Shannon laid out, not quite sure what to say.

"Max, Charlotte, and Lucas," Shannon said, "you and the rest of the family need to let this percolate awhile, talk among yourselves, see what questions and issues come up for you." She paused. "We've taken the first step, but we're still in decision mode to prove if this can work. Nothing lost, nothing gained—yet. I should be able to get back here in a few months, and we'll see where we stand."

She rose from her chair. "Are we in agreement on the next steps?"

The others were still seated, their mouths agape, even Greg. Only Alex's face showed no reaction.

Shannon adjourned the meeting, and climbing the stairs to their rooms, Alex took Shannon's elbow and whispered, "The family just got a full blast of 'Shannon, both barrels, up close and personal'." She giggled. "You might need to give them a little time to take all this in."

* * *

Family Partnership

AS THE OTHERS filed out of the room, Max called another meeting for family members only. he closed the doors to his study. The room erupted.

By breakfast, the family had crafted a handwritten proposal. Lucas led the presentation. "The family agrees we don't want outside investors, and we want to figure out how we can come up with the operating overhead ourselves. We'll use our banking connections for a loan on capital expenditures, like the materials, equipment, furnishings, and so forth. We propose a family partnership with ownership of the entire business as follows: 8% to Mom and Dad, 8% each to Dexter and Jude, 10% to Greg, 15% to me, and 51% to you."

Shannon studied their list.

Lucas continued, "Max and Charlotte won't put money in but will contribute the land and construction. My share is larger than the others because of the amount of my time I anticipate will be required—providing the grapes and getting the winery licensed and accepted in South Africa."

He pointed to the names on the list. "When Dexter, Jude, or I die, our shares will go to our children so it stays in the family."

Shannon nodded.

"After we see the numbers," Lucas said, "we'll get together and see how we can come up with the cash to cover costs until revenues kick in and we start turning a profit."

Shannon's eyes scanned the page, as Lucas continued. "Since the Thorneside Farms winery bears our name and is on our farm, we share ownership. You provide whatever financial incentives you need to attract the key people, like the cooking school chef or B&B operator. That becomes a budgetary concern for approval of the board."

"How does Helen fit in?" said Shannon.

"If you feel you must give Helen some ownership, it comes out of your 51%." He paused. "It's a pretty safe structure for you. As soon as the project produces revenue, those involved in day-to-day operations, especially you and Alex, will get a salary. We will pay Greg fees for his time when we can afford it, as it looks like his time will be substantial, at least in the early years."

"What about the board of directors?"

"We agreed that each family member should have a seat on the board and a vote, together with you and Greg. You and Dad will co-chair the Board."

"Is that it? No one else?"

"That's it for the board. No one else is entitled to ownership. This way, we all have some skin in the game and a voice in the operation. Every board member is invested in the project's success." Lucas cleared his throat. "Keep this in mind. You own 51% and are the majority stockholder. When Mom and Dad pass away, their 8% will be distributed equally among all four of us, so even then, you will retain majority ownership."

Max tapped his index finger on the tabletop. "Shannon, I've kept Thorneside entirely in the family, all 10,000 acres. Whenever we needed anything, we took care of it ourselves. When we borrowed money for major equipment or building a barn, whatever, we did it without giving up ownership. It's the only way we'll do this project. We agree with Greg's 10% because he's putting in money and his skills in managing this monster. His voice of experience and objectivity add balance to a family-owned-and-operated business. That can get out of hand unless there is an objective voice on the board. Quite frankly, we need him. You need him!"

Shannon nodded again, as much for herself as for Max and the others.

"When Charlotte and I pass away," Max said, "Graeme's share of the farm, minus the land we're giving the project, will be put in trust for his three children." He paused. "What do you think of these terms?"

Shannon sat up straight. "Max, my goal is to build a legacy for Graeme's children, one where he is never forgotten. As for me, this is not a get-rich-quick scheme, and Greg's initial numbers prove that a long road of hard work and risk lies ahead of us. What you've outlined doesn't alter that goal one iota. Your proposal is fair, and I accept it—in concept. Of course, a legal mind needs to alert us to any pitfalls we don't see here, or other questions may come up that none of us has thought about."

"I hope we can keep it simple and clean, as free of legal meddling as possible," Max said. "I never met a lawyer who solved anything."

"Fortunately, we have a family lawyer!" Shannon said with a grin. "Alex's whole purpose for getting her license to practice here is to advise Thorneside Farms and keep us out of legal trouble. She has as much at stake as any of us to protect the interests of the business."

Max looked at Alex with a wistful smile. "That's very true."

"I speak for my other children," Shannon said, "and we agree to this kitchen contract."

That Was the Easy Part

Greg's documents outlining revenue projections and costs for all three businesses showed optimism after operating the B&B and cooking school for two years. With that encouragement, the entire team got behind the project, full steam ahead.

The next few years were a blur of frenzied activity.

Alex enrolled in the University of Cape Town's law school. She roomed in a dormitory during the week and spent her weekends at Thorneside. It took a full year for Alex to obtain her license. As the only female student, she endured more than her fair share of hazing and discrimination. Like Shannon, she had little patience for this nonsense and couldn't wait to finish and return to Thorneside and get to work on the winery.

Ivan Hart's response to Shannon resigning from the company surprised her. She assumed he would be upset, but he was enthusiastic about Shannon's plan for the winery, the entrepreneur in him unleashed.

"It's perfect, Shannon!" he said. "You've got the land free, and vineyards that have been producing grapes for years—the two biggest hurdles resolved right off the bat. The ownership structure is sound for you and your children. And you've got the business skills to make it happen. It's perfect! I wish I had thought of it!"

"So you're okay with my—"

He waved a hand across his face, as if shooing a fly. "Now about your leaving Hart Hotels, I'm disappointed, of course. But things will go on here. Shannon, this is the opportunity of a lifetime, and what an incredible legacy you are building for your children. I'm jealous!" he said. "I wonder if you might let me invest. I've always wanted to get in the wine business."

"The family wants no outside investors. But who knows what the future holds and what unknown challenges lie ahead? One day I might just come back to you about that offer."

A trip to Texas was first on her list, to see Helen face-to-face. After hours of conversation and many glasses of wine, Helen became infected with the same enthusiasm for Thorneside Farms Winery as her best friend.

Shannon showed restraint, however, wanting Helen to decide for herself what was in her best interests. She committed that Helen and Cece would have their own home, separate from the B&B, completely private, and Helen's to decorate any way she liked. Helen wouldn't have to pay for housing until the B&B showed a profit, and it would be far less than housing in the U.S. Shannon promised a share of profits from the B&B in addition to a salary. The convincing carrot was 50/50 shared ownership in the B&B, coming from Shannon's portion of the family partnership.

Like Shannon, Helen engaged an accountant confirming her overall living costs would be a lot lower. At the same time, her income potential was much higher.

Talking to her own family in Johannesburg, however, was the deciding factor. Their assessment of the country following repeal of the apartheid laws assured Helen that change indeed was happening.

In the end, Helen agreed to move to South Africa.

* * *

A STRONG SELLER'S MARKET netted a healthy profit on the New York home, closing in less than a month. With help from Ivan's legal team, Shannon secured immigration documents and visas for herself and the boys, and she packed what she intended to ship to South Africa.

Three months later, Shannon was back at Thorneside. Max had made fast progress on the house. The foundation was laid and the framing up. Shannon and the kids stayed with Max and Charlotte in the meantime, and Charlotte wasted no time in getting Nathan into a disciplined homeschooling routine.

Isabel was waiting for Shannon's call; she needed no convincing. She required a visa classification permitting her to hold a job that couldn't be filled by a South African. That would take some work, and Alex's legal skills were already in demand.

"Now I've got to find our chef," Shannon told herself. "Time to revisit Italy and France."

* * *

LUCAS TURNED OUT to be an invaluable partner. He arranged introductions to the winemakers' inner circle as he high-fived with the best of them, and shared beers to win their influence on the permitting process.

"We were wondering when you'd finally get in the business for yourselves," one winery owner said to him. "We're not afraid of a little competition."

Lucas neglected to mention, however, the detail that his sister-in-law would be running the business.

Shannon traveled to Europe often, meeting with Graeme's business contacts and telling the story about Thorneside Farms Winery. Members of the press, who had known Graeme as a tennis professional and later as an outspoken activist, interviewed Shannon. Favorable articles appeared about Graeme Thorne's family starting a winery at his South African birth home.

Only one incident interfered with the winery's development. The top candidate for the cooking school chef had flown in from Italy. She was an expressive, young woman who spoke English with that lilting Italian accent. She bolted from the room during her interview with Lucas and told Shannon she would not work with such a boor of a man.

"Let me talk to Lucas, Paola. I am sure it's a simple misunderstanding," said Shannon. "Wait here for a minute, please."

To Lucas in private, she said, "What in the world did you say to her?"

"I was just honest. She spouted all that sophisticated Italian bullshit, acting so high and mighty, and I just told her, 'There will be none of that Euro-trash business here'."

"Look, it's our job to convince her to join us, not run her off. She's the most qualified candidate we have, and her references are impeccable. The Italian style that puts you off is what our customers will gladly pay for. If it means adapting to cultural differences, then that's what we must do."

He shrugged.

"You and I have found a way, Lucas, so I know we are both capable of bending a bit. She's outside on the terrace. Now please, see if you can turn this around and persuade her to come. We need her," she said as she grasped his arm and ended their conversation in a much more moderated tone than the Shannon of the past.

She didn't know what passed between the two of them, but Paola accepted the job as the chef at the cooking school, and Lucas never bullied or berated staff again.

Over time, Shannon and Lucas became close allies as they learned to respect each other's strengths. Lucas respected Shannon for her business acumen, and she admitted she could never have made it without Lucas's first-quality grapes and his business connections throughout the country. They even grew quite fond of one another.

Shannon's new home was perfect. The wrap-around balcony far exceeded her hopes and evoked childhood memories of playing on her aunt's wrap-around porch, pretending it was her special place in the world. Her kitchen was a smaller version of what the cooking school would need: a massive center counter for meal preparation, a five-burner gas stove, double ovens, and plenty of cabinet space for Shannon's everyday and formal dishes and extensive cookware collection. She couldn't wait to get in the kitchen and prepare meals for her family and guests.

Upstairs, French doors to all the bedrooms opened onto the balcony, capturing the sun rising over the mountaintops as it cast its shimmering orange glow on the vineyards, still wet with morning dew.

"It's exquisite," Shannon said to herself, as she stood on her balcony with a cup of coffee and caught the sunrise.

Downstairs the terrace turned out to be every bit as big as Charlotte's, accessed by French doors from the kitchen, formal dining room, and living room.

Shannon was thrilled.

Max turned his attention to the winery's master plan, starting with a gravel drive connecting the main road to the tasting room. The winery and inn construction began at the same time, stretching the budget to include the house for Helen and Cece.

Isabel needed a working laboratory to experiment and develop formulas and test blends for the varietals, using all manner of flavors from the farm's fruit orchards. She learned which South African wines customers preferred and kept a stocked cellar of the country's best. Wine presses were in place as soon as possible so she could get grapes into casks for aging. Isabel worked from first light until dark, setting a high standard for the other workers.

Shannon and Max walked the grounds every day when she wasn't traveling, updating Max's punch list.

"Shannon, I don't know how much longer I've got left on this earth, so I want to do my part to get the master plan completed as soon as possible," Max said. "That's my commitment to you and the children—and to Graeme."

Shannon couldn't believe this was the same harsh man who had clashed so with her husband. "If only Graeme could have known his father as he is now," she thought.

"I'm glad to see you and Lucas getting on so well, but I've got to make sure you and the kids are protected when I'm gone. I asked

Alex to ensure the ownership structure stands up legally and you maintain 51% control. But I'm still a bit worried."

"What's troubling you, Max?"

"What about making Alex managing director?" Max said. "She's got the fire in the belly, she's a blood relative, and she's learning the business from every angle."

"That's a wonderful solution, Max. I'd like that for Alex, and she will be perfect for it. But it's too soon," Shannon said. "She needs more time. Perhaps at the board meeting, we can talk about that as the path for succession, for her to succeed you as co-chair and ultimately me as Chair of the Board."

Helen and Cece arrived within the year and settled themselves in their new home. Max was as attentive to its design as he had been with Shannon's. A large breezeway and patio separated the Inn from Helen's home, ensuring her privacy.

Helen threw herself into the tasks of designing the Inn's interiors, using her talents to make each room unique, welcoming, and cozy. She wanted guests to feel they were in a private home, not a hotel.

Cece, now out of high school like Gabriel, enrolled in a Cape Town university that offered a degree in hospitality management, intent on helping her mother with the B&B.

Within the year, Paola arrived and got right to work selecting equipment and furnishings, designing menus, establishing vendors for her products, and planting an outdoor garden. Until Thorneside wines were ready to uncork, Paola would offer the best South African wines to her guests.

Shannon established a routine for her team to drop by in the evenings for cocktails or wine. Sometimes it was just one or two of them, other times the whole group, including Max, Charlotte, and Lucas. If Shannon was away, Alex welcomed them instead. The camaraderie grew tight, and Shannon felt very protective of all of them.

The B&B opened its doors a year after Helen and Cece arrived. Helen held a formal grand opening for the entire community and invited the local press. Paola used Shannon's kitchen to prepare an elegant cocktail reception for over 100 guests. For overnight guests in the new B&B suites, Paola served a hearty breakfast on the inn's vine-covered patio. With Alex' help, Max ensured the ownership structure would endure past his death. The board approved the succession plan for Alex to be named Chair of the Board and Managing Director, at a date Shannon would determine. Until then, Shannon held the reins.

Max lived long enough to see the grand opening of the bed-and-breakfast. They found him slumped over the wheel of his tractor, the engine idling. At 85, he still worked in the fields of his beloved farm every day. He didn't live to see the cooking school finished, but it was well on its way.

Charlotte and her husband had at last carved a comfortable life together. Their sons were often caught off guard by the open affection they expressed for one another.

"How will I survive without him," she cried. "He's all I've ever known."

"We are here for you, Charlotte. We will help you through this." Shannon hugged her beloved mother-in-law. But she knew what little others could do when grief clenches, making it difficult even to breathe. As if it were yesterday, she remembered her sorrow when she lost Graeme.

Charlotte lived another five years after Max passed away. She devoted her remaining years to children and grandchildren as she always had, but her light had dimmed. Her trusted housemaid found her one morning, peaceful and still, regal even in death.

All of Thorneside went into mourning, and they were grief-stricken at losing the heartbeat of the entire family. Next to Helen, Charlotte was Shannon's closest friend as well as her mother-in-law. She didn't know what she would do without this woman's generous spirit and unconditional love. Charlotte was buried next to Max in the family plot at Thorneside Farms.

* * *

Mandiba

ON A TRIP TO Johannesburg, Shannon attended a reception for Nelson Mandela, where the newly-elected President made a speech. Soft-spoken, self-effacing, observant, and highly intelligent, Mandela seemed unfazed by the adulation that surrounded him.

His 27 years of imprisonment honed his steely character. Mandela had nothing left to fear. He had endured all the punishment man could throw at him. While Mandela was pleasant to everyone around him, he allowed no compromise on his vision for his New South Africa.

At the reception, Shannon met her hero face-to-face.

"You're the American I've heard so much about," the President said while shaking her hand, "the one who is breaking the rules of what a woman can do in this country. I understand you've formed quite a strong team of like-minded women who are shaking up the status quo around here."

Shannon was speechless for a moment. "I don't know what to say, Mr. President. I had no idea you heard of our little enterprise in the Cape."

"You're much too modest. A winery, a cooking school, and I hear the nicest bed-and-breakfast in the country—all started and managed by women. You've got the old boys shaking in their boots."

"We could not have attempted this, Mr. President," said Shannon, "without your many years of work and sacrifice to change South Africa and its policies."

"I hope you will get involved in helping women's equality in South Africa," Mandela said. "We have a long way to go. Get in touch with my office, and we'll give you the names of people who are active in the women's movement here. Our work has only begun in building the New South Africa."

"Mr. President, I'd love to get involved. I always fought

discrimination in my career, and there are similarities to what the blacks face. Of course, I never went to prison, but if it hadn't been for my husband, I might have," she said with a laugh.

"Yes, Graeme Thorne. I admired him so much. He was a great tennis player, and he made our country proud. Of course, I'm a soccer and boxing man myself, but I still loved watching him play. What made me most proud was when he took brave stands against apartheid whenever he had an audience, though it made him very unpopular with the regime here. I read some of his newspaper interviews that were smuggled to me in prison."

Shannon beamed at him.

"I can see why he was attracted to you," Mandela said. "He would expect a strong woman at his side. His death was a loss to us all."

"He's our motivation behind everything we're doing at Thorneside. Please, Mr. President, if you ever want to visit us, you would be our honored guest. We would love for you and your wife to come and stay with us."

"I might take you up on that, Shannon. It is indeed a pleasure to meet you."

Alex, Helen, and Cece couldn't contain themselves when Shannon told them about meeting Nelson Mandela.

"Can we go with you to the President's Palace?" they said. "We want to be involved too?"

The four of them met with the head of Mandela's Human Rights Commission. Alex and Cece were enthusiastic about getting involved in the movement and volunteered to work with the Commission. Shannon and Helen were content to let their daughters carry the banner, supporting their efforts in the background. Shannon and Helen always looked for exceptional women, including women of color, to employ at Thorneside Farms. They felt their most significant contribution would come from helping women attain economic success and independence through jobs with a future.

Paolo established a relationship with the Prue Leith Chef's

SHAPING SHANNON ◆ 311

Academy. Their students were a steady flow of interns as sous chefs in her kitchen. Isabel benefitted as well from students working on their Cape Wine Academy certification. Through Cece's contacts, Helen had access to black female graduates of the hotel school. Thorneside Farms was abuzz with intelligent, enthusiastic young men and women, black, white, and Asian, who had chosen hotels, wine, or food as their career path. These young people kept everyone on their toes.

One day Shannon received a phone call.

"Shannon, hello. This is Graca Machel Mandela calling. We've been reading about your beautiful Thorneside Farms, and Mandiba and I would like to come for a few days. Now that he's out of office, we're trying to take time to enjoy some of the beautiful places in South Africa."

They came for three days and nights, and Helen put them in their best room. Their privacy was protected, allowing them to enjoy well-deserved rest and quiet time. Still, they invited Shannon to join them for breakfast one morning. Mandela set Shannon at ease while she chatted with one of the most admired men in the world.

He asked how Alex and Cece were doing in their efforts for women's equality in the country. Graca told Shannon about Mandiba founding an organization called The Elders, made of independent global leaders unified in their vision for peace, justice, and human rights.

"Mary Robinson is a member who is active on women's rights. She's the former President of Ireland and served as United Nations High Commissioner for Human Rights. She's fearless and makes her voice heard throughout the world."

Mandela was well into his 80s by this time, showing his age and appearing quite frail. Shannon didn't dare ask, but at one point, Mandela asked if Shannon would like to take a photo of the three of them.

"I don't know if it will help or hurt, you be the judge, but you have our permission to say we were your guest here at Thorneside Farms."

Alex came at once and took the photo, which hangs in the Inn's lobby for all to see. Although proud of it, Shannon seldom used the image, not wanting to commercialize the visit of one of her lifelong heroes.

"Wouldn't Graeme be proud!" she thought.

* * *

Graeme's Reserve

AS ISABEL DEVELOPED her formulas for the Thorneside Farms labels, Shannon invited her to dinner on her terrace. While enjoying hors d'oeuvres prepared by Paola, Shannon opened two bottles of cabernet sauvignon. One was South Africa's highest-rated cabernet, and the second one was a California cabernet that had been a favorite of hers and Graeme's. She poured them a glass of each.

"Isabel, I want to tell you about my husband."

Isabel nodded.

"Graeme was passionate—about life, about his wife, children, and family. He loved with abandon and without reservation. His intelligence far surpassed his contemporaries, and he could hold his own in any conversation. He listened to others intently, never shirked a lively debate, yet was slow to voice an opinion until he was resolute. He laughed quickly and often, and he engendered trust by those who knew him."

"Your marriage must have been very unique."

"Graeme had the perfect physique. His years of playing tennis honed his muscles to perfection. On the court, he was as graceful as a gazelle and quick as a cheetah. His face had chiseled features like a Greek statue. His hair was thick and curly, and his eyes were dark and intense."

"I've seen his photos. He was very handsome."

"These are the qualities I want you to capture in Graeme's Reserve. I don't know how you accomplish this, and I won't presume to teach or show you. But when we are ready to release Graeme's Reserve to the world, I want it to be the best cabernet in the country and to reflect Graeme's qualities that I described to you."

She pulled out a piece of paper to show Isabel. "Look. I even have the label in mind for Graham's Reserve. I had it designed a few years ago."

It was the shadow of a leopard, and she told her the story of Graeme's grandfather who had once wrestled a leopard on the farm many years before.

In time, Isabel produced five South African varietals, blends suited to the climate and consumers' tastes. She offered the favorite of the Cape region, the pinotage, as well as a syrah, a pinot noir, a chardonnay, and her best wine, a cabernet sauvignon. The lighter, whiter versions were ready first, while the cabernet required longer to age.

By the year 2009, the winery had been open for five years. The first four labels of Thorneside Farms were in the market, and sales were satisfactory, mainly within South Africa.

Meanwhile, Graeme's Reserve had been aging in casks and bottles. Until the day Isabel announced to Shannon that Graeme's Reserve was ready.

For this significant occasion, Shannon gathered those closest to her for a sunset dinner on the terrace. She made sure they were all there: Alex, Gabriel and Cece, Nathan, Helen, Paola, Lucas, and of course Isabel and herself. Max and Charlotte were the only ones missing.

Isabel shipped a case of Graeme's Reserve to Greg, and Shannon asked Greg and Sylvie open a bottle at about the same time they were opening theirs at Thorneside.

Isabel opened a bottle of Graeme's Reserve, 2004 vintage, and offered the first taste to Lucas. He shot Shannon a glance, a small smile on his lips, showing he was visibly moved at the honor of this gesture. He accepted the goblet and tasted the wine, allowing it to linger in his mouth. He smiled and nodded to Isabel to pour glasses

314 ◆ Jo Ann Swahn

for everyone else.

Shannon lifted her goblet and twirled the deep burgundy liquid, noting the vertical lines forming on the glass. She brought the goblet to her nose and, with eyes closed, inhaled its aromas. She took a healthy sip and allowed the liquid to linger on her tongue, savoring the taste, then swallowed, feeling the thickness of the wine as it went down her throat. Eyes still closed, tears spilled down her cheeks.

"Thank you, Isabel," she whispered. "You've done it! I don't know how you managed it, but you did. You've honored Graeme better than I could have imagined."

To the group, she raised her glass. "This is the culmination of all our dreams, our hard work. Each of you has made Thorneside Farms what it is today and will be tomorrow, a living reminder of our beloved Graeme and a legacy to a life well-lived. Thank you, each and all, for your hard work, your sacrifice, your persistence, and your love. To you and to Graeme."

Over the next few days, Shannon and Isabel hand-delivered complimentary bottles of Graeme's Reserve to the wine critics in Cape Town and Johannesburg and asked Greg to do the same in the UK. She also shipped bottles to wine journalists in the United States, including *Food and Wine* and *Bon Appetit* magazines.

Soon after, she received a call from a Food and Wine editor. "We received the bottle of Graeme's Reserve you sent us, and we'd like to do an article on your winery. Could we send one of our writers who is currently touring the country?"

The article on South African wines became the featured story with a photo of Thorneside Farms Winery on the front cover. The world was hungry for stories about post-apartheid South Africa, and Thorneside Farms made a fascinating story. About the American widow who built a winery on her husband's family farm as a lasting legacy for Graeme Thorne. And her daughter, a lawyer, on track to be the winery's CEO and Chair of the Board. About Shannon's best friend, a naturalized American citizen who returned to her native South Africa to run the bed-and-breakfast inn. About the female vintner from The Netherlands, the first woman winemaker in South Africa. About the Italian chef who heads the Thorneside Farms cooking school, modeled after famous schools in Italy.

This all-female team shattered glass ceilings in South Africa, blazing trails for women and blacks alike in the country once dominated by white males.

After that story appeared, every bottle of Graeme's Reserve was sold. Orders flooded in for the 2005and 2006 vintages, still in their casks. Isabel and Lucas planned to increase the production of the grapes used in Graeme's Reserve to yield more bottles in the coming years.

"We must be cautious not to inundate the market," said Shannon. "Sometimes it's better to raise prices and drive up demand."

Bon Appetit soon sent their writer to stay at the B&B and attend the cooking school. Their high-profile article put Thorneside Farms on the map as a top travel destination.

"Just look at how many reservations are from out of the country," Helen said to Shannon. "Many coming for safari and starting or ending their trip with a few nights at Thorneside Farms."

From that time forward, Thorneside Farms enjoyed international recognition. Business was brisk, and so were profits. With confidence and pride, Shannon nominated Alex to succeed her as Chair of the Board and Managing Director. The decision was unanimous.

* * *

Empty Nest

WHEN IT CAME time for Gabriel to declare his college intentions, no one expected he wanted to become a park ranger and game manager.

"Ever since Dad took me on safari as a kid, I've wanted to return to Africa and work with animals, but with South Africa's political mess, I didn't believe it would ever be possible."

"Gabriel, I am so proud of you. You've been accepted into the world's best university for wildlife conservation," Shannon said.

"Yeah, it's exciting, Mom. Even though the main campus is in England, their curriculum will place me in game parks all over Africa. But my goal is to manage a game reserve in my father's home country. When I graduate, I plan to get a job at a game park here in South Africa."

Everyone expected that Gabriel and Cece would marry. They had grown up together and, as adults, were inseparable. After completing his studies, Gabriel landed his dream job as a ranger for a South African game park. He proposed marriage before the ink was dry on his employment contract. For their wedding, all of Thorneside Farms closed for the occasion. Guests celebrated through the entire weekend, enjoying Paola's cooking and Thorneside wines.

Gabriel and Cece started married life at the game preserve, and the birth of two daughters followed in quick succession. Their parents were determined to raise the girls in the backcountry. However, they spent as much time as their parents would allow at Thorneside with their grandmothers. Shannon often visited the safari lodge they called home. She adored the girls and taught them about the wide world outside the bush—and about their grandfather.

When it came time, Nathan chose medicine, true to his compassionate nature to care for others. He was accepted into Oxford premed and completed his medical degree and residency in Johannesburg. He joined an NGO clinic in a teeming black township outside the city. Shannon didn't see him as often as she wished. His practice required most of his time.

Shannon had continued the American holiday of Thanksgiving, serving a traditional turkey dinner for all the Thorne family. One Thanksgiving Alex brought home an African colleague.

"Shannon, family, I'd like you to meet Michael Brown," Alex said as she beamed at her new beau. "He's working with Mandela's Human Rights Commission, and in my spare time, I've volunteered on the reconciliation efforts."

Soon, Alex announced that she and Michael were engaged. The laws against interracial marriage had been abolished in 1985.

"Long-held grievances and prejudices will confront them in the future," Shannon thought. "But it is so like Alex to take the road less traveled."

She also couldn't help thinking, "My, my! A daughter running a successful winery, hotel, and cooking school with 75 employees, and engaged to an African lawyer and activist. A son who is a wildlife conservationist and game park ranger, married, with two daughters. And another son, a doctor, committed to caring for the sick and needy in poor black communities. Graeme would be quite proud of his children."

Shannon sat back and sighed, "My job as a mother is done, and our children are now masters of their own ships."

V. HARVEST

S hannon's nest was indeed empty.

She lost Helen. A vicious, unstoppable cancer had spread through her body, and Shannon's best friend for almost 50 years left the world. Shannon's touchstone, the one to whom she turned whenever in doubt or need, was gone.

Alex was married now and lived in a home not far from Shannon's, and she ran the day-to-day operations at Thorneside Farms. Alex had a devil of a time replacing Helen to run the B&B, whose legendary hospitality had established a loyal clientele. She found it impossible to replace this witty, intelligent, efficient woman who had endeared herself to customers and staff alike.

Instead, Alex hired a young graduate from the university's hotel school who made up for a lack of experience with unbound energy. No one could keep up with her. She embraced the traditions started by Helen, and maintained the quality and warmth that their guests expected.

Isabel's reputation as a vintner was now established throughout the wine industry, thanks in large part to the successful Graeme's Reserve. Paola's cooking school held its head high with the best in Tuscany, and she had a waitlist for every scheduled session.

At board meetings, Alex listened to discussions about expansion, with members talking often about increasing the numbers of rooms at the Inn. Shannon kept her own counsel, trusting the future direction was in Alex's capable hands.

Gabriel and Cece enjoyed a full life on the game reserve. Their daughters were naturalists in the making, and loved their connection to the land and the animals.

Nathan joined a practice closer to Johannesburg, serving both black and white patients. He was in a relationship with a woman who had two children from a previous marriage, and they visited Thorneside from time to time.

Lucas stepped into his father's shoes as the undisputed head of the family. Though family members attended Board meetings, Lucas was their appointed spokesperson. Lucas' wife had passed away, and he involved himself in Thorneside Farms even more than before. He and Shannon often met at the end of the day, enjoying wine on the terrace, and reminiscing about their years of butting heads while developing Thorneside Farms. They shared a rich history, and they had succeeded together. Now in their older years, the two often accompanied one another to business events. Never as lovers, but now old friends. Lucas, the crotchety reformed bully. Shannon the moderated liberal feminist. The two of them helped fill an emptiness that each felt.

* * *

Awakening

SHANNON BECAME ACTIVE in an Episcopal church in Trelwyn. She liked it. The church was small, and the people were welcoming. During one Sunday service, a parishioner read the Parable of the Talents from the twenty-fifth chapter of Matthew.

It was the story of a wealthy landowner who left his fields in the care of three workers, dividing the land among them and instructing them to reap healthy harvests while he was away on a journey. When he returned, he summoned the three workers to show him the rewards of their labor.

The first had worked night and day and produced three times what the previous year had yielded. The second doubled last year's harvest. The third explained that he was so afraid of harming the master's land that he didn't plant a crop and therefore had no yield. The master was furious with the third servant and cast him out.

For a reason Shannon couldn't explain, the Scripture seemed as though it was written for her. She saw herself as that third servant, as someone who only looked after herself, who had never helped people in need. Had not planted seeds for future harvest.

That night she tossed and turned, reflecting on her life. She saw the faces of people she hurt who got in the way of her success. She remembered the years of struggle to accomplish goals at any expense. She saw herself fighting, fighting, fighting—all her life.

Her one exception had been the years with Graeme. Then, she was centered, content, happy. But the years before she met Graeme and her life since he died were consumed by struggle. She had worked tirelessly, creating a false front to protect herself from the world. High ideals. Perfection. Success. Nothing less would keep her darkest fears at bay, that she would fall into a pit like her parents and never escape, that persistent, gnawing fear of failure.

The opportunity of immigrating to South Africa was a chance to pursue financial success—with a vengeance. But again, she had to fight. Fight Max, Lucas, and South Africa itself to prove that a woman could be successful.

Shannon recalled those conflicts with Lucas in the early years, both trying to exert one's will over the other.

She had succeeded. In spades! But in all those years of struggle, Shannon had never prayed for God's help, had never asked His guidance, had never expressed gratitude for her success. Nor had she devoted energies toward anything but serving her inner monster to succeed, to avoid the fate that doomed her parents.

But something else at last dawned on her as she reflected in this new light. Yes, her tenacity through the years was motivated by fear of failure, seen through the lens of her parents' lives. With sudden clarity, she realized not all of her characteristics and behaviors sprung from just her parents. She had other genes as well.

Her father's family had immigrated from Sweden to a new country, risking a perilous Atlantic crossing to an uncertain future, never seeing their homeland again. They built an entire farming community out of barren plains east of Austin, survived wars, the

Spanish flu, and economic collapse—but they endured. Her great-grandfather was a famous Texas Ranger who helped tame Texas. Her great-grandmother was a Delaware Indian whose parents had survived the Trail of Tears. Together they raised eleven children on a sprawling ranch in Central Texas. Her maternal grandmother and grandfather were born on ranches and lived that rugged life until the Great Depression forced them to become nomadic sharecroppers, seeking any work to feed their family.

These people were fighters, too. And survivors. These ancestors shaped Shannon as much as her parents had. She thought about the people she now most admired who replaced those magazine-cover women of her youth. Men and women whose lifelong struggles changed the world. They were fighters too, but what mattered was what the fight was about.

"Knowledge and wisdom are hard-won, and it comes with time," Dr. Ross had said to her. A new emotion now gripped Shannon, one that had eluded her for her entire life. Humility.

Still, her fighting spirit wasn't all bad, though often misguided. Without it, she would never have overcome that home that roared every night and imprisoned those living the nightmare.

Mo's wisdom, spoken to her as a child, echoed in her mind: "All fam'lies got they own ways, Miz Shannon. You just gotta decide what way you gonna be, don't matter what other folks do. You be awright, I reckon."

She now admitted something else. She recognized how extraordinary, how rich her life had been.

"My life has straddled two centuries, and I've witnessed—no, participated in—enormous changes. I survived a childhood worthy of a Dickens novel. I've seen wars and recessions and racism. I've seen social norms dissolve into dust and experienced firsthand the advances women made that bear no resemblance to a century ago. I've known a love few women will ever have, and I've raised three beautiful children on two different continents. I've built an all-woman business in a male-dominated country, creating jobs for over a hundred people. So, yes, my life has been extraordinary."

Welcoming the next dawn, watching the sunrise over her beautiful mountains, Shannon knew her life had changed. With a new clarity of purpose, she felt calm. She resolved that for the rest of her life, she would endeavor to help and love others. Not just her family! That came easily.

Shannon set up a school for first graders through middle school and hired an ex-pat from the States to provide an education superior to the local public schools. She taught some classes herself and recruited Alex, Isabel, and Paola to do the same. Even Lucas and Dexter taught courses in carpentry and mechanics from time to time.

Shannon built a church for her expanding community, and a pastor emerged from the ranks of the workers. On Sundays, when the wind was just right, sounds of joyful Gospel singing reached Shannon's home.

She chuckled to herself, remembering Lucas worrying about her building a shopping center at Thorneside Farms. "No, no shopping center, but we do have a thriving community."

* * *

The Final Lesson

"WHY DID IT take me so long to look to God, and ask His guidance," Shannon often wondered. "All those years, I fought so hard, relying on my will and determination. Imagine if I had His guidance, what I could have accomplished."

She reflected on Mandela's council of Elders that included half a dozen Nobel Peace Prize recipients: Mandela himself, Jimmy Carter, Mohammed Yunas, Kofi Annan, and others.

"Mandela and Carter were devout in their faiths and would never have had the courage to speak truth to power without guidance from Above," Shannon thought. "Their efforts and sacrifice made a lasting impact on racial equality, women's rights, freedom, and justice throughout the world."

Always her own most harsh critic, Shannon scolded herself, "My life hasn't even made a ripple compared to others. I've bumbled and stumbled through life, making more mistakes and messes than I should've been allowed and hurting people along the way. I always wanted to do something big. Even Dr. Ross saw that in me in my twenties when I was trying to save the world."

She shook her head. "If only I had sought God's help, maybe then. If only…"

She considered her achievements small potatoes, but she was learning to be at peace with herself, her past, her life.

She just finished writing a card to Gabriel and Cece. They announced another pregnancy, hoping, of course, for a boy this time.

"Just think, Graeme. Another grandchild on the way, and if it's a boy, they're naming him after you."

She often talked out loud to Graeme these days, or her dog, her constant companion, or to herself. Living alone allowed her that eccentricity, no one around to complain.

"This makes four so far," she murmured. "No signs yet from Nathan. He's too busy with his patients to think about a family just yet, but he has plenty of time."

Shannon liked to write personal notes, for birthdays and special occasions like this one to Gabriel and Cece, congratulating them on their happy news. As she was sealing the envelope, she noticed her hands.

"My goodness," she cried, as if seeing her hands for the first time. "They look like my frail Grandma Alma's hands." She hadn't noticed all the sunspots or the translucent skin stretching over knobby knuckles.

"Well, at least the fingers are still straight, and no signs of arthritis. These hands have done me well, and I still have enough strength in them to do what needs doing."

Shannon poured herself a glass of Graeme's Reserve, raised her glass, and said aloud, "To you, Graeme, and Helen, and our next grandchild. May they be as blessed and loved as the others." She reserved the cabernet for special occasions and tonight qualified.

She made herself a light supper that she planned to enjoy in bed while watching TV. She liked this part of living alone, eating when she wanted, going to bed when she wanted, without adjusting her schedule to someone else. As she walked toward her bedroom, plate in one hand and her glass of wine in the other, a sudden massive pain hit the back of her head.

"Oh, m… my. That's… different," Shannon whispered.

Never having suffered from headaches, this indeed was a new experience. It felt as if someone had hit her in the back of the head with a baseball bat. She set the plate and goblet back on the counter and sat for a few minutes. The pain subsided, but a sudden onset of nausea sent her to the bathroom to vomit into the toilet. After that, chills and shaking took hold of her. She wanted nothing more than to get under her covers and warm up.

She took two painkillers and called Nathan in Johannesburg. It was around ten in the evening, and her call went into his voicemail.

"Hi, Hon. It's Mom. Nothing urgent, just wanted to tell you something odd happened. I just had a sudden, terrific headache. It felt as though I was hit in the head. Then I threw up. The headache's gone now, although it's painful to move my head. I'm better but have chills. So I've taken a couple of Tylenol and am going to bed to sleep it off. I'll talk to you in the morning."

Shannon pulled the covers around her neck, still shivering.

Then she saw Graeme standing at the foot of her bed. He looked as handsome as ever, impeccably dressed in all black—blazer, silk shirt, trousers, black loafers without socks, just like their unforgettable dinner date at LaSalle in Paris.

Graeme held out his hand to Shannon, took hers in his, and said, "Shannon, will you come with me? I have one more thing to show you."

Shannon took his outstretched hand, noticing how her skin was now smooth, unblemished, without the wrinkles and sunspots she had complained of earlier. She grasped his hand, holding it tight, and went to sleep.

THE END

ABOUT THE AUTHOR

Jo Ann Swahn is a native Texan, born and raised in Austin. Her desire for adventure led her to New York where she lived for a time, pursuing a successful corporate career and extensive travel for work and fun. She is the mother of two sons and grandmother of three. In retirement, she returned to her beloved Texas, where she lives on the outskirts of Austin, devoting time to her extended family, including brothers, nieces and their offspring, friends, and her beloved sheltie, Angie. When she's not writing, she's likely golfing, cooking, or spending time with friends, church, and charitable endeavors.

ACKNOWLEDGMENTS

Sandy King Lankford has held an important part of my heart for over fifty years. Throughout our history together, she has always encouraged me to write a book, reminding me I've talked about doing just that for most of my life. My life and career took me in different directions, but during Covid lockdown of 2021, she told me, "Now you have no excuse. Write that book!" To her, I owe the inspiration and motivation of writing *Shaping Shannon*.

Jan Dryden, sister of my dearest friend, Lou, read my first draft, a clumsy, rambling attempt. With her intellect, objectivity, and trademark tact, she let me know I had a long way to go before *Shaping Shannon* was ready for readers.

Lu McCann, another dear friend, read the tenth and final version. With all my fingers crossed while my baby was in her hands, Lu said she loved the story. Her keen editing eye found a number of assaults on the King's English before turning the finished manuscript over to my ultimate judge and mentor, my editor and publisher, Cynthia Stone of Treaty Oak Publishers.

These women have provided incredible support, encouragement, and patience through the two years of writing *Shaping Shannon*.

Thank you, Ladies!